The Riddle
of
THE SHIPWRECKED

SPINSTER

PATRICIA VERYAN

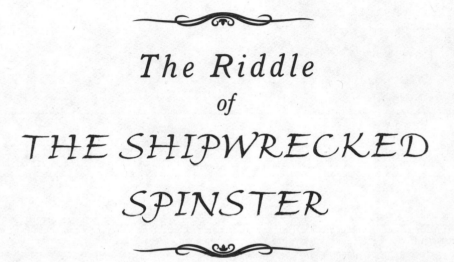

The Riddle
of
THE SHIPWRECKED
SPINSTER

ST. MARTIN'S PRESS
NEW YORK

www.stmartins.com

ISBN 0-312-26942-0

First Edition: April 2001

10 9 8 7 6 5 4 3 2 1

For Sheri
My very loved daughter-in-law

1

London
Autumn 1747

*D*espite the oppressive heat of the September evening, the ball given by the Dowager Lady Hall-Bridger was a success. Fans might flutter in a constant attempt to cool pretty but flushed cheeks, fine linen handkerchiefs might be plied surreptitiously by gentlemen far too elegant to be so coarse as to perspire, but nonetheless the ballroom floor was crowded, the dancers merry and clearly enjoying themselves.

The ball was in honour of the come-out of Lady Hall-Bridger's granddaughter, and to please that very indulged maiden, a larger than usual number of the younger set had been invited. Many of these were variously frolicking or flirting their way through a country dance. Two young ladies, however, stood chatting in a secluded archway that gave onto a corridor adjacent to the ballroom. Their murmurous conversation was frequently interspersed with soft laughter. Both were pretty enough to have attracted male attention, but neither appeared distressed by the lack of a dance partner. Long-time friends who had been separated for some months by the Grand Tour of one family, they were mutually delighted to have discovered each other at this Society function and had slipped away to share the more noteworthy events each had experienced while parted. Their merry chatter turned very soon to *ton* gossip, mostly of a nature that their respective chaperones would have frowned upon.

Miss Maureen Coffey uttered a gasp and threw one lace-mittened hand to her cheek. Big brown eyes wide with awe, she exclaimed, "You never *did?* But—but he is *by far* the most adored and adorable gentleman in London!"

Miss Angela Alvelley giggled and agreed, adding pertly, "And the most pursued, though for his fortune rather than his good looks; at least that's what my aunt says. Every mama in Town with an unwed daughter is on his trail."

"And some with daughters they'll never be able to fire off. Like poor Cordelia Stansbury, for instance."

"That little dowd?" Miss Alvelley patted her powdered hair coquettishly. "Much chance that hatchet-faced mother of hers has."

Behind them a large potted palm rustled suddenly, but the two damsels were so intent upon their well-bred character assassination that they were unaware of this odd occurrence.

Miss Coffey, who had a trace of kindness in her otherwise selfish heart, said, "Poor Cordelia. I cannot but feel sorry for her, she has such a frightful harpy for a mama! And she has been in love with him forever, you know."

Incredulous, her friend stared at her. "With Gervaise Valerian? *Cordelia Stansbury?* You never mean it! Why, how prodigious stupid! She must know he can take his pick of all the beauties in the Southland. As if he would so much as glance her way, much less flirt with her!"

"Not with you in the same room, I'll own. Though he has not seemed particular in his attentions this evening."

Quite aware that she was judged one of the loveliest maidens in London Town and well on the way to becoming an acknowledged Toast, Miss Alvelley stiffened. "He can scarce flirt with me while my grandmama is here, watching me like a hawk. She holds him to be dangerous."

"As does every mama in Town. But they will risk a little flirtation if it may lead to his fortune!" Lowering her lashes, Miss Coffey added archly, "Even so, far from flirting with you, one might suppose he does not even know you are here."

"Of course he knows, you silly thing! And when you look so smug, Maureen, I vow I yearn to scratch you! I could have him flying to my side in the wink of an eye, Grandmama or not, if I so wished. I will tell you in strict confidence that we had planned to meet here tonight." The angry flash in her blue eyes faded. She said thoughtfully, "Still, you are right; he has been ignoring me. He is playing one of his sly little games, is all, keeping me waiting. Well, I think I shall teach the so much admired Gervaise Valerian a lesson!" She beckoned a hovering footman, and having captivated him with her delightful smile, sent him off.

Miss Coffey asked curiously, "Why do you want paper and seals? Are you going to write to him?"

"Yes. And beg that he meet me in the green ante-room."

"Heavens! Angela, you must not! It is the farthest room, and very isolated. If anyone should see you alone with him you would be quite ruined!"

Miss Alvelley's smile was bright with mischief. "*Do* try not to be so silly! I will be least in sight, and when he gets to the ante-room he can cool his heels waiting for the kiss he will think to win, while you and I enjoy the next dance with less conceited beaux."

The footman returned, the fatal note was written and despatched, and the conspirators melted into the throng, aglow with the pleasurable knowledge that London's most courted young bachelor was about to receive a well-deserved set-down.

Mrs. Regina Stansbury had chosen the small sofa in the corridor because it was tucked away, half-concealed by the fronds of a large potted palm, and offered privacy. She had retreated here to control her temper, sadly frayed by the barbed hints of two "friends" regarding her hopes for "Cordelia, poor child." A lady of strong opinions and uncertain temperament, she prided herself on her impeccable lineage, which she judged superior to most of those present at this function. Her taste in dress was as impeccable as her lineage, and tonight she had chosen to wear a splendid mauve satin ball gown. A diamond-and-amethyst necklace was spread on her bony chest, and there were two curling feathers in her wig, which was of the latest French style. More diamonds sparkled in the bracelets she wore on her gloved wrists, and only a close inspection by an expert would reveal that the gems in both necklace and bracelets were paste.

Her sharp tongue and abrasive hauteur tended to limit the ranks of her friends, but she was acknowledged to be good *ton,* and as one of the leaders of fashion, was seen "everywhere." Despite her husband's rapidly shrinking funds, she refused his every plea for economy and persisted in patronizing London's most talented (and expensive) modistes. Tall and thin, and blessed with a tiny waist, she wore her clothes well and presented an impressive appearance, but not the costliest gown or the richest jewels could soften the harsh line of her lips, or warm the glitter in the hard dark eyes.

Almost, she had confronted those two insolent girls when they'd dared to name her "hatchet-faced" and a "harpy," and said she would never be able to "fire off" her "little dowd" of a daughter. How fortunate it was that she had succeeded in controlling her justifiable wrath and had continued to "overhear" their wicked conversation.

Looking after the plotters, her tight mouth became tighter. So Gervaise Valerian would "not so much as glance at" Cordelia! Thanks to a succession of profligate heirs and the hopeless financial ineptitude of her spouse, the Stansburys no longer possessed a comfortable fortune, but insofar as lineage went, a Valerian might think himself fortunate to win a Stansbury for his bride. From time to time she had attempted to impart such awareness to young Gervaise, but he always contrived to slip away just as she was coming to the point. Once, while at a musicale, the rascal had been so gauche as to pretend not to have met Cordelia. It was a rare mis-step on his part and she had seized the golden opportunity at once, insisting upon introducing him to her daughter. She'd fancied that good manners would compel him to keep beside them, but he'd bowed politely to Cordelia and suddenly recalled he was promised to join another party. She had boxed her daughter's ears when they returned home, and told her a few home truths about speechless, spotted, and fat females. Almost, she had despaired of Valerian, but now, that conceited little witch Angela Alvelley (whose aunt was *not* good *ton* and gave card parties of questionable repute) may well have given her the very tool she needed to catch the insolent young rake—and his fortune! Provided, she acted swiftly.

To that end, Mrs. Stansbury went in search of a footman, wrote a hurried note and, along with other instructions, ordered that it be delivered *at once!* Then, with a rare and triumphant smile curving her lips, Regina Stansbury returned to her sofa, from which she might watch the corridor, unobserved.

⌒✿⌒

He was here tonight! She had seen him come in, accompanied, as always, by a jolly group of friends. Tall and dashing and— oh, so very handsome.

Miss Cordelia Stansbury, short and inclined to plumpness, with a regrettable tendency to throw out a spot when she was nervous, watched him from a distance. How becoming was the powdered wig concealing his hair, which she knew to be a softly curling dark brown. How enchanting the clear grey eyes, slim nose, firm mouth and chin. If some named him a Dandy, it was no more than jealousy. Suppose he was fastidious about his dress, why should he not be? His valet was known to be proud of him, for he was tall and perfectly proportioned and had a fine pair of broad shoulders.

Miss Stansbury sighed and edged a little closer, thrilling to the sound of his deep laugh and noting every graceful movement. How immediate was the heightened sense of excitement in the ballroom now that he had arrived. And how hopeless her love for the man so sought-after for the very qualities she admired, and even more sought-after for the great Valerian fortune. It was believed that despite his estrangement from his father, Gervaise had not been disowned and remained the sole heir to Sir Simon Valerian. Much she cared for that, thought Cordelia sadly. But Mama cared. Mama never ceased to remind her that she was twenty now, and if she did not bestir herself to become less of a shy and colourless little dab, and master some of the tricks that even pretty young ladies employed to catch themselves a husband, she would be a spinster all her days. Mama had said—so often—that she did not propose to support her for the rest of her days, and that Cordelia owed it to her to make a good match.

She sighed. She'd always thought life would be easier once she left the schoolroom, but if anything, it was more difficult. If Papa were in London, it would be different. But Mr. Nathan Stansbury, a renowned authority on antiquities and a gentle soul, had escaped his wife's shrewish tongue by retreating to the less exhausting heat of the Egyptian sands, thus abandoning his only daughter to the machinations of her ruthless mother.

With a twinge of guilt, Cordelia glanced around. Mama had gone off somewhere, probably to find Lady Hall-Bridger and demand she provide a partner for her plain and timid offspring. How horrid that would be. And how humiliating. The other young ladies would giggle behind their fans, as they always did, and she would wish the floor might open and swallow her.

"Miss Stansbury?"

A footman, making a far more elegant appearance in his livery than did she in the ornate ball gown Mama had insisted she wear, was holding out a note. A summons, she thought with sinking heart, but she nodded and he gave her the note together with the admonition that she was requested to destroy it as soon as it was read.

Curious, she broke the seal. The writing was an unfamiliar scrawl, and the message brief.

> I am in great distress and appeal to you for the
> kindness I judge you to possess. I beg that you
> will do me the honour of meeting me in the green
> anteroom, at the end of the west corridor.
> On my oath, I will detain you no more than a
> minute or two.
> In the sure knowledge that you will respect my
> confidence,
>
> > Anxiously,
> > Valerian

The green ante-room was unoccupied. Pushing the door wider, Cordelia started to call, but he had stressed confidentiality and she crept inside, bowing to convention by leaving the door open but crossing to the inner room where he might wait so as to be out of sight of the corridor.

She was a little flushed with excitement, her heart pounding madly. Of all people, in his trouble—whatever it was—he had turned to her! Had he guessed that she had adored him from the first moment she saw him? She'd been thirteen then, accompanying Papa to a dusty old bookshop. When Gervaise had strolled in it had seemed to her that the shop lit up. He had also been with his father, for this was before the terrible quarrel that had driven them apart. Sir Simon had spoken briefly to Papa and Gervaise had made his bow, smiled on her kindly, then wandered about and not glanced her way again. Why should he, an already acknowledged prize on the marriage mart, glance at a chubby girl not yet out of the schoolroom? But if he'd been scarcely aware of her, she had never forgotten him or that dazzling smile. The altar in her heart that was built that day had remained, undimmed and unshakeable, so that, while knowing he would never choose her, having met the man of her dreams, she was determined to marry no one else. Never had she hoped for this evening's wonderful turn of events; never had she dreamt he noticed her, much less judged her to be kind-hearted.

She was somewhat surprised to find that the inner chamber was empty also. It was her own fault, of course. She could never seem to master the little tricks of flirtation. Mama would likely box her ears again and shrill that a lady did not rush to meet a gentleman, but kept him waiting for a decent interval lest he judge her over-eager. "Cordelia," she murmured, starting back to the outer room, "you are such a silly—"

"Where are you, little lovely?"

The soft call sent her heart leaping into her throat. For an instant she could not move, and her voice was unwontedly husky when she gulped, "In . . . here."

"Aha!"

She heard his quick tread and knew she was pale and trembling.

He said lightly, "Discretion is, they say, the better part of—"

Then he was in the room, had taken two strides, checked abruptly and gasped, "What—the devil . . . ?"

"I c-came as soon as I received your note, Mr. Valerian," she stammered. "In—in what way can I be of assistance to—"

The flaring dark brows twitched into a frown. "I sent you no note, madam," he said icily. "Be so good as to let me see it."

8

Horrified, she gulped, "You asked that I destroy it, so I threw it in the fire."

"If ever I heard such a silly—" Suspicion dawned then. He whirled about and ran to the outer room.

Bewildered, Cordelia followed. "What is it? Have I—"

The door to the corridor was closed. Groaning a curse, he sprang at it, but his tug at the latch was unavailing. "Treed!" he snarled inexplicably. "Devil take me for a fool!"

Gripping her hands together, Cordelia whimpered, "I don't understand. Why would you have come if you had not sent for me?"

He rushed past her and threw back the window draperies, only to be thwarted by locked casements. Again he ground out an oath of frustration, then exclaimed, "Send for *you?* Why the deuce would I send for *you,* madam? A pretty web you've woven, thinking to catch me in parson's mousetrap, is that it?"

Aghast, she cried, "No! No, sir! I swear—" She shrank back as he advanced on her, eyes blazing with wrath, hands clenched. Sure that she was about to be strangled, she gasped, "You—you are mistaken, sir. I—"

A shrill screaming put a stop to her desperate denial. The outer door was opened. Mrs. Regina Stansbury, the picture of outraged and vengeful motherhood, stood there, weeping hysterically and surrounded by a shocked and growing crowd.

Very white, Valerian said harshly, "Madam, you must know I did not think to find your daughter here! If truth be told—"

"Truth?" she shrieked. "Do you deny that you had locked yourself in here with my poor innocent child?" She looked pleadingly at the titillated but disapproving spectators. "Only see how wickedly he tries to deny what is all too obvious—"

Somehow regaining her voice, Cordelia half-whispered, "Mama! Mr. Valerian did not—"

"Trick you into coming here . . . alone?" wailed Mrs. Stansbury. "Oh, I am faint! My sweet little girl . . . so shy and—and

9

innocent. She would not know . . . He has *ruined* her . . . !"

"Nonsense!" snapped Valerian, but he read condemnation in the faces at the door.

The crowd separated suddenly. Lady Hall-Bridger, large and opinionated and a power in Society, pushed her way through and took in the situation at a glance. "Is this how you serve me, Gervaise Valerian? A fine scandal for my granddaughter's come-out! Be so good as to explain."

He met her eyes and read the stern warning that told him there was no explanation. He had been neatly trapped. Fuming, aware that there was also no escape, he thought savagely that it would have been bad enough had it been that saucy little hussy Angela Alvelley, at least she had some liveliness, but this plain and dim-witted creature had been born for spinsterhood! She was croaking something.

"It is—is not what you think, Mama. Someone must have—"

Her hostess hissed softly, "Quiet, you little widgeon!" And in a louder tone, "Well, Valerian? You are surely aware that you have compromised the gel. You must set things to rights."

Helpless, he said in a voice that shook with rage, "I apologize, Mrs. Stansbury for my—impetuous haste in—in courting your daughter. And I—beg you will permit me the—the honour of—of offering for Miss Cordelia's hand in . . . marriage."

From the corridor came a chorus of relieved exclamations.

Mrs. Stansbury dabbed a tiny square of cambric and lace at her tearless eyes, and moaned that she accepted Mr. Valerian's offer. "Though, it should have been made in a less scrambling fashion, you naughty boy."

Valerian barely restrained a shudder.

Lady Hall-Bridger fixed him with a stern stare, then smilingly urged her guests to return to the ballroom. They drifted away, chattering happily over the juicy *on dit* they would be able to relate to those unfortunates who had not witnessed the downfall of the popular but naughty young rake, who deserved just what he had come by.

Several people, excited, failed to keep their voices down. Their comments would haunt Cordelia's nightmares:

"Poor Gervaise! Who'd have dreamt he would be snabbled by such a plain and dull chit! . . ."

"Gad, but London's hopeful beauties will yearn to murder her! . . ."

"He was caught by her *mother,* my dear! That poor little mouse has neither the courage nor the wit to set such a trap. For trap it was, of that I am certain! . . ."

"Cordelia Stansbury! The last one I'd thought Valerian would look at, much less compromise so blatantly . . ."

"I feel for Gervaise. Only last week he told me he meant to remain a carefree bachelor till he reached thirty-five, at least."

"The more fool he, to be so indiscreet. Well, he's stuck with the chit now, poor fellow . . ."

Sick with shame, Cordelia wept, and longed for an early grave.

⌖

"Less than a month!" Mrs. Evaline Coffey tucked in her several double chins and poured her guest another cup of tea.

Comfortably seated on a rose velvet overstuffed chair in the private parlour of the Mayfair house the late Mr. Coffey had provided for his family, Miss Saphronia Aymer's finely drawn brows arched higher. She was a thin lady on the far side of middle age, and her powdered wig, which was somewhat out of the present style, framed an angular face not improved by a very sharp nose and chin. "As the sister of a well-known clergyman," she said in a fluttery high-pitched voice, "I should not really comment on the matter. But . . . one cannot help but ask oneself what on earth could have possessed the lady—especially such a lady as Regina Stansbury—to allow her daughter

11

to go off and visit friends and then leave the country with them so soon after the announcement of her betrothal. Has she given any explanation, Evaline?"

Mrs. Coffey refilled her own cup and stirred the tea briskly. "She tells everyone the gel was eager to visit her papa and obtain his approval of her betrothal. Stuff!"

Blinking at such vehemence, although she agreed with the sentiment, the clergyman's sister was struck by a sudden thought. She caught her breath, leaned forward and half-whispered, "But—but surely, this was Mr. Valerian's duty? Never say he accompanies the girl?"

"Gervaise? Certainly not! Lud, Saphy! That young scamp is in enough trouble with half the *ton* believing he was in his cups and really did try to seduce Cordelia!"

"And the other half suspecting Regina Stansbury set the scene and won herself a wealthy son-in-law. But if that were so, Evaline, what a fool she would be to send her daughter halfway around the world almost before their betrothal was safely established. If Valerian has really been entrapped and now Cordelia is gone away for many months, he is liable to cry off and claim—oh, desertion or some such thing. No?"

"Exactly so. I'll own Cordelia was devoted to her father and probably did want to see him, but I'd stake my life her mother would have fought such a plan tooth and nail. She knows Valerian, and would not risk losing her prize catch. Unless . . ." Mrs. Coffey set down her teacup and stared at it thoughtfully.

Miss Aymer leaned forward again and hissed avidly, "If the gel really sails to Egypt she will be gone—at least nine . . . months?"

Mrs. Coffey said with a slow smile, "You've a quick mind, Saphy. Naughty, but quick."

"Oh, my goodness! Do you really think . . . But Cordelia cannot have sailed alone. Who escorts her?"

"A Mr. and Mrs. Gerald Walters and family. Close friends, so Regina claims. I never heard her mention the name before, but now she purrs that it was "so very dear" of the Walters to allow her "beloved child" to travel with their party. And do you know, Saphronia, those hard eyes of hers fairly hurl rage when she says it. No—there's more to it—far more than we are told!"

Miss Aymer drew back, her own eyes wide. "The morals of today's youth appall one, Evaline! My dear brother—he is Chaplain to Sir Brian Chandler, you know—Nathaniel would be sick at heart were I to hint at this latest scandal." She saw her friend's disapproving frown and added hurriedly, "Not that I would, of course, for we really have no proof, have we? But—that poor child! Just think, she is on the high seas at this very moment. An East Indiaman, I suppose?"

"As you say," said Mrs. Coffey, then added with a titter, "Or as her dear mama says!"

Extract from Notice posted at the East India Company in Leadenhall Street:

It is with deep regret that the Company adds the following names to the previously published list of those who perished when *The Sea Horse*, 500 tons, outward-bound for Egypt, foundered off the Cape of Good Hope during a violent storm on the night of May 2nd, 1748:

Dr. James Johnson and family.
Mr. and Mrs. Samuel Jurgens and party.
Sir Kenneth and Lady Lindall and Miss Lindall.
Mr. and Mrs. Horace Needham.
Mr. and Mrs. Gerald Walters and party.

Three other vessels in the fleet sustained heavy damage, but so far as is known there was no further loss of life.

2

January 1749

*H*ampshire had received a light fall of snow during the night, but with the dawn came a weak but welcome winter sun. The ground was hard and the air was still cold, but for the most part the wide-spreading acres of Muse Manor were green again, the patches of white fast retreating to lurk in shady spots and among the woods.

Suddenly, the hush of early morning was shattered by the pounding of hooves. Two horses, one a tall and powerful bay stallion, the other a dapple-grey filly, galloped neck and neck over the brow of a low hill and thundered down the slope. The riders, superb horsemen, were also twins, and at seven and twenty were so alike that until recently it had been difficult to tell them apart. They both were tall and well-built, their features clean-cut, the chins firm, the eyes wide-set and of a deep blue. Neither wore a wig but the thick dark hair of each was powdered and neatly tied back.

Exhilarated by their race and the rush of cold bracing air, they crouched lower in their saddles, urging their mounts to greater speed. The river came into view, winding its broad and gleaming ribbon through the lush meadowland, and the brothers turned their mounts towards the bridge that spanned the fast-flowing waters and marked the end of the contest. The bay horse was powerful, but gradually the filly began to pull ahead until, when the bridge was reached, she was a full length in the lead.

With a triumphant shout Piers Cranford drew her to a halt, patted her firm neck and told her that she had done splendidly, as usual. His brother came up with a whoop and a scattering of dirt clods and the big bay reared as if indignant that he'd been beaten by the smaller animal.

"Jolly well done!" Peregrine Cranford dismounted, revealing the fact that he wore a short wooden peg-leg in lieu of his right foot. He stroked the nose of his stallion and advised him breathlessly that he must not be put out because a young lady had bested him. "For you must admit, Odin, that she's a very beautiful lady." He turned his head, smiling up at his twin as Piers swung from the saddle. "Though how Tassels achieves her astonishing speeds, I cannot fathom."

Piers was proud of his horse, and, always pleased when she received a compliment, he said with a grin, "Nor can anyone else, though a surprising number of fellows are ready to relieve me of her keep."

"Don't blame 'em at all. Would you sell her?"

Piers shrugged and answered carelessly, "Oh, perhaps. If the price were right."

They led their mounts onto the bridge side by side, and Piers scanned his twin obliquely. They both had served as lieutenants with the King's forces during the recent Jacobite Rebellion. Peregrine's foot had been crushed by a gun carriage when its panicked crew deserted the disastrous Battle of Prestonpans, and two days later, under harrowingly adverse conditions, his foot had been amputated. Later, infection had set in, necessitating a further amputation. Although he had recovered, the ordeals had weakened him, and during the past three years, there had been several close brushes with death. "He's going along much better now," thought Piers, for if suffering had left its mark on the fine features, Peregrine had recently found his lady, and happiness glowed in his eyes.

Peregrine glanced at him. "Well?"

"Well—what?"

"Yes, I thought you were wool-gathering. I asked what you would consider an acceptable price for Tassels."

"She is beyond price." Piers patted the mare fondly. "As you know very well."

Peregrine found no fault with this remark, for he himself would like to have owned the mare. Perfectly formed and of a most affectionate nature, she was a pretty creature and attracted attention wherever Piers rode. Her coloration was a rare pearly white, splashed overall with small round circles of softest grey, remarkably uniformly spaced, with only her head and tail being a solid pale grey. Neither colouring nor conformation were Arabian, her barrel and hindquarters being more rounded and her back short and strong, but Piers believed that she had some Arab blood, evidenced by the delicately shaped head and large expressive eyes.

"Thought you might be in the basket and had changed your mind about selling her."

Peregrine had spoken in jest, but Piers said a scornful "Gudgeon!"

They came to a halt and stood looking up at the wooded hill that rose some half-mile to the north-east.

Piers asked curiously, "Now what are you grinning about?"

"I was thinking of how furious old Finchley must be. He wants Tassels so badly he can scarce contain himself. Has he thrown another offer at you?"

Major Gresford Finchley, their southerly neighbour, was a quarrelsome individual, harsh of voice and manner, and recalling their most recent encounter, Piers nodded. "He has. He gets alarmingly red in the face each time I refuse."

"The monstrous major is a man who likes his own way. Does he bellow at you?"

"Bellows at everyone. Last time, I had all I could do not to laugh at him. He knew it, and for a minute I really thought he was going to strangle me. The silly fellow went so far as to howl that she had belonged to him originally."

Indignant, Perry exclaimed, "Why, that sour old skinflint! After you saved his scrawny neck? That's at the root of it, y'know. He can't bear to admit he let such a prize escape him. If he'd dreamt when he gave her to you that she would develop such speed, you'd never have laid a finger on her!"

"Oh, I don't know." Piers chuckled. "He may have thought that having dug his precious person from under that landslide, I rated a magnificent prize."

"Any decent fellow would've thought that, I grant you. Not many men would have risked crawling under that slope on Hound's Tooth Hill to dig him out with their bare hands. The rest of the slide could have come down on you at any second— and did come down scant minutes after you freed the ingrate!"

"I can scarce name him 'ingrate' when I look at Tassels."

"The clutch-fist only gave her to you because he thinks— or thought then—that bay is the only colour for a horse, besides which he judged her days were numbered. And a mighty sick creature he gifted you! I'd have wagered a thousand guineas you'd never be able to cure her foot. I used to marvel at all the hours you spent caring for her and then training her with such patience. Well, you've been rewarded. Seriously, how many offers have you had for her?"

"Very many. And you'd be surprised by the anger levelled at me when I refuse." As if sensing that they spoke of her, the filly nudged her soft lips against his neck. Piers caressed her and said scoffingly, "And where would you get a thousand guineas, twin?"

The smile faded from Peregrine's eyes. "If I had such a sum, I'd build Zoe a house atop Quail Hill."

17

Piers gazed thoughtfully at the hill that rose a short distance to the north of the bridge, but he made no comment.

Peregrine stifled a sigh, then said a quiet "You've gone away again. What's wrong?"

"You are what's wrong, Sir Perry." Still unused to his recently conferred knighthood, Peregrine flushed. "D'you realize," Piers went on lightly, "that you dozed off last evening having raved about your affianced all through dinner and given poor Aunt Jane and me not a word of the *ton* gossip. Cruel! You know full well that we rusticate here and know nothing of what is going on. Has any more been heard of that nest of traitors you and Rossiter and Morris outwitted last autumn? Have Falcon and Gwendolyn announced their betrothal? Has a date been set? How does—"

Mounting up again, Peregrine laughed and begged for mercy. " 'Tis only a month since we were lucky enough to defeat the League of Jewelled Men. There has been no further word of them—beyond the fact that Smythe faces execution. You did know that."

"Dear Reginald Smythe." Swinging into the saddle, Piers mused, "I still find it hard to believe that slimy little toad was the mighty 'Squire' and led those madmen in their lunatic plan to topple the government. Our monarch did well to confer a title on my intrepid little brother."

"Pish! Falcon's the one should have been knighted, not me, and their betrothal will be announced next month, which is— Who's that?"

Between the bridge and crest of the hill where Peregrine had dreamt to build his house the land rose in a series of gently undulating folds. On this sunny morning the landscape offered a charming picture, its various shades of green threaded by the silver of the river. The new owners of the parcel had erected a cottage on the eastern side of the property, but were seldom in residence. Today, however, the emerald meadow was enlivened by a splash of pale pink.

"Aha! A lady," said Piers. "I suppose she must be one of the Westermans."

They rode down the bridge and Peregrine asked, "What are they like?"

"I've no least notion. Why they bought the place is more than I can understand."

"Jupiter! Haven't we even paid a courtesy call? What shocking neglect of our new neighbour! You should have cultivated their acquaintance long before this."

"Even you, Sir Perry, would have found it difficult to cultivate the acquaintance of folk who are never there."

"Well, there's someone there now. We must seize this chance to introduce ourselves."

"Not while she's alone, you block. If two strange men go galloping up to her unannounced, she'll likely faint dead away!"

His words fell on deaf ears. The more impetuous of the twins, Peregrine was already cantering Odin across the bridge and into the north meadow. With a snort of exasperation for his brother's impatience with protocol, Piers followed.

Far from fainting away, the young lady who sat on the rise amid the meadow grasses was allowing Peregrine to assist her to her feet. Riding up, Piers noted that the ringlets peeping from under her ruffled cap were an unpowdered soft light brown. Her eyes were hazel, not particularly large, but with a sparkle; she had a small uptilting nose, high cheek-bones and a clear but rather tanned complexion lacking the pale pink-and-white daintiness so carefully cultivated by ladies of the *ton*. A country maiden, he deduced, whose mama had not warned her against the sun. She was of average height, and when she bent to pick up something her cloak was blown by the wind and revealed a pink gown and a shapely figure. Pretty enough, he thought, dismounting, if not a beauty by London standards. But as she turned to him in response to his brother's introduction, he noted that she possessed a charming little mouth and a warm and unaffected smile.

19

Without a trace of shyness she told them that she was visiting relations in London. "But my aunt sent her woman to collect some things she'd left in the cottage, and I was permitted to accompany her. I've never seen the cottage. Such delightful surroundings, and the countryside so green and beautiful. Just as I remember . . ."

Her eyes had become sad and remote. Watching her curiously, and wondering that an unwed girl was allowed to roam about without so much as a maid to accompany her, Piers said, "Then you have been here before? I must have mistaken. I thought you—"

"Said I'd never seen the cottage?" She smiled and nodded. "Well, that is true. I mean that—that I remember the countryside. I've been abroad, you see. But our groom told me about you gentlemen." She looked from one to the other approvingly. "You are twins, I think? How very nice that must be. Unless you squabble all the time, of course."

Peregrine laughed. "Acquit us of that, ma'am. Not that we've never come to cuffs, my brother being so elderly he must always rule the roost, and—"

"And *my* brother being harum-scarum," interposed Piers with a grin, "and incorrigible and lacking all respect for his seniors. But I think you have broke your beads. May we be of assistance, Miss—er . . . ?"

"I am Miss Mary Westerman." She offered a demure little curtsy, and glancing down at the green bead she held, added, "I did not notice it right away, and I fear I must have trod on the poor thing, for as you see it is all mud, but I can have it repaired, so 'tis not—" She broke off as a large woman came toiling towards them, waving her arms and panting breathlessly. "Oh, dear! Here is poor Brownie and will be quite out of curl because I am talking with you. Pray excuse me, gentlemen. I must hurry."

Their offers to intercede for her were answered by a brief wave as she fled.

Looking after her, Peregrine said an amused "I think Miss Mary is getting a fine scold from her maid. And what did you think of her, Gaffer? I saw none of the town airs and graces you so dislike, and she's a pretty little creature, no?"

"Charming, certainly." Again, Piers swung into the saddle. "And if you are at your unrelenting matchmaking, for mercy's sake, give it up. I have but now met the lady. And besides, I'm not in the petticoat line at the moment."

"At the *moment?* You've been saying that for years, and only because you spend every waking second worrying about Mitten and me, and the estate. Your time for worries is done, twin. Shut 'em all away. M'sister's happily wed, and I'll soon be off your hands, so you'll have time to concentrate on finding a nice bride. Now, in my opinion, Miss Westerman is—"

"—Not one to simper and be shyly coy, as damsels are supposed to be," Piers commented, taking care not to notice his brother's difficult climb into the saddle. "Certainly the lady is not an arbiter of fashion."

Peregrine sighed resignedly. "We are in the country, I'll remind you, where a lady don't have to dress as if she's going to a Town party. Are you become sufficient of an expert in female attire as to criticize her dress?"

"Gad, no! And I had no business saying such a thing."

"Why did you? You ain't usually so critical."

"I hope not! But it struck me that—well, her gown was pink."

Throwing a hand to his brow, Peregrine moaned, "Frightful! She should be pilloried!"

"Bacon brain! Seriously, I never yet met a lady who'd wear a green necklace with a pink gown."

"Well, that's told her tale, poor lass. To the darkest cell in the Tower with her!"

Piers swiped his tricorne at his aggravating brother. With a whoop, Peregrine was away, and at the gallop the tall bay and the dainty grey filly thundered down the hill once more.

21

"Much better." Miss Jane Guild set a French knot in her embroidery and gave it an approving little nod. "Finding Zoe has made Peregrine very happy and I think she is a darling girl, no matter what your great-uncle says."

The withdrawing-room at Muse Manor was a spacious but comfortable chamber, warmed, on this chill evening, by the flames of a fine log fire. Piers rose to move a candelabrum closer to his aunt. After the tragically early deaths of their parents in a shipping disaster some sixteen years ago, Miss Guild had been father and mother to the orphaned twins and their sister Dimity. She was plump now, and her hair, although luxuriant, was greying. Her features reflected good nature, and if she had never been a beautiful woman, they all had known she'd given up her chance for a suitable marriage and chosen instead to care for her dead sister's family. The children's terror of being parted was thus banished, and their gratitude had very soon deepened into love.

"Great-Uncle Nugent hoped each of us would make what he calls 'gratifying alliances,'" said Piers, resting a hand on her shoulder fondly as he returned to his chair. "The old fellow approves of Mitten's husband, since Tony Farrar has a title and a respectable fortune. But Zoe Grainger has little to recommend her—in his eyes, at least."

Miss Guild put down her embroidery and blinked at her tall nephew near-sightedly. "I suppose her dowry is not large, but you've always planned that Perry will have a share of the Manor property, no?"

"If I had my way, he'd have an equal share, but he won't hear of it. Says the estate must remain intact and that he'll accept 'a few acres only,' the silly numps."

"What have you in mind, dear?"

Piers hesitated briefly, then said with slow deliberation, "My twin has been through several kinds of hell since Prestonpans. He'll have his happiness now, by heaven, but he will! I mean to deed him three hundred acres where he can build Zoe the house he's always dreamt of."

"That is so like you, my dear one," said Miss Guild. "Have you decided which area to give him?"

"The north-east acreage. He's always longed to build a house on Quail Hill."

Startled, his aunt pushed the spectacles higher on her small nose. "But—that's on the river parcel! You had to sell that property years ago."

"Yes. I mean to buy it back."

"But—but I thought you were planning to sell the estate."

"Sell Muse Manor? Now why in the name of— Why ever would you think such a thing?"

"Perhaps because I heard you tell Florian only yesterday that you've had many offers and that one was very tempting."

"Aye." Frowning, he said slowly, "And I'd give something to know who made it. The solicitor is blasted secretive about his mystery would-be buyer. Not that it matters. I've had lots of offers for Tassels as well, but I'd no more sell her than sell this estate. Even if Perry and Mitten would hear of it—which they would not!"

Miss Guild blinked over the spectacles, which had slipped down to the end of her nose again and asked if they could afford to buy the river parcel, even if it were put up for sale.

"Oh, it's for sale," Piers said airily. "Old Finchley is hot after it."

"Then I do indeed hope we are able to buy it back! I do not like to speak ill of anyone, you know that, but Gresford Finchley is a nasty bully and makes our Florian's life miserable only because he takes him for a gypsy—which he is not and if he were 'twould make no odds. How shall you go about it, dear? Do you mean to ask Sir Anthony for a loan? I expect he would be only too glad to help."

"Perish the thought! Tony is a grand fellow and I couldn't

23

wish a finer husband for Mitten, but to beg money from a relatively new family member—ugh!"

Amused by his revulsion, she shook her head and chided him for "foolish pride."

He laughed and kissed her, and refrained from divulging that he'd already applied to their banker for a loan. Old Seequist had been agreeable and beyond saying that he'd have to obtain the approval of the directors, had promised to have the papers ready on Friday. It would mean delaying the repairs to the Home Farm this year, but it was much to be preferred over breaking his brother-in-law's shins. Why, poor Farrar would wonder what kind of family he'd married into!

". . . all of a twitter, and you've heard not a word I said!" Miss Guild clicked her tongue and observed that Peregrine had been right. "He was sure you were fretting over something. Am I allowed to know what it is?"

"It is that my twin borrows trouble where there is none. If my attention wandered just now, 'tis because I am wondering who is 'all of a twitter,' as you claim."

"Had you been attending me, child, you would have heard me say that this morning I received a letter from your Aunt Clara."

"Aha. Cousin Adam up to his tricks again, is he?"

"If he is, she did not mention it, though that wretched boy has led them a merry dance these past few years. No, my sister-in-law was big with *ton* news."

With a lift of the eyebrows, Piers said, "Never say my Uncle Harvey ventured out of Leicestershire at last? I'd not have thought anything could lure him from his precious farm."

"A surgeon lured him, poor soul. He will trust no one but the man he's always gone to in London, so they went but only for two days, and Clara had not time to come down and see us. She was able to take tea with some old friends who gave her all the latest news of the *ton*. Society is evidently agog because a young lady of Quality, who was lost at sea a year or so ago, has been rescued from some island or other and is back in Town again. You can imagine the scandal!" Miss Guild sighed. "How I feel for the poor child."

Piers looked at her curiously. "I'd think you'd be glad for her. I fancy her family must be overjoyed, unless she is ill, perhaps?"

"Ruined, rather. No, never look so betwattled, Piers. Do but consider: a young spinster, unchaperoned, cast up on an island inhabited only by savages, and living with them for a year and more! Goodness gracious! You can imagine what . . ." She broke off, her gentle face rather pink.

"*I* can," said Piers with a chuckle. "But I don't believe *you* can. Or in fact, should, dear Aunt."

Her blush deepening, Miss Guild took up her embroidery hurriedly and resorted to the only appropriate comment. "Men!" she said.

The large coach shot round the bend, taking up the centre of the lane with the team at a full gallop.

Piers Cranford, who'd been gazing through the window, lost in thought, was hurled to the side as his own carriage swerved violently to avoid a collision.

On the box, Florian Consett howled an incensed "Hey! Get out of the way, dimwit!"

The coachman driving the larger vehicle responded with a flood of fiery profanity as his wheels skidded from the road surface. The coach lurched and almost overturned, the horses snorting and squealing in terror. Enraged, the coachman scrambled from the box, seized the bit of the off-leader and attempted to drag the team back onto level ground. His loud curses and brutal hands further alarmed the animals, and he resorted to his whip, cutting savagely at the panicked bay as the horse reared in pain and fright.

"Stop that at once!" Florian secured the reins, leaped from

25

the box and ran to seize the coachman's whip and attempt to wrest it from him.

Cranford wrenched the door open and jumped down. He recognized the other coach as belonging to his neighbour, Gresford Finchley. He hadn't seen the face of the coachman, but the man's bulk and temperament identified Grover, the Major's head-groom, in which case the fat would be in the fire. Sidney Grover shared his master's loathing for the youth they referred to as "the thieving gypsy," and he and Florian had already come to blows. Cranford swore and ran to them; he'd not wanted any more disputes with the cantankerous major, but he had no intention of allowing anyone in his service to be abused. Florian had been of inestimable aid to Peregrine, who valued him highly; he had become a friend as well as an employee and, aware of his background, Piers could understand and sympathize with his present behaviour.

As a child the boy had been stolen by gypsies. His early years had been nightmarish, but his attempts to run away had resulted in such cruel retaliation that he'd given up hope. A kind-hearted man, much respected in the tribe for his artistic abilities, had "adopted" him, given him his own name, and a love of books. For a while he'd been protected, but as he grew into young manhood, his eager pursuit of knowledge and cultured way of speech had irritated many; his reluctance to steal caused him to be viewed with suspicion; and his dark good looks, while winning the hearts of several girls in the tribe, had earned him the increased enmity of the men. In desperation he had at length succeeded in escaping, but had been close to starving when a chance encounter with Peregrine Cranford had led to his being taken into that young ex-soldier's service.

Of late, Peregrine's involvement in diplomatic affairs, and his approaching marriage, made it necessary for him to spend much time in London. Piers, in need of a man with the potential to take on the duties of steward at Muse Manor, had offered Florian the position. Peregrine had protested with much indignation, but he was aware that Florian was happier in the country than in the great City. When the youth's loyalty had caused him to refuse the offer he yearned to accept, Peregrine relented and encouraged him to make the move. Since then Piers had been well pleased by the young fellow's industry and intelligence, and he'd made such progress that he was already assuming some of the duties of steward.

Even as Cranford ran up, a swipe of Grover's large fist sent Florian reeling. Cranford ran to steady him and demanded furiously that the big groom control his temper. "Had you not been hogging the entire lane, you'd not now be in this predicament!"

"And did your pretty gypsy know how to handle the ribbons, *Lieutenant,* sir, there would be no predicament!"

Cranford turned to face the owner of that harsh and belligerent voice. "My coachman—who is not a gypsy—knows more about horse-flesh than your clumsy bully will ever learn, Finchley," he responded coldly. "What a pity you do not instruct your people on the unwisdom of schooling a frightened horse with a whip."

Major Finchley was a stout individual of late middle age and choleric disposition. He stamped closer, his intense dislike of Piers Cranford causing the hue of his habitually red face to deepen. "I've a whip of my own," he bellowed. "And I give you fair warning, Cranford: If that gypsy whelp you call a servant dares cast his greasy eyes in my daughter's direction again, I'll use it to flay him raw; be damned if I don't!"

"Nonsense." said Cranford contemptuously, and glancing at Grover, snapped, "Tend to your cattle, fellow—and try if you can make your master proud of your skill. Which I doubt."

"Curse your insolence," snarled Finchley. "Don't use that tone to me, or—" Incoherent, his clenched fist lifted.

Grover grinned hopefully and stepped beside his employer.

Florian, pale and his mouth bloodied, all but sprang closer to Cranford.

The contrast between the opponents was marked, Cranford and Florian looking slight compared to the bulk of the major and his groom.

Standing very straight as Grover raised the heavy horse-whip, Cranford drawled, "Threats, Finchley? Rate your marksmanship high, do you? Or does your temper outweigh your instinct for self-preservation?"

The Major started. Losing some of his colour, he said un-easily, "Think to trick me into a duel, do you? Well, you'll not succeed, damn your eyes, for I'll not fight over a filthy gypsy."

"Indeed?" Cranford enquired curiously, "What will you fight over, I wonder?"

"You'll find out soon enough, curse you!"

"What a pity that I cannot wait for you to reach a decision. Come, Florian. We mustn't hang about like this."

Finchley sent more insults after them as they walked back to their coach, but both the whip and his volume had been lowered.

"You called his bluff, sir," said Florian admiringly as he opened the carriage door.

"They're a pair of bullies, and bullies retreat when someone faces up to them. But you'll do well to heed his warning, my lad, and restrain your admiration for his daughter. Both the Major and the charmless Grover would be happy to do you a mischief."

Florian said a meek "Yes, sir," and climbed back onto the box.

───※───

The bank manager's office was very quiet now, only the shifting coals of the small fire disturbing the silence. It was a mellow, pleasant sort of room, the panelling and the mahogany furnishings reflecting the dignity of its function and imparting an air of polite affluence but not luxury. Cranford thought inconsequently that it smelt like the lair of a bank manager.

A gust of wind rattled the casements. He glanced out at the lowering skies of early afternoon. It was raining again.

He knew that Seequist watched him, and he had a hold on his temper now. Meeting the man's anxious eyes, he said slowly, "Perhaps you will be so good as to tell me why I must see my great-uncle before you will confirm the loan? I am not under the hatches, I believe?"

"No, no, Mr. Cranford. Your credit is as good as ever, I promise you." Mr. Seequist was a stout individual, but his clothes were well-tailored and from the buckles on his shoes to his discreetly unpretentious wig he was neat as a pin. He had cultivated a jovial, almost avuncular manner, but today his laugh was as strained as his smile. He said carefully, "But— since his lordship is Executor of your parents' estate—"

"He *was* until I attained my majority," said Cranford impatiently. "At which point he became our adviser." An adviser in absentia, he thought cynically, for General Lord Nugent Cranford had been much too busy with his own affairs to concern himself with problems at Muse Manor.

"As you say, sir." Mr. Seequist removed his spotless spectacles and concentrated on cleaning them with his handkerchief. "The thing is, you see—an oversight, no doubt—but since we have never received notice of the termination of the Trust . . ." He shrugged, put on his spectacles again, and spread his pudgy hands apologetically. "You can—ah, understand our predicament. I feel sure you and your brother will have discussed the enlarging of your estate with his lordship, and it will need only—"

"You mistake it. I have not discussed the matter with Lord Nugent. Nor do I propose to enlarge our estate."

"Er—but I understood you to say—"

"Yes—well, it *will* enlarge the estate in a sense, I suppose, though the parcel I'm after was once Muse Manor property. Furthermore, my brother knows nothing of this, and I do not want him approached in the matter."

29

Seaquist's eyebrows went up.

Again, Cranford strove to control his irritation. The man was an old friend and was bound to protect the bank, after all; no need to get starched up about it. He said levelly, "Peregrine is soon to be wed. I want him to have the river parcel. It's been his lifelong dream to build a house of his own on Quail Hill when he married."

"Ah." Seequist beamed. "A happy occasion. I felicitate him. Your wedding gift, eh? What a splendid surprise it will be."

Cranford took up his gloves. "Does that clarify the matter, then? You will approve the loan? I am nigh eight and twenty, as you know, Seequist, and I assure you the Trust has long since been terminated."

"Of course, of course." The bank manager rose and came around the desk to shake the hand of this young man for whom he harboured a deep admiration. Opening the door, he said gently, "All we will need, Mr. Cranford, is a clarification from General Lord Nugent, and we can proceed."

A few minutes later, watching from the window as Cranford's coach splashed through drenched Basingstoke, Mr. Seequist shook his head ruefully.

"Proper vexed, he was, sir," murmured his assistant, carrying a sheaf of papers into the office. "Not like the Lieutenant to swear."

"We may be thankful it was Piers Cranford I'd to deal with," said Seequist, turning from the window. "If it had been that young hothead, Sir Peregrine, you'd have heard a deal more language, and a sight sooner!"

"I fancy he's off to see the General. Then he'll come back, eh, sir? You don't think he'll take offence?"

"I hope not." Mr. Seequist took up the top letter and looked at it unseeingly. "I'd no choice in the matter, but I would hate to lose his business—or his friendship. For such a young fellow to be saddled with the responsibilities he's had to cope with all these years . . . He saved his twin's life during the Rebellion,

30

did you know? Went back from the retreat at Prestonpans, crossed enemy lines to find him, then carried him out, got him home and managed to keep him alive when we all thought Peregrine was doomed. The estate was heavily encumbered and 'tis thanks to his efforts it wasn't lost to them. He's worked like a Trojan to keep things running smoothly—or at least to make it appear that way."

"Is it not—er, 'running smoothly,' sir?"

"Let us say, rather, that it has been a close-run thing. I honestly thought several times he was dished and would never be able to keep the property, but he juggled this, and manoeuvred that, and somehow hauled them out of the River Tick. It was an impressive feat for so young a man. I doubt his family knew the half of it . . . I just hope there's not a cockroach in his ale, is all."

His assistant watched him curiously. "Do you believe something is seriously amiss, sir?"

Mr. Seequist summoned a smile and declared in a rather hollow voice that he never entertained gloomy thoughts.

3

The following afternoon was ushered in by a blustery wind that carried occasional flurries of cold rain. Once again seated on the box of Piers Cranford's rather shabby coach, Florian tucked his chin into the scarf about his throat and narrowed his eyes against a chilly gust as he guided the chestnut pair towards Mayfair. It was a pity, he thought, that they'd had to leave Muse Manor, but the Lieutenant—he still thought of Cranford by his military title although he'd left the service two years ago—had been in a fine rage yesterday when they'd reached the country home of his illustrious great-uncle, so it was perhaps as well they'd been advised that General Lord Nugent Cranford was not in residence, and was instead occupying his Town house.

This philosophical outlook came less easily to Cranford. Seequist's polite but immovable request for a letter from his great-uncle had at first astonished, then infuriated him. The General, in his typically high-handed fashion, had likely deemed it unnecessary to remind the bank of the full details of the Trust. Irritated as he was, he knew he would have to tread carefully around the old fellow. General Lord Nugent had been decidedly testy of late. A distant relative of his late wife had tricked him into an involvement with the infamous League of Jewelled Men, and in all innocence he had enabled that traitorous group to further their plans. It was all smoothed over now, of course, but Lord Nugent had bitterly reproached himself for having been gulled. 'I'll have to bear that in mind and keep calm,' thought Cranford. He tried always to be polite to his seniors, but this confounded stumbling block with the loan was enough to—No. He would be calm and not allow his temper to get the best of him.

He glanced idly at the passing traffic, noting that Florian was driving with his usual skill. Didn't want the horses slipping on London's wet cobblestones; a grand fellow with a horse was Florian.

The coach slowed, and here they were at last, pulling into the porte-cochère beside the General's imposing Mayfair house, and the footman running to open the door of the carriage.

In the warm hall, Spiers, his great-uncle's elderly butler, pink and round and unshakeable, greeted him with his customary suavity and assisted him to remove his cloak. He was advised that Lord Nugent would be pleased to see the Lieutenant. Perhaps he would care to wait in the morning-room?

Cranford knew the signs. "Another caller, Spiers?"

"As you say, sir." The morning-room door was swung open. Spiers bowed and withdrew but not before Piers had glimpsed the twinkle in the faded brown eyes.

The morning room, a rather spartan chamber, was brightened by a small fire and two branches of candles. A tall young man was sprawled in a chair before the hearth. He turned his head and peered over his shoulder.

'Oh, egad!' thought Cranford. 'The Deplorable Dandy!'

Gervaise Valerian rose with supple grace and bowed low. "My very dear coz," he drawled. "But what a coincidence."

Sauntering forward, he held out one slender white hand on which gleamed a great sapphire ring.

Cranford returned the handshake reluctantly. At least the fellow did not have a limp grip, but that was the most that could be said in his favour. There were those, he knew, who would disagree with his sentiments, if only because Valerian wore his clothes well and, typically, was today the epitome of elegance. His wig was a work of art, as was the dark blue coat that hugged his broad shoulders as if molded to them. Beneath a paler blue satin and exquisitely embroidered waistcoat his breeches were pearl-grey, his stockings ornamented with blue clocks, and aquamarine buckles graced his high-heeled shoes.

Cranford ran a contemptuous glance over this magnificence, and thought, 'Faugh!' He met the light grey eyes then— famous eyes, darkly lashed under thick, soaring brows, set in a lean face that created havoc in innumerable female hearts and loathing in as many male ones.

Valerian sighed and waved his jewelled quizzing-glass in exaggerated dismay. "Alas, but I offend. As usual. Should you wish that I take myself off, coz?"

Feeling like a graceless oaf, Cranford said shortly, "Why should you think me offended? I am not master here. Nor, to the best of my knowledge, am I your cousin."

"But my very dear fellow, we *are* related. So sad for you, I know. But my lovely grand mama was, I believe, second cousin—or was it once removed?—to the late Lady Eudora Cranford. Your great-aunt, that is. Or rather, that was." Valerian smiled sweetly as he returned to his chair. "Forgive if I continue to offend by failing to pour you a glass of wine. I am a trifle fatigued, you know. Boredom, no doubt. Ah—" He waved the quizzing-glass gently at Cranford and drawled, "You are going to reiterate that you are not offended. But how am I to think otherwise when you scowl at me with such ferocity? I fancy it comes from your military background, but I declare 'tis quite frightening to a gentle individual of peaceful disposition. I shall probably be forced to seek a more serene atmosphere."

Cranford stalked to the sideboard, and, refraining from suggesting the atmosphere that he considered to be most appropriate for this dandified wastrel, poured himself a glass of claret. "My apologies if I appear—disgruntled," he said insincerely.

"But, of course, coz. You have—as usual—so much on your poor mind. I quite understand. And for you to be summoned . . . Oh, dear me!"

Well aware of the mocking laughter in Valerian's eyes, Cranford chose a chair on the far side of the hearth and sat down. "Would you care to elaborate?"

His alleged "cousin" blinked. "How so? Ah, you mean as to your having been summoned! Well, you were, weren't you? I mean, if not—why come?"

Cranford sipped his wine. "You came."

"I am all dutiful obedience. Whereas you, although two— or is it three years?—my junior, are a dauntless and gallant war hero whom I had fancied impervious to the whims of aging tyrants."

"I was not summoned. If you were, the General will doubtless wish to talk with you privately, so I'll leave you to—"

"But the old gentleman and I have already—er, enjoyed our little *tête-à-tête;* I had supposed that was why you were called into the breach, as it were."

Cranford stared at him. "If you've already talked to his lordship and are so averse to his company, you are doubtless eager to leave. Or do you stay to dine?"

With an artistic shudder, Valerian said, "Perish the thought! His *cook,* my dear! Dreadful! And with your usual perspicacity you guessed rightly, I am eager to depart. But I was shattered, quite levelled by my—er, great-uncle's choler. Such language you soldiers use! Though I comprehend that you are no longer—how is it the Scots say?—of that ilk! So quaint. Where was I? Oh, yes—being shattered, so that I judged it necessary, nay, vital for one of my delicate constitution, to rest and—ah,

35

recuperate before venturing into the rain. And when I saw your coach roll in, I felt it my bounden duty to stay and warn you."

"Indeed?" drawled Cranford, not bothering to conceal his boredom.

"But yes, coz. I am a very loyal fellow, you know. And it seemed unfair to let you go trusting and unarmed, as it were, into the lion's den. Especially since my own regrettable moral standards have brought about—" He paused as the door opened and Spiers returned, followed by a maid carrying a tray of buttered scones, sliced cold meats and cheese, and little cakes.

"Aha!" Valerian sat straighter as the girl blushingly set the tray before him. "Bless you, my pretty one! The condemned man—or should that be the reprieved man? Yes, I feel that is more apropos. The reprieved man shall eat a hearty meal!"

The maid's giggle ended in a squeak and she moved hurriedly from the vicinity of the chair, shaking her head chidingly at Valerian's grin.

Fixing the clearly unrepentant culprit with a stern stare, the butler dismissed the girl and said, "His lordship will see you now, Lieutenant Cranford."

Valerian quoted softly, " 'There is no witness so dreadful, no accuser so terrible as the conscience that dwells in the heart of every man . . .' Sadly, I acknowledge it. Do pray keep that in mind, coz."

Ignoring him, Cranford followed the butler.

In the wainscoted withdrawing-room General Lord Nugent Cranford stood before the mantelpiece, hands clasped behind him as he gazed into the fire. A man of large frame, he dressed conservatively, his one bow to the current whims of fashion being the high French wig he wore. The Indian sun had weathered features more often described as "daunting" than "handsome," an impression heightened by a large nose and prominent chin. Above a pair of keen hazel eyes, bushy eyebrows betrayed the fact that earlier in life his hair had been red.

He turned as the door opened and his flushed countenance told Cranford that this would be a stormy interview.

"Thank you for seeing me, sir," he began, coming forward to endure the older man's numbing handshake.

"Glad you're here," boomed the General. "Would have sent for you at all events." He motioned his grandnephew to a fireside chair and offered a glass of Madeira, which Piers declined politely. Pouring himself a glass, his lordship grunted, "But I forget m'manners. A courtesy call, m'boy?"

"One is certainly overdue, sir." Piers could almost feel the older man's wrath, and he said cautiously, "I'm glad to find you well."

The General glowered, took a deep breath, and barked, "And what of you and your charges? Dimity, or Mitten, as you call her, has done well for herself, eh? A title and a fine estate. All serene in Farrar's household, I trust? And Peregrine? Going to wed the Grainger chit, still? Could have aimed higher, there."

"They are deep in love, sir. In fact, it's partly because of their impending marriage that I've come to consult you." Piers added hastily, "Besides wanting to visit you, of course."

Lord Nugent occupied an adjacent chair and waved his wineglass impatiently. "Why should you seek my opinion of your twin's marriage now? Shutting the barn door after the horse has fled, is it not?"

Nerving himself, Piers launched into his carefully rehearsed explanation. Those heavy and expressive eyebrows shot up when he mentioned "three hundred acres" and drew down sharply when he spoke of his plans for the river parcel, the proposed bank loan and the necessity to confirm the dissolution of the Trust. "For, as you know, sir, my father intended those provisions to remain in force only until I attained my majority."

The General uttered two deafening barks of sound that vaguely resembled coughs. "Are you not forgetting that I funded the educations of yourself and your twin?"

Startled, Piers replied, "No, indeed, sir! We both are extreme grateful, and—"

"And that it was my generosity that bestowed a decent dowry on your sister?"

"We are very aware of that also, Uncle, and will never forget your kindness. Which is why I did not approach you for a loan in this matter, but—"

"But plunged ahead with ill-considered plans to purchase another parcel of land without even determining whether it might be more to the point to sell the estate?"

Stunned, Piers stared into the eyes that glared ferocity. "*Sell*—Muse Manor?" he gasped. "Absolutely not! Under *no* circumstances! It has been home to our family for centuries, and—"

"Times change!" The General stood and stamped over to the mantel again. In a rasp of a voice he said, "There was a codicil to your father's will that I kept from you. I admired the way in which, despite your lack of experience, you took on the responsibility for your brother and sister, and I had no wish to interfere until—or in case—it became necessary."

"A—codicil, sir?"

There was steel in the young voice now, and a glint of anger in the blue eyes. 'Natural enough,' thought the General, and the level of his own voice rose as he said, "You did not know, perhaps, that a year or so prior to his death, I loaned your father a large sum, with Muse Manor estate as collateral. I could be said to have a—a vested interest in the property."

Speechless, Piers watched him.

"Which is why," resumed Lord Nugent, I was appointed legal counsellor to my nephew's children until the eldest reaches thirty years of age."

"Legal counsellor?" Recovering his wits, Piers exclaimed, "But—even if that were so—"

"Do you *dare* doubt my word?" Lord Nugent's boom rattled the prisms on the lamp. "By God, sir, but you're an impertinent young bounder! Were you under my command and had implied—"

"I apologize. I—I can only suppose there is some misunderstanding here." Struggling to comprehend this sinister development, Piers said, "I have the most profound respect for you, Uncle. But this is so—new to me, and—and at all events, I doubt a legal counsellor has the right to—"

"He can counsel *against* any hare-brained decisions that would work to the detriment of the estate. And he can—if necessary to protect the heirs of his deceased nephew and in his own interest—order the property sold. In case of—er, emergency."

Piers sprang to his feet and demanded explosively. "What emergency? I've worked like hell to restore our finances! I do not know the sum of these vested interests you speak of. Indeed, I was unaware that my father had borrowed 'gainst the estate. But you will be repaid, sir! And you may believe I'll challenge in the courts if *anyone* tries to take the estate away from us!"

The General stamped to face him, and roared, "And *you* may believe, Lieutenant Sauce, that if I so decide, Muse Manor *will* be sold! In its entirety! And I promise you that, when the facts become known, no court in the land will oppose me. On the other hand . . ." He sat down again, and avoiding his great-nephew's enraged glare, said in a calmer tone, "If you are willing to abide by my wishes, that would, of course, change matters."

Piers, who had been about to demand the "facts" the old gentleman had implied, was thrown off-stride, and asked instead, "And what are these "wishes" of yours, Uncle?"

"They concern— But sit down, m'boy, so we may be comfortable."

Still seething with shock and resentment, Piers thought, *'Comfortable!'* but he took his seat again, and waited.

The General pondered a moment, then said heavily, "It is a matter of honour, I regret to say—or the lack of it! A matter involving your cousin."

Piers ran the faces of his cousins through his mind's eye. His mother's two brothers had families, one residing in Wales, and the other in Leicestershire. He'd never met his Welsh cousins but knew there were a sickly youth and three girls. The Leicestershire Guilds were a successful farming family, and Aunt Jane, who corresponded with her brother's wife several times a year, had sometimes remarked that their elder son, Adam, had been "a source of worry" to his parents.

"Adam Guild?" asked Piers thoughtfully. "I'd heard he is a handful."

"Who the deuce is—Oh. Your mama's brother's boy, eh? No, no. I refer to Valerian."

"Valerian? That fellow is scarce a cousin of ours, sir! I fail to see how—"

"Evidently. I wish I could agree. Gervaise Valerian is a mountebank, a rogue, a—a posturing popinjay, the despair of his unfortunate sire, and all but disowned by his lovely mother, whom he drove to live in France rather than endure his nonsense! Regrettably, his grandmama was cousin to your grandmother, and the confounded disrespectful here-and-thereian means to drag our proud reputation through the mire!"

"What—another duel, Uncle? Which lady's husband is after his blood this time?"

"The lady has no husband. And if her father weren't off frippering around some pesthole t'other side of civilization, he should be calling out the young scoundrel! I see you are confused. You surely knew that Miss Stansbury has been rescued?"

Once again mystified, Piers stared at him blankly.

"Gad! Do you pay no heed to Society affairs—er, matters? Cordelia Stansbury. She is betrothed to Valerian. Oh, I make no doubt he was trapped into the match. The chit is no beauty and I have to admit don't compare to the incomparables he usually takes under his protection. But that is neither here nor there. The fact is that the gel's mama, a scheming harridan if ever there was one, contrived to discover your cousin most improperly *tête-à-tête* in a locked room with Miss Cordelia, and quick as a wink rushed off a betrothal announcement to every newspaper in Town."

"Yes . . . I do recall something of the sort," said Piers slowly. "But that was more than a year since, I believe?"

"Just so. Mrs. Stansbury claims that the gel felt duty-bound to obtain her father's consent to the match, so she sent her off to Egypt, where Nathan Stansbury putters about in the sand. A stupid move, because the ship was lost in a fierce storm. Went down reportedly with no survivors."

"Poor lady. Then Valerian escaped? How does this—"

"If you'll hold your tongue for a minute, I'll tell you how. If Valerian had an ounce of wit, he'd have chose himself a more acceptable bride at once, just in case. He didn't. Now, the Stansbury chit has been rescued from some God-forsaken uncharted island, and has come home. He's honour-bound to wed her. All England knows of their betrothal."

This, Piers thought, must be the affair Aunt Jane had spoken of. So Valerian was properly caught. Amused, he asked, "Does Miss Stansbury not want him? Has she found someone else, perchance?"

"A cannibal chieftan, per *no* chance! But that matchmaking mama of hers has no intention of taking her claws out of Valerian. He and his sire have been at daggers drawn for years, but the boy is the legal heir, and when Sir Simon goes to his reward, Gervaise inherits the title and the fortune. Mrs. Stansbury will use every means at her command to force Valerian to honour his promise."

41

"Then I'd say he is properly caught."

"So would I. So would any man of honour. Not *that* worthless rake!"

"Gad! Do you say he means to draw back? Surely not. The poor girl will be ruined."

The General snorted, "Of course she's ruined. Nigh a year on a desert island! Unchaperoned! With only heathen savages for company? You may be sure her virginity is a thing of the past. That she would dare show her face in England at all is beyond belief."

"She's *here,* sir? In London?"

"Aye. And every gabble-monger in the three kingdoms in transports over the juicy scandal and agog to see what Valerian will do. Any other female would pack the gel off into a convent, but not the Stansbury tabby! She'll force the slowtop to wed her daughter if she can. And he flatly refuses even to call on her. If it were left to him, our family name would be trampled in the mud!"

"So that's why he's here," murmured Piers thoughtfully.

"You've spoken with him?"

"Briefly. I gather you were unable to change his mind."

The General said nothing, but stared at him with grim fixity.

In belated and horrified comprehension, Piers exclaimed, "No, Uncle! You never mean to suggest that *I*—"

"Why not? You are unwed, and to the best of my knowledge your heart has not been attached. For many reasons it is imperative that our name not be linked to any more scandal."

"But—but Valerian does not share our name."

"That don't mean the *ton* is unaware of the relationship. I've already been kindly reminded of it. Damned gabble-mongers! I'll not have it, I tell you!"

"Because of your contretemps with The League of Jewelled Men?" asked Piers with blunt daring.

The General's face became near purple and he fairly gulped with rage. "I said—*many* reasons," he rasped, as if fighting for

42

control. "And it is my understanding that you wish to buy the river parcel for your brother."

Also enraged, Piers came to his feet. "Your pardon, sir. I mean no disrespect, but I cannot think Perry would expect me to offer for the lady under such circumstances."

"The decision is yours, of course." With a smile that held nothing of mirth, his lordship snarled, "And must depend on the depth of your fondness for poor Peregrine, and for Muse Manor."

"He never did?" Lounging on the morning-room sofa, brandy glass in hand, Gervaise Valerian threw back his handsome head and gave a shout of laughter. "Why, the slippery old codger! I hope you drove a hard bargain, coz."

Cranford directed a narrow-eyed glare at him. "Do you," he said savagely. "So you waited here to enjoy the outcome of your damned disgraceful antics."

"But of course. Best pour yourself some of this excellent cognac, dear boy. You look—ruffled."

Advancing on the sofa, Cranford said with soft menace, "I'll ruffle you—*coz*!"

"Temper, temper!" With a lithe twist Valerian darted away. "Only play your cards right, and you can wheedle whatever you want out of the old curmudgeon."

"You lecherous blackguard—"

"Oho!" Dodging Cranford's advance, Valerian chuckled. "We resort to name-calling. Unfair. Did I not most gallantly stay here to warn you? Had you only paid heed—"

"To what? Your miserable treachery? *You're* the one offered for the poor lady. Had you an ounce of decency, you'd honour your word!"

"And so I would have, had she not rushed off to sea and disappeared for a year or so." Valerian winked and hooked one leg over the far end of the sofa. "That gave me my chance to

43

outwit her dreadful mama and escape the bonds of matrimony with— No! Stay back! Only put yourself in my shoes, Cranford. I didn't want a fat and spotty bride in the first place, and—"

"But, spots or no, you weren't averse to so compromising her that when you were caught you had no choice but to offer for her. And now you mean to jilt the poor lady and complete her ruin!"

"She's already ruined. I'll not wed some heathen savage's cast-off! No one would expect it of—Whoops! Almost had me there, dear old boy!"

"You are—despicable," snarled Cranford. "The lady may be dishonoured, but so will you be! All London will scorn you for the unscrupulous libertine you are!"

The faintest frown disturbed Valerian's classic brow and for an instant a steely glint replaced the mockery in his eyes. "Do you know—I really dislike to be named a—libertine," he murmured. "But, have no fear, coz. Our proud old General will never let the whole tale be told. And since you feel so pious in the matter, you'll be more than willing to ride to the rescue and save the maiden, eh?" He sprang up to put an armchair between them, and with eyes again alight with laughter, said softly, "Spots and all . . ."

Cranford was so infuriated when he left the morning-room that he stamped across the entrance hall and snatched his hat and cloak from the hands of the footman without a word. It was unlike him, and the footman exchanged a glance with the housekeeper as she came in her soft-footed way from the kitchen passage.

"Has something upset you, Mr. Piers?" she asked, watching him anxiously.

He took a deep breath and managed a smile. Eliza Turner had been housekeeper here for as long as he could remember. She was nearing fifty now; a plump, sad-eyed woman with greying hair who bore little resemblance to his childhood memories of her. She'd been a pretty widow in those days, and proud of the little son whom Lord Nugent allowed to live with her. Herbert had been a fine lad then, but at the age of ten he'd been severely injured in a riding accident. He had recovered his health, and at twenty was a splendid-looking young fellow, but his mind remained that of a child and all too often he was the target for cruel taunts and mockery.

Bending to kiss the housekeeper's cheek, Cranford said, "Nothing I cannot deal with, Eliza. And before you ask, as I know you will, my brother is well, and soon to be wed."

She gave a little cry of delight and clung to his hand. "I am *so* glad. I was afraid his lordship was vexed with you. Of late he has been rather—er—" She broke off, stepping back a pace as Valerian sauntered into the hall. "Are you leaving us also, sir?" she asked, her eyes admiring as they rested on the dandy's elegance.

"I must tear myself away, alas," he drawled, directing a sly grin at Cranford that said he knew he was safe from reprisals in front of the servants.

The footman hurried to offer Valerian's cloak and enquire if he wished a chair to be summoned.

"I was about to ask my cousin to take me to my club," said Valerian, adding with a heavy sigh, "but I see he is not in a generous mood this afternoon, so, yes, you'd best call up a chair."

"I'll be main glad to pole up a pair and drive you to the Madrigal, sir." The offer came from Mrs. Turner's son, Herbert, who stood humbly in the kitchen passage, his hopeful gaze on his idol.

"Thank you—no," said Valerian curtly.

Cranford had started towards the front door, but the small exchange brought him to a halt. It was typical of Valerian's arrogance that he should snub the lad who so obviously adored him. And it was typical also that this revolting individual could

45

so easily send his own temper flaring. He turned back and asked kindly, "How do you go on, Herbert? Well, by the look of you—"

"Oh—well enough, thank you, sir." The tall youth gazed wistfully after Valerian's departing figure and when the door had closed behind him, walked despondently back along the passage.

Mrs. Turner sighed, and driven by a sense of responsibility for the unkindness of his alleged "kinsman," Cranford said, "Your son has a fine pair of shoulders, Eliza. Does he still tend my great-uncle's garden?"

"Aye, sir. And loves doing it, though I wish he would find a situation that might offer a better future for him."

"No, but the grounds here do him credit. If ever he leaves his lordship's employ he could very well become the head gardener on some great estate. Or else you may send him to me. We would be glad of him at Muse Manor."

She brightened at this and patted his arm, murmuring that he was "very good."

Leaving her, he stepped out into the rainy afternoon. Florian stood at the heads of the pair, talking with Valerian, who turned abruptly and strolled to join Cranford. "I could not depart without wishing you joy of your wooing," he taunted.

Yearning to deck him, Cranford held on to his temper. "You might better bring some to young Turner. The poor lad worships you and you begrudge him so much as a kind word."

With a curl of the lip Valerian said, "To worship any man is to be a sorry fool. He fits that role, certainly. Besides which, dear coz, the last time I gave him a kind word I'd to endure a stammered lecture on the delights of ferns. Ferns! Gad! And here are my chairmen. Adieu, your nobility!"

As he bent to enter the sedan chair, Cranford yielded to temptation. He took a long step and "slipped." His boot rammed home on the seat of the dandy's breeches. Valerian uttered a howl of rage as he was slammed forward and barely avoided shooting out of the far side of the chair.

"My *poor* coz," called Cranford, walking towards the grinning Florian. "A stumble, alas. I was clumsy past permission. You cannot guess the depth of my . . . distress."

He climbed into his coach, hearing Valerian's profane assessment of his "distress" fading into the distance.

Leaning back against the squabs, he chuckled to himself. His day, he decided, had not been a complete loss.

4

*M*y *poor* little girl." Regina Stansbury sighed deeply as she poured tea for her afternoon caller. "Who ever could have imagined such a frightful tragedy would chance?" she mourned, refilling her own cup and indulging a mental sneer as she heard the creak of her guest's corset. She had not expected Mrs. Coffey on this wet afternoon, though had she known the woman was in town she'd have guessed the old busybody would come nosing around. Wanted to earwig out how they were to escape this hideous fiasco into which Cordelia had plunged them, that's why Evaline Coffey had come, purring like the smug tabby she was! Much good may it do her! Still, thought Regina, it was fortunate that she had worn the rose-pink *robe à la française* with the wide Watteau back pleats; her gown was far more fashionable than the purple satin over those great hoops that made poor Evaline look even more monstrous. It was quite comical to hear her creak as she moved. If she would but put off five or six stone, she'd still be a fat old—

"So affecting," said Mrs. Coffey, her sharp eyes taking in the ridiculous French wig affected by her hostess. As if any wig could render those hatchet features one whit less harsh. And Regina Stansbury might simper and sigh all she pleased, but the pushing creature couldn't hide the fact that she was seething—positively *seething*—because she'd not only lost a fine catch for her mouse of a daughter, but was now saddled with the disgraced gel and with not a chance to fire her off respectably. "I suppose that wretched boy has seized his opportunity to cry off," she said sadly. "Poor Cordelia would be heartbroken if she had cared for him deeply. But I fancy she's forgotten all about Gervaise after the excitements of her— adventures . . . eh?"

'Horrid *cat!*' thought Mrs. Stansbury. Her temper was seldom far from the surface and betrayed her into saying with a snap, "Cared for him *deeply?* Why, the sweet child *adores* him! She always has. When he offered she was in alt. I promise you, ma'am, that through all these months he has been enshrined in her heart."

"Oh, the poor *dear!*" Mrs. Coffey held a tiny handkerchief to her tearless eyes and enquired brokenly, "How *ever* shall you . . . comfort her, Regina?"

Yearning to slap her, Mrs. Stansbury uttered a shrill titter. "But why should I feel obliged to *comfort* her, dearest Evaline? Although the gossips among us whisper their wicked lies and insinuations, my Cordelia is as innocent and—*untouched* as the day she was born. Gervaise Valerian would not dare to cry off, for he would certainly be held in contempt by all London if he did so dishonourable a thing!"

"*Untouched?*" Mrs. Coffey blinked. "But—my love! Surely . . . all those months . . . alone on an island with only savages for company . . . and no one to protect the child . . . ?"

"Ah." Mrs. Stansbury gripped her teacup so hard that it was remarkable the handle did not break. "But you have been listening to a lot of fustian. You should not do so, naughty girl. The savages *worshipped* my lovely Cordelia! They'd never before seen a lady with fair hair. Quite logically, they thought she

49

was a goddess and laid not a finger on her. Not one!" Her rather large teeth were bared in a smile, but a hard stare challenged her guest.

Undeterred, Mrs. Coffey drew a deep breath and fired off her next volley. "How splendid, my love! You will, I am assured, have explained matters to poor Gervaise, and all those unkind rumours about his crying off are—"

"So much jealously! Valerian *adores* my Cordelia, and knowing of her unswerving devotion, has uttered not a hint of drawing back." (Which was no lie, she thought, since the graceless wretch had not had the common decency to call upon Cordelia since her return!)

"I am *so* glad! Then—may we look forward to bridals in the near future? I fancy Gervaise will be anxious to make Cordelia his own. Now she is so—ah—famous, she will have awoken the—um—the interest of other young rascals, I am very sure."

"Much chance they will have. Cordelia is as loyal as she can stare, and nothing would induce her to settle for another!" Mrs. Stansbury sank her teeth into a macaroon and thought, 'He had *better* wed the stupid chit, or he'll rue the day!'

Mrs. Coffey was quite aware of the frustration simmering behind that awful travesty of a smile. Gratified, she soon took her leave, eager to advise her friends that poor Cordelia Stansbury was hopelessly on the shelf and that her mama might very well strangle her.

As she was leaving the entrance hall, another caller arrived. He bowed politely and stood aside to let her pass. A tall, good-looking young fellow with a hint of the military about his bearing. It was a simple matter to claim to have mislaid her glove, and while a lackey was searching about for it, she heard the newcomer answer the butler in a pleasant voice, "I am Piers Cranford. Would you be so good as to take my card up to Mrs. Stansbury and say I beg a private word with her?"

Mrs. Coffey's ears tingled. "A *private* word!" It was a word she longed to overhear, but the glove having been discovered with irritating promptness under the credenza where she had kicked it, she was obliged to depart. Walking out to her waiting carriage, she was titillated by the knowledge that she had another fascinating *on-dit* to impart to her cronies. The name "Cranford" was familiar, though for the life of her she could not place it just now. Still, someone would know who he was, and all they'd have to learn then would be why he was calling on Regina Stansbury. Was it possible this young gallant cried friends with the dashing Valerian and had come to convey the rascal's regrets and end the betrothal? She gave an involuntary little squeak of excitement. That was the root of it, no doubt. Poor dear Regina must have known it was inevitable. Still, she would be enraged, and, shrew that she was, one could only feel sorry for her unfortunate daughter.

⸎

"I am well aware of your connection to the Valerian family." Mrs. Stansbury's tone was acid.

Cranford, who tended to be shy in the presence of unknown females, felt transfixed by her piercing glare, and noting the two spots of colour high on her cheeks, dreaded lest this volatile lady fly into one of her famous rages and succumb to strong hysterics.

"I collect you are here in behalf of dear Gervaise," she went on, "to arrange the terms of the marriage settlement."

Her fierce stare dared him to deny this, but he said quietly, "No, ma'am. It was my understanding that you had been advised of the termination of the betrothal between Valerian and your—"

"What?"

Deafened by her screech, he shrank back in his chair.

In full cry, Mrs. Stansbury left no doubt as to her opinion of Gervaise Valerian, his ancestors and all his relations. Shrill sobs and wailings followed.

Desperate, Cranford sprang up and snatched for the bell-pull.

"Do not dare!" hissed the outraged matron.

"But—but you are clearly overset, ma'am. Surely, you will need your maid to—"

"Sit—*down!*"

The words were a snarl; almost, she crouched in her chair, the thin hands crooked as though preparatory to attacking him. Obeying, Cranford thought, 'Dear heaven, what a dragon!' But he managed to gather his wits and say, "My deepest regrets if I have brought you grief, ma'am. I'll go and leave you in—"

"Oh, no, you don't!" She leaned forward, teeth bared and eyes glaring fury even as she wiped savagely at tears of frustration. "I do not hesitate to say I am appalled to find that a well-bred gentleman, such as you appear to be, would stoop to come here with so—so *despicable* a betrayal! *Appalled,* I say! And you may be sure the *ton* will sympathize with the shock and grief of a mother whose—whose precious child has been abandoned . . . Cast off like—like an unwanted—" She disappeared into her handkerchief once more, her words muffled.

The uproar had not gone unnoticed, and Cranford drew a breath of relief as the door was flung open and a young lady hurried in, followed by a maid and a footman. His hope that a rescue party had arrived was short-lived, however. The maid, clearly frightened, hurried to the side of her mistress; the footman paused just inside the door, eyeing Cranford truculently.

Turning from Mrs. Stansbury's wilting form, the young lady demanded, "What has this—person—said to so upset you, Mama?"

Cranford thought numbly, 'So this must be the shipwrecked spinster,' and his heart sank. He had stayed at his club in London these past two days, avoiding his friends while struggling to decide whether to accede to his great-uncle's demands. Having arrived at a most reluctant decision, it had been all he could do to summon the fortitude to act upon it. En route here he had tried hard to be comforted by the knowledge that his self-sacrifice would rescue an unfortunate girl from social ruin, besides ensuring that Muse Manor would not be wrest from his family.

He'd not been sufficiently noble to be comforted, but he had thought himself prepared. Valerian had described his erstwhile fiancée as being "fat and spotty." Not an inspiring picture, but preferable in his opinion to the young female who now faced him. She was not at all fat, being actually very slender, and in spite of the fact that she was taller than the height deemed desirable in a female, her extremely elaborate wig, of the latest French style, was very high. She wore a great deal of paint for so youthful a lady (perhaps to conceal the spots), and although her features were not unattractive, both mouth and eyelids drooped disdainfully and her expression was so haughty that he feared she must have inherited her mother's disposition. All in all, Miss Cordelia Stansbury was a far cry from the shamed and humble girl he had expected to meet. She looked, in fact, more likely to strike him than to be grateful for the rescue he meant to offer. Considerably unnerved, he bowed, and said, " 'Twas not my intent to upset—"

Mrs. Stansbury interrupted rudely, "Was it not, indeed! Then what *was* your intent, pray? Why are you here, Mr. Cranford?"

It was a home question. He glanced uneasily at the younger lady. "I had hoped to discuss the matter with you in private, ma'am."

Miss Cordelia fluttered her fan and uttered a shrill laugh. "Fie, but you need not coat your words with sugar on my account, sir. I know well enough what people say of me."

Her mother cast her an irritated glance, and having dismissed the servants, performed curt introductions.

Miss Cordelia selected a chaise and sat down; no mean feat considering that her pink velvet skirts were not worn over rounded hoops, English fashion, but were spread instead over the great flattened panniers now in vogue in France.

"Mr. Cranford is cousin to Gervaise Valerian," barked her mother. "You had best leave us, my love, for you will not like to hear what he has come to say."

"I should very much like to hear what he has to say, if you please, Mama," argued the girl. "Is it an apology, perhaps, for Mr. Valerian's failure to call upon me?"

"More likely an offer of recompense for—what do those sly solicitors call it nowadays?—breach of promise?" Mrs. Stansbury tucked in her chin and added malevolently, "It had best be a *large* amount! He can certainly afford it!"

Astonished by such vulgar presumption, Cranford glanced again at the notorious spinster. She sat very still and did not comment, and with the windows behind her it was difficult for him to see her expression. "Scarcely, madam," he responded drily.

"*Indeed,* sir? *Indeed?*" Mrs. Stansbury's enraged screech made him wince. "And how will he justify such stark cruelty to a stricken and innocent maiden, I should like to know? I wonder Lord Nugent Cranford allows any kinsman of his to display such a rampant lack of honour and responsibility! Well, all Society will hear of it, I promise you, sir! And your name will be—"

Cranford stood and lifted one hand. This loud-voiced, hard-eyed woman appalled him but he managed to gather his courage, and in a cold voice that cut off the tirade, he said, "Have done, madam! I am indeed sorry that Miss Stansbury has suffered such a sad—accident. But you know as well as I why Valerian has drawn back. And— No! Pray hear me out. You know also that while the *ton* may not approve of his action, neither would they condemn it. However—" He had to raise his voice to override her spluttering indignation. "However, my great-uncle is indeed aware of our family responsibility, and I am here today, ma'am, to ask if I might be permitted to—to call upon your daughter. In my own behalf."

It was done. The die was cast and his fate sealed. He could

feel perspiration starting on his brow and had to restrain the impulse to wipe it away.

After a breathless pause, Mrs. Stansbury said incredulously, *"You?* But, but— We don't even know you! Or," she added in a rush, "what your prospects may be."

"I can furnish you with any information you may wish, ma'am. I am not a rich man, but I have no need to apologize for my name or my home. If I may be permitted to call and take Miss Stansbury for a drive tomorrow, perhaps we can learn more about one another, and—" He stopped, staring.

The ruined and disgraced young spinster was laughing hilariously.

"Unkind!" Miss Laura Finchley pulled away from the strong arm that held her close against a muscular chest and turned fiercely on the man she loved. "You use too gentle a term, Florian! I hold it to be nothing less than disgraceful! Cordelia is a living, breathing, lovely human being, yet is being placed on the auction block just as if she were a—a cow or a sheep! Much her mama cares whether she knows or even likes the man she will wed! Her only concern is that he must be rich!"

At nineteen, Laura Finchley was a quiet damsel whose only claim to beauty was a pale complexion that appeared almost translucent and was the envy of her friends. Slightly below average height, she did not indulge herself at table, but no amount of tugging and lacing could create a satisfactory waistline, and her bosom was too slight to compensate for this defect. The velvet gown she wore on this windy day, although of the latest fashion, did not become her, the pale green giving her a washed-out appearance. Her hair, of an indeterminate brown, was inclined to frizz, her face was more square than the oval she so admired, and she described her looks, ruefully, as "humdrum." The sweetness of her nature was evidenced by the kindness in her soft brown eyes and gentle voice, but despite

55

her timidity, she had a firm chin and on occasion would exhibit a determination that startled her relatives. On this chill afternoon, when she was believed to be reading in the luxurious parlour of her suite, she was instead deep in her father's woods, sitting on a fallen tree-trunk improperly close to her most "unsuitable" suitor, Mr. Florian Consett.

Florian lost no time in replacing his arm. Smiling fondly into his lady's flashing eyes, he pointed out that Mrs. Stansbury had tried to arrange a match between her daughter and Gervaise Valerian. "And you say Cordelia loves the gentleman—no?"

Laura sighed and nestled close against the handsome young man whose jet hair and olive complexion reinforced the opinions of those who held him to be of gypsy birth. "She has loved him all her life," she said sadly. "But . . ."

"But Miss Cordelia is neither beautiful— No, do not fly into the boughs, my loyal little love! Be honest."

"Are you being honest? When did you last see her?"

"I think I have never seen the lady. But I've heard that despite the fact she is judged rather plain and has now come home in deep disgrace, she rejected Mr. Cranford when he was so gallant as to offer for—"

"Ooh!" Laura wrenched away again and declared, "I would think, of all people, you would understand her feelings!"

Florian's dark eyes hardened. "Of . . . all people . . . ? Do you mean that because your sire judges me a—what did he call me the last time?—'a thieving gypsy bastard' who has not the right to polish your shoes, much less aspire to your hand—"

Distressed, she pressed her fingers to his lips and murmured, "Never say such things, my dearest love. You know I do not share my papa's prejudices. What I meant was that— because we are sadly denied our happiness I think you might sympathize with my poor Cordelia's predicament. When she laughed at Mr. Cranford's offer—"

Florian gave a gasp. "She *laughed?* Oh, Jupiter! Small wonder my Lieutenant had a face like a thunder-cloud when he came back home! I do not understand, Laura. If her admired Gervaise don't want her—and mind you, he's not a quarter the man Mr. Cranford is—one might suppose she'd be grateful to— Whoops! I've done it again! You're gnashing your teeth at me!"

"You deserve that I should! What is she to be grateful for, pray tell? An offer from a gentleman she knows has not the smallest interest in her, and would wed her purely to save the face of that puffed-up uncle of his?"

"Great-uncle, love. And Miss Cordelia's face would thus be saved also, I think. But we have other things to talk of then—"

"Than my poor friend?" Miss Finchley uttered a lady-like snort. "Who is offered a marriage made in heaven, no less! Small wonder she refused to accept such a loveless bargain."

Florian sighed, but lifted her hand and kissed it tenderly, "And what of her fierce mama? How did she view this—bargain?"

"She boxed poor Cordelia's ears and said she had thrown away her last chance for a respectable marriage—which was the most she could hope for now she has ruined herself. And that she does not intend to support a spinster daughter for the rest of her days."

"The lady would seem to have a hard heart. I collect Miss Cordelia has no choice but to apologize and accept my Lieutenant, which would be in her best interests at all events. Now can we not talk of our own—"

"You mistake it!" overrode the single-minded Miss Finchley. "Cordelia is proud—too proud to spend her life kissing Mr. Cranford's boots and whining of her gratitude and—and repentance!"

"As if he would expect such slavish behaviour," said Florian indignantly. "Piers Cranford is one of the finest men I know. He may not possess a great fortune, but as his wife Miss Stansbury would be treated with a kindness she'd likely never have been shown by that strutting popinjay Valerian!"

Laura pulled the hood of her cloak tighter against a gust of cold wind and said slowly, "You may be right, dear. But I think Cordelia will never wed any other, however her mama may plot and scheme."

"Gemini! Do you fancy Mrs. Stansbury will try again to—"

"To entrap another hapless bachelor? Most definitely! Cranford didn't really suit her, at all events. She says he is a nobody and not to be compared with Gervaise Valerian for looks or fortune."

"Which is why every matchmaking mama in the *ton* is on the catch for him. One might think she would have realized her daughter was, er"—Florian hesitated and finished cautiously—"not likely to catch his eye."

"True, I suppose. Gervaise is everything most girls dream of—handsome, charming, wealthy, and heir to a baronetcy. Mrs. Stansbury knew he could have his pick of London's beauties and that there was no chance for Cordelia unless he were forced into offering. Oh, Florian! If you but knew how *mortified* she was at that dreadful ball."

"What do you suppose she will do now? Life with her mama must be insupportable, I'd think. Has she relations who would take her in?"

"I rather doubt it. Mrs. Stansbury quarrelled with all of them and they have been completely estranged ever since."

"Even so, Miss Cordelia must live *somewhere*, dearest. Surely her mama would not dare turn her out into the street, and she is too young to set up her own household."

"She told me she has—a Plan." Laura looked solemn. "And—oh, my goodness, I know her—Plans. Faith, but I dread to think of what may happen."

Florian kissed her cheek and tightened his arm about her. "Then turn your thoughts instead to what may happen to us, my love."

She leaned her head against his shoulder and said sadly, "I

dread to think of that as well. If my father should ever find out that I sometimes slip out to meet you! . . . "

"He would have my ears, I know. And in truth I cannot blame the gentleman. You deserve a splendid match, rather than to be tied to a young fellow who cannot even claim a legal family name and has no fortune whatsoever!"

Smiling at him fondly, Laura said, "You will succeed, I know it. You have looks and charm and—"

"And had it not been for the Cranford twins I would have starved by this time." He said without enthusiasm, "Perhaps I should take the King's shilling and enlist in the Army. I might work my way up—"

"And in the meantime I would never see you!" Seizing him by the collar of his coat, she cried, "And you might be killed! Oh, Florian! I could not bear it if I lost you! Only think, dearest, Lieutenant Piers has already made you his steward—a splendid achievement for so young a man!"

"And that achievement would render me acceptable in the eyes of your sire? Hah!"

"But—but I am growing older, Florian! I am nineteen already. We have only to wait until I am of age. Papa cannot forbid me to marry you then." She tilted up his chin and peered into the eyes that had been turned from her. "Dear one—you *will* wait? No, look at me! And promise you'll not go rushing off into the Army."

He forced a smile and kissed her and gave her his promise. Soon afterwards, watching her scurry across the park towards her father's great house, he was all too aware that meeting her against Major Finchley's wishes was dishonourable conduct. Lieutenant Piers had warned him repeatedly against coming here. Yet what other hope had they for ever seeing each other? Piers Cranford was a fine man, but if he had ever loved deeply, he would understand. Still, the need for all this secrecy brought a troubled frown to his face, and returning to the shrubs where he had tethered his horse, he acknowledged wistfully that he and his beloved had small chance of ever finding their happiness.

⁓

"It's agin me nature to come frettin' ye with it, Mr. Cranford." Oliver Dixon perched on the very edge of his chair in the Muse Manor study, turning his hat in gnarled, agitated hands as he gazed across the littered desk at his young landlord. "If we hadn't had so much dratted rain, the river likely wouldn't've backed itself up, nor the bridge wouldn't've fell itself down. But as things are, sir, I be powerful glad you're home again."

"Yes." Cranford smiled and said bracingly that he would ride over to the farm in the morning. "And we'll see what's to be done, Oliver."

Dixon looked even more distressed. "If ye could possibly come today, sir," he pleaded. "The fields are gettin' flooded, and me cows be already hock-deep in water, and the feed's gettin' soaked and turnin' mouldy, and I cannot haul feed in wi'out Hound's Tooth Bridge!"

Cranford nodded worriedly. "I wish I could come today, but I've two fellows waiting to see me, and there's no point in my riding out to the farm after dark. Have you been able to discover what caused the river to back up? We've come through more severe winters than this with no trouble."

"By what I can tell, sir, the side of Hounds Tooth Hill just give way and slid down. Blocked the whole channel and sent the water rushin' into my fields!"

"Did it, by Jove! Then until we can clear the river-bed, there's nothing for it but you must haul your supplies over the east bridge. It's the long way round, but—" Cranford paused. "What now?"

The farmer shook his head and said glumly, "Can't be done, sir. We'd have to cross the Westermans' property. I rid over,

60

but there's big signs bin put up, and it's more'n I dare do to go past 'em and open the gate."

"Gate?" Cranford stood and came around the desk to ask frowningly, "What gate?"

"The gate in the fence round that there great house they call a cottage. Fence went up whilst you was away, it did, and they've stuck up a sign saying as trespassers will be shot! *Shot!* But I 'spect—if *you* was to go, sir? . . . "

Taken aback by this news, Cranford concealed his vexation and said lightly, "Are you trying to be rid of me, you rascal?" He swung the door open, and calmed Mr. Dixon's protests, assuring him he spoke in jest, that there must be some misunderstanding on the part of the Westermans, and that he would ride over first thing in the morning, inspect the damage and then call at the Westerman cottage.

His tenant departed, looking somewhat gratified, but Cranford's reassuring smile faded. Why the deuce would anyone put up so grim a sign in this peaceful countryside? The sooner he came at the root of it, the better. Despite what he had told Dixon, he was of a mind to ride out as soon as he finished here, if the light held. Glancing up, his heart sank. Aunt Jane was talking with the curate, who had joined the two villagers waiting to see him. They all looked anxious. So much for riding out soon. It would be, he thought stifling a sigh, a long afternoon.

⁓⁓⁓

"I would not trouble you with it, dear," murmured Jane Guild, watching her nephew carve the roast pork, "but it drips right onto my bed, which I cannot like, you know."

"Well, of course not, love," answered Cranford, wondering where he could find sufficient funds to repair the bridge and the damage to the Home Farm, and rebuild Ezra Sweet's cottage, which had unaccountably caught fire three nights ago— thank God the poor old fellow had not been hurt! And now the bells of St. Mark's Church must be replaced, to say nothing of dealing with the havoc they'd wrought on the choir loft when they'd come crashing down.

"Piers! Thank you, but that's quite enough!" said Miss Guild, taken aback by the increasing mound of sliced pork on her plate.

"It's so old, you know," muttered Cranford, adding yet another slice.

"The pork?" asked his aunt, eyeing it uneasily.

He looked up at her. "Pork? No! St. Mark's, of course. Didn't I—" He broke off, flushing as he saw the massive serving he had prepared for his aunt, who was not a large lady. With an embarrassed grin, he said, "What on earth am I about? Your pardon, m'dear." Removing some slices, he handed the plate to footman Peddars, who smiled indulgently as he delivered it to Miss Guild.

"You will think me properly wits to let," said Cranford ruefully.

She was thinking that the poor boy had a great deal too much on his shoulders, but she smiled and evaded, "How did you find Lord Nugent? Were you able to enjoy a comfortable chat with him?"

"Not . . . exactly. Valerian was there."

"Sir Simon? Such a delightful gentleman. I hear that London seldom sees him since he came home from Paris."

"Not Sir Simon. His heir."

"Gervaise? Good gracious me! Then I quite comprehend why you were unable to enjoy a comfortable cose! Nugent likes Sir Simon. We all do, come to that." She waited until Peddars had finished serving them, and when Cranford had sent him away she said indignantly, "But to hear Gervaise speak of him, one would fancy Sir Simon to be a hydra-headed monster—which I do assure you he is not! That wretched boy should hang his head in shame for distressing his father so."

"I agree, but I doubt Gervaise Valerian would ever—" He

closed his lips over that caustic remark, then said, "Never mind about the silly fellow—what were you trying to tell me while I was carving you such a gargantuan meal?"

Miss Guild put down her wineglass and looked at him steadily. "The roof leaks. Over my bed."

"Oh, egad! And you've told me of it before!" Remorseful, he said, "Forgive. I'm really a woodenhead not to have—"

She leaned to pat his hand. "No such thing. Piers, what is amiss? And do not tell me 'nothing.' You're worrying. I can tell. You must let Perry help if we're in deep trouble."

"What? Pull my lovesick twin down from his rosy cloud? And only because we've a little difficulty with the river, and the church steeple has chosen to join the choir? Scarcely 'deep trouble,' love."

Miss Guild was not deceived by his charming smile, and in her gentle but determined way demanded to know what else had him "into the hips."

Cranford teased her and accused her of "borrowing trouble," but he was relieved when Peddars came in to announce that Lord Glendenning had called and was waiting in the library.

Horatio, Viscount Glendenning, was a lifelong friend of the family, and one of Miss Guild's favourites, and she was as delighted as her nephew to welcome their unexpected guest and insist he overnight with them.

His lordship raised small objection. He interpreted Cranford's sidelong glance correctly and stepped into the breach, joining them at table as another cover was called for. A skilled *raconteur,* his light-hearted tales of Town and mutual acquaintances brightened the meal, banishing Miss Guild's apprehensions and bringing her often to laughter.

Not until the good lady had gone to her bedchamber and the two men were alone before the library fire did his lordship demand bluntly, "All right, Piers. What the devil's going on here?"

"Some wretched weather, mostly, and—"

The viscount's lips compressed and a spark came into his eyes. "Never try to fob me off as if I were a casual acquaintance. I've known you since we both were in short coats. If I can sense there's a rat in your pickle barrel, you may be sure Perry will."

Alarmed, Cranford exclaimed, "Jove! Is he on his way here?"

"Not to my knowledge. But I've a decided feeling he should be. And if you mean to play the strong and silent chivalrous knight, be damned if I don't ride to Town and fetch him!"

Cranford swore softly, but he was in really desperate need of a friendly and sympathetic ear, and Horatio was, beyond all doubt, the best of friends. Suddenly exhausted, he put back his head and drew a hand across his eyes.

Watching him, Glendenning's apprehension deepened. Over the years he had seen this man overcome one drawback after another so as to keep his family together and turn the estate into a paying proposition. Piers was not one to be easily crushed, but at this moment he looked nigh foundered. "Come on, old fellow," he urged in a gentle voice. "If it weren't for you and Mitten and Perry risking your own necks, my foolish head would even now be grinning from a spike on Temple Bar. I owe you my life. The least you can do is allow me to help, if 'tis only to offer my far from sage advice."

Cranford turned his head against the sofa cushion and for a long moment regarded this man he knew so well. Powerfully built, though not above average height, the viscount could not be described as handsome, but he had a fine pair of green eyes edged by the laugh lines that spoke of a sunny nature. His loyal friends declared that his nose, if not of slim and classical proportions, was "strong." The mouth below it was wide and humorous, though the chin had a stubborn jut. Freckles hinted at the auburn hair that today was powdered and tied back, and which had sufficient red in it to speak of the impetuous and rebellious spirit that during the recent Jacobite Uprising had almost cost him his life.

All in all, thought Cranford, it was a good face, and the depth of concern in the eyes was touching. "Very well," he said wearily. "But not a word to Perry. I'll have your promise, Tio."

"You have it."

And so Cranford told him of his hopes for the river parcel. He saw the viscount's expression change from understanding to astonishment when he described the banker's evasiveness. Glendenning did not interrupt until he spoke of the interview with his great-uncle, at which point he exclaimed, "The devil you say! He really wants you to pull Valerian's chestnuts out of the fire?"

"Not quite how he worded it, but in effect, those are his wishes."

Glendenning scowled, rose, and crossing to the sideboard, carried over the decanter of port to refill their glasses. Sitting down again, he muttered, "Jupiter! I thought my sire was difficult, but—"

"And I'm an insensitive clod not to have enquired about your lovely lady. How does Miss Consett go on, Tio? Is the earl—ah—"

"Reconciled to my taking a lady with neither fortune nor high title for my bride?" The viscount grinned happily. "Amy has wrapped him quite around her little finger. The dear old fellow dotes on her."

"Splendid, and she's taking the Town by storm, I hear. Your stepmother's doing?"

"Yes, bless her. Though Amy charms everyone, and— Enough of that, slyboots! We are discussing your kettle of fish, not mine—"

"For a change," inserted Cranford with a twinkle.

"True enough. No, seriously, you never mean to offer for Miss Stansbury? You'd do better to call Valerian out. The *ton* would then consider your family honour vindicated and—"

"The deuce they would! And much good would it do me if I were dead! He may be a dandy, but I've heard it said that he's a damned fine swordsman."

Glendenning sighed and said heavily, "Aye. He is that."

"You've seen him fight? He's really good?"

"Good enough that I'm glad I was not the one to face him."

Cranford turned to scan him curiously. "A duel? When?"

Reddening suddenly, Glendenning shrugged, and answered with exaggerated nonchalance, "Och, I disremember. 'Tis of no import. The thing is—"

"It was on the *battlefield!*" breathed Cranford, his eyes widening. "By heaven, you faced his steel at—where? Prestonpans? Culloden?"

Glendenning stared into his wineglass in silence, his face sombre.

Lowering his voice, Cranford persisted, "Do you say that mincing dandified fop fought beside you?"

"No."

"Then—he was for King George?" Glendenning's eyes met his own levelly, and Cranford said, "I'd not have believed he had that much gumption! And—he was really a man to be reckoned with?"

"I told you I'd not care to have faced him."

Coming from this man who was a skilled swordsman, it was high praise. Cranford whistled softly and there was a pause before he murmured, "Tio—have you ever wondered what we'd have done if Perry or I had faced you?"

"Aye. 'Twould have been a—sticky wicket, old lad. What do you think *you'd* have done?"

"I suppose—tried to disarm you . . ."

"And then—taken me prisoner? To be dealt Cumberland's hideous 'justice'?"

"Lord forfend! But—suppose you'd overpowered one of us? What then? A swipe of your claymore?"

They looked at one another askance for a moment, then Glendenning chuckled. "What claymore? Did you ever try to heft one of those monstrous swords? I doubt I could lift one, much less swing it. And you're trying to lead me off the subject again. You will never do as your great-uncle demands?"

"If I do not, Perry won't get his acreage or his house."

"Then let me, or my father—" His answer was a flashing glare, and he sighed and dared not finish the offer, saying instead, "Can you not build Perry's house on another parcel? Ah! I see you've not told me the whole. What more, my buck?"

Reluctant to speak of his humiliating encounter with Mrs. Stansbury and her daughter, Cranford evaded, "Only that we seem to have run into a flock of disasters. The steeple and bells of the village church tumbled into the choir loft; one of my tenant's cottages burnt down; the river has decided to change its course and in so doing has flooded the Home Farm; and just for a small bonus—this roof is leaky as any sieve! If I don't satisfy the old gentleman and get my loan, I'll be dashed fortunate to hold on to Musc Manor, much less buy back the river property. Do you see?"

Glendenning pondered, then asked slowly, "When do you mean to offer for the unfortunate lady?"

Cranford flushed and was silent.

"Jove!" gasped the viscount. "You silly block! You've already paid your addresses!"

Cranford muttered, "Say rather I made the attempt."

"Made the *attempt*? Do you mean— You cannot mean— You offered the poor creature the only chance for a respectable alliance she is ever likely to receive and . . . and she *rejected*— No, that cannot be the case, of course. Her mother is a dreadful battleaxe. Likely, she still hopes to entrap Valerian and all his lettuce. Is that the way of it?"

Cranford answered slowly, "The lady threatened to bring suit 'gainst my ignoble cousin for breach of promise."

"Ha! She'll catch cold at that! Valerian's no green boy."

"True. I believe it was an empty threat. She appeared to me to be thunder-struck when her daughter found my—my offer ludicrous. Oh, it's quite true, Tio. I am really sorry for Miss Cordelia Stansbury, and have no wish to speak ill of her, but I fear . . ." He hesitated, then said, "I tell you in confidence that the lady is extreme proud. She is quite attractive and most elegant, and affects the very latest French fashions. In short—a far cry from the shy little waif I had expected to meet."

"But—but she's *disgraced!* Utterly ruined! Does she not realize that?"

"So far as I can tell, she has not a vestige of the shame or humility one might expect from a lady in her predicament."

Incredulous, Glendenning exclaimed, "Can I credit it? She *really* rejected you?"

"Not in so many words. She just . . . laughed."

"Laughed?"

Squirming at the recollection, Cranford said bitterly, "Until she cried. I took my leave at once, feeling several kinds of a fool, as you may imagine. All the way out to my carriage I could hear her mother screeching."

"I can scarce blame her. But—rejoice! You're free, old lad. You tried. His lordship will have to accept that your offer was rejected. Have you seen him since?"

"I called on him before I left Town this morning." Cranford scowled. "He says Miss Stansbury was likely 'overset' and that I must try again."

"You're never going to? Now that is above and beyond the call of duty! You cannot seriously contemplate taking such an ill-mannered creature for your wife?"

"You may be sure it is not my wish." With a rueful sigh, Cranford said, "And that is an ungentlemanlike thing to say, is it not? The fact is—dash it all, Tio! I think the girl is still mad for my worthless dandy of a pseudo-cousin!"

"Good! But I suppose you were too mannerly to say as much to Lord Nugent."

"I told him she'd have none of me." Cranford paused, looking glum. "He said I was not forceful enough, and that a lady likes to be pursued."

Lord Glendenning's opinion of that edict was as forceful as it was impolite.

5

Riding with the viscount to the Home Farm next morning, Cranford's worst fears were verified; the south field was now a wide lake and the water in the farmyard was ankle-deep. They located Oliver Dixon in the stables, hard at work with two of his farm-hands. He looked exhausted and admitted he'd had little sleep. "It do be sad to see the place like this, sir," he said wearily.

His own heart heavy, Cranford agreed, and asked if they had lost any livestock.

"Not so far as I know, sir. Not in the barns and stables, anyhow. But I've got my three boys out to the pastures in case any beasts are in trouble. I mean to join them soon as I finish here."

"I'd sooner you get some sleep, before we have *you* in trouble," said Cranford. "Your lads will give you a full report, I've no doubt."

Pleased by this compliment to the sons of whom he was justly proud, Dixon invited Cranford and Glendenning to go up to the house, where his lady wife would be "only too glad" to prepare them breakfast. Mrs. Dixon was a fine cook and Cranford was tempted, but he was anxious to get to the site of the slide, and having reluctantly declined the offer, he and the viscount rode out again.

They negotiated the muddy ground with care and skirted the flooded fields, both men dismayed by the extent of the damage. When they reached the source of the blockage, Horatio Glendenning reined his mare to a halt, leaned forward and viewed the bare gash in the hillside, below which labourers were industriously clearing rocks and debris from the river. "It appears to me that some of those large boulders were dislodged by the rain," he said. "And when they came down it started a tidy little avalanche. Your fellows will have their work cut out to clear the beastly mess, even if it don't rain."

Cranford glanced at the sky. The early-morning was chill and overcast but it was bright and there were no heavy clouds. "It's going to take a week at the very least," he agreed. I've sent Florian down to Short Shrift to hire more men and another team and waggon to haul away the rubble."

"Where d'you mean to put it? In The Teacup?"

The Teacup was a deep depression not far from the manor. As children it had been their secret meeting-place, and two years ago, when the viscount had been a wounded Jacobite fugitive, he'd taken shelter there and been aided by the Cranfords despite the knowledge that their lives would be forfeit if they were caught helping him.

Piers said musingly, "It might be as well to fill it up, if only to keep out rascally rebs." He ducked the tricorne Glendenning swiped at him, and with a wry grin took out his pocket watch. "I'd expected Florian before this. He'll be sorry to have missed you."

Amy Consett, the viscount's beautiful affianced bride, had been stolen from her nurserymaid by the same band of gypsies who had later kidnapped Florian. Both she and the boy had only sketchy memories of their early childhood and neither

71

knew their true parentage, but having grown up together under the protection offered by Absalom Consett, a respected member of the tribe, they considered each other to be "family."

Glendenning was fond of the youth, whom they now guessed to be about nineteen, and he asked, "How does he go on with your people?"

"Very well, in most respects. He has a fine mind and learns quickly. If he can just control his pride he'll make a good steward."

"I thought he'd subdued that famous pride of his. I know it bought him trouble aplenty while he was with the tribe. Amy told me that the young bucks resented the height in his manner. Does he still tend to treat others as if he were the king of the castle?"

"If he does, I've not seen it. But he certainly aims high in— other directions."

They rode on, side by side, the bright coat of Flame, Glendenning's chestnut mare, shining in the pale light and making a fine contrast with Tassels' softly mottled grey.

In an attempt to turn his friend's thoughts from the disastrous flood, Glendenning said lightly, "The direction of the ladies, eh? Or should I say 'lady'? D'you fancy he made a detour in that 'direction' en route home?"

Cranford's lips tightened. "If he did, he'll hear from me!"

"Jove, what a spoil-sport! Florian is no longer a child, y'know."

"True. But still too young to have formed a lasting attachment."

"I don't see that. He's a fine-looking lad, and if his heart is given—"

"Then he has given it most ill-advisedly."

"Why? Is Miss Finchley an antidote?"

"I've only seen the lady in the village, or at church occasionally, but she's certainly not an 'antidote.' Her father loathes me, and is the kind to judge all gypsies as thieves and vagrants

72

who should be shot as soon as may be. He's already warned Florian off."

"Even as the girl beckons him on, eh? How is it that I've not the pleasure of her acquaintance?"

"She was at a seminary for several years after they moved here. You met him, though. Last autumn."

"So I did, and was glared at with pronounced disapproval. He fought at Culloden, as I recall, and made clear his suspicions about my loyalties. Didn't he once offer you and Perry some advice about your 'treasonable' friendship with me? He likely judges me to be as expendable as young Florian."

"Oh, I'm sure of it. He's the type to nurse his prejudices. Do you care to come and have a look at our collapsing bell tower?"

The viscount said he would be glad to see Muse Village again. " 'Fraid I'll have to leave you afterwards, old lad. I'm to dine with my parents and Amy, and I've not left myself a deal of time."

"What you mean is that you can scarce wait to get back to your lady. You poor besotted lovers are all alike."

"Oho! Listen to the crusty old bachelor expound on something he knows nothing about! If you're lucky, one of these days *you* will fall in love, Mr. Indifference, and discover the joys of being 'besotted.' "

"But not today," said Cranford. And he thought, 'And certainly not with Miss Cordelia Stansbury!'

They enjoyed a gallop through the crisp cold morning, and reached Muse Village neck and neck, with Glendenning boasting that his splendid chestnut had held her own against the much-praised Tassels, and Cranford declaring that he had very kindly held the filly back so as not to embarrass Tio's "red-headed lady."

The air now carried the tangy aroma of burning wood, and smoke drifted from the chimneys of the thatched cottages. A few villagers were to be seen on the winding lane; hats were raised and greetings called to "the Squire." Two women busily hanging out washing responded to Cranford's greeting by saying shyly that they had to catch "a dry day." A shabby but sturdily built man, his laden donkey cart nearby, was attempting to interest Mrs. Franck, the blacksmith's wife, in the charms of a flat iron implement he called a girdle. Glancing at it curiously, Glendenning muttered, "Is the poor lady supposed to wear that thing?"

Cranford chuckled. "It's a cooking pan, you lunkhead! They're suspended over the fire and used for cooking cakes and suchlike. If you've never tasted a little cake still warm, with butter melting in the middle, you've missed—" He broke off, mildly irked when his friend rode on, obviously having paid no attention to his explanation.

Children came running along the lane, whooping with excitement, eager to greet their hero, "Left'nant Cranford." Always an object of delight, Tassels was made much of, and betrayed no signs of alarm when many small hands stroked and caressed her. Glendenning was popular also, Flame came in for her share of admiration, and the two young men were soon surrounded. The viscount liked children, but it seemed to Cranford that today he was rather brusque and a tense look had driven the customary smile from the green eyes.

The horses were placed in the care of two of the older boys and led off to the stable while the younger children scattered to homes and breakfasts. Walking towards the church, Cranford said, "I hear something rattling around in your brain-box. Are you finding me solutions, Tio?"

" 'Fraid not." Glendenning glanced back. "That pedlar. D'you know him?"

"If you mean have I bought any of his goods—no. But he comes to the village now and then and makes a few sales. I'm told he's an amiable-enough fellow. Why?"

"Does 'now and then' cover several years?"

"Be dashed if I know. But . . . a few months, anyway. You don't look pleased. Is he a slippery customer?"

"I wish I knew. I've seen him before . . . somewhere . . . Can't remember where. Only that he gives me an uncomfortable feeling. No—don't look round. He's still watching us."

"Mercy! You never think he's after *you?* I thought you had escaped that sticky wicket."

"So did I. And very likely I'm borrowing trouble. Still, I'd be wary of him, your Squire-ship. Speaking of wariness, I'm surprised that old Perry ain't come charging up here, and— Oh, egad! Only look at your poor church!"

St. Mark's, although small and unpretentious, was much admired and usually presented a charming example of a rural place of worship. The graveyard lay behind the church. On either side of the building were velvety lawns and oak trees that imparted an aura of serenity to the old structure. Today, however, the lawns and front steps were littered with debris, several stained-glass windows hung in shreds, a thick dust covered leaves and grass, and the missing top of the bell tower gave the church an oddly "headless" appearance.

Cranford paused to view the damage in dismayed silence.

Beside him, Glendenning muttered, "Jove! Another mess for you, Piers! Beastly luck you're having."

Joseph Barrick, the curate, hurried to join them. A pale and rather high-strung young man with a nervous twitch, he expressed his gratitude for Mr. Cranford's prompt arrival and led them inside, warning of the hazards of fallen masonry, glass, and splintered beams. Carpenters were busily erecting a makeshift cover over the hole in the roof, but Cranford realized sadly that most of the ancient and beautifully carven choir stalls were past saving. Glendenning, a fine amateur architect, was asked to comment on the work of restoration and delighted Piers and the clergyman by declaring that he knew some skilled artisans who could copy the carvings "so that you will scarce know the difference." He became so interested in the details that eventually Cranford had to remind him of the time.

They left the much-cheered cleric and reclaiming their horses, rode side by side until the viscount asked idly which cottage had burnt. Cranford shot an oblique glance at him and did not answer. Suspicion dawned in Glendenning's eyes. Halting his mount, he demanded sharply, "Piers? It's never old Ezra Sweet's house? Gemini, but it is! Farewell, you unprincipled rascal!"

Piers leaned to snatch Flame's bridle. "Wait! It won't hurt you to delay another minute or two, and if you're with me the poor old fellow is less likely to—"

" 'Poor old fellow' my Aunt Samantha! He's a perpetual raincloud, and crusty at that! Why you tolerate the creaking curmudgeon is more than I can—Hi! This is your chance, Piers! Build him a cottage on that piece of land you own outside Basingstoke! The Muse villagers will thank you, I'll go bail!"

"As if I could do such a thing! It's little more than a swamp, and besides, he'd die of loneliness away from everyone he ever knew! And I 'tolerate' him, as you put it, because after we lost our parents, Dimity nigh went into a decline. It was Sweet who took her with him about the gardens and—"

"And told her stories by the hour. Yes. I remember her speaking of it, but that was long ago, and he hadn't turned into an argumentative old gaffer."

"Who put the joy back into the girl you wanted to make your wife at one time, as I recall."

"Well, and why not? Your sister is a very special lady." Glendenning smiled nostalgically. "Fate has her own schedule, eh, Piers? Who'd ever have dreamt back then that Mitten would wed Tony Farrar?"

"Or that you'd have found your beautiful Amy."

"To whom I must make haste!" Jerking his reins free, Glendenning said laughingly, "Go on, then. Listen to his moanings. But don't say I didn't warn you!"

76

"Fair-weather friend!" Cranford watched as the viscount rode off towards Windsor and Glendenning Abbey, but checked his speed after a minute to turn and wave a farewell. Returning the wave, Cranford guided Tassels to the north end of the village to inspect the charred ruins of his elderly tenant's home. It was all too clear that the cottage was past restoring, and would have to be razed and rebuilt.

"I 'spect as you be a-sittin' there and blaming poor old Ezry. And thinkin' as old Ezry went to lie down on his bed and left the fire burnin' and no screen up," wailed a scratchy voice beside him.

Cranford smiled down at the lined and sunken features of the frail, bowed old man who had once delighted his mother with his expert care of her beloved roses. "Now why would I think such carelessness of you?" he asked. "I know how conscientious you are, Ezra."

"So you *says,* Mr. Piers," argued Sweet, feebly brandishing a gnarled cane. "But I sees that there frown in yer eye, and I knows what ye was a-thinking. Old Ezry be too doddlish t'be trusted any more, ye was thinking to yerself. Don't mean to build me another house, I shouldn't wonder. Not as it wouldn't be shame on ye to kick a poor old soul out in all weathers, wi' nowhere to rest his poor weary bones, nor no one to give a button whether he lives nor dies! Arter all the years he served ye, and yer father afore ye!"

Dismounting hurriedly, Cranford promised, "Of course we'll build you another cottage. And as for putting you out in the weather, I had understood you were staying with that pretty granddaughter of yours."

"Bessie don't want her old granfer taking up space in her fine new house what were give to her by her new father 'law. A real house *that* be, with a fine deep hearth and no draughts comin' in the winders or round the door like my poor old place. Fair froze I were in the winter-time the way they draughts come whistlin' in, nigh deafenin' me ears! But did I complain? Never!

And who cared? Not one single soul! Lone and lorn I be. Lone and lorn and outlived me usefulness."

He turned away, only to stagger a little, so that Cranford threw an arm about his shoulders. A tear gleamed on the weathered cheek and Cranford said bracingly, "Come now, Ezra. Cheer up. Mr. Consett is already having plans drawn for your new cottage. I'll send him down to talk to you and find out how we can make things more to your liking."

"Aye, well, that young gypsy sprig had best come quicklike, fer poor old Ezry's days be numbered, an' chances are he'll be called to his reward long 'afore that there new cottage is built. Though even if it's got better winders an' more cupboards an' a fine deep hearth it'll be a lonely place fer a solitary soul, now that Bessie's gone orf an' turned hersel' into a wife, an' deserted her old granfer."

"Now, Granfer," said a gentle voice. "What be ye a-saying to Mr. Piers?" Bessie Sweet, now Mrs. Tom Kayne, was a comely, soft-voiced young woman, rosy-cheeked and bright-eyed. Flaxen curls were inclined to escape from beneath an immaculate frilled cap, the apron that encompassed her plump self fairly glowed with cleanliness, and there was about her an air of vibrant youth and health. Her fondness for her grandfather was well known, and she said with faint scolding, "Ye knows sure-ly I hasn't deserted ye, but has begged ye to move in with me and Tom; only you said you'd be more comfortable with Auntie Peg."

"And so I would. Who wants to move in with a pair o' lovebirds, billin' and cooin' night an day? Bad enough yer Auntie Peg's comin' to chit and chat and plague me mornin' to night! Enough to turn the stomach of a sensible man. And likely she'll do nought but grouse about the new cottage Mr. Piers *says* he means to build me. Not as a humble workin' man can trust anything as 'ristocrats promises. So—"

"So that'll be enough o' that sort of talk," chided Bessie, winking at Cranford, but sounding very stern. " 'Tis past time

78

for the cordial the Widder Macaveety wants ye to be taking, so stop yer grousing and come home now, do."

She took the old fellow's frail arm and with a ruefully apologetic smile at Cranford led him off, nodding patiently through a snorted tirade about midwives "what don't know peas from beans," and gypsies who "only knows houses what a horse pulls!"

Reprieved, Cranford decided to discover what was delaying Florian. He rode south, across-country, his mind wrestling with the various problems that faced him and the need to resolve them before his twin sensed that all was not well at Muse Manor.

There was no sign of his young steward and he was approaching the stand of poplars that marked the southern boundary of his lands when he heard sounds of conflict: Major Finchley's nasal bellow, and a younger voice, ringing with indignation, that told him he had found Florian.

Emerging from the trees, he saw the horse and cart nearby and his new steward struggling in the grip of Sidney Grover and a sturdy stable-hand, while their employer laughingly egged them on.

Cranford thought an irritated, 'Not again!' and sent Tassels cantering across the meadows to his neighbour's drivepath.

Catching sight of him, Finchley howled, "Off with you, Cranford! I warned this little rat what I'd do if he dared set foot on my property!"

Florian's face was bloodied and he looked white and spent. He panted, "There was a sign on—on the lane for a detour, sir. I followed, and—"

"Cor, what shockin' lies!" Grover, the Major's head groom, threw a saintly glance at the heavens. "You knows as there weren't no sign, Major, sir. Fact is this worthless gyppo was creepin' 'round to annoy Miss Laura again."

"Not true," gasped Florian. "The sign said—" He broke off, flinching as Grover twisted his arm savagely.

Cranford said curtly, "I've no slightest doubt as to the truth of the matter, and if I discover you've tampered with a public right-of-way, I'll have you in Court, Finchley." He turned to Grover. "As for you—let him go!"

"Ho, yus, I won't." But despite the snarled defiance, the big groom hesitated, looking from Cranford's stern face to his scowling employer.

Cranford sent Tassels dancing forward. "I've no wish to trample you," he warned, "but my mare is fond of Mr. Consett, and if she thinks you're harming him I may not be able to control her."

A light tap of his spur and Tassels' ears went back. She reared, then plunged forward, teeth bared.

Grover and the stable-hand swore, but released Florian and retreated hastily.

"I could have your gypsy shot for trespassing!" brayed Finchley. "And if you've trained that filly to be a man-killer, she'd best not threaten my people again, or I'll not wait for the law to take action. I know how to deal with rogues—men or beasts."

"You certainly surround yourself with them." Cranford dismounted and threw an arm about Florian, who swayed unsteadily. "And I've seen how you 'deal with' horses, which is the reason I'll never sell you my mare."

All but gnashing his teeth, Finchley howled, "She was mine before she was yours! I wish to God I'd never given her to you!"

"I'll remember that the next time you get yourself trapped in a landslide." Guiding the youth to the cart, Cranford called, "Now I come to think of it, you were on *my* land that day, and you never did say what you were about."

Aware that his men knew Cranford had saved his life on that occasion, Finchley waved them away and answered tauntingly, "If you want to know, I was looking over the Quail Hill property you'd just sold. Decided then that I meant to have it."

So the belligerent Major was indeed after the river parcel. 'Damn!' thought Cranford, boosting Florian onto the seat of

80

the cart. "You seem to make a habit of coveting my property," he drawled. "Another disappointment for you."

As always, the younger man's cool self-control was fuel to Finchley's temper and the hue of his cheeks deepened. "It ain't your property now, confound you! I've made the Westermans a generous offer, and they've as good as accepted."

Cranford gave him a scornful glance but did not comment as he climbed to the seat, whistled to Tassels, and took up the reins.

Watching with burning resentment as the mare trotted daintily to the cart, Finchley shouted, "No point in pretending you don't believe me. The river parcel's as good as mine! What d'ye say to that?"

"Giddap, Sport." Cranford slapped the reins on the broad back of the ageing but still reliable bay gelding.

Finchley heard a distant hoot of laughter. So his men were laughing at him behind his back! A pox on the lot of 'em! His temper soaring, he shouted, "Your day is done, Mister High-and-Mighty Cranford! We all know you're properly in the basket. You'll be wise to sell Muse Manor and get out. We want no traitor-lovers in this neighbourhood!"

Driving off, Cranford stiffened. Finchley was referring to Glendenning, of course, but as yet no one had been able to prove that the viscount had actually taken up arms under the banner of Charles Stuart. Tio's remark about the pedlar re-echoed in his ears: "I've seen him before somewhere ... he gives me an uncomfortable feeling ..." If he hadn't been so preoccupied with his own concerns he would have stayed in the village and spoken to the pedlar. It would be just like Gresford Finchley to resent Tio's rank and his assured manner and inform Bow Street or even the Horse Guards of his suspicions.

Watching his grim face anxiously, Florian said, "I'm sorry, sir. I know you told me to avoid Finchley Park, and I swear I wasn't trying to see Miss Laura! What it is ..."

"What it is, a trap was set for you, and you drove right into it. The Major's a man who enjoys violence, and Grover's cut from the same cloth. He marked your face, I see. Are you much hurt otherwise?"

"They caught me a few good ones across my back when they dragged me from the cart. No worse than I used to get in the tribe."

"We'll have Miss Jane look at you when we get home. Tell me, were you able to hire another waggon?"

"Yes, sir. And two brawny ex-soldiers who are eager for work. They'll bring the waggon out first thing in the—" He broke off, looking intently to the east. "Isn't that Mr. Valerian?"

Cranford followed his gaze. Some half-mile distant, a tall black horse was galloping up the rise. The rider was unmistakable: Gervaise Valerian, and going like the wind for once. What in Hades was the fellow doing here?

Florian muttered, "Jove, but he can ride!"

Cranford made a mental note that the next time he met his alleged "cousin," he'd demand an explanation for the man's presence on his land. His land . . . Muse Manor belonged to all of them. He was merely the guardian of the estate. He looked north-east across the meadowland to the distant swell of hills beyond the bridge. A pale winter sun threw cloud shadows onto the slopes and set the river sparkling. It was so green and quiet and lovely, even though the trees did not yet wear their leaves and the meadow flowers still slept. By heaven, but they would *not* lose the dear old place! Miss Cordelia Stansbury would be duly pursued, and Perry would have his house and his acres! There would be snowdrops and crocus appearing to greet the bride, and spring would carpet the woods with bluebells and—

His dreaming introspection was cut off by a tug at his arm, followed immediately by the sharp crack of a musket. Florian uttered a startled shout. The retort reverberated deafeningly, as thunder tended to do among these hills. Sport snorted and shied, and Tassels neighed in fright.

"What—the devil . . . ?" gasped Florian.

82

Cranford was already turning the cart into the shelter of a copse of trees and calling Tassels to them.

Florian exclaimed, "You never think—"

"Some fool, hunting, belike."

"But—the ball passed right between us! See—it tore your sleeve!"

"Stay here!" Cranford sprang down from the cart, and, as far as possible keeping to cover, sprinted up the slope. He scanned the countryside narrowly, but there was no sign of anyone, riding or afoot.

Florian came to join him, breathless and pale, but clutching a sturdy branch with resolution. "Do you see him, sir?"

"No. He'll be far off by now."

"Mr. Valerian must have heard the shot. He'll come back."

"Very likely. Let's get you home."

Climbing painfully into the cart, Florian muttered, "Poachers don't usually carry muskets—too loud."

Guiding Sport back towards the Manor, Cranford glanced down at the tear in his sleeve. The ball had come damnably close. If somebody had actually been aiming at him, he must be a fine marksman. But why should anyone want him dead? He glanced instinctively to the south, although it was unlikely that Finchley could have saddled up and ridden ahead in time to stage an ambush. It was also unlikely that, despite his ferocious disposition, the man would stoop to murder by stealth. He was crude and a bully, but although he had drawn back from a prospective duel, he was not a coward. If he meant to take revenge he'd call his opponent out, like a gentleman. And at all events there was no sign of a rider in that direction. Perhaps it really had been unintentional. A poacher who'd missed his shot, then hidden away for fear of being caught. But—a poacher with a *musket*? As unlikely as a poacher riding a horse!

Valerian had been riding. At speed; but he must have seen them and heard the reverberations of that shot. And Valerian had not turned back . . .

Echoing his thoughts, Florian said, "We have no real quarrel with Gervaise Valerian, have we, sir?"

Cranford told him sternly to disabuse his mind of any suspicions in that quarter, adding that he was not to mention the incident to anyone at the Manor.

"I only wondered," said Florian meekly.

Bringing Sport to a faster trot, Cranford grinned as he recalled how his boot had "assisted" the dandy into the sedan chair. It was possible that his disliked and distant cousin might consider that they did indeed have a quarrel.

Florian had more than his share of courage, but by the time they reached the Manor he was near exhaustion. Cranford half-carried him into the house. Jane Guild came running and, horrified, took charge, and Mrs. Burrows, their cook, was summoned to assist. She was a tall woman, built on generous lines, her disposition unfailingly cheerful. The handsome youth had won a special place in her heart, however, and she bristled with righteous indignation over the brutal treatment he had received.

Cranford went up to his room. Blake came to him at once. A spare, rather taciturn individual who had never been known to betray emotion, he was the younger brother of General Nugent's housekeeper, Eliza Turner. He had contracted a fever while serving with the Army in India, and had been sent home. In the spring the General had written to Piers noting that Johns, who had valeted the twins for several years, had now left them. If Piers had not as yet hired a new man, he was urged to consider Blake, "a most superior servant." Piers had hired Blake on a trial basis, but had not since regretted it. The man was enigmatic and exhibited none of the possessive airs of a devoted retainer, as did Cook, and Peddars, the footman, and Sudbury, the head groom, and even Florian, who was, of course, more friend than servant. Blake might have no affection for his employer, but he was as efficient as he was silent, and Piers, who tended to be impatient with tardiness and small talk, was well satisfied.

Blake's eyes lingered on the tear in Cranford's coat, but when he was informed that it was the result of "a clumsy accident," he murmured woodenly, "As you say, sir."

Having washed, been provided with an undamaged coat and clean neckcloth, and brushed his wind-blown hair, Cranford hurried downstairs. His aunt was waiting for him in the breakfast parlour, where luncheon had been set out. She looked pensive and he said bracingly, "Cheer up, m'dear. The lad's not badly injured, surely?"

She returned his smile and confirmed this, but while accepting the bowl of cream-of-leek soup that Peddars placed before her, she remarked that Major Finchley was a most disagreeable man. Cranford glanced at her sharply, but she kept her eyes lowered. Freshly baked rolls, a platter of cold meats and cheeses, and a bowl of fruits and nuts were carried in, after which he told Peddars to serve two tankards of Kentish ale.

Miss Guild looked at him in surprise.

He said gravely, "You need it. You have to tell me of something distasteful, I think, ma'am."

She shook her head in wonderment. "It never fails to amaze me, Piers, how you can sense things—and 'tis not as if you were *my* twin."

"No. Gad! Must I expect Perry to arrive at the gallop? I particularly asked that he not be told of all these trifling—vexations."

"He has not been told, dear. But I'm afraid . . . well, you boys have always been able to know somehow if the other is in trouble."

It was a truth that had been nagging at the edges of his mind for some days. The last thing he wanted was for Perry to come charging home and become caught up in all these worrisome problems when he should be happily preparing for his nuptials. On the other hand, it would be a touch odd if his twin did not at least make an enquiry.

He asked quietly, "What now, ma'am?"

Miss Guild sighed. "This was not Florian's first encounter with that horrid Sid Grover."

"I'm aware. Had you a specific incident in mind?"

"Several, unfortunately. And—"

She broke off as Peddars returned with two tankards of foaming ale.

Cranford told the man he would ring if he needed him, and when the door closed he raised his tankard, saying smilingly, "A toast, Aunt Jane. To our Perry and his new house!" She lifted her eyebrows but made no comment and drank the toast willingly enough.

He said, "Now, you were saying that you're afraid. Not of Sidney Grover, surely?"

Miss Guild put down her tankard and stared at it worriedly before replying. "I'm afraid there is real trouble brewing. That nasty creature took Florian in deep dislike last year, if you recall, when poor Herbert Turner drove Blake here from Town. I own the Turner boy is slow-witted, but he's gentle and devoted to his mama."

"And to Valerian."

"Yes. So pathetic, poor creature. But that is no cause to make mock of him, and Mrs. Franck told me that Grover was horrid to him when they met in the village. Florian stood up for him, but poor Herbert was practically in tears because Grover had everybody laughing, and when Herbert tried to defend himself he was clumsy, you know. Grover had fine sport mocking him and making him look ridiculous."

"Aha! So that's why Florian decked him!" Piers grinned. "I never did have the straight of it. 'Twas jolly well done. Especially when you consider Florian is half Grover's size."

His aunt uttered an exasperated but lady-like snort. "How can you say that it was well done? Do you not see what has come of it? Sidney Grover is the type of ruffian who will do anything to even the score, and I fear he's not a man to play fair."

He watched her thoughtfully. She was clearly upset and nervous, which was unlike her. He said, "It seems to me that Florian was in the right of it to defend a boy who is in a round-about fashion one of our people, and I'd guess the village folk would agree. Speaking of whom . . . Have you had any dealings with that pedlar who's taken to wandering about the village?"

"Not many. Why? Do you disapprove of the man?"

"I know nothing to his discredit. He must be doing a good trade, since he is here so often."

Miss Guild looked dubious. "I doubt he shows much profit. His prices are reasonable enough. He called here a few times. His name is Joshua, and I must say he was very polite and respectful, in fact he gave me a bargain on some wool for—" Her eyes sharpened and she interrupted herself to demand, "But what has that to do with Florian defending Herbert Turner?"

"Nought," he said, offering her another slice of cheese. "I suppose my mind wandered, love. It happens as we grow older, I've heard." She laughed and told him to speak for himself, and he said lightly, "The fact is that we chanced to see your pedlar friend in the village today, and Tio had the notion he knew him from somewhere but couldn't recall where. Since you ladies always manage to learn everything about anyone new . . ."

Undeceived by his nonchalant manner, she interposed keenly, "*Tio* thought he knew him? Oh, heavens! Do you take Joshua for—for some kind of government spy? If that is the case, I cannot be of much assistance. He is always ready for a chat, but never speaks of himself or his background. Do you want me to see what I can find out?"

"There's probably nothing to it, but—yes, you might poke around a little. Carefully. Just in case, you know. May I peel an apple for you?"

"You may stop trying to make light of the business. Dear, oh dear! I *knew* you were worrying about something!"

"Not so. I may err on the side of caution, but I never worry. You should know that."

"Fiddlesticks! You worry about all of us and guard us, like—like a hen with her chicks!"

Revolted, he exclaimed, "No! That's a horrid simile, Aunt Jane! At least name me a rooster!"

"Well, you know what I mean. You work day and night and seldom take time for yourself and your own interests—"

"You are my interest," he teased, quartering the apple and passing it to her.

"And that's another thing. You should be looking about for a pretty lady to marry, but you so seldom go into Society that the hostesses have given up asking . . ." The smile had left his eyes and his face was suddenly stern; noting which she broke off and said apprehensively, "Forgive. I don't mean to be a nag, but—"

"But my lack of a lady is not what's really disturbing you, is it? Out with it, love."

She hesitated, then said miserably, "Oh, Piers—I wish I had not to bring you more bad news, but . . . Oliver Dixon was here while you were out—"

"What—again? Tio and I rode over to the farm this morning and saw the flooding. It's an ugly mess but Florian has hired another waggon and two extra workers, which should help, if— Ah. There is something else, I see."

With a heavy sigh, she said, "It's the new plough you bought, dear. One of the farm-hands found it in a ditch. It had been smashed. Deliberately, so Dixon believes. And—and, oh my, it is so sad, but . . . They have found Gertrude and her calf.

88

The poor creatures drowned sometime during the night."

Piers sat very still and seemed scarcely to breathe. His aunt saw the colour drain from his face, leaving him very pale. He had purchased the strange-looking black-and-white heifer from a Dutch farmer who had shipped four beasts to Sussex, saying they were Friesians and demanding a high price. Piers had been among the very few men willing to meet that price. It was one of the rare occasions when the twins had disagreed. Peregrine was against the purchase, but Piers had stuck stubbornly to his convictions. It had been a struggle to raise the funds, and many there were who had scoffed and said he'd thrown his money away. Jane had named the new arrival Gertrude after a friend who had always worn black and white, but others named the animal "Cranford's Folly" and laughed because they thought her ungainly. Peregrine had resented the jeering but Piers had taken it all in good part. He'd been proud of the heifer when she grew to be larger than other cattle, and, confident that he'd be well rewarded for his investment, had searched carefully for a worthy mate. He'd paid another high price as stud fee, and again there had been laughter and criticism. But Gertrude had presented him with a fine bull calf and the scoffers had been silenced when she became a splendid milk producer. Other landowners had begun to show an interest in the animal and Piers had planned to show her at the Summer Livestock Fair in Short Shrift. Her loss was more than a financial matter, however. Gertrude had become an affectionate creature, and would invariably wander across the pasture to greet whoever approached. They had all been fond of her, even Peregrine admitting that his twin had done well in his risky investment.

Watching her nephew's stricken face anxiously, Miss Guild patted his hand and said, "My dear—I am so sorry."

He thanked her and said gruffly that he would ride over to the Home Farm at once.

89

Miss Guild walked to the stables and waited with him while his mare was saddled up. Watching his supple mount, and the way Tassels came almost at once to the gallop, she found herself praying that this latest disaster would be the last to worry him.

6

The air was chill by the time Cranford left the Home Farm, and the dark clouds that were climbing up the eastern horizon matched his mood. Oliver Dixon had looked grim and had little to say about the loss of Gertrude, but Mrs. Dixon, a tender-hearted woman, had shed tears. Dixon had accompanied him to the field where the cattle had been found and pointed out the spot where the flood waters had concealed a ditch into which the animals had blundered. Folding his arms across his broad chest, he'd tucked in his chin and waited in silence.

Investigating, Cranford formed his own conclusions, saying at length, "Does it not seem odd to you that Gertrude would wade so far into the water? Surely, a beast would instinctively keep to higher ground?"

"Aye! And so I do think, sir." Obviously gratified that his suspicions were shared, the farmer had growled, "Nor her bull calf wouldn't have gone paddling in that muck. Not," he added meaningfully, "less'n he was druv! Mischief, it were, sir! Plain wickedness! Likely done by some o' they vandals and tramps as curate were speaking of last Sunday; them what took William Goode's pig. 'The wicked shall not go unpunished,' he said. And no more should they! Trying to make off wi' our Gertrude, they was, mark my words, and druv her into the water, being iggerant and not knowin' how to herd cattle. Be ye goin' to tell the constable what we thinks and about our smashed new plough, sir?"

Cranford had promised to do so, and had then left the farm and ridden towards the Westerman property to see the new fence. Dixon's solution to the puzzle did not satisfy him. He was plagued by a suspicion that the gunshot which had so narrowly missed him could be connected to this series of calamities and had to tell himself sternly not to allow imagination to get the best of him. If he allowed himself to believe the worst he'd have Perry sensing his alarm and posting down here! Deep in thought, he paid little attention to his surroundings until he found they were atop the Quail Hill Bridge. He swore in disgust and reined Tassels to a halt. The old hump-backed bridge was not blocked, but at a short distance from the north end a fence had been erected, running from the water's edge northward across the lane for twenty or so yards, then swinging in a wide curve back to the east, where it connected with a taller fence around the Westerman house. There was a narrow gate barely sufficient to allow a single horseman or a pedestrian to pass, and a pair of wider gates, now closed, allowed access to the house. A tall sign positioned outside the house bore the warning that had so angered Oliver Dixon, painted in bold red letters.

"Be damned!" exclaimed Cranford. "Did ever you see such an ugly mess, Tassels?"

The fence was indeed unlovely, consisting of unpainted boards and rising to a height of about four feet. It had not been designed for beauty but to keep traffic out, and this it very efficiently did, for the river was too deep at this point to allow a team to wade across, and few men would go to the house braving that ominous sign.

Cranford's jaw set. He started Tassels towards the cottage, but upon glancing up saw that once again a lady wandered about the high meadows. Perhaps Miss Mary Westerman was here with her maid and there was no one else to speak with. He hesitated briefly, then turned Tassels down the bridge, flung open the smaller gate and rode towards her, raising his hat as he came up. "Searching for more of your beads, Miss Westerman?"

She swung around, looking startled. "Oh! Good day, sir. Yes, I—er, was, as a matter of fact."

Her sunny smile had dawned almost at once, it was an infectious smile and his dark mood was lightened. With an answering smile he said teasingly, "And alone again! Do you not fear that your militant abigail will take you to task?"

She gave a little rippling laugh and declared that she was in truth shaking in her shoes. Reaching up to caress the mare, she said, "You were riding this lady the first time we met. Is she your favourite? I'd not be surprised. I never saw a prettier creature. How do you call her?"

"Her name is Tassels. Thank you, but pray do not flatter her. She is so much admired that she is already far too impressed by her own consequence." Miss Westerman's eyes, sparkling with amusement, met his own. He said, "No, really, it is truth. I am forever rejecting offers for her." He put his hand over one of Tassels' ears and half-whispered, "Some are quite tempting, but she is a managing female, and won't allow me to consider them." Tassels shook her head as if in confirmation, and releasing her ear he said, "There! Do you see how she voices her opinion?"

"I do, and I am quite in sympathy with her. But don't worry, Miss Tassels. I think your master is a great tease and has no least intent to ever let you go."

Watching her, in some unaccountable fashion he was reminded of Cordelia Stansbury; yet how different they were. Mary Westerman was such a friendly, cheerful damsel. Her fresh young face was innocent of powder and paint, and the glossy curls that peeped beneath the hood of her cloak were her own. Nor did she wear hoops, and the small feet that he glimpsed below her gown were encased in sensible half-boots. No paint and wig and high Spanish heels for this young lady, and in his eyes she was far more attractive for the lack of them.

He swung down from the saddle. "Perhaps I can help? Is this where you broke your beads? I had thought it was over there."

"You are likely right, Mr. Cranford. Thank you."

He accompanied her up the rise and Tassels grazed as they talked and searched about. It was easy to talk to Mary Westerman, and before he knew it Cranford found himself telling her about the flood and the loss of his prize cow.

She halted and touched his arm with ready sympathy. "Oh, the poor dear thing! However did it happen?"

He felt a rush of gratitude for her understanding, and told her what he knew of the matter and of the suspicions he and Dixon shared. He was not given to betraying his feelings and was embarrassed to realize that he had been rambling on for several minutes and that his voice sounded hoarse and strained in his own ears. He stopped speaking abruptly, and feeling his face grow hot, exclaimed, "What a fool I am to babble on like this! I apologize, Miss Westerman, and hope you will believe that I have not quite taken leave of my senses. I do apprehend that she was, after all, only a cow."

"Not so! I saw her and her calf one day. Such an unusual animal, and when I called to her she came over to chat with me in the most friendly way. 'Tis no wonder you considered her to be more of a pet. I know little of cattle but I thought her very beautiful and can appreciate that you had such plans for her. It is indeed a great loss. I am so very sorry."

Overwhelmed by such warm kindness, he thanked her gruffly and there was a brief but not uncomfortable silence as they walked on side by side.

94

With his head bowed he exclaimed, "Jove! I believe I've found another of your beads!" He retrieved the small stone and wiped away the mud that coated it. "No—I think this cannot be—"

Miss Westerman took it from his hand eagerly. "It is! What keen eyes you have!"

"Are you sure, ma'am? It is red, and the other was green, as I recall."

"My necklace is of mixed stones. Very old, and quite unusual." She shivered. "Goodness, how cold it has become. I must start back, sir."

He whistled Tassels to him. "I'll walk with you, if I may."

"Thank you, but you have a long ride before you. Had you to come all the way up here to use this bridge? Is the one near your farm impassable?"

"It is unsafe for any but a single rider. My tenant farmer cannot get his waggons and supplies across until we have turned the river to its proper course. Actually, I rode this way to see the fence and the signs your family has put up."

She frowned. "Not so, Mr. Cranford! The fence and that horrid sign were put up by the gentleman who desires to buy our property. To my mind it was a great piece of impertinence since the sale is not yet finalized."

"It sounds unlawful as well as impertinent." And sure of her answer, he enquired, "A local individual, ma'am?"

"Yes. He is called Major Finchley."

───◦❦◦───

The Westerman cottage was larger than Cranford had supposed. He was too angry to pay much heed to the half-timbered exterior or the wainscoted entrance hall, and when Miss Westerman left him he stamped, glowering, after the neat footman. He was ushered to the withdrawing-room, and advised that Mrs. Westerman would be with him "in a moment." He snapped, "I wish to see *Mr.* Westerman!" The footman bowed,

95

smiled in an irritatingly supercilious manner, and withdrew.

Several "moments" slipped past. Pacing up and down, seething with impatience, Cranford had to acknowledge that this was a charming room, furnished for comfort rather than elegance. The sofa was large and covered in a red velvet that bore the marks of use. He decided to see if it was as soft as it looked. He sat down and at once had to spring up as Mary Westerman came in. She had tidied her curls and wore a simple primrose-yellow gown that became her very well. Accompanying her was a matron whose age he guessed to be in the neighbourhood of fifty.

He was presented to Mrs. Caroline Westerman. Inherently shy, he usually found older women less intimidating than young damsels, but this lady was truly formidable. She stood half a head taller than he, and without being stout, was built on a grand scale that put him in mind of Horatio Glendenning's step-mother, Lady Bowers-Malden. Unlike the countess, however, Mrs. Caroline Westerman could not be described as a handsome woman: her nose was too large, her mouth a thin line above an up-curving chin, and the light hazel eyes that might have been a redeeming feature held a fierce and belligerent glint. Moreover, she presented a very untidy appearance. Wisps of greying hair escaped a cap that sagged crookedly on her head. Her gown of purple velvet, worn over very large hoops, was not enhanced by an outsize multi-coloured shawl that appeared to have been crocheted without the aid of any pattern or design. Bowing before her, he caught a glimpse of muddy riding boots and was almost undone. With an effort he collected his wits, and began, "I have come, ma'am, to—"

Her arm flew up and he had to step back quickly to avoid the flying shawl. "We are not blind," she said in a deep booming voice, and wrenching the shawl about her as if she subdued a determined enemy, she added, "We will wait, if you can contain yourself, for our sister. Ah, Lucretia, this impatient young fellow is Lieutenant Piers Cranford. You may make your bow, sir, to Mrs. Lucretia Westerman."

Cranford turned to face a very stout lady who smiled at him as she extended her hand. Bowing over it, he scarcely dared look up. Mrs. Lucretia was probably a year or two younger than Mrs. Caroline, and there could be no doubt but that she had once been very pretty. Her powdered curls were neatly dressed under a lace-trimmed cap, she had a small up-tilted nose, and eyes of china blue; unfortunately, they, together with her mouth, were almost lost in the swell of her cheeks, and as for a chin, she now had four of them. She wore a green gown trimmed with swansdown that would have been becoming save for the fact that it had been made for a lady of far less ample proportions. Cranford could all but hear the seams straining, and wondered in awe how her abigail had ever managed to fasten the buttons. Her bosom was generous, much too generous for the very *décolleté* bodice that struggled to contain it, and fearing that at any second the struggle would be lost, he averted his eyes, and said rather hoarsely, "I am here to—"

"How droll." Mrs. Lucretia lowered herself cautiously into a wing chair beside her sister and panted, "But it is quite correct, Caroline. He *is* here."

"Yes, and keeps telling us of it, as if we did not know. I wonder why," said Mrs. Caroline, regarding Cranford with suspicion.

"To find—" he began.

"Oh! A game! But how droll!" Mrs. Lucretia clapped her plump hands. "I love games! He has lost something!"

"Try not to be so foolish, sister."

Cranford, who had sat down, sprang up again, beginning to feel surrounded as a new voice was heard.

The lady now entering was tall and graceful, beautifully gowned, and at least ten years younger than her sisters. Her hair was powdered and dressed in the latest style, and her features were delicate. She wielded a large feathery fan as she advanced with a faintly sinuous sway into the room, her fine hazel eyes fixed admiringly on Cranford.

Mrs. Caroline flung her shawl about her shoulders so violently that she then had to fight her way out of it, and emerged growling irritably, "This is—"

The latest arrival raised a delaying hand. "I *know* who he is, Caro."

"If you have met him before, you should have told us." Mrs. Lucretia put her fan over her lips concealingly, but did not trouble to lower her voice as she said to her elder sister, "Is it not just like her to keep him all to herself? He is very handsome, of course."

Mrs. Caroline's fan was also brought into play while above it her eyes fixed the embarrassed Cranford with a hard stare. She said quite audibly, "We do not judge him especially handsome. And she likely has never met him."

"I am—" began the latest arrival.

"Miss Celeste Westerman," her sisters-in-law chorused triumphantly.

She sighed, and from behind her fan said to Cranford, "Poor dears. They like to think they know everything." She extended her hand, her eyes flirting with him in exaggerated roguishness, and as he touched her fingers to his lips, murmured, "You will think it foolish, Lieutenant, the way they fancy they cannot be heard if they hide behind their fans."

Since she was doing precisely the same, he merely smiled and asked evasively, "Forgive, but did we meet in Town, Miss Celeste?"

Seating herself on the red sofa, she said archly, "I will forgive you—if you sit here beside me."

"Aha!" cried Mrs. Caroline, her shawl agitated, "she has *not* met him! We knew it!"

"They think I don't know why you have come," purred Miss

Celeste, patting the cushion beside her. "But I do."

"To pay a courtesy call, of course," declared Mrs. Caroline.

"And long overdue," agreed Mrs. Lucretia, tugging at her bodice in a way that terrified Cranford. "But he wants to know about the fence; that is his true reason for calling." Up went the fan as she leaned to her sister and confided loudly, "Only see how she flirts with him, Caro! I declare it is most droll!"

"I am *not* flirting with him," argued Miss Celeste, pouting, and then adding provocatively, "But I'll own I've ever had a soft spot in my heart for gentlemen with curling hair and such very blue eyes."

"Or with no hair," appended Mrs. Caroline waspishly.

"And a squint," tittered Mrs. Lucretia.

They put their fans together and, "safely hidden," laughed hilariously.

Miss Celeste shrugged and said with disdain, "Pay no heed to them, Lieutenant Cranford. They are silly and jealous, is all."

Sure that his face was scarlet, and considerably off-stride, Cranford stammered, "No, but—but Mrs. Lucretia is quite right, ma'am. I—"

Miss Celeste rapped her fan across his knuckles and uttered a piercing shriek. "Oh! You horrid thing! I am *not* flirting with you! How dare you presume so!"

Aghast, Cranford looked about helplessly for Miss Mary and saw that she stood just inside the open door, watching him, her eyes alight with mischief. Realizing that rescue from that quarter was unlikely, he said, "No, no, ma'am! I did not mean— What I meant was—I—er, I came hoping to have a few words with Mr. Westerman."

Three fans were lowered, three pairs of eyes regarded him wonderingly.

"Now this is *very* droll," murmured Mrs. Lucretia.

Mrs. Caroline said with a snigger, "Is that so? We wish you well of it, sir!"

"Why?" demanded Miss Celeste.

"Because he don't wish to deal with *us,* you ninny," said Mrs. Caroline. "He fancies us too foolish."

Miss Celeste fluttered her lashes at Cranford, and again patting the sofa cushion beside her, said wistfully, "Is that why he will not sit here?"

Cranford sat down gingerly, and said in a nervous rush of words, "I feel sure you all are very capable, ma'am. But I want—"

"What, you dear man?" gushed Miss Celeste, leaning towards him. "You shall have anything you ask. *Anything!*"

'Dear God!' thought Cranford. "It is a—a legal matter concerning the sale of this property and that confoun——"

Mrs. Caroline howled and threw her shawl over her head. "No swearings! No cursings! Remember you are in a ladies' withdrawing-room, sir!"

"Yes. Yes, indeed! I apologize," he gasped. "What I mean to say is, it's that—er, revoltingly ugly fence and—and the sign. I understand they were put up by Major Finchley, and I want to know by what right—"

Mrs. Caroline's shawl flapped wildly. Emerging from it, she struggled to restore her cap, which had fallen over both eyes. "Oh, there you are!" she said breathlessly. "How should we know about Major Finchley? What a foolish question! Waste of time! Waste of time!"

"Why would he come here to waste our time?" asked Miss Celeste, bewildered.

Mrs. Lucretia suggested, "He is a spy, perhaps."

"Or a revolutionary," contributed Mrs. Caroline, adding solemnly, "Lots of young fellows are these days. Too much time on their hands, so they occupy themselves with mischief and mayhem, fighting for lost causes they know little about and that no one else gives a fig for."

"It is too *droll*," remarked Mrs. Lucretia, clearly washing her hands of the issue. "Speaking of which, it is time for tea."

With an emphatic nod Miss Celeste declared, "He will want brandy in his."

"Good gracious me," exclaimed Mrs. Lucretia. "Well, I suppose there must be some in the house, though he should have warned us ahead of time. Are you sure, dear?"

Miss Celeste said, "Well, of course I am sure. He is a gentleman, and they *all* do."

"No—please," gulped Cranford, yearning to be elsewhere. "I thank you, but—"

"Here is dear Mary come with the tray," said Mrs. Caroline, beaming.

Mary Westerman came into the room, followed by a maid bearing a laden tea-tray.

"Our guest demands brandy also," panted Mrs. Lucretia, sitting up straighter and then making a frantic grab for her wilting bodice.

With an anguished glance at Mary, Cranford said, "You are very good, but I must be on my way; if you could just—"

"You see?" exclaimed Miss Celeste. "Because we did not bring the brandy at once, he will go off in a huff!"

"Men!" snorted Mrs. Caroline.

The maid gave the culprit a censuring look, set the tray on a table before the sofa and hurried out.

Mary Westerman murmured dulcetly, "But of course he shall have some brandy, and Lieutenant Cranford would never be so ill-mannered as to go off in a huff." She slanted a twinkling glance at him. "Would you, sir?"

Mopping his brow, he summoned a smile. "Certainly not, ma'am. It will be my pleasure to drink tea with you—but without brandy, if you please."

"I declare," said Mrs. Lucretia, eyeing him curiously, "How very . . ."

Cranford waited, although he was sure of the final adjective.

Mrs. Lucretia did not disappoint him. ". . . droll," she said.

"It would have been kind in you to give me a little warning!" Walking to the stables beside Miss Mary, Cranford was glad of the chill breath of the wind. After the arrival of the tea-tray, another hour had passed before he could decently escape, and he still felt considerably shaken.

Mary Westerman drew the hood of her cloak closer. "Warning of—what, pray?" she asked pertly. "My dear aunts have the kindest hearts in the world. If they offended, sir—"

Cranford groaned, "Do not! You know very well that I am in no state to cross swords with you."

She gave a throaty little chuckle and it occurred to him that although he had known her for a comparatively short while, he felt quite at ease in having made such a remark, as if she were a close friend. "I've no doubt your aunts are very kind," he said. "But you must own they are rather—er—"

"Unusual? Yes. But it is gauche in you to say so!"

He pulled aside her hood, and searching her face anxiously saw that her eyes again held that sparkling look of mischief. Relieved, he pointed out, "I didn't say it."

"But you were thinking it." Again came that soft little chuckle. "If you could have seen your face when Aunt Celeste said you were going off in a huff because we'd not supplied you with brandy! Yes, I know I am naughty to tease you so. They are darlings, but I'll admit that on first meeting they can be rather . . . startling. I really did try to—ah, prepare you, but you were having such a lovely time indulging your wrath that you would not listen. Are you quite wrung out? I had thought an Army officer—even one with revolutionary tendencies— would be accustomed to dealing with ladies."

"So had I," he said with a grin. "But never in my life have I met such an—to use your own term—an *unusual* trio! I mean no offence, but—are they—always like—er, that?"

"They are held to be a trifle eccentric, but they liked you."
She added with a dimple, "Especially Aunt Celeste."

Cranford said ruefully. "She is a beautiful lady, but—"

"I know. Poor Aunt Celeste. She is my mother's youngest
sister and has never married. Aunt Caroline and Aunt Lucretia
were married to Mama's elder brothers. They are both widows
now. Truly, I doubt they had any thought to frighten you."

"Frighten me? Ma'am, I was terrified! There must surely
be a gentleman in your family with whom I can discuss business matters? I want to bid on this parcel of land, and I want
that ugly fence and the sign torn down. You spoke of your father, I think?"

"Yes. Papa is a fine scholar, but he is from Town at present."

"Do you know when he will return? Is he perhaps at University? I could ride up there, if—"

"I meant that he is out of the country. He does not teach,
though he could. He has a great interest in antiquities. In fact,
he is the one gave me my necklace. If you wish to find out
about the sale of this property, our solicitor can probably help
you. I believe he lives in Lincoln's Inn, or has offices there. His
name is—um, let me see now . . . Shorey, or is it Story? No!
Shorewood, that's it!"

He thanked her and swung open the door to the small barn
and stables. Inside, it was warm and fragrant. Two lanterns
hung from beams and a stove held small glowing logs. A groom
came running, and Miss Westerman stayed to stroke Tassels
while the filly was being saddled up. She said admiringly, "She
really is a beauty. Did you buy her from someone, or was she
bred on your estate?"

The groom gave an amused snort and she glanced at him
curiously.

Cranford said with a smile, "Tassels was bred on Gresford
Finchley's land."

Her eyes widened. "And he sold her? How very odd!"

"Matter of fact, the Major gave her to me."

"Good gracious! He *did?* Now that I find even more odd. I see you know all about it, Thomas."

The groom nodded. "Everyone in these parts knows, miss. Lieutenant Cranford dug the Major out of a landslide, and was give the filly as a reward. Her being two short jumps from being sold fer hoss-meat."

"This lovely lady?" Miss Westerman stroked the velvety nose gently. "I find it hard to believe that."

"She weren't a lovely lady then, miss," explained the groom. "A very sick little hoss, she were. The Major thought as he was givin' nothing away." He barked a laugh. "They do say as he's never fergive hisself—nor you, sir!"

"People say too much." Cranford pressed a coin into the man's hand as he took the reins. "Thank you."

Walking beside Cranford to the door, Miss Westerman said, "Laura Finchley had told me her father almost died in a landslide a few years ago. Had you a great struggle to save Tassels?"

"It was touch-and-go for several months, but we were able to pull her through, fortunately."

"Small wonder she so obviously adores you. Did you train her yourself?"

"Yes. Although my steward has a magical touch with horses, and he worked with her also. She's incredibly fast." He prepared to mount up. "Well, I must be on my way, ma'am, so—"

She put a small detaining hand on his arm. "You meant Florian Consett. He is your new steward, I think?"

"And bids fair to be a good one. Do you know Miss Finchley well, ma'am?"

"Very well indeed. We were at the same Young Ladies Seminary for two years and became best of friends. Laura is a wonderful girl, and as good as she is lovely. Some lucky man will win a very special wife when she marries."

He said with a slight frown, "Someone like Florian Consett, for example?"

"Ah! So you know. I wasn't sure. Do you not approve? They are ideally suited, and deep in love."

"And very young."

"Perhaps, but Laura has a sensible head on her shoulders, and Florian somehow seems much older than his years."

"He's had a hard life. If you know this much, you must be aware that her father regards him as a thief and a vagrant, and will have none of him."

"Major Finchley thinks he is a gypsy, but if he were a very rich gypsy, I suspect he would sing a different tune. Oh, do not put up your brows at me! I know I should not say such things, but after all, Florian was stolen as a child. How can anyone know his ancestry? He might be just as well-born as the Major. Certainly, he has a more agreeable nature! I'd hoped you wouldn't hold his lack of family background against him."

"You may believe I do not. I count him a good friend. And if I 'put up' my brows, as you say, Miss Westerman, 'twas because you echoed my own thoughts."

She said eagerly, "Then you will help them?"

"To—what? Heart-break? Certainly not! And if you have any influence with Miss Finchley, I beg you will warn her. If she continues to encourage Florian, she may well be inviting tragedy. Jove! Is that what is meant by 'looking daggers'?"

"If it is not, then I have failed," she said darkly.

"I consider myself properly slain." Failing to win an answering smile, he said, "Try to look at their situation reasonably, Miss Mary, and don't be too vexed with me. Whatever you or I may think of the Major, he is her father and has a right to want the best for her future."

She tossed her head and did not comment.

Mounting up, he said, "It's getting dark. May I escort you back to the house?"

"You may not!" With a swirl of her cloak, she walked rapidly away.

Cranford watched her for a moment, then turned Tassels towards Muse Manor. Miss Mary Westerman was properly cross with him. How like a woman to be so swept up in a romantical involvement that she could not see the danger looming right under her pretty nose. Still, she was a nice little lady and had, for a time, taken his mind from his own troubles, now made so much worse by the tragic loss of poor Gertrude and a perverse worry because, while not wishing his twin to be troubled, he could not dismiss the feeling that it was unlike Perry not to have at least posted off an enquiry as to the state of affairs at the Manor.

A white square loomed up. In large red letters the word SHOT stood out. He swore softly. Finchley's revolting warning. If he carried an axe or a rope on his saddle . . . But he didn't, and he could scarcely shoot the thing down. If he asked Tassels to kick out at such a narrow post she'd probably do her best but might damage her legs in the process. Several unused fence-posts had been piled to one side. A thought came to him. It wasn't a windmill, exactly, but . . . Laughter danced into his eyes and he dismounted.

He muddied his cloak when he took up a likely-looking post, but he cared not a button. "I've always wanted to try this, Tassels my love," he said. Mounting up again, he balanced his impromptu "lance" carefully, rode off a short way, then reined around. His first attempt at "tilting" failed; he grazed the post but almost lost his "lance" and his seat and had to turn the mare swiftly to avoid running into the fence. Tassels snorted and pranced as if she entered into the spirit of this new sport.

Boyishly exhilarated, he muttered, *"Nil desperandum,"* gave the mare a longer run, then yelled, "On with the joust, lass! Now!" They thundered at the "enemy" and the "lance" hit home squarely. The shock of the impact almost knocked Cranford from the saddle, and splinters from the "lance" drove through his gloves, but the signpost lay vanquished in the mud, and he gave a whoop of triumph.

A squeal rang out. Guilt-ridden, he turned and saw Miss Mary Westerman jumping up and down and clapping her hands. "Bravo, Don Quixote," she called gaily. "So end all villains!"

He swung from the saddle and swept her a low and flourishing bow, to which she responded with a deep curtsy.

Mounting up again as she ran to the cottage, he told himself sternly that it had been a childish prank as a result of which he'd ripped his gauntlets and put some nasty splinters in his hands. Miss Mary would be justified to judge him a proper fool. Still . . . she hadn't seemed to think that. In fact she had entered into his scenario merrily. He grinned at Tassels' ears and began to feel that in a small way he had struck a blow against tyranny. Also, there was no denying he was quite absurdly pleased that Miss Mary had not been disgusted by his nonsense.

When he rode into the Muse Manor stables it was dark and very cold. Bobby Peale, their young under-groom, ran out to take Tassels and as usual commented on her exceptional qualities. Reaching for the saddle-girth as Cranford started towards the Manor, he remarked, "They say lots of gents want her, sir. And that some has offered a high price."

Cranford heard the note of anxiety in the young voice. Frowning, he paused and demanded, "What else do 'they' say? That the Cranfords are on the brink of losing their lands, perhaps?"

The youth flushed and answered nervously, "Meanin' no disrespect, sir, but . . . yes, that's what tavern talk says. Gawd ferbid, I says, Mr. Cranford. Not none of us here wants to lose our—our family. An' if 'tis true—"

"That will do!" Florian had come into the barn and said sharply, "Tend to your duties, Peale, and keep your tongue in your pocket!"

Cranford said, "Don't listen to tavern talk, Bobby. I appreciate your loyalty, but we're far from losing the Manor, I promise you!"

Walking beside Florian into a rising wind, he scolded, "You should be laid down on your bed!"

"I was. All day. I mend fast, as you know. My apologies for Peale's hasty tongue, sir. He's a good lad, but—"

"But he's afraid he's about to lose his situation. Your friend Finchley has apparently spread the word, in which case I fancy the rest of the staff is worried."

Florian hesitated.

"Blast the varmint!" Cranford stamped up the back steps angrily. It was doubtless a waste of time, but tomorrow he would see the village constable and at least make a report of trespass, the deliberate destruction of his new plough, and malicious cruelty to animals. He knew what old Bragg would say. "There just bean't no proof, Lieutenant, sir. And without proof—what can a body do?"

⁂

Cranford's early-morning visit with Constable Bragg was as fruitless as he had anticipated. The constable, on the far side of sixty, flabbily slow but honest and well-meaning, was horrified by the facts laid before him. He blinked his drooping eyes, clutched his sagging cheeks, and moaned his sympathy, but having made copious notes said sadly that Squire Cranford, for whom he entertained the deepest respect, had neither witnesses nor proof to offer. "Such dreadful things, sir, to happen on your own lands! Ungodly, is what it is! Downright evil! But, without proof, sir"—he sighed—"whatever is a body to do?"

Cranford worked off some of his frustration by riding at the gallop to the nearby hamlet of Short Shrift. The day was cloudy but dry, and the rush of cold air past his face was invigorating. The splinters his jousting had earned him were becoming a nuisance. With a mental note that he must soon make an effort to remove them, he went directly to the cottage of the stonemason where Florian and the sturdy craftsman were deeply involved in a discussion of the rebuilding of Ezra Sweet's cottage. Cranford listened to the opinions of his steward, and having requested that the construction of a new steeple and bell tower for St. Mark's be accomplished, wherever possible, by workers from Muse Village, he left Florian to arrange the details and made his way to The Spotted Cat tavern for a late breakfast.

The tavern had been built a century earlier. The coffee-room was small and low-ceilinged, the floor had a decided slope to the east, and the settles and tables were dark with age, but a fine fire blazed on the hearth, and as usual, Cranford was greeted warmly by the host. He had no sooner been shown to a window table, however, than with a great blaring of the yard of tin and a thunder of twenty-four iron-shod hooves, the Royal Mail coach rolled into the yard. At once all was confusion: Ostlers rushed about to change teams, the coachman and guard roared orders for luggage and shipments to be taken off or put on the stage, continuing passengers hurried inside to gather what sustenance they might before the coach left again, disembarking passengers were met by friends or family and joined the breakfast quest, would-be passengers jostled for the coachman's attention, and the solitary serving maid struggled to help everyone at once without much success.

The host wrung his hands and apologized. The serving maid rushed a mug of coffee and a flirtatious giggle to her "very fav'rite gent" and promised to bring Cranford's breakfast at once. "At once" became twenty minutes, contributing to the fact that he reached the Manor at half past eleven rather than the ten o'clock hour he'd anticipated. During the long wait he had decided to consult with his solicitor, Barnabas Evans, and try to pry some information from him about the Westerman cottage sale. That meant he must go to Town, which was as well, since while there he could visit his twin and assure himself that Perry was suffering from nothing more than an agitation of the nerves due to his imminent marriage. He thought without much enthusiasm that he would also have to call on his great-uncle and make a final effort to convince him that Miss Cordelia Stansbury wanted none of him.

He slipped into the Manor by a side door and went up to his room. His aunt had seen his stealthy arrival, however, and when she caught Blake apparently "sticking pins" into her nephew, nothing would do but that she inspect his hands. She was appalled to see the splinters he'd collected, and having scolded him for not attending to them before this, insisted on dealing with them herself.

His answers to her questions were evasive and feeble at best, and when he realized that she was really provoked with him, he confessed his venture into jousting. Jane Guild was not without a sense of humour; she laughed heartily and forgave him. If she suspected that he was worrying about his brother's absence she did not speak of it, but instead made an unsuccessful attempt to persuade him to let Sudbury or Florian drive his light coach on the journey to London. As always, he preferred riding to being confined in a carriage. He told Blake to pack his saddle-bags with sufficient necessities for a possible stay of two or three days, and soon afterwards, having promised to overnight in Woking and hire a coach in the event of rain or snow, he gave his aunt a farewell kiss and at last rode out mounted on Tassels.

7

The man's an idiot!" General Lord Nugent Cranford, hands clasped behind his broad back, stood before the windows of his study, scowling at London's steely late-morning skies. "He's more suited for the position of church sexton than a minion of the law. You should not have wasted your time with him."

Watching his great-uncle from the wing chair, Piers stretched out his legs to the comfortable warmth of the fire. He had passed the night at an excellent posting-house outside Woking, and having reached Town early had intended to go first to Peregrine's flat. However, it was very early and he went instead to call on his solicitor. By the time he had finished his interview with that gentleman he was ready for breakfast, and having fond memories of the skills of the General's cook, had come here where, sure enough, he had been served an excellent meal.

Now, thinking that the old gentleman looked more haggard each time he saw him, he said, "It was necessary that I file a report of the crime, at least. Though I guessed what poor old Bragg would say."

"In which case you were not disappointed. You'd have been better advised to take your complaint to the chief constable at Basingstoke."

"I rather suspect the outcome would have been the same, sir. The chief constable would likely refuse to investigate the death of a cow and her calf."

"Perhaps. But he'd be less likely to refuse an investigation of the bastard who shot at you. Have you turned up anything on that score?"

"Nothing. Nor any proof that our Gertrude was drowned deliberately."

The General turned and regarded him with a frown. "Do you say that the fire at Sweet's cottage, the collapse of St. Mark's steeple and bell tower, and the landslide were also deliberate? If that is the case, you've a cunning and murderous enemy, my boy." He went to his desk chair and asked, "Whom do you suspect?"

Piers said slowly, "Lord knows. We certainly had some vicious opponents in our battle with the League of Jewelled Men, and I suppose there could be members of their ugly little army who still mean to even the score."

The General, who had squirmed and turned pale at the mention of that traitorous organization, exclaimed, "Balderdash! The ringleaders are all safely under lock and key. Besides, your brother was more involved than you were. Came out of it with a knighthood, lucky fella. Have you no other candidates? Men you've offended in some way?"

"Probably there are plenty of those." Piers said with a smile, "Some of the fellows who are determined to buy Tassels turn downright ugly when I refuse 'em."

"Understandable. She's a fine animal, but I doubt a man would resort to murder only to buy a horse. Nobody else who has a score to settle? And I trust your list does not include your cousin."

112

Piers frowned, but said nothing.

His heavy brows bristling, the General growled, "Gervaise Valerian is a selfish, spendthrift young ingrate, with not a soupçon of filial loyalty. But I'll not believe him capable of harming a helpless beast, or of planning your murder. He's far more likely to call you out, if you've really annoyed him. Who else has grounds for violence? Someone from the Rebellion, perhaps?"

"I doubt it. I'm rather short of suspects, in fact. There's Finchley, of course, who holds a deep grudge against me. And perhaps this anonymous would-be purchaser of the estate is trying to run me off. I called on Barnabas Evans before I came here, but in spite of the fact that he's our legal representative, he's close as a clam and will tell me only that he has received another offer from the same source. I've already turned it down three times. Why he refuses to identify himself I cannot think."

The General grunted. "I asked Evans about it last week, but received the same nonsense he threw at you. He says he cannot violate the confidence of a client."

"We are his clients! What legalistic flummery! I think I'll engage another solicitor! Meanwhile, I have the direction of the Westermans' man of affairs and will try and pry something from him. Be damned if I'll allow Muse Manor to fall into the hands of a man who is ashamed of his identity!"

"Bravely said, but it will take more than your oaths and preferences to prevent it. And if the estate continues to be plagued by these ugly incidents, the value will fall."

"Aha! Perhaps that's what is behind the disasters! Planned deliberately in an attempt to bring down the value of Muse Manor!"

The General pursed his lips and said, "Don't sound very likely to me. In your shoes, m'boy, I'd forgo seeking out the Westermans' lawyer and instead concentrate on pursuing my courtship!"

113

Piers nerved himself and said firmly, "Sir, the lady has made it abundantly clear that she does not want me. I've no wish to—"

Lord Nugent rose from his chair and roared, "Then you must do as you please, but you know my terms, nephew!"

—◦⁂◦—

Cranford was still mulling over the General's "terms" when he rode into Lincoln's Inn Fields, the rather gloomy home of so many gentlemen of courts and the law. Enquiry of a porter took him to the north and brighter side of the buildings and he left Tassels with a hopeful page-boy who promised, crossing his heart several times, to let no one come near her.

Henry Shorewood, Esquire, had upstairs chambers into which Cranford was shown, with much bowing, by an elderly clerk. A few minutes later the barrister came into the room with a rush, and kicking the door shut advanced upon Cranford at such speed that his robe billowed out behind him. He was a big burly man, with heavy features and small pale eyes that contrasted sharply with skin so bronzed that Cranford thought he resembled a farmer rather than a learned man of the law.

"Shorewood!" he announced as though a hundred people listened eagerly in the courtyard below, and glancing at Cranford's calling-card he boomed, "Cranford, eh? Heard that name before! Got a crippled brother, ain't you? Did damned well in that sticky bit of treason last year! Damned well!" A ham-like fist shot out to enclose Cranford's outstretched hand like a vise, then he marched to his desk, swept all the papers onto the floor and said, "Sit down, sit down!" while lowering his bulk into the large chair behind the desk.

"Now," he said with a broad grin, "I can give you my undivided attention. Have to do it, y'know. Anything left on the desk, I start to look at it, then forget where I am! How the hell have you managed to hold on to that pretty estate of yours?"

'Phew!' thought Cranford. "You've seen Muse Manor, Mr. Shorewood?"

"Several times. A client drove me down there to look over a parcel of land. Wants to buy it. Finchley. Made several offers to the Westermans. Know 'em? An interesting lot. Are you in the basket?"

Cranford stared at him resentfully. "Absolutely not. Why would you think we're in trouble?"

Shorewood's great boom of a laugh rattled the casements. "Blunt, ain't I? Don't have time for backing and filling. Why are you here, then?"

"To try and discover if the Westermans have accepted an offer. I called on them but was unable to talk to Mr. Westerman."

"Be remarkable if you were! Been dead these ten years!"

Taken aback, Cranford said, "But—Miss Westerman said he was out of the country."

"Miss Celeste Westerman?" Shorewood chuckled. "Have a care, friend. She's a huntress if ever I saw one! Pretty, though."

"I meant Miss Mary Westerman."

"Hmm. Ain't met that one. Why d'you want to know about the offer? Want the property yourself? Understood you'd sold it."

"We did, but I want it back. I'm—negotiating the loan now, but of course, if an offer has been accepted . . ."

"Ain't, so far as I'm aware."

"Did you know Finchley erected a fence around the cottage that fairly blocks access to the bridge, and has put up some damn great sign threatening to shoot trespassers?"

The pale eyebrows went up. Shorewood tore off his wig suddenly and hurled it across the room. "Has he, by God!" His eyes narrowed. With a sly grin he said, "I'll wager it ain't up now."

Cranford chuckled. "You must have a crystal ball. The sign

appears to have—er, fallen down. Can I be hauled up before a judge?"

"Not unless the sign went up by permission of the owners."

"Miss Westerman said it was Finchley's idea and she called it a great piece of impertinence."

"Then the ladies likely think you did 'em a favour. That all?"

"No. I'd like to know who is bidding on our estate. Can you find out?"

"Don't need to. I know. Can't tell you though unless I'm give leave."

Irked, Cranford said, "Can you tell me if there is more than one would-be buyer?"

The solicitor contemplated his wig thoughtfully. "Have you discussed it with your own solicitor?"

"Yes. He wouldn't tell me."

"What's his name?"

"Barnabas Evans of Clifford's Inn."

"You hire him?"

"No. My great-uncle did, when he was made Trustee of the estate."

"Hmm. Poor choice. Don't like the fella, so I'll tell you— yes, there are two interested parties. That's all I can say."

"My thanks. But as for the river parcel, if the ladies can't do business, then who—"

"There's a brother who lives abroad. At the moment they're still arguing over the pros and cons. They enjoy arguing. If they ever make up their minds I can act for 'em. Liable to be a long wait unless we hear from the brother. Good day, sir. You can pay my clerk on your way out. I've another client due any second."

Cranford was ushered out. Shorewood was irritating, but he found that he liked the man, even so. The liking was evidently mutual, because as he closed the door, Shorewood said, "If you change attorneys, sir, pray keep me in mind."

Outside, it was cold and a thin mist had drifted from the

river. Cranford acknowledged to himself resignedly that there was no use procrastinating; he must get on with his pursuit of the frigid Miss Cordelia Stansbury. The page-boy was some distance away, holding Tassels and talking with a gentleman who was stroking the mare. Cranford strode to them. "Are you—" he began.

Gervaise Valerian whipped around. "The devil! I didn't expect to find you here," he said, his dark brows twitching into a scowl. "But it's as well I did! We've a score to settle, cousin! No man kicks me and runs away clear!"

The page-boy drew back, looking frightened.

Cranford tossed him a coin and thanked him and the boy fled. "I didn't run away," he corrected. "And you deserved kicking, if only for the way you treat young Herbert Turner."

Valerian pulled off his gauntlet and said softly, "Need I throw this in your face? Or are you man enough to meet me?"

"I am meeting you. Much against my better judgment. No, you can put back your glove. Since you're challenging, I've choice of weapons and time and place—no?"

Valerian brightened, and bowed mockingly.

"Very well," said Cranford. "I choose fists. And—here and now."

Valerian stared at him glassy-eyed. "That—that is *disgusting!*" he declared in a near squawk. "Gentlemen don't fight with *fists!* You're bamming me! Come now, Cranford, you must have *some* small knowledge of civilized behaviour. Swords or pistols?"

"I don't consider duelling to be civilized behaviour. And from what I hear, you could kill me with either weapon."

"Oh, yes." A gleam came into the grey eyes, and pursing his lips, Valerian said, "Might not, y'know. I'd give you a sporting chance."

"Thank you, but the odds are not in my favour, I think. I'm no amateur with pistols or steel, but I've not made duelling my career, as you appear to have done."

117

"Fiend seize you—" snorted Valerian.

Cranford overrode his indignation. "On the other hand, I'm pretty fair with my 'fives' and it would do my heart good to squash that dainty nose of yours and, as my groom would say, 'darken your daylights.'"

"Barbarian!" With a shudder Valerian fingered his slim nose tenderly. "Tell you what," he said, recovering as they walked across the courtyard side by side. "I'll give you my word not to do you a serious injury if you'll sell me your mare."

Cranford halted, staring at him. "What, are you after her, too? Why? I've seen your black and he's a dashed fine— And that reminds me! What the deuce were you doing riding across my land the other day?"

"Short cut from—ah, here—to there," drawled the dandy airily. "Besides, I wanted to look over your estate. Member of the family, y'know."

"If you consider yourself a member of my family, I wonder you didn't stop and say hello. Certainly you saw us."

"I caught a glimpse of a fellow in a horse and cart. Was that you, coz? But how degradingly rural. I'd have rid over and enjoyed a good laugh had I only known. That's what comes of not paying attention, alas. But I was in a hurry."

"Too much of a hurry to come back when you heard that shot?"

"I assumed the yokel with the cart was shooting rabbits. I collect I was mistaken. Never say some bad man means to put a period to you? Zounds! What if he should try again and hit your pretty mare instead? I must save the dainty darling. See here, Cranford, I'll double my offer. If you value her safety you'll be eager to accept!"

"I value her too highly to entrust her to a dandified hedgebird like you!" Starting to mount up, Cranford was astonished when Valerian caught his arm. Wrenching clear, he growled, "You silly block! Be off with you!"

"No! I tell you I must have her! Name your price!"

Puzzled, Cranford said, "There is no price on Tassels. Lord knows, of late I've had offers enough. Some even more dashed persistent than you!"

"And you cannot guess why?" Valerian said impatiently, "For the *steeplechase*, you clod. If you had an ounce of sporting blood you'd know of it. Several gentlemen have put up the purse. Last I heard it was a thousand guineas."

"Jupiter! I collect every horseman in London is riding!"

"It's a limited field. Competition is fierce and the word's gone out that your Miss Tassels is very fast. I saw you at the gallop when your brother was at the Manor, and I believe it."

"So that's why you've been lurking about! You're entered, I take it?"

"Of course. I can put that fat purse to good use, and I'm a sportsman to the core."

"Not how I'd describe you—cousin. And much you need a fat purse. You're heir to one of the largest fortunes in the land and spend money like water."

"Untrue." Valerian added broodingly, "My old curmudgeon of a sire gives me a niggardly allowance."

Cranford doubted this. He had met Sir Simon Valerian on a few occasions, and both he and Peregrine admired him as an honourable gentleman with a kindly and generous nature. Scarcely the type to begrudge adequate financial support for his son and heir. Unless rumour spoke true and Gervaise had broken his father's heart.

"Your father being a man of impeccable morals, you likely brought it on yourself," he said. "I'll wager you offended him by refusing to honour your promise to Miss Stansbury. If that's the root of it I'd think your logical course would be to marry the girl."

Valerian scowled. "Logical for a dull dog like yourself, with little to offer any lady, except perhaps a Cit's daughter. No, when *I* take a bride she will be a diamond of the first water, afflicted by neither baby fat nor spots."

119

"Charming," said Cranford drily. "But while your lack of gallantry is only to be expected, it is somewhat surprising. I found the lady to be slender and er—spotless. And quite as foolish a slave to the whims of fashion as your so elegant self."

Ignoring the contemptuous mockery in Cranford's words, Valerian stared at him and said incredulously, *"Cordelia Stansbury? Elegant?* By Gemini, your judgment is even more faulted than I'd suspected! The chit is a mouse!"

"She may have been when you knew her. She's no mouse now."

"Nor is she an heiress," jeered Valerian. "And you need an heiress, do you not?"

Someone was hailing them in a weak, warbling tenor.

Valerian exclaimed, "Curse it all! I forgot my appointment with the strident Shorewood and he's sent his ancient clerk tottering after me. Last chance, Cranford! Name your price and I'll double it!"

"A hundred thousand gold doubloons," said Cranford, laughing at him. "And I give you fair warning, if the steeplechase offers such a large purse I just might ride Tassels myself."

Valerian scowled, then laughed and started away, walking trippingly on his high heels. "I hope you do, dear coz. Truly, I hope you do."

Cranford called, "Your sire is a superb horseman—does he ride in this steeplechase?"

"If I thought there were a chance of that," declared Valerian bitterly, "I'd not venture within a mile of the course!"

Cranford thought of his own father, loving and loved, and so sadly missed down through the years. Gervaise Valerian didn't deserve the fine gentleman who had sired him and for whom he could never find a good word. His lip curled. "Ramshackle court-card," he muttered contemptuously, and turned Tassels in the direction of St. James's Park and the home of the redoubtable Mrs. Regina Stansbury.

120

There had evidently been some kind of event at the Opera House; traffic was unusually heavy. Horsemen, carriages, and carts jostled for space, and apprentices and lackeys darted recklessly among the vehicles. Tassels tossed her head and snorted, and Cranford muttered, "I agree, my lady," and turned off the Strand onto a quieter thoroughfare. It was no better paved than the pot-holed and muddy streets he'd traversed since leaving Lincoln's Inn, but there was less traffic to be contended with.

The scattering of elegant shops seemed well patronized; a young couple was entering a jewellery shop, two gentlemen escorted an elderly lady from an emporium with a discreet sign in the window announcing a specialization in "Rare and Precious Items from the Mystic East." A luxurious carriage pulled up outside the establishment of a modiste—a shop he recognized since his sister had once asked him to collect a package from there. He glanced idly at the matron who was handed from the carriage. The door to the shop opened as she approached and a young lady came out and stood aside respectfully, allowing the older woman to pass. Aside from a haughty glance, she received not so much as a nod of thanks.

'Shabby treatment,' thought Cranford, and then grinned as the young lady dropped a distinctly mocking curtsy to the closing door. She turned about, clearly vexed.

"Now, by Jove!" he muttered, and reined Tassels into the kennel. Swinging from the saddle, he raised his tricorne and cried eagerly, "Miss Westerman! What luck to meet you here!"

She halted, staring at him. He had a momentary impression that she was flustered, but she smiled warmly as they shook hands. "Yes, indeed. Are you often in the City, Mr. Cranford?"

"Not really. May I carry your bandbox? Or is this your carriage approaching?"

She relinquished the box and said that the carriage was not calling for her. Cranford glanced about and she added mischievously, "No, I have not brought my abigail or footman. Nor am I a green girl."

The afternoon was chill, and noting that she slipped both hands into the large muff she carried, he asked if she had far to go. "Perhaps I should call up a chair for you?"

"I might take a chair in a little while, but I enjoy to walk about London. There is so much to see."

The lady did not bow to convention, evidently, but with those three shatter-brained aunts to guide her, one could scarce wonder at it. "Very true," he agreed. "Am I permitted to accompany you?"

"Please do. I heard the King may drive out today. Is that why you came this way? I never have seen him wearing his crown and riding in his coach and eight, with all his high officers and the guards around him."

"I believe he only takes the whole lot when he's bound to or from Parliament, ma'am." Leading Tassels, he walked on beside her. "His other jaunts are a little less ostentatious. As for me, I went to see your solicitor, Mr. Shorewood. Quite an interesting fellow."

"Yes." There was an outburst of shouting nearby and she had to raise her voice slightly so as to be heard. "Was he able to tell you about the sale of our property?"

"Not really. He confirmed that Gresford Finchley has put in a strong bid, but until your uncle returns or your aunts make up their minds, he cannot act."

She glanced at him from under the hood of her cloak. "My—uncle?"

"Yes. No! What a clunch I am! I suppose he must have been referring to your father. Do you correspond with him, Miss Mary? Dare I beg that if I am able to make a decent offer you will intercede for me?"

"I will be glad to do whatever—" The level of commotion had been rising and she abandoned her attempt to finish the sentence. As they reached Whitehall and turned the corner, they became part of a noisy throng. People were all about them, pushing and shouting in good-humoured excitement. Cranford drew Miss Mary closer to him, and edged Tassels back.

"What's to do?" he asked a man who had climbed the rail fence around an area-way and clung rather precariously to a flambeau. "Is the King to pass by?" The response was incoherent, but a bright-eyed linkboy said, "That's it, guv'nor. Big weddin' at St. George's, there was. All the 'ristocrats like to get leg-shackled there, 'cause it's new."

Mary climbed two front steps, but wailed that she couldn't see above the crowd.

"Whyn't yer give the lidy a 'eave-up, yer worship?" shouted the linkboy.

Cranford said with a smile, "Good idea, lad. By your leave, ma'am," and handing the bandbox to the boy, he lifted Mary to his saddle.

She gave a squeal, but did not protest, and when he had retrieved her bandbox and rewarded the boy he climbed the steps and had a fair view of the procession.

As he'd expected, the King rode in a sedan-chair today. He was preceded by six gorgeous footmen. Six Yeomen of the Guard walked majestically on either side of the monarch. The sedan-chair was an elaborate affair much embellished with gilded scrolls and the royal arms. Miss Mary would be disappointed, thought Cranford, because the King did not wear a crown. A powdered wig of the latest French fashion lent distinction to his heavy features and a blue coat richly embroidered with gold thread did its best with the florid royal figure. Leaning back against the squabs, King George smiled fixedly and raised a languid hand from time to time in acknowledgment of the shouts of his subjects, though not all those shouts were complimentary.

Next came the coaches of the officers-in-waiting, and since there were many of these and the pace of the procession was not rapid, Cranford began to think they would be trapped in the crowd until dark. At last, however, the parade came to an end, the onlookers began to disperse, and he was able to lift Miss Westerman from the saddle.

She showed him a sparkling smile and, apparently not in the least disappointed, said ecstatically, "Was it not wonderful? Oh, I am so glad I saw it! Thank you so much, Lieutenant Cranford."

"It was truly my pleasure, ma'am. I'm only sorry His Majesty did not wear his crown for you. I fear all this pomp has delayed you. Shall I call up a chair now?"

She looked doubtfully at the crowded streets. "I don't see any, do you? Truly, I've not very far to go now. I fancy you also have business to attend to."

The business he had intended to "attend to" had lost its urgency in the face of a deepening anxiety for the well-being of his twin. At first attributing his unease to the naturally distracted state that seemed to plague bridegrooms, he could no longer dismiss the feeling that something was very wrong.

Watching him, Miss Westerman said, "You are troubled, I think? You don't appear to look forward to whatever— Oh, how very thoughtless of me! You were likely on your way to see your brother, and I have delayed you! Do pray, go at once! I shall be at home within ten minutes, I promise you."

She looked distressed. Her kindness touched him, but he had no intention of allowing her to walk alone in this noisy crowd. He caught a glimpse of an unoccupied sedan-chair and waved the bearers to him. "Now I can know you will get home without mishap," he said, handing her inside despite her protests.

"You are very kind." She leaned to the open door. "I do hope you find Sir Peregrine improved."

Cranford tensed. "Improved? Is he ill, then?"

"You did not know? You looked so anxious, I thought—"

"We are twins. Sometimes we can sense if the other is in trouble. I have feared something was wrong, but ascribed it

124

to— Well, that is neither here nor there. I think Perry is not in deep distress— Do pray tell me I'm right."

She said wonderingly, "What a remarkable gift. I believe you are quite correct, Lieutenant." She saw how intently he searched her face and she went on quickly, "Sir Peregrine and his future brother-in-law were walking home from the Bedford Coffee House last night when they were knocked down by some lunatics racing their horses. After dark, of all the ridiculous things!"

Shocked, he said, "But you heard my brother was not badly hurt? My great-uncle said nothing of it this morning."

"I doubt 'tis widely known yet. I only heard of it because a friend of my aunt chanced to ride by and saw it happen."

"Forgive, ma'am, but I must see him at once."

"Pray go. I'll give the chairmen my direction."

He thanked her and mounted up, guiding Tassels along the Strand while cold fingers seemed to close around his heart. The unease he'd experienced when Perry hadn't come to Muse Manor had deepened into anxiety today, but he'd been so busy with their various disasters that all he'd done was concoct a tale he'd hoped would fob Perry off. 'Fool!' he thought remorsefully, and urged Tassels to a faster gait.

Peregrine occupied a ground-floor flat in a charming house on Henrietta Street. Now that he was about to become a benedick, he was looking for a suitable house, but Piers had urged him to bring his bride to Muse Manor, where there was plenty of room for them to live comfortably until a permanent home was found. The page-boy ran out to take charge of Tassels as Cranford dismounted and in two long strides was atop the front steps. The porter already had the door open and greeted him with a nod and the observation that he was not surprised to see him.

Townes, his brother's new valet, answered his knock and with a faint welcoming smile took his hat, cloak and gauntlets. As always, he was immaculate, his wig neatly combed and his cravat like snow. For fifteen years he had served aboard some of the finest vessels in the East India fleet, valeting various captains. He had left the Company when he'd fallen in love with and married a passenger who had been returning to England with her soldier father. Sadly, influenza had claimed his bride less than a year later, leaving him heart-broken and without hope or purpose. A tavern brawl had led to a friendship with Enoch Tummet, Mr. August Falcon's unorthodox valet, who had encouraged him to apply for the position vacated when Florian Consett left Peregrine and moved to the Cranfords' country estate. Townes had adjusted well, but he appeared older than his thirty-five years and the deeply lined face gave mute testimony to his personal tragedy. He said in his well-modulated voice, "Miss Grainger will be pleased you have come, sir. She is in the parlour."

"Thank you. No need to announce me. Please tell the page to take my mare around to the stables and see she is fed and watered."

Townes bowed and went outside and Piers hurried into the small parlour.

Zoe Grainger uttered a cry of relief and rose from the sofa to greet him.

"My poor girl." He took her hands and held them strongly. "How bad is it? Can I see him?"

Zoe shook her auburn curls and lifted tear-wet green eyes to meet his. She was somewhat below average height, and pretty rather than beautiful, but with a shapely figure and usually a bright and cheerful disposition. Now, however, her voice trembled as she said, "Not too bad, I pray. Dr. Naseby is with him now, and has asked me to wait here. He said yesterday that Perry was lucky to have escaped serious injury, but one of the horses' hooves struck his bad leg and—and we don't know yet what—what the outcome may be."

He thought an anguished, 'Dear Heaven! Not more surgery?' and it was an effort to say calmly, "What a dreadful shock

126

for you. I understand your brother was injured also? Not seriously, I hope."

"Travis was cut about the head and suffered a sprained wrist, but— Oh, Piers! I'm so afraid!"

Still holding her hand, he sat beside her on the sofa. "If I know my twin, he will do nicely, as he always does. I just wish I'd come sooner."

"I wonder you arrived so quickly. I suppose you sensed he had been hurt. You must have rid all night. The thing is . . . It was so senseless, Piers! Those wicked creatures had not the common decency to stop and help. In fact, Travis was getting to his feet, when one of the riders turned back and beat him down with his riding crop. That's how his head was cut. If Perry had been able to get up—or if a coach hadn't driven up at that moment . . . Oh, I dread to think what they may have done."

He stared at her pale little face. Another disaster . . . Could it be tied to all the rest? And if so—what was the purpose?

Zoe said, "Might it be more reprisals from that evil League of Jewelled Men? I thought that was all behind us, but who else would wish to harm Perry?"

"No one," he said firmly. "And the tale of the League is told—forever! I'll wager it was a matter of drink coupled with two irresponsible young bucks looking to prove their manhood."

"That's what the Bow Street Runner said," she murmured doubtfully.

He was at once tense with apprehension, but knew his brother would keep any private concerns from the girl he loved. He asked gently, "The Runners were here? What did they have to say?"

"Nothing to the point, or so Perry thought. They as good as said he should have been more vigilant and that any citizen in these lawless times should exercise caution when walking after dark. He is not a peer, of course, else they might perhaps

127

have been more thorough. I believe Perry is more concerned that something is amiss down at Muse Manor." Searching his unwontedly stern face, she asked, "Is that the case?"

He summoned a smile. "Is my brother fretting himself to flinders?"

"He is, that's what frightens me so," she said, appearing not to have noticed the evasion. "He's no coward, Piers."

"Lord! I know that!"

"But he dreads more surgery, poor darling. And he says that thanks to him our—our wedding might have to be post-poned. Piers, he is making himself even more ill with all this anxiety."

In which case, thought Piers grimly, Perry must know noth-ing of recent events at Muse Manor.

He sprang up as Dr. Naseby hurried in.

"How is he?" he asked, shaking hands with the plump little physician.

Naseby smiled over the big round spectacles that gave him an owlish look. "Not good, but not bad enough to cause you to be in despair. You got here promptly, which don't surprise me in view of the odd mental link you share with your twin. He told me he was on the verge of coming up to your estate, fret-ting that something is amiss." He scanned Piers shrewdly. "Is it?"

Irritated, Piers said, "Nothing of import. But let me have the tale with no bark on it, if you please. I understand his maimed leg is damaged."

Zoe half-whispered, "Are you going to operate again?"

The doctor glanced at the decanter. Remembering his man-ners, Piers stifled his impatience and poured a glass of Madeira and Naseby sat down and accepted it with a murmur of thanks and the observation that "it has been a busy day." He took a mouthful of wine, sighed with gratification, and said, "Your brother is quite battered, Mr. Piers, but I suspect he got off lightly. The main damage is to his leg, which is lacerated. At first I'd feared surgery was indicated, but I'm happy to say I don't think we'll have to resort to that, if all goes well."

Zoe wept with relief. Putting his arm about her, and saying a mental prayer of thanks, Piers gave the doctor a steady look. "I can go in and see him now?"

Interpreting that glance correctly, Naseby said, "Yes. But just yourself, if you please. Young Grainger is with him and I don't want his nerves overset. One visitor for a few minutes only. I'll come with you and haul Mr. Grainger out." He patted Zoe's hand and went with Piers into the corridor.

Piers said softly, "There was a qualification, I think."

"I didn't want to alarm the lady. The nature of the wounds leads me to wonder if this was a random accident. I suspect your twin knows more than he has said, and fears for the safety of his fiancée. His anxieties are hindering his recovery."

"Miss Grainger says he dreads that his injuries may cause them to delay their wedding."

"Nonsense. He is in a deal of pain, but if he can just be convinced to stop worrying and get some sleep, he will do splendidly. I tried to give him laudanum, which was a forlorn hope, as usual."

"Yes, he loathes the stuff. I think it reminds him of all the misery he endured when he lost his foot."

The doctor nodded. "Understandable. Well, do what you can to make him more tranquil. That's the best medicine for him just now. I'll tell Miss Grainger her brother will be out directly, I fancy you want a quick word with him. A *quick* word, mind!"

Piers nodded and opened the bedroom door. Peregrine gave a whoop and shouted gaily, "About time you arrived, old slowtop!"

Travis Grainger rose from the bedside chair. Six years Zoe's senior, he had the same auburn hair and green eyes and the family resemblance was strong.

Shaking hands, Piers noted that he was pale and looked

wan. "Hello, Hops," he said warmly. "Has my graceless twin dragged you into trouble again?"

Amused by the schoolboy nickname, Grainger confirmed this, and Piers moved past him to bend over his brother. The blue eyes were, he thought, too bright, but the hand that reached out to him was no more than normally warm. He thought, 'No fever, thank the Lord!' and chided, "Well, halfling? What possessed you to allow two drunken bullies to put you flat on your back again? I can't be running up to Town every other day, you know."

"No more can I be trudging into the country," said Peregrine.

Grainger said quietly, "We doubt they were drunken bullies, Piers, though don't tell Zoe I said so."

Piers sat on the side of the bed. "What, then? If they were the League's assassins you'd both be dead."

"Very true. But"—Peregrine glanced to the door warily— "it was no accident."

Grainger said, "We thought at first it was attempted robbery. Mohocks again. You know what a plague they are for violence and thievery in the City. But these two varmints were mounted."

"On fine hacks," put in Peregrine, shifting restlessly in the bed.

Piers asked sharply, "What kind of animals? Were you able to see?"

"Well enough to note that one was a splendid black." Peregrine said. "Reminded me of August Falcon's Andante."

Dr. Naseby stuck his head around the door. His dark eyes glinted, and he remarked testily that there were too many people jabbering at his patient.

Grainger said, "Aye, aye, sir!" and hurried out.

Piers scarcely noticed him leave. He was thinking, 'A splendid black . . .' Falcon wasn't the only man who owned such a horse—their alleged "cousin" Gervaise also rode "a splendid black." He made no comment and kept his face expressionless, but watching him narrowly, his twin said, "All right, now you can tell me what's wrong at home. And don't say "Nothing." I knew days ago that I should come down there. Would to heaven I had! As soon as this stupid leg improves—"

"Lord, what an ego," said Piers, laughing. "D'you suppose we cannot handle a few minor problems without screaming for your sage counsel?" He saw Peregrine flush and look irked, and hurried on, "If you must know, your friend Florian came to cuffs with old Finchley's head-groom and—"

"Grover? Florian's no match for that ruffian. Was he hanging around the Finchley preserves again? I warned him the charming Major would take exception to his interest in Laura. But—there's more, I think. What aren't you telling me? I am still part of this family and I've a right not to be shut out of—"

"All right, all right!" Piers said resignedly. "We have had a small problem at St. Mark's—the steeple and bell tower fell into the choir loft, but I promise you we're in a fair way to rebuilding, so there is no cause for you to be into the boughs about it. Aunt Jane sends her love and will doubtless want me to drive her to town so as to visit you. Is that sufficiently sinister to warrant your morbid imaginings? . . . "

"It is sufficient to cause me to beg that you not tell her of this fiasco! Seriously, twin, it was bad enough having the Runners hover over me, but poor Aunt Jane would be in a state over something that may be, as the Runners implied, laid to my own lack of alertness. And—for Lord's sake, don't tell our great-uncle of it! If he should come stamping and bellowing over here I would truly be driven to the ropes!"

Piers grinned but warned that if the attack should get into the newspapers he would have no way of keeping Lord Nugent in the dark.

Nodding gloomily, Peregrine demanded more details of the estate, and Piers obliged him at some length, teasing his brother and making light of events at Muse Manor, his performance so convincing that by the time he left, Peregrine was comfortably asleep.

I am very sorry, Mr. Cranford." A sleek and slender individual, with a tendency to flourish his gloved hands in elaborate gestures, the Stansbury butler looked bored rather than sorry as he explained that Mrs. Stansbury was attending an afternoon musicale and Miss Cordelia Stansbury was from home.

The short winter afternoon had already faded into dusk; Cranford was cold and very aware that he had not as yet enjoyed luncheon. He could return to Perry's flat, where he knew he'd be offered a meal, or go to his club, but he was eager to put this unpleasant task behind him.

He said, "I am most anxious to talk with Miss Stansbury. Do you know where I might find the lady?"

The butler's pale eyes slithered over him in a swift appraisal, then blinked at the ceiling as he imparted that he "could not say."

Recognizing the signs, Cranford took out his purse.

Doncaster Close was located in one of the newer areas that were springing up west of Hyde Park. The houses were neatly kept and of a good size, but there was no central private garden, and the Close conveyed an impression of comfortable affluence rather than the aura of great wealth which pervaded an adjoining square. Cranford's tug on the bell of number fourteen was answered by a large and gorgeous footman. His protuberant eyes swept the caller briefly, and although he appeared to be somewhat deaf, he was sufficiently impressed by Cranford's card to admit him to the entrance hall, and having bowed him to a stone bench sailed away, desiring that he "be so good as to wait" while he ascertained whether "the ladies" were at home.

Cranford watched the footman's majestic progress to the stairs and resigned himself to a long wait. He glanced around the hall. Empty, it would have been a large chamber, but it was so crowded with furniture that it appeared to be quite small. The pieces were seemingly unrelated and of such widely diverse styles that he was put in mind of a second-hand furniture warehouse. Although far from being an expert in such matters, he was able to recognize that an elaborate credenza on one wall was of the baroque style, while beside it was a tall mahogany coat-stand such as might be found in an English country house. The bench he occupied looked to have been culled from a garden; the enormous gilded mirror reflecting his curiosity would have been more suited to a ballroom; and a marble-topped sideboard appeared to be of Italian origin. He was gazing in fascination at a purple velvet chaise supported by black marble griffin's legs when footsteps sounded from a staircase at the rear of the hall and he sprang to his feet.

The lady who tripped to greet him was tall and willowy, her height accentuated by the large blue feathers that bobbed above her French wig.

"Miss . . . Celeste . . . Westerman . . . ?" he stammered incredulously.

Wielding an outsize fan of matching blue feathers, she advanced, hand outstretched, eyes gleaming with delight. "Lieutenant Piers Cranford! Why, you *dear* thing! You have sought me out!"

He bit back the instinctive denial, which could only offend, and dropped a reluctant kiss on the hand that was thrust at his lips. "The—er, pleasure is mine, ma'am, but—"

"Silly boy. We are *alone* at last. You may call me"—she lowered her voice and purred provocatively—". . . Celeste."

"Thank you," he gulped, edging back as the fan whisked across his nose. "I had—"

"And I shall call you . . . *Piers*," she said throbbingly. "Such a lovely, *lovely* name. I think—"

"If you did, sister," growled Mrs. Caroline Westerman, coming heavy-footed from a corridor that apparently led to the back of the house, "you would know that Mr. Cranford probably has not come to see you, but rather—"

Miss Celeste uttered a shrill titter. "But how foolish you are, *dear* Caro. You surely do not flatter yourself that he has come to see *you*? La, but I declare 'tis positively amusing." Her long eyelashes fluttering, she lowered her voice once more and urged, "Tell her why you are come, *dear* . . . Piers," and behind her fan said clearly, " 'Tis not kind to tease the poor creature."

Mentally, Cranford groaned. "I think I am in error," he said. "It is my pleasure to see both of you charming ladies, but I had hoped for a word with—" He broke off as a laughing voice declared:

"Aunty Caro, I have torn the hem of my gown. I am still unused to these wretched heels . . . and . . ." Entering the hall holding one very high-heeled slipper and walking jerkily on the other, Miss Cordelia Stansbury came to an abrupt halt. The laughter vanished from her eyes and the colour from her cheeks as she saw Cranford. "Oh . . . my . . ." she whispered.

"Just so, *Miss Mary,*" said he sternly.

The wig she wore was dishevelled and a curling tendril of

golden-brown hair had escaped. She had not applied her paint and patches, and she seemed smaller and only half-dressed minus all the jewels she'd worn when first they met.

Raising a hand to straighten her wig, she forgot the shoe she held, with the result that the wig was knocked sideways. Scarlet-faced but recovering, she snatched at it frantically, and gabbled, "Lieutenant—Cr-Cranford. How—er, charming that you have called upon—"

"Me!" interposed Miss Celeste sharply.

"Nonsense," barked Mrs. Caroline.

"I was under the impression I had called upon Miss Cordelia Stansbury—or is it Miss Mary Westerman?" said Cranford, his eyes bleak.

"Why, you silly boy," teased Miss Celeste, preparing to take his arm. "Don't you know—"

"We know that we must ask Cook to prepare tea," said Mrs. Caroline, in a voice that brooked no argument. "Come *along*, sister. Be so good as to show the Lieutenant into the withdrawing-room, Mary."

Miss Celeste's squeaked protestations faded as her sister took her firmly by the arm and all but dragged her from the hall.

Cranford said, "May I help you with your shoe, Miss Stansbury?"

For answer, Cordelia kicked off her other shoe, gathered up her trailing skirts and said defiantly, "Oh, come along and do stop looking daggers at me. You have found me out. You know perfectly well who I am."

Following her along an over-furnished corridor into an even more over-furnished withdrawing-room, he said, "You would appear to be two ladies, ma'am, both of whom have been playing a game with me."

She was silent until they were seated on either side of a merrily crackling fire. Watching the flames thoughtfully, she murmured, "Yes. You are entitled to an explanation, I suppose.

My mother, you see, never liked the name Mary. My father had chosen it and my aunts liked it well enough, but Mama judged it too—ordinary. She refused to call me anything but Cordelia. Mama judged my aunts 'ordinary' as well. Which they knew. There were—disagreements and eventually a sad rift. Afterwards, my aunts insisted on calling me Mary Westerman, and of late I've not minded using that name since my own is so sadly disgraced. Family nonsense, you see, but I trust you are not going to claim that I have broke your heart, sir."

"It would be foolish in me, considering that we had never met prior to the day I called upon your mama and you saw fit to make mock of my offer."

Her hazel eyes lifted and scanned him with a candid and unwavering gaze. She nodded. "I apologize for being so gauche. But now you must please be honest. Do you even like me?"

He hesitated, then said, "I like Miss Mary Westerman."

"But not Miss Stansbury. Did you dislike Cordelia on sight?"

"I—er, I try never to rely on—on first impressions, ma'am."

"Now you are evading. You strike me as being the type of man who would form immediate first impressions and seldom revise them." She saw the slow smile that crept into his extremely attractive blue eyes. "In which case, Lieutenant," she said with a small chuckle, "why ever did you offer for me? No! You are a soldier, I'm aware, but pray answer me honestly and do not exercise tactful diplomacy."

She had asked for honesty, but if, as he suspected, she was deep in love with his revolting "cousin," he had no wish to hurt her. He said, he hoped nonchalantly, "I have sold out and am no longer a soldier, ma'am. I will tell you that I stand in need of a bank loan which I cannot obtain without the consent of my great-uncle."

Her brows lifted. "General Lord Nugent Cranford?"

"Yes. He is a very—proud gentleman and will fight tooth and nail to protect our family from any hint of dishonour."

She said with a faintly sardonic smile, "And you are, I believe, related to Mr. Gervaise Valerian?"

"Unfor——er, I mean—distantly, ma'am."

"Ah. I see that you do not like the gentleman."

He shrugged. "As you say."

"But you have been commanded to—what is it you men say? To 'pull his chestnuts from the fire' by offering for the lady he rejected, and thus restore the family honour. Is that the case, Mr. Cranford?"

Her candour would be judged by many as scandalous, but she was reacting calmly and sensibly, thank goodness, and he was emboldened to admit, "You are in the right of it, ma'am."

"*Right* of it!" She sprang up, eyes flashing suddenly and cheeks flushed. "*Right* of it? I would say rather you have the *wrong* of it! It is *disgusting! Indecent! Immoral!*"

Startled, he said jerkily, "You asked for—for an honest—"

"Beneath *contempt!*" Her voice shrill with fury, she cried, "Not caring a button for the poor creature, you were willing to take her for your wife only to secure money for—"

He had stood also, and gripping her shoulders, interrupted harshly, "You insisted upon the truth. Try using some yourself. I am no matrimonial prize, I grant you. But I could have offered the lady a good name at least—"

"To cleanse her sullied reputation? I wonder so proud and upstanding an officer would stoop—"

"Be quiet! I know she—you—are in love with my cousin."

Her head bowed at this, and she stood silent and passive in his grasp.

"But I would have made no demands upon the lady," he declared. "However much I—"

"Lusted for your rights as a husband?" she shot at him.

"I was going to say, however much I deplored Miss Cordelia's taste in men," he replied, taking his hands from her shoulders.

She turned away and walked to a window, her careful dignity marred by an occasional trip, since her gown had been fashioned for wear with high heels. Reminded of Dimity as a child dressing up in one of Mama's gowns, he smiled faintly.

"Have you ever been in love, Mr. Cranford?" she asked in a calmer voice.

"Surely every man has been in love at some time during his life."

"You are skilled at evasions, sir, but I wonder if you know what it means to . . . really . . . love someone."

"The same thought occurs to me regarding Miss Cordelia and her—passion for Valerian."

She swung around and regarded him smoulderingly. "You almost said 'unrequited' passion."

"Ill-judged, rather."

"If you admit it to be genuine passion, how could you endure life with a lady who loved another?"

"Probably by finding myself—'another,' as you put it."

She said with a curl of the lip, "A splendid basis for a happy marriage, I do declare!"

With a nonchalance he did not feel, he responded, "We live in a modern age, Miss Cordelia. I am—" He paused as a maid entered, carrying a tray laden with tea-time paraphernalia which she proceeded to set out on a low table.

Returning to her chair, Cordelia took up the teapot, then slanted a glance at Cranford and murmured, "Alas, you will not care for it. No brandy, Lieutenant."

His eyes were fixed hopefully on a plate of steaming buttered crumpets, but meeting her gaze and finding a sparkle of laughter there, he grinned in response. "Ma'am, I am too famished to quibble for such unorthodox seasonings."

"Famished? A late breakfast, perchance?"

"No lunch. After we parted I went to see my brother and then to your—Miss Cordelia's home."

She at once handed him a plate and offered the crumpets and strawberry preserves. "I trust you found Sir Peregrine not badly injured?"

"He goes along better than I'd dared hope. The attack was stupid and pointless." He said thoughtfully, "At least, I think it was pointless," and sank his teeth into a deliciously juicy crumpet.

Conversation languished as they enjoyed their tea, but when his hostess offered to ring for more crumpets, Cranford declined and asked her instead to tell him about the island where she had been cast away. "If 'tis not too painful for you, ma'am."

"Oh, no. Not at all," she answered, so blithely that he looked at her in surprise. "Well, of course, it was terrifying— the storm, I mean," she amended hastily. "But the island was lovely. So sunny and warm. And the natives were very kind."

"They did not—er— That is to say, you were not—ill-treated?"

"If you mean was I ravished," she said outrageously, "I was not, sir." She saw the lift of his brows and her chin went up. "You are thinking that ladies do not make such remarks, but I will tell you that I was in fact treated with far more respect than I have received here in London."

Her defiant flare faded into a wistful resignation, and Cranford waited, saying nothing.

"I suppose," she went on, running a fingertip around the handle of her cup, "you are wondering why I did it."

"Did—what? Come back to England?"

"No! This is my homeland; of course I would come back. I meant—why I set out."

"I understood your mama sent you to Egypt."

"Not so, Mr. Cranford. The truth is that—that I was so humiliated when poor Gervaise was entrapped into offering for me . . ." Her voice trembled a little. She took a deep breath and said, "I—knew he didn't care for me, you see. And I—I just could not bear it."

Awed, he asked, "Do you say your mother did *not* send you? That you ran away?"

"I did." With a sideways glance at him, she said, "Are you greatly shocked?"

He was certainly taken off-stride, but he managed to say, "It must have taken a great deal of courage, I think. But—you never managed it alone?"

"My aunts helped me, the dear things. That was the worst part of it for me. Knowing how worried they must have been, and blaming themselves."

"Well, you're safe home now, so they may be happy again. But if you won't have me, what shall you do? Or have your aunts decided to confront Valerian and oblige him to—er—"

"Force him to honour his word, do you mean? Good gracious—no! That is the very reason I ran away in the first place. I have my pride, Mr. Cranford. I want no gentleman to marry me as a duty, and having no affection for me."

"But—your pardon—if you care for him . . ."

"I do," she admitted, her face saddened. "I always will. But—I know I am socially 'beyond the pale' now. And even if I were not, I would never condemn him to a loveless marriage. Or you to an even more loveless marriage, since in our case there would be love on neither side."

"Then . . . you will live here? With your aunts?"

"For the time being." She nodded, then said with one of Miss Mary's michievous smiles, "Never look so troubled, Lieutenant Piers. I have—a Plan, and if all goes well, shall do very nicely."

Whatever her Plan, it would almost certainly be judged brazen by most of the *ton,* but he could not fail to be impressed by her resourcefulness. He said, "I hope for your sake it does go well. But if it should not, my offer still stands. Arranged

141

marriages sometimes turn out to be the best, so they say. And you like my country home."

"Indeed, I do. But— Oh my! Will you really lose it if I refuse you? Surely the General would not be so unkind?"

"To say truth, ma'am, I also have a Plan that may save Muse Manor for us. I am obliged to admit, though, that were you ever to consider me, I could not offer you all the elegancies that Valerian would provide. Our finances are at a low ebb at present, and we've to cope with several costly repairs."

He looked rather grim, and she probed curiously, "We? Do you mean you and your twin?"

"Yes." Scanning her face in sudden anxiety, he said, "If you should meet Perry again, I must beg you not to mention the little difficulties that—"

"That require 'costly repairs'? The truth is that you've not told him of the flood, or your poor cow, or any of it, have you? Why not? I thought you said he was not badly injured, in which case you could have at least discussed the situation and asked his opinion. Or is he fumble-witted?"

Indignant, he exclaimed hotly, "Certainly not! If you'd been in England last year, you would know he was knighted for gallantry."

"Ah. So he has become too high-in-the-instep to help with your difficulties."

"Not so! Good heavens, ma'am, how you do take one up!"

"Do I? Perhaps. But I would have to be foolish indeed not to realize that there must be some reason why you won't allow him to help, and shut him out as though he were a child."

His temper flaring, he said, "If you must know, he's had a miserably painful three years because of a war injury. He has found his lady now, and is soon to be married. God knows, he deserves his happiness."

"And you mean to ensure that nothing spoils it. I see." Her sudden smile beamed at him. "I think Sir Peregrine is a lucky man to have you for a brother, Lieutenant Piers."

Her eyes were very kind, so that he said with a grateful but rather embarrassed smile, "Thank you. Now that you have evidently put me on a most undeserved pedestal, are you quite sure you won't reconsider my offer?"

She shook her head. " 'Twould be unkind to both of us. But I will very much like to have you for a friend—if you have any use for the friendship of a disgraced lady."

"I would be honoured," he said, and was mildly surprised to realize that he meant it.

Her aunts did not reappear, and soon afterwards he bade her good night and took his departure.

Outside, it was dark and cold, but he felt the need of some exercise and, refusing the footman's offer to call up a chair, he set off at a brisk pace. A chill wind moaned between the buildings and whipped the flambeaus that blazed beside most doors. He scarcely noticed the lowering temperature; his thoughts were on the house he'd just left and the incredible story Miss Stansbury had told him. She was a courageous little lady, but he wondered if she fully comprehended the enormity of what she had done and the inevitable judgment of a Society that could be merciless. In his opinion, Mrs. Regina Stansbury was responsible for her daughter's rash action, but for a young and pretty girl to be, as she herself had said, 'beyond the pale,' was a sad fate. The kindest of the *ton* hostesses would not invite her to their parties or pay her morning calls. She would be shunned and avoided and all Society's doors would be closed to the poor girl. There would be only two avenues open to her: she must either wed someone of good family, or a powerful *ton* hostess must defy public opinion and take the outcast under her wing.

He chuckled to himself, recalling the way her eyes had flashed when she'd stormed at him and labelled his offer for her hand as being "disgusting, immoral, and indecent." As he turned onto the New Road to Kensington, he could almost hear her saying she would not condemn him to a marriage in which there would be love on neither side ... Surely, most ladies caught in so unenviable a situation would have jumped at the chance of a respectable alliance, and have given not a button about saddling a gentleman with a "loveless marriage." A *rara avis* was Miss Mary ...

The gust of wind was so strong, it broke through his introspection and sent his cloak billowing. He pulled it closer, finding that he was shivering with cold. Hoofbeats were coming up behind him and he turned sharply, hoping to find a hackney coach. This coach, however, was large and far from being a vehicle for hire. By the light from a flambeau he saw that the coachman was holding his team to a walk. Briefly Cranford had a strong impression that he was being watched, then he had to leap back as the coachman cracked his whip and the carriage plunged past so close that it brushed his cloak. He caught a glimpse of the man inside and his instinctive shout of anger died away. It was a brief glimpse and the passenger jerked back at once, but Cranford's eyes were keen and he stared after the fast disappearing carriage curiously. The likeness had been truly remarkable. If he didn't know better, he'd have sworn it was the pedlar fellow who came so often to Muse Village.

He shook his head and scolded himself for such foolishness. As if an impoverished pedlar could have ridden in that fine coach—or even be in Mayfair.

A hackney carriage approached, the jarvey slowing his horse and peering hopefully at a possible fare. Cranford waved his cane and the coach was turned smartly and pulled up alongside. Directing the jarvey to the Madrigal Club, Cranford settled back against the worn squabs. At once Miss Mary again occupied his thoughts. Did she really intend to strike out on her own? Surely, such a daring course was unlikely. It was also unlikely that she would be "on her own" for long. She was a taking little creature, and if a match in her own strata of Society was not forthcoming, she would probably win the admiration of some worthy Cit and be perfectly happy living in obscurity.

For some reason that solution irritated him. He shrugged impatiently and turned his thoughts to Muse Manor.

Not until he was enjoying a fine supper in the Madrigal Club did he recall Tio Glendenning's reaction to the pedlar, Joshua somebody, they'd seen in the village. Tio had been markedly uneasy. "Be wary of him," he'd warned. His own efforts to cope with the various calamities that demanded his attention had driven that warning from his mind. Now, in the act of lifting a forkful of succulent roast beef, his hand stilled. If Joshua Pedlar was in truth an Intelligence officer, he might very well have been in that carriage just now! And if he had been ordered to monitor Piers Cranford's activities, he was likely aware of the close friendship that existed between him and the hot-at-hand viscount. A chill shivered between Cranford's shoulder-blades. He'd thought they were clear of that terrible threat. But if the Horse Guards and Bow Street were still on Tio's track, then they all were at risk. Dimity and her fine young husband, Perry; Aunt Jane; and himself; for each one of them had given aid to a man they knew to have followed Prince Charles Stuart and would share his cruel fate if that fact were proven.

Cranford lowered his fork slowly. The roast beef had lost its flavour.

"Mathieson?" Comfortably settled on the sofa in the drawing-room of his flat, Peregrine looked up at his twin curiously. "I knew he was back in Town, but you didn't say you'd met him."

"Forgot." Piers concentrated on the stubborn shell from which he was struggling unsuccessfully to extract the nutmeat. He had originally intended to ride straight to Glendenning Abbey and warn Horatio of his misgivings concerning the alleged pedlar. It had dawned on him, however, that if he was indeed under surveillance, to rush down to Windsor would surely add weight to whatever suspicions of Tio already existed. He had therefore penned a very carefully worded letter and sent it off to Windsor via a fast messenger. He had left the club directly and walked to a coffee-house from which he had a clear view of the club. The messenger had left without so much as a hint that anyone had followed. Relieved, he had settled down to enjoy his breakfast, and when some acquaintances had arrived and looked about for a table, he'd been only too glad to invite them to join him. His enquiries about the forthcoming race had given rise to eager questioning, and when he'd confirmed that he hoped to be allowed to enter, there had been whoops of excitement. Several of the avid young sportsmen had accompanied him to White's, and Roland Mathieson, who was on the Steeplechase Committee, and had afterwards shared a boisterous celebration of his acceptance as a rider.

He had not intended to share any of this with Perry, and could cheerfully have throttled Travis Grainger, who had just come breezing in, unannounced, and advised his prospective brothers-in-law that he'd stopped in at White's earlier. "I'd have joined you, Piers, but you and Mathieson were surrounded, and there was so much uproar I could not reach you." Perry, of course, had pounced on it at once.

He carried his uncooperative nut to the hearth and smashed it with the poker. "Where did your man find these things?" he grumbled. " 'Twould be easier to peel a one-minute boiled egg!"

"Never mind about that," said Peregrine. "What's all this about 'uproar'? Is Roly ill again?"

Grainger remarked with a grin, "He don't look it. As elegant as ever, despite the loss of his eye. What a remarkable fellow. Did you notice that eye-patch of his, Piers? Dashed if it don't have a sapphire in one corner!"

"It was a diamond the last time I saw him," said Peregrine. "Trust Roly not to let his injuries throw him into despair. He's a good man."

"Good-looking, certainly," put in Grainger, appropriating a

nut from the bowl. "A bit of a rascal, wasn't he? Tony Farrar told me that half the damsels in London were mad for him before he fell into the hands of a jealous Army captain. Is that why he was almost beaten to death? Jealousy?"

Well aware of his brother's apparent lack of interest in the subject, Peregrine said, "Something of the sort. Much good it did Captain Lambert, eh, Piers? Mathieson is quite recovered and the ladies seem to find him even more attractive, though we don't see him in Town very often nowadays."

In an attempt to change the subject, Piers said, "Can't fault him for that. Fiona presented him with a fine heir, and gentlemen tend to dote on their first-born, as you'll likely discover, twin. Speaking of which—"

"Rather, let us speak of this alleged 'excitement,'" interrupted Peregrine sternly. "What's Mathieson about, Travis?"

"He's on the Steeplechase Committee," said Grainger. "The talk is that he has a grand horse himself."

Peregrine nodded. "Rumpelstiltskin, better known as Rump. A sizeable purse, is there, Travis?"

"Roly don't need a purse," Piers interjected, striving. "He's Marbury's heir, and—"

"Sizeable, indeed," exclaimed Grainger, his youthful face alight with enthusiasm. "A small fortune! I heard 'tis in the neighbourhood of a thousand guineas!"

"Is it, now?" Peregrine's narrowed eyes searched his brother's expressionless face. He said, "You mean to ride Tassels!"

"That's the rumour," confirmed Grainger. "Is it truth, Piers?"

Abandoning his efforts, Piers admitted that he had applied to and been accepted as a rider in the forthcoming steeplechase. "So many fellows tried to buy Tassels, and were convinced she could win, that I decided to ride her myself."

"And the purse was of secondary interest, of course," murmured Peregrine sardonically.

147

Piers laughed. "I'd be a liar if I agreed. It was of *some* interest."

"Well, I think it's jolly good, and I hope you win," said Grainger. "Whether or not you need the lettuce."

"No one could scoff at *that* much lettuce," said Piers.

"As you say," agreed Peregrine, but his steady and unsmiling stare told his twin that he had better prepare himself for some home questions.

He was quite correct.

9

"One might, Miss Mary, judge me to be the most savage criminal!" Cranford reined Tassels around a gorse bush and sent a rueful glance at the girl who rode beside him on this frosty morning. She was warmly clad against the cold in a dark blue hooded woollen cloak worn over a riding habit of lighter blue. Her cheeks glowed rosily and her hazel eyes sparkled with amber glints so that he thought those who judged her less than pretty should look again. Admittedly, she was not beautiful, but she was a most taking little creature. He knew now that her name was Cordelia Mary Westerman Stansbury, but he continued to think of her as Miss Mary. Since the race was to take place on the coming Saturday, he had remained in Town, and for the past two mornings had managed to persuade her to accompany him on his early rides. Knowing that she was so notorious as to almost certainly be dealt a cutting snub by any member of the *haut ton* they might chance to encounter, he had chosen to avoid the much frequented equestrian paths through Hyde Park and had ridden farther west into the open and largely deserted fields.

Mary said with a twinkle that while she did not judge Lieutenant Cranford "a criminal . . . exactly," she could not blame his brother for being put out. "I know you wish to protect him, but he is a grown man and as a member of your family has a right to be consulted—even if 'tis on a matter that must disturb him. He is bound to think you have no confidence in his judgment."

"So he told me," Cranford admitted glumly. "You should only have heard him carry on. Threw questions at me like a barrister for the prosecution! Dashed if I didn't feel I was on trial!"

She chuckled. "So the end of it was that you told him all of it?"

"Gad, no! He would have likely called off the wedding and ridden *ventre à terre* for Muse Manor! I managed to fob him off with some details of the necessary repairs to our roof and to the village church."

"Then he is satisfied there's nothing more? My goodness! I don't envy you when you must confess the whole!"

She did not know the whole, he thought, for he'd not told her of the shot that had come so close, nor of the sinister pedlar who haunted Muse Village. He groaned and said, "True! I dread to think of—"

"Do you know those men?"

There was a note to her voice that made him turn swiftly in the saddle. They had seen less than a dozen other people thus far, the few riders venturing out having for the most part kept to the trails in the park. Now, however, three horsemen had emerged from a copse of trees and were coming up fast. With hats pulled low and collars turned high, their faces were too hidden to be identifiable but their rapid and silent approach and the business-like clubs they brandished left no room for doubt as to their intentions.

"Mohocks!" Cranford shouted. "Go back, Mary! Go back!"

There was no time for more; the three were upon him even as he heard her fierce "No!"

He ducked the long club that flailed at his head, and gripping his riding crop by the thong, he swung it hard at his attacker. The man swore, clutched his jaw and veered off. A tall rogue snatched for Tassels' bridle and she reared, whinnying to the brutal tug. Managing to keep his seat, Cranford lashed out at the tall man's arm and felt the shock as the handle of his riding crop struck home. There was an outburst of profanity.

He heard Mary cry out and sent a frantic glance her way. She was beating furiously at the third thief, who now turned on her and attempted to push her from the saddle. Cranford drove home his spurs. Frightened, Tassels plunged forward, caroming into the thief's hack. "Go!" yelled Cranford.

Mary started her mare away, then pulled up, screaming, "Look out!"

Whipping around, Cranford saw that her attacker had levelled a pistol. He ducked even as the man fired. A blinding flash, a violent shock and a strange, thickening mist, through which he seemed to hear a vaguely familiar voice howling something about "... name of the law ..."

❧

"'Tis one thing to attempt a robbery in broad daylight," growled the deep voice. "But—murder? The varmints must have been crazed!"

"Never heard of such a thing," snorted another man.

A third and feminine voice implored, "Oh, *do* be careful."

Whoever was mauling him about was clumsy, and made his head throb even more wretchedly. "Yes, pray do." Cranford blinked one eye open and as the haze cleared saw Mary's white face, seemingly disembodied, hovering over him. "Are you? ... " But he found speech to be so ridiculously difficult that he was unable to finish the sentence.

"I am quite all right," she declared, "thanks to you!"

"No thanks at all to him," argued the deep voice. "Whatever possessed you to bring Miss Stansbury into this desolation, Cranford? You fairly begged to be robbed!"

"He did it for my sake," Mary said staunchly. "To keep me from being embarrassed by London's kindly aristocracy!"

Peering at the blurred individual who was offering her a large white handkerchief, Cranford asked, "Is that . . . you, Shoreham?"

"Shorewood. Hold your head up, sir; you've taken a nasty rap on your brain-box. If your head ain't broke it won't kill you, but the ball scored along your scalp and you're bleeding like a pig. Keep you out of the race, I shouldn't wonder. Pity. I'd like to have seen your mare run. Recognize any of those bas—— er, rascals?"

"No." Trying not to flinch as Mary bound the handkerchief about his head, Cranford asked, "Tassels . . . ?"

"She's not hurt, but I think she was very frightened." Mary added ruefully, "As was I, alas. A fine heroine!"

"Had it not been . . . for you, the ball would have . . . have gone through . . . my stupid head. What a fool to have . . . to have brought you out here."

"Glad you agree with me," grunted the barrister.

The unceasing throbbing in his head was beginning to make Cranford feel sick. He tried to see more clearly, and said, "There was someone . . . else just now, I think?"

Shorewood barked, "Right. Odd sort of duck. Was exercising his hound, and ran up with me when we heard the lady scream. Gone for help." He stood, assuming giant-like proportions as Cranford blinked up at him. "Here he comes, with a coach. Hopefully there's a sawbones inside." He waved and shouted, "Can you not move faster, for God's sake?" the strident howl reverberating excruciatingly inside Cranford's battered head.

"Oh, poor soul," exclaimed Mary, holding her own gory handkerchief to Cranford's brow. "I am so sorry."

He managed, "Thank you. Don't tell..."

"I know. Don't tell Peregrine." She shook her head at him chidingly.

Faint but defiant, he murmured, "But it won't keep me... from... the race," and fell asleep.

"Why did you bring me here?" asked Cranford, with an uneasy glance at the bedchamber door in his great-uncle's Town house.

Mr. Shorewood, who watched him from the foot of the bed, said, "Couldn't take you to the home of Miss Stansbury's three lunatic aunts."

"No, by Jove! Heaven forbid!"

"What she wanted. Said you was staying at your club, but I didn't know which one enjoys your patronage. She wouldn't hear of us taking you to your brother's flat."

"Good for Mary!" At once anxious, Cranford said, "You haven't sent him word of this—this nonsense?"

"No." The lawyer rubbed his chin and asked shrewdly. "Is it nonsense?"

"Have you reason to think it anything more?"

"Zounds, how you delight to dance around an answer! Well, invalid or no, I'll not wrap it in clean linen for you. No one with half a brain would judge it anything but an attack carefully planned and directed 'gainst you personally! You certainly cannot suppose that any thief worthy of the name would hang about deserted fields hoping for some wealthy rider to wander past? Oh, no, m'dear fellow! You have either a very vindictive enemy, or someone means to keep you out of the race. Ah, I see you have your suspicions. Care to voice them?"

Cranford hesitated. "They are suspicions only. But I am in

153

your debt, sir, for coming to the rescue. Now, if I might ask, who was the other fellow who you said ran to help? I didn't see him."

Shorewood said with a grin, "That's only part of it, I think. You really want to know why *I* was hanging about an empty field."

Cranford was becoming very tired, but meeting the light eyes levelly, he said, "Just so."

"Very well. You are, or were, a soldier. By and large, your life was ruled by comparatively clear issues: You obeyed orders, you gave orders; you fought or retreated, as circumstances and your superior officer dictated. Everything neatly defined and straight from the shoulder. Now, I'm not so—shall I term it 'fortunate'? In my business one is often obliged to proceed at variance with established rules and regulations, in the course of which—er, proceedings, individuals of less than savoury morals or—um, ways of life, have to be dealt with, or bribed, or frightened into divulging information that may be vital to whichever case is under way. D'you follow me?"

"You mean you were in the fields to meet a disreputable character with information for sale."

Shorewood bowed and said admiringly, "Succinct, and correct. Remarkable for a fellow with a broken head."

"And this unsavoury individual was the man you met who was walking his hound when Miss Mary and I were attacked?"

"Correct. And don't ask me his name. I wouldn't tell you, even though I suspect he'd given me an alias."

Cranford tried to ask the barrister to describe his "unsavoury" individual, but in the middle of his question he fell asleep again.

～∞～

"He looked absolutely nothing like Gervaise!" Mary jabbed her needle at the ruffles she was replacing on Cranford's shirt-

154

sleeves and added stormily, "Whatever reason would he have for doing such a—Ow!"

Cranford, who had been allowed to borrow his great-uncle's dressing-gown and lie on the morning-room sofa today, said, "Now you have pricked your finger, which was unnecessary, because I didn't say it *was* my reprehensible cousin—"

"Why must you always speak of him so—so—"

"Contemptuously?"

"And behind his back," she snapped, her accusation losing some of its force since the damaged finger was at her lips.

"I say much worse things of him to his face," he said, truthfully if not diplomatically. "And if you will cast your mind back, you'll remember that I merely said if the man with the hound had resembled Valerian, you'd have been able to describe his looks in great detail."

"A snide remark if ever I heard one! Do you fancy ladies can only describe handsome gentlemen?"

"I wait with bated breath to be proven wrong."

Mary frowned and set two more stitches with care.

Amused, he watched closely and, as he'd anticipated, she hummed a little tune and the tip of her tongue touched her upper lip. He'd learned to recognize those signs of concentration and he smiled to himself. It was kind of her to have visited him again. And it was good of the General to permit an unwed girl to be alone with him, even if he was now classified as an invalid—which was ridiculous because, aside from a persistent headache, he felt perfectly well today. He thought sardonically that Great-Uncle Nugent was allowing this breach of manners willingly enough, hoping that Mary's presence indicated she looked more favourably upon his nephew as a prospective bridegroom.

"He wasn't very tall," she murmured at length.

"Aha! We progress! Dark? Fair? Well-bred? Well-dressed?"

"If you keep nattering at me I'll forget him altogether!"

155

He said meekly, *"Peccavi.* I shall natter not."

"Good. I don't think he was dark . . . especially . . . though I did notice that his eyes were dark. Certainly, he was well-bred, but—um—neat but not elegant, is how I'd describe his garments."

"Which could describe a thousand gentlemen," he commented impatiently. "Surely you can recall *something* of his features? A large nose, perhaps, or a scar on his cheek?"

"Or a cutlass between his teeth and a hunchback? Your 'natter not' didn't last very long! If I cannot recall more details it was, I suppose, because he was so . . . nondescript."

Nondescript. A prime quality for an Intelligence officer. Cranford frowned uneasily. God send Tio had received his warning. The individual he'd glimpsed in the coach and the man with the hound might not have been Joshua Pedlar, of course, but—

"If 'tis so important that you must scowl like a cannibal," said Mary, watching him, "you should have asked Mr. Shorewood to describe the gentleman."

"I intended to. But I very stupidly fell asleep. Do cannibals scowl?"

She laughed her musical little trill of mirth. "Good gracious, how should I know?"

"I thought there might have been some on your island."

"Oh. Well, there were not. My natives were very gentle people, else I'd likely have been eaten long ago."

"You'd not have provided many meals," he teased. "You're too small and thin."

"I wasn't then. Polite friends told me I was plump. Honest acquaintances said I was fat." She puffed out her cheeks. "Like that."

He chuckled. "Tell me about the natives. Did you have any friends amongst them?"

She slanted a sideways glance at him and he corrected, "Among the female population, I mean."

"Ah. As a matter of fact— Oh, no! Now see what you've made me do!" She held up the shirt-sleeve, the ruffles firmly sewn together.

He laughed, and regretting it, instinctively raised a hand to his pounding temple.

"Serves you right," she said. "There is no cause to make mock of a simple mistake. I think you want for gratitude."

"No, but I truly am grateful, and it was a splendid effort, ma'am." Sitting up, he said, "Never mind. Mrs. Turner will remedy matters."

"I can remedy my own matters. I'll have this undone in no time. Lie down again."

"You are more than kind." He stood and said with a smile, "But I really must be on my way."

She stared at him blankly. "On your way—where?"

"Firstly, to see my brother and—"

"And fib to him that you fell off your lovely Tassels, I suppose."

He bowed and restrained the impulse to hold his head on when he straightened up. "Besides which, I must call on Mathieson and discover the route they've laid out."

"What fustian!" Standing to face him, she exclaimed, "You are white as a sheet and cannot seriously mean to ride in that stupid race?"

"But of course I shall ride," he said gravely.

She clasped his arm and protested, "No, Piers! You heard the doctor forbid it! You must not!"

Touched by her anxiety, he smiled down at her and patted the small hand on his arm.

From the open doorway, General Lord Nugent said, "But he must, Miss Stansbury. Your solicitude for my grandnephew is appreciated." Briefly, his gaze rested on the hand that clasped Piers' arm. With a broad smile he reiterated, "Greatly appreciated, but there have been wagers placed, and Piers is promised to ride."

157

Mary stepped back, and looking from one to the other, argued, "But what if this rain persists? They'll postpone the race, surely?"

"I expect they will," lied Piers, striving to ease her kind concern.

The General spoilt his effort, saying with a snort, "Nonsense! I hope the Steeplechase Committee is not so wits-to-let as to wait for a sunny day, else we'll wait till the months lose their *r*'s!"

Mary said dubiously, "I suppose that would mean May, at the soonest. But Tassels is such a dainty lady. I think she is not what my father would term a—a mudder?"

"Nor is this a really gruelling cross-country race, m'dear," argued the General. " 'Tis a difficult course, I grant you, but at this time of year will be held to not more than five miles. Piers has accomplished much longer rides at the gallop, and under fire, to boot!"

"Even so, I am sure that if the Committee knew he had been shot they would never expect it of him."

"I don't want it known that I was so clumsy as to put my head in the way of a bullet," said Piers quietly. "Besides, the race is to be run on Saturday. I cannot withdraw at this late date. Do you see?"

"I see that you are eager to be rid of me," she grumbled, gathering up the sewing-basket she'd borrowed from the housekeeper.

"Never that. You are more than kind to have come and kept me company."

Mary tossed her curls and walked to the door, where she paused and turned back. "Don't expect me to come and see you fall off Miss Tassels."

He chuckled. "Such a blunder would make your friend happy. Perhaps you should come."

She stared at him. "My—friend?"

"Valerian," he teased.

His great-uncle gave an exasperated snort.

"Oh—pooh!" exclaimed Mary, and left them with her small nose held high.

"My goodness! These modern damsels want for manners," murmured the General, looking askance at the swing of her skirts. Recovering, he amended hastily, "But at least her mama has failed to crush all the spirit from her."

"She has spirit and to spare," agreed Piers.

Brightening, his great-uncle asked, "You like her?"

Piers said slowly, "She is a delight."

The General rubbed his hands together happily. "By Jove, but that's much better, my boy! You'll win her yet, or I'm a Dutchman!"

⁂

"I tried to stop him." Sitting beside Peregrine in the parlour of his comfortable flat, Zoe Grainger watched her brother hand Piers a glass of Madeira. "He was convinced something had happened to you," she said. "If you'd not come just now, he would be on his way to Hampshire."

Fully dressed, but looking very worn, Peregrine eyed his twin without approval. "You look as if you'd been dragged through a blackberry bush," he said bluntly. "And what the deuce have you done with your hair? If that's the latest style, I'll not bow to it!"

Piers had been cautioned by the doctor not to wear powder, and had persuaded Lord Nugent's valet to so arrange his thick hair that it would conceal the only partially healed gash on his head. Mrs. Turner had said the final effect was "charming." Piers did not share the loyal housekeeper's opinion, but it was the best they'd been able to achieve. "Unkind!" he said in an injured manner. "You should pay more heed to fashion, twin."

"Fashion, my eye! Don't try to fob me off! You've been in

a turn-up, or something of the sort. I sensed it yesterday, but when I sent Townes around to the Madrigal, they claimed not to have seen you since Tuesday."

The blue eyes were stern. Piers abandoned his carefully constructed tale of a fall down some area-way steps. Perry was far from well yet, but the bond between them was too strong for him to be hornswoggled by an outright fabrication. He said, "It's to do with this upcoming race."

"Jupiter, but all the south country is wagering on it," exclaimed Travis Grainger. "I'd give anything to be entered!"

Peregrine said, "I hear Tassels is a favourite. Are you still besieged by offers? Or did some enterprising rogue try to steal her?"

"I am most certainly still receiving offers. Even Gervaise Valerian tried to buy her. I refused, of course."

"Does he mean to ride, then?" asked Zoe.

"So he says."

Travis refilled Peregrine's glass, then sat on the end of the sofa, still holding the decanter. Clearly taken aback, he said, "You never think *Valerian* tried to steal her?"

"That would be pointless," said Peregrine. "Her colouring is too well known; he wouldn't dare to ride her."

"Is it possible," asked Zoe, "that he meant only to keep her from running?"

Travis said, "I cannot believe that of Valerian. Whatever else, he is a gentleman. And you've no proof he was behind it, have you?"

"I don't accuse our graceless cousin." Piers shrugged. "But *somebody* sent ruffians out to steal her. When I objected, my head paid the penalty."

"So that's why you look out of curl," exclaimed Peregrine, leaning forward intently. "Did you recognize the louts?"

"No, but Miss Stansbury had a better look at them than did I."

Intrigued, Zoe said, "Cordelia Stansbury? You know the poor lady?"

Piers nodded, and Peregrine murmured, "Wasn't Valerian betrothed to her? Or am I thinking of someone else?"

"No. You're in the right of it. But they are no longer betrothed."

"To his shame," said Zoe with disgust.

"Aye. Well, I grant you he has small acquaintance with that word," said Piers drily.

Peregrine grinned. "And that properly throws him into the discard! But then you've never liked him, and I'll own he's harum-scarum. In the opinion of our venerable great-uncle he is a conceited, dandified popinjay."

"Bravo," said Zoe. "The old gentleman is a good judge."

Travis laughed. "Well, I like him, even though I am outnumbered."

Piers put down his glass and stood. "Forgive this short visit, but I've to send word to Florian to bring me funds and more clothes. Cannot keep borrowing your wardrobe, twin. And then I must get to the stables."

Disappointed, Peregrine grumbled, "Must you rush off? I'd hoped you might stay for luncheon. I want to hear all that is going on at home."

"Your brother is concerned for his horse, dear," said Zoe, and added demurely, "At least, I *think* 'tis his horse he's hurrying to . . ."

Followed by hoots and laughter, Piers fled.

~❦~

Despite the unremitting pounding in his head, Cranford instructed the chairmen to set him down at a good distance from the stables. This morning's rain had stopped, but the afternoon was cold and a mist was beginning to swirl over the wet cobblestones. London looked grey and wintry, and already flambeaus

161

were being lit here and there, creating small islands of brightness in the gloomy afternoon. Cranford walked slowly, apparently deep in thought, but with his keen gaze alert for any suspicious loiterer or vagrant.

He reached the stables without incident. Tassels had been well cared for. She greeted him fondly, and the head-groom assured him that there had been no sign of anyone watching the stables.

"No strangers lurking about?" asked Cranford.

The groom's eyes widened and he shook his head. "Not that 'zackly, sir. One new customer, is all. An' the gent only left his hack here fer a coupla hours."

Cranford tensed. "Did you know the man?"

"Never see him afore, sir."

"What did he look like?"

The groom, who had for a time been a prize-fighter, watched him curiously. "Nothin' outta the way, sir. About yer height, but not a 'top o' the trees' like yerself. A well-built cove, though. I says to meself as he'd likely peel to advantage. Nice spoken and perlite. A gent, certain."

"Hmm. What kind of hack?"

"A fine beast. Sixteen hands; full of spirit; black as pitch."

"When was this? What was the gentleman's name?"

"Why, 'twere day afore yest'dy, Mr. Cranford. As to the gent's name—le'see now ...'Twere Gordon—or ... Grant ... Began with *G*, that I do recall."

'Valerian,' thought Cranford, 'surely would not leave his first name?'

"Judge!" exclaimed the groom, triumphant. "That's it, sir. Mr. Judge!"

Unable to wring any more details from the man, Cranford thanked him, and gave strict orders that two grooms were to stay in the stables all night, as there had already been an attempt to steal his horse. The groom, much shocked, promised faithfully that Tassels would be guarded "like she was royal!"

162

Tipping him generously, Cranford left. The "gent" with the pitch-black horse may very well have been Valerian. On the other hand, there were many black horses in Town. If Mr. Joshua pedlar was in fact a very different article, he might also own such an animal.

Cranford walked slowly up the steps to the Madrigal Club, wondering if it was purely coincidental that in the Bible, "Judges" was the book that followed "Joshua."

10

The Golden Goose was a modest inn prettily situated on the banks of the river Wey not far from Woking. During the winter months it was a sleepy hostelry, most of its desultory trade derived from travellers suffering the poor road to or from London. On this cloudy Friday, however, the cobble-stones of the yard rang to the stamping of impatient and high-bred hooves; the chill air was rent by the snorts and whinnies of horses, the rumble of carriage wheels, and shouts of greeting as friend met friend. The solitary ostler had been augmented by three farm lads who shouted also as they rushed from one arriving coach to another; and all was noise and bustling good-humoured confusion.

Florian Consett turned from the window of an upper room that overlooked the courtyard, and exclaimed as the door opened, "Good morning, sir! Blake packed some clothes, as you asked. What a crush! It's almost as crowded as was the Fair on Mitcham Common last summer! I'd never have—" He broke off, regarding his employer in alarm, "Are you well, Mr. Piers? You're extreme pale and look—"

"Never mind how I look," said Cranford, smiling as he threw his saddle-bags on the bed and crossed to slap his steward on the back. "You've worked miracles, as usual! However did you manage to secure a room for us? From what I could tell, half London is down here, and I was warned there's not a bed to be had from Redhill to Windsor! I had visions of us sleeping in the stables!"

The praise brought a pleased flush to Florian's lean features. "You gave me advance warning, sir, else there'd have been no hope. I fancy you were the cause of that howl I just heard." He started to unstrap the saddle-bags. "You're one of the favourites."

"You mean Tassels is. No, leave that, if you please. I want you to go down and be sure she is well-quartered. And we must guard her tonight."

With his hand on the latch of the door, Florian paused and glanced back.

"Trouble, sir?"

"Yes. Some Mohocks—perhaps. Tried to make off with her near Hyde Park several days ago. Miss Stansbury and the General think 'twas an attempt to keep her from running."

Florian's dark eyes had widened at the mention of Mary's name, but he said only, "And you were able to spoil that attempt. But you didn't come off scot-free, I think?"

"The important thing is that Tassels wasn't harmed. I've left her with Sudbury; I'm glad you brought him, but you'd best go and look to her, then I want to hear all the news from home."

Florian nodded and left. Cranford crossed the small chamber and peered out of the window. In the yard below, a group of young Corinthians moved towards the back door, conversing merrily at the tops of their lungs. Cranford recognized Bertie Crisp, a well-liked and wealthy marquis, whose round and cherubic features gave no indication of his passion for sports of all kinds.

A splendid coach was being tooled deftly through the press

165

of vehicles and the liveried footman ran to let down the steps and hand out a most elegant older gentleman, who glanced around idly, then raised a belaced hat to Cranford's window. Opening the casement, Cranford called, "Welcome, Your Grace. Does your grandson ride, then?"

"He does," answered the Duke of Marbury. "Come down, Piers. I wish to see your famous filly."

Hurrying down the stairs, Cranford was swept into the boisterous crowd. Many of these sportsmen were old friends who thumped him on the back and shouted greetings, assured him their bets were on him, or warned that the odds were against him, since Roly Mathieson's grand Rumpelstiltskin was entered.

Cranford responded as best he might while attempting to win through to the door without offending anyone. He caught a glimpse of carelessly powdered red hair and a pair of blue eyes set in a freckled and familiar face that grinned at him, and he managed to dodge around an argumentative trio seeking to detain him. Shouting that he'd return directly, he gripped Duncan Tiele's arm and pulled him into the passage leading to the kitchens.

"Whew!" he gasped breathlessly. "Well met, Duncan. What a crush!"

"The price you have to pay for being a favourite," said Tiele as they shook hands. "You still mean to ride, then? Heard you'd been hurt by Mohocks and was likely to cry off."

Cranford's gaze narrowed. "Who told you that?"

"Hi! Don't slay me with that steely glare! Be dashed if I can recall who . . . Yes, I can, by Jove! It was Valerian. Leastways, I think it was . . . Kin to you, ain't he? Claims he is, at all events." Watching Cranford, the redhead chuckled. "Don't like the dashing dandy, eh?"

"The relationship is a distant one." Cranford bit back the following "Fortunately!" and asked instead, "Are you entered to ride?"

"Yes, but I know my chances are slim. Don't have a hack who'd hold a candle to your Tassels. Or Mathieson's animal, come to that. But strange things can happen during a cross-country race. I was surprised to hear you'd been accepted, not— No, do come down from the boughs, man! Egad, but you're crusty today! I only meant that you don't leave your place in Surrey very often; I'd not have thought a steeplechase could drag you away."

"Hampshire," corrected Cranford. "And a fellow has to put in a social appearance occasionally, lest he fade from the memory of the mighty *ton*. We don't all have flaming locks like yours to render us unforgettable. Speaking of which—who else is here? I saw Bertie Crisp, and Marbury just arrived."

"So he did. With his ladies, the old rascal."

"Ladies? I saw no—"

Interrupted by a roar of laughter and recognizing a raucous howl, Cranford's dark brows drew down briefly.

"I see you've identified those strident tones," said Tiele with a sly grin. "Finchley. Your neighbour, ain't he? A former military man, like yourself."

Cranford grunted. "I resent the comparison. Is he riding, d'you know?"

"Yes. And winning no admirers with his boasts that his bay cannot lose. It's a grand brute, I have to admit. What, are you off? Stay and hoist a tankard with me."

"Gladly. Later, though. I've kept Marbury waiting as it is!" With a grin and a wave to his friend, Cranford started away, then turned back to ask with proper nonchalance, "Have you seen Tio Glendenning?"

"Yes, indeed. He's entered, in fact. Fine chestnut mare called um . . ."

"Flame. Yes, I know." Turning to the door, Cranford's smile died abruptly. He thought, 'Tio, you *idiot!* Did you not get my warning? . . .'

The stables were crowded and buzzing with talk; the race,

the odds, the points of the various horses, the merits and expertise of the riders being the only topics of conversation. In a centre stall the Duke of Marbury was caressing Tassels and chatting with Daniel Sudbury, Muse Manor's head groom. A sturdily built man in his late forties, Sudbury curried the mare and answered the duke respectfully. As Cranford made his way through the throng and came up with them, he heard Marbury say, ". . . doesn't appear capable of showing her heels to my grandson's Rumpelstiltskin, but the word is she's a very fast little lady."

" 'Tis a word you may believe, sir," said Cranford. "And speaking of ladies, I'm told you have several in your party."

The duke smiled faintly as they exchanged a handshake, but said nothing. His early marriage had been disastrous. After his wife's death, many handkerchiefs had been dropped for him, for he was the possessor of a great fortune. He had eluded every "parson's mousetrap" set for him, however, although through the years several beauties were known to have enjoyed his protection. Only five months ago he had astonished Society by wedding the widowed Lady Clorinda Ericson, his childhood sweetheart.

Wondering if the ducal eye was already wandering, Cranford dared to murmur, "I suppose I must not ask if one of your fair companions is your charming lady wife?"

"Certainly not," declared the duke. "Can you believe I would bring the duchess to an event intended for vulgar male creatures?"

Tassels snorted and tossed her head, impatient for Cranford's caress. He moved at once to stroke her velvety nose and assure her she was as lovely as ever. The duke looked amused and Cranford said with a grin, "She is all female, sir, and demands her share of affection."

"Yes, I can see that your Miss Tassels is properly devoted to you, though I suspect the feeling is mutual. What a pretty creature she is, to be sure. And you are agog with curiosity to know whom I have escorted today. I promise you, my boy—" Marbury glanced around and lowered his voice. "I promise you I have—er, mended my ways. I refused to offer these ladies my escort unless they were veiled as propriety demands, and I've no intention of revealing their identities." He chuckled and dug an elbow in Cranford's ribs. "There are very few of the fair sex here today, and Roland will be beside himself with curiosity. Now tell me: Is it truth that you are in the basket?"

The duke had spoken softly, but the abrupt and typical shift of subject took Cranford off-stride. He flushed and glanced around, embarrassed. "Not quite that, Your Grace. The fact is that I am in hopes of enlarging the estate but seem to have encountered some determined opposition."

"From Lord Nugent? Why? Yes, am I not the rude old gentleman? Never mind, here come my ladies, so you are reprieved."

Cranford's relief at the timely interruption was short-lived. Two ladies approached, each with a hand tucked into the arm of the gentleman who walked between them. They wore warm cloaks and were, as the duke had said, heavily veiled. Their cavalier, the epitome of elegance, minced along on high red heels and made no attempt to restrain the mocking grin that curved his beautifully shaped mouth.

"Valerian!" thought Cranford with revulsion.

"How glad I am that the look in your eyes is not aimed in my direction," remarked the duke *sotto voce*. "But I'll warrant you cannot name the lovely creatures on the arms of the—er, 'deplorable dandy.'"

So His Grace knew of his sobriquet for his unwanted kinsman. Irritated, Cranford wondered if these ladies, who defied convention by coming here, were the latest victims of Valerian's much-vaunted "charm."

"Well, well," drawled the dandy. "If it ain't my gallant military cousin come to lose the race."

A familiar giggle sounded, and one of the mysterious ladies trilled, "How *droll* you are, Gervaise!"

"Deuce take it!" gasped Cranford, the mystery resolved. "Mary! What on earth are you doing here?"

A plump little hand emerged from its muff and Lucretia Westerman scolded teasingly, "Naughty, naughty boy! You should address me first, you know."

Ignoring his cousin's amused chuckle, Cranford bowed over Mrs. Lucretia's fingers and apologized. "But you should not have brought her, ma'am. This is not a suitable meeting for a lady to attend without inviting notoriety."

Miss Mary twitched away a corner of her veil and briefly her eyes twinkled at him. Small wonder her eyes were so sparkling, he thought. She must be in *alt* to be on the arm of her idol.

"I am already notorious," she asserted pertly. "Besides, the duke was so kind as to offer us his escort. You will surely not find fault with His Grace for bringing us here?"

"Touché!" exclaimed Valerian, laughing. "Well done, Cordelia. Wriggle out of that, if you can, cousin mine."

Cranford ignored him. "Of course I don't find fault with the duke's kindness, but you must be aware, Mrs. Lucretia, that it is not—"

"—the thing," interposed Miss Stansbury. "La, but what a piece of work you make of it, Lieutenant. I'd think you might be grateful because we came to cheer you on when your lovely Tassels wins."

"He wants for gratitude, my love," trilled Mrs. Lucretia. "Did I not say it?"

Valerian shook his head. "Such lovely creatures to come so far and be spurned for their loyalty! For shame, coz!"

Feeling a veritable ingrate, Cranford flushed and declared that he was most grateful for the support of the ladies.

"Good, for we have put down some guineas on you, thanks to Muffin," imparted Mrs. Lucretia, evidently sufficiently acquainted with the duke to use his nickname. "Oh, but it is *such* fun to be naughty!"

"Alas, but your fun will cause you to lose your money," said Valerian. "Although my cousin tries to pretend I am not here, he will have no choice but to see me win."

"I very much doubt that," snapped Cranford, yearning to wipe the smirk from those classically perfect features.

Valerian said thoughtfully, "No, you're probably right. I doubt you'll stay the course. I am banking on it, in point of fact."

"Betting on yourself, eh?" inserted the duke, amused by the barely contained animosity between the two young men.

"I'm not that sure of success, sir," said Valerian. "I am betting, however. Large wagers. Against my cousin."

His Grace's eyebrows lifted.

Cranford gave a contemptuous shrug.

Mary, however, drew away from the dandy, and said sharply, "What an unkind and disloyal thing! To wish harm to your own kinsman!"

Valerian said with a grin, "I did not say I wish the poor fellow harm, my dear Cordelia. To judge from those bruises, one might suppose the harm to have been already done, but—"

"I am not your 'dear' anything!" she intervened.

"My apologies." With a low bow, Valerian went on, "I am merely wagering that your self-righteous friend will either come in last or be thrown and not come in at all!"

Disgusted, Cranford said, "Spoken like a true sportsman. Or did you perhaps attempt to secure your wager by employing the London vandals who tried to do Tassels an injury?"

"The devil!" exclaimed Marbury, shocked.

Valerian's smile vanished and for an instant his face was very grim. Then he drawled, "Dash it all! I never thought of it!"

His fists clenching, Cranford stepped forward.

Marbury said sharply, "I feel sure you will remember there are ladies present, gentlemen!"

171

"Mr. Valerian," said Mary icily, "you are the one should hang your head in shame. I wish I could think you knew it. Lieutenant, your arm, if you please."

Cranford's anger was replaced by delight. Offering his arm with a flourish, he said—and meant, "My very great pleasure, ma'am."

The duke crossed to Mrs. Lucretia, who was stroking Tassels. Accompanying him, Valerian murmured an amused "Who'd have dreamt the little wallflower could show such spirit?"

"I think you've missed a good deal more than dreams," said the duke softly. "Including your chance to win a genuinely delightful young woman."

Cranford's hopes that he would be invited to dine with the duke's party were dashed when His Grace said that tonight they stayed at the nearby home of his bride's cousin and must not arrive late for dinner. His footman announced that a fresh team had been poled up and the ducal coach was ready at His Grace's convenience. There was a small embarrassment when Mrs. Lucretia managed somehow to trip despite the Duke's supporting hand, and the contents of her reticule scattered and had to be gathered up again. Predictably, she giggled, and accepting the hair comb the footman handed her, remarked that all in all it had been "an interesting day. A very droll day!"

Cranford was disappointed by their early departure, although Mary made a point of wishing him every success in tomorrow's race. He handed her into the coach and said his farewells, acknowledging to himself that it was as well, since he must at once seek out Tio Glendenning.

Lost in thought, he watched the coachman guide the team from the inn-yard, and was startled when a voice purred in his ear, "I'll thank you to guard your tongue, cousin. Miss Stansbury defies convention, but may yet establish herself creditably, unless this latest little escapade should be bruited about, and—"

"Now damn your eyes, how dare you!" exclaimed Cranford, swinging around to face Valerian's sardonic grin.

"Is that a 'thunderous look,' I wonder?" The dandy tapped a jewelled quizzing glass against his chin and said musingly, "Faith, but did one couple your lovesick gaze with that fiery reaction, one might—almost—suppose you nourished a *tendre* for the lass."

"As opposed to your inability to nourish a *tendre* for anyone save your magnificent self?"

"Aha! An attack, which is, or so I'm told, the best means of defence."

Turning away, Cranford said curtly, "Good day to you."

"Now you don't really mean that, do you, cousin?" murmured Valerian. "And will mean it less if I 'enter the Lists,' as it were, in declaring my admiration for a lady I appear to have most short-sightedly underestimated."

Cranford paused, his jaw tightening. He said pithily, "But then you admire so many ladies, Valerian, that 'twould be hard to know which one is to be so singularly honoured. I can say only that she has my sympathy."

He bowed and walked away, somewhat mollified to note that the smug grin had quite vanished from his cousin's handsome features.

His search through the uproarious coffee-room and the adjacent gardens drew a blank. In the stables Glendenning's fine mare, Flame, was being curried by a groom who was unable to shed any light on his master's present whereabouts. Cranford wandered back inside and joined the group he'd left earlier. He was welcomed so heartily that the pounding in his head increased, but while answering a barrage of eager questions about Tassels he contrived to scan the crowd often. There was nothing to indicate that he was being watched. He had sufficient experience with Military Intelligence, however, to know that if agents had indeed been set to observe his movements he'd have small chance of spotting them.

173

Florian joined him and they found a comparatively quiet spot in the coffee-room and ordered a light supper. Florian had brought a note with a fond message from Jane Guild, who wrote that she enjoyed her usual good health but missed him. His young steward then launched into a detailed report on the progress at Muse Manor. Plans for the repairs to the roof of St. Mark's were almost completed and would be ready for Cranford's approval when he returned. The rebuilding of Ezra Sweet's cottage was being delayed because of the old man's constant fault-finding and interference. "If he had his way, sir," said Florian wryly, "you'd be building a palace rather than a cottage! When you come home, you'll be able to reason with him, I'm sure." Work on clearing the debris from the river was going well, the flood waters were receding, and the rebuilding of the bridge had proved to be less involved than originally feared. Oliver Dixon and his men had succeeded in clearing out the farmyard and barns. His report on the roof of the Manor was not as favourable; preliminary repairs had begun, only to be halted when it developed that there was more damage than they'd hoped.

Florian hesitated at this point.

Apprehensive, Cranford prompted, "More costly, I take it."

"I fear so. Will I tell the builder to postpone, sir?"

"Heaven forfend! My poor aunt has been dripped upon for too long!"

Wondering how on earth he was to pay for it all and still buy the river parcel for Perry, Cranford adjusted his plans and said cheerfully that his steward should at once return home and be sure these various projects went along smoothly. He was mildly surprised when Florian did not put in a very strong bid to be allowed to stay until the race was run. Not until the youth had left did it dawn on him that Major Finchley was entered in the race and would certainly have left his daughter at home. "Blast!" he muttered, and could only hope that Florian would heed his warning and keep away from his admired lady.

There was still no sign of Glendenning and he embarked on another stroll through the various rooms, meeting ever more raucous enthusiasm. The wine was flowing freely, which had much to do with the increased volume of the celebrants. He accepted a glass and carried it about with him untouched, very aware that he must keep a clear head for tomorrow's race.

Major Gresford Finchley had no such inhibitions. Catching sight of Cranford, he deliberately blocked his path through the crowded tables and stood weaving before him, declaring thickly that he had placed a large wager on his "goo' neighbour." Having said which, he broke into howls of mirth and added, "T'lose! V'ler'an an' me! Both goin' t'make lots a money, on my goo' neighbour!" His hilarity at this fine joke was not shared. Never popular, this unsportsmanlike behaviour caused many to turn from him in disdain. Cranford shrugged and attempted to pass. Resentfully aware that he had little support from these men, Finchley's hot temper soared. He seized his "good neighbour's" arm and started to snarl threats and insults. His speech was blurred and for the most part incoherent. Cranford gave him a sharp push and the Major reeled back, collapsed into a chair, and promptly fell asleep.

Cranford's hand was gripped and held high by Lord Bertie Crisp, who pronounced his friend "the winner and (hic!) new champion!" Cheers rocked the rafters and seemed to split Cranford's head. He abandoned his search, and as soon as he could decently manage it, escaped and retreated to his room.

Suddenly he was crushingly tired, and it seemed to take an inordinate length of time to reach the upper landing. Arriving at last, he negotiated the passage, opened the door, and stopped dead.

Looking up from the newspaper he was reading while lounging on the bed, Lord Horatio Glendenning waved a tankard at him.

175

Cranford whipped the door shut. "Are you gone demented?" he demanded angrily. "Or did you not receive my message?"

"I did. And I thank you, dear boy." Sitting up, the viscount drawled, "Thing is, I was already entered. Couldn't in good conscience draw back."

It was a decision Cranford had also faced. Crossing to the chest of drawers and the decanter and glasses Florian had left there, he poured himself a glass of Madeira and sank into the solitary wooden chair, saying testily, "But my life wasn't at stake."

Mystified, Glendenning stared at him and swung his legs over the side of the bed. "What the deuce are you talking about? You must find another barber, Piers. Your hair looks as if it harbours a bird's nest."

Instinctively, Cranford ran a hand through his untidy locks, then winced and swore.

The viscount said shrewdly, "Been in another turn-up, have you? Unwise, just before a race, y'know."

"I'd a turn-up all right, with some rogues who tried to steal Tassels."

"Did they, by Jove! When was this?"

"In—or rather—near Hyde Park, two days since."

Glendenning whistled softly. "Since they broke your head but didn't get your mare, I presume someone was with you to lend a hand?"

"Miss Stansbury."

"You surely don't mean Cordelia?"

"Yes. Though I know her as Miss Mary." Cranford brightened. "Gad, but she was splendid, Tio! Had it not been for her, you'd be burying me today!"

Incredulous, the viscount exclaimed, "That slip of a girl drove the thieves off?"

"Don't be a gudgeon. She warned me so that I was able to avoid taking a ball through my head. Luckily, her family solic-

176

itor chanced to be nearby. He's the one ... the one who drove off the ruffians." Cranford's head was throbbing so viciously that he found it difficult to think, and he paused frowningly. "There was something else, though ... Ah, yes. I remember now. It was the fellow who was with him. I think you were right about the pedlar in Muse Village."

Dismayed by his friend's obvious confusion, Glendenning said uneasily, "Do you? In what way?"

Cranford glanced to the closed door and lowered his voice. "I've a notion the fellow is either from Bow Street, or is Military Intelligence. I saw him having what looked to be a very serious talk with Valerian a week or so ago."

"Hmm. I know you've little use for your cousin, but what the deuce does Valerian have to do with my—er, checkered past?"

Cranford said impatiently, "You must know the answer to that. You told me you'd seen him on the battlefield, which means he probably saw you also and would be aware you fought for Prince Charles. He's the kind of unprincipled rascal would sell any information for a price. Of late he seems to make a habit of riding across my lands. When I taxed him with it he gave me a nonsense answer, but if he's seen you and—"

"Great heavens, man! What if he has? Everyone knows we're friends of long standing. True, I did see Valerian at Prestonpans, but I doubt very much that he saw me, since I was flat on my back at the time. He ain't in need of the ready—rolling in it, I believe. And what could he tell the authorities regarding my more recent indiscretions?"

Cranford was frowningly silent and the viscount said carefully, "Y'know, Piers, you're one of the most honourable fellows I ever met, and I've never known you to judge unfairly. But—well, in this particular instance I think you allow your dislike of Valerian's kinship to ascribe more villainy to him than he warrants."

"And you admire him, do you? Just what about him do you

find admirable? His behaviour to his unfortunate sire? His treatment of poor Miss Stansbury? Scarcely sterling qualities, Tio."

"No. And I didn't say I admire him. Certainly, he's a rake and a dandy and wildly irresponsible. I just don't think those traits indicate murderous treachery."

Cranford's headache was becoming more and more intense. Trying to ease his discomfort, he shifted uncomfortably in his chair. "I hope you may be right. And I shouldn't have said what I did. The fellow just . . ." He drew a hand across his brow and said wearily, "But aside from that, I've thought to see the alleged pedlar—who goes by the name of Joshua, by the way—watching me since I came up to Town."

"In London? You never mean it!"

"Oh, yes, I do. I thought—I thought I'd told you he may have been with the lawyer fellow who helped us after the attack in the park."

"You saw him?"

"Er—no. I was knocked out of time. But the description could well fit him. And I'd swear he was in a coach that followed me back to my club on Tuesday evening."

Glendenning swore softly. "A simple pedlar don't drive about London in a coach. I wish to heaven I could recall where I've seen him before. If he *is* a Runner, or with Military Intelligence, I take it you assume he's following you to get at me."

"It's a possibility I think we can't afford to ignore. You'd be well advised to stay out of tomorrow's race, Tio."

"Aye. And so would you, old fellow." Watching this lifelong friend anxiously and deciding he was properly gut-foundered, Glendenning said, "You're not exactly at the top of your form."

Cranford responded to that concerned scrutiny with his slow smile. "Tassels is, which is the important thing. And to echo your own remark, I can't very well back out now, can I?"

"You could let Florian ride in your stead. He's a lighter weight and a better rider than—" Glendenning dodged the cushion that was hurled at his head and said with mock indignation, "Just for that piece of savagery, I shall retaliate by asking how it came about that you were riding in the park with Cordelia Stansbury."

"You know the General's orders."

"Yes, but I'd understood she don't want you. Are you colouring up because you've taken a fancy to the notorious spinster? Have a care, Piers. If her heart still belongs to—Aha! So *that's* what is adding to your dislike of the Dangerous Dandy! Our confirmed bachelor has succumbed at last to Cupid's—"

Fortunately another cushion was within Cranford's reach.

An hour later, sitting on his bed while pulling on his riding boots, after an all too brief sleep he pondered the viscount's taunts. Mary Westerman's bright image was clear in his mind's eye. He had to own that he found her a pleasant companion—and a courageous one, at that. Faced with a future that would crush most gently born girls, she put up her little chin and refused to be crushed. She was not blessed with a kind-hearted mama, and her sire, who might have shielded her, appeared to have retreated from his obligations and the social world. Her aunts, eccentric as they may be, were evidently fond of her; at least she had that consolation. But she'd implied that she did not mean to accept their hospitality on an indefinite basis. She had a Plan, she'd said. He wondered what it might be, and found himself hoping it was not another outrageous escapade that would sink her even farther beneath reproach. Not that he had anything to say in the matter. Admire her he might, and certainly he was grateful for her kindnesses, but he had no intention to give his heart to a lady who was deep in love with another man. And of all men, his revolting cousin! Besides, what had he to offer a lady? Neither title nor fortune, and an estate so encumbered it would be a miracle could he hang on to it.

Inevitably, his thoughts turned to the Manor. He'd sent Florian off with a brief letter to Aunt Jane. Despite her cheery note he knew that good soul would be worrying. So would old Ezra

Sweet, and the curate, and Oliver Dixon, poor fellow, struggling to recover from the flooding. And there was his twin, to whom he'd made a solemn, if silent, vow that he would have his beloved Quail Hill and build his house . . .

So many people relying on him, trusting him . . . He tossed his shoulders back, fighting the need for sleep. Almost he could hear again the voice of young Bobby Peale, his under-groom: "None of us wants to lose our family."

He thought fiercely, "Well, you won't lose us, lad! I have Tassels, and no one can beat her! We'll win tomorrow, and the purse will solve all—or almost all—our problems! Come hell or high water, we'll win!"

Yet it was not the image of his beautiful dapple-grey that brought the slow smile to his lips, but a very different beauty with a delightfully curvaceous figure, a bewitching mouth and hazel eyes full of mischief.

11

The urgency of Cranford's need to talk with the viscount had caused him to allocate the first two-hour shift of the night watch to Sudbury, the second to himself, and the last to Glendenning, since Tio had insisted he also had a highly valued horse to be guarded. It was a quarter past midnight when Cranford hurried down the stairs, reproaching himself because he was late, having come near to falling asleep while pulling on his boots.

Despite tomorrow's race many of the inn's guests were still celebrating, the sounds of their revelry following him as he closed the side door.

The night was very dark, low-hanging clouds obscuring the stars. But a cold wind blustered about, setting the naked tree branches to rattling, and occasionally chasing a cloud away so that the half-moon's silver radiance could brighten the sky.

Walking swiftly to the stables, Cranford was wide awake now and alert for signs of trouble, but he heard only the wind, the distant and desultory barking of a dog, the muted noise from the inn, and a loose shutter somewhere that creaked and occasionally slammed when caught by a stronger gust.

Everything looked calm and comparatively peaceful. His taut nerves and the sense that all was not well could likely be ascribed to his desperate need to win tomorrow, and to the knowledge that so many relied on him. "Don't borrow trouble," he told himself sternly. But he stood well to the side as he swung the barn door open with one hand, and kept a grip on his pocket pistol with the other.

A sleepy voice called, "That you, Lieutenant, sir?"

"It's me," confirmed Cranford. "Twelve o'clock, and all's well!"

The response to his light-hearted impersonation of the Watchman was silence and then a loud snore. Irked, he strode into the circle of light cast by the lantern that hung from an overhead beam. Sudbury was sprawled on a bench, leaning back against Tassels' stall. The sturdy groom was indeed asleep. Beside him, a tankard of ale had fallen over and deposited a puddle on the straw-strewn planks. It was behaviour quite foreign to the faithful groom, who at times had a tendency to become too explicit in his descriptions of his "contrary innards" and had for years declared it not worth the price he had to pay if he dared take more than one tankard of ale.

"Wake up, damn your eyes!" cried Cranford angrily.

His only answer was an even more resonant snore.

A grown man didn't usually subside into a drunken stupor after one tankard of ale—less, since half the contents of the tankard appeared to be soaking into the floor-boards. Cranford bent over the groom, gripped a sturdy shoulder and shook him hard.

Sudbury opened a bleary eye, peered at him without recognition, muttered something unintelligible and went back to sleep.

Impelled by a sudden and strong sense of danger, Cranford drew his pistol and spun around.

There was no one behind him, but then a dark shape, all

arms and legs, plummeted down from the hayloft. The pistol was smashed from his hand before he had a chance to fire. They were both down. He lashed out fiercely and felt his blows strike home. A knee rammed into his middle, driving the air from his lungs and doubling him up. Boots were running at him. Something struck his head with brutal force, bringing an exquisite anguish. The scene became blurred . . .

From far away, a hoarse voice snarled, "Damn him, but he's quick! Knocked me bloody tooth out, he done! Scrag the perishin' nob!"

A second man argued, "Nah. The guv'nor don't want no killin'!"

And a third voice put in with a breathless laugh, "No killin' of two-legged nobs, anyways!"

"Who'd 'spect this here cove to come out in the cold when he'd set his groom here?"

"Not us, mate. We thought as he'd be in the tap, guzzlin' ale or whatever nobs guzzle, an leavin' us to do our work in peace. That's the trouble with them there Army officers. You can't never tell what they're gonna do next! You got the oil ready yet, Willum?"

"Yus. And if you was to ask me, I'd say he *oughta* be scragged. He might've see me. *Or* you."

A brief and thoughtful pause. Then the second man agreed, "You got a good point, ain't he, Dick? An' why should we be blamed if the silly bastard fell into the fire?"

Tassels was stamping in her stall. She neighed ringingly.

The first voice said, "Look sharp, mates! We don't wanta be caught here!"

A sentence was echoing in Cranford's dazed mind: "No killin' of two-legged nobs . . ." They meant the horses! The filthy swine meant to burn down the barn and destroy the horses!

Rage possessed him. He managed to drag himself to his knees, but he felt sick and for an indeterminate space couldn't see anything clearly.

183

Struggling to stand, he smelt smoke and then was dazzled by a brilliant glare. Curse the murderous louts, they'd fired the barn! At once frantic with fear, the horses began to neigh shrilly and mill about, but those raucous merry-makers in the tap probably wouldn't hear anything until it was too late!

He got to his feet somehow. Dense clouds of smoke were spiralling up. A corner of his mind registered the awareness that several fires must have been set for the blaze to have spread so quickly.

He reeled to the stall and fumbled at the latch, then flung the half-door wide.

Tassels neighed and galloped for the barn door.

Cranford glimpsed a dim outline on the floor, and closing his eyes against the searing smoke, dropped to one knee and felt about. His groping fingers closed over cold steel but when he tried to stand again the pain in his head defeated him and he lacked the strength to get to his feet. His favourite psalm came to mind and he whispered it as he'd done often during battle . . . "The Lord is my shepherd . . ."

His head cleared a little and he got to his feet and stumbled through heat and flame to the door. Aiming his pistol towards the inn, he fired. It was all he could do. Now he must get Sudbury out. The rogues must have drugged the poor devil.

Staggering back into the smoke, he heard a shout, then someone pushed past him. He caught a glimpse of a red and contorted face. Finchley. "Help me get my groom out," he called. The Major gave him a contemptuous glance and rushed on. Less than astonished by this callous reaction, Cranford groped his way forward. The smoke was billowing, the air becoming hotter. It was difficult to see farther than a few feet. Coughing, he persisted and at length found Sudbury again. He was dragging him out when Roland Mathieson ran by, leading his beloved chestnut horse and shouting something about "flames in there!"

Cranford hauled his groom out into the paradise of the

damp cold night and stood over him, gulping sobbing breaths of the pure air, and thinking with dull resentment that he didn't need Roly to remind him about the fire. Men carrying buckets were running from the inn now, shouting to each other. Abruptly, he thought, 'Flame! My God! *Tio's* Flame!'

He ran back inside again. The smoke was even more acrid, searing his lungs and his eyes. Peering through smarting tears, he recollected that Glendenning had stabled his mare in the end stall, gloating that she was "out of the draughts." It was just like Tio, he thought, to have chosen the spot most difficult of access.

The roar of the fire was deafening now: He groped his way between the rows of stalls, surrounded by heat and flame. A frantic animal kicked down the gate of its stall and plunged at him, sending him sprawling. As he clambered to his feet, a scrawny feline shape flew through the air at his face, apparently having been propelled by a boot. He heard a terrified yowl and sharp claws drove into his shoulder.

Finchley ran past, a cravat tied over his horse's eyes. "Out of my way, curse you, cat!" he shouted.

Cranford staggered on, vaguely aware that there were others here now. He thought to recognize Valerian, leading a blindfolded stallion, then he had reached Flame's stall, and between racking coughs was calling soothingly to the plunging mare as he struggled to open the gate.

A familiar voice howled, "Stand away, Piers!"

He thought, 'Tio! Thank the good Lord!'

Afterwards, he could never quite remember leaving the inferno, but he was outside at last, sitting gratefully in the rain, breathing the sweet fresh air while the hastily organized bucket brigade fought to save what was left of the barn.

Bertie Crisp came up, wiping soot from his face. "They're fighting a lost cause," he spluttered breathlessly. "The barn's nigh gutted. Did you fire that shot, Piers? I say, jolly well done!"

"If it hadn't been for you, Cranford, I'd likely have lost

Rump." A lean hand was thrust at him, and Roland Mathieson, still strikingly handsome despite the loss of his left eye, said earnestly, "I am forever in your debt."

Reaching up for the handshake, Cranford realized that the cat still clung to him. He detached the emaciated little creature, but it voiced a strident wish to remain and transferred its claws to his arm.

Glendenning took the cat and held it up. "A black moggy," he said. "You need a home, poor fellow." He shoved the animal at Valerian, who was scanning his tall horse anxiously. "Here, Gervaise. Another lost soul to join you, and it matches your black brute."

Valerian gave him a narrow-eyed stare, then observed that the viscount was "too kind! But my Walker don't like cats any more than I do—black cats especially. Besides, cats don't have souls."

"I wouldn't be too sure of that," argued Duncan Tiele, picking up the refugee and stroking it, awakening gritty purring sounds. "He brought us luck tonight, you have to admit."

"Nonsense," jeered Valerian, walking away. "If you are so foolish as to believe such stuff, you're the one should adopt the wretched little brute. You'll need plenty of luck tomorrow!"

Tiele grinned, and as Valerian passed, slipped the adoptee onto the back of his black stallion.

Cranford watched the cat cling desperately to Walker's saddle blanket. "Poor little mog," he muttered. "Finchley gave it a hard kick that likely will put an end to it. If it survives, I'll take it back to the Manor. My aunt will take it in, I'm sure."

Glendenning said, "I think you've just found another mouth to feed, dear boy! Now, what the deuce are we going to do with the nags? Can't leave 'em out in the rain the night before the race!"

This problem was solved by the host, who fortunately had an old barn in his back field that was now used for storage and was still fairly weather-proof. Grooms and ostlers were summoned, the various horses were led to their temporary quarters, and a generous sum was collected to pay the men who were to guard the animals through the remaining hours of darkness.

❧

Very few occupants of the Golden Goose slept late the following morning. Cranford was up and dressed by seven o'clock, and already the old inn was full of movement and bustle. The few hours of sleep had refreshed him, and aside from a burn on his right forearm, bruised ribs and a dull headache, he was little the worse for the night's violence.

He opened the side door and stepped into an early morning heavy with clouds, and chill air that was stirred by occasional icy gusts. A few men were gathered about the charred remains of the barn. He joined them to look at the ruins, grimly aware that he had been meant to perish there and wondering which of the contestants was so desperate to win as to be willing to incinerate Sudbury, himself, and some very fine horses. So far as he was aware, Finchley had been first and very fast on the scene. Nor had Roland Mathieson lost any time in rescuing Rumpelstiltskin. Valerian also had arrived promptly to lead out his black stallion. Any one of them, having foreknowledge of the fire, could have come quickly to the rescue of his own mount. Yet it was difficult to believe that any gentleman, even so unpleasant an individual as Gresford Finchley, would have put the other horses at such terrible risk.

He made his way across the field to the makeshift stables. The skies were lighter now and the ground was comparatively dry, but there was a misting on the air and banking clouds on the horizon held a promise of rain to come.

Inevitably, his thoughts dwelt on last night's fire. It was possible, of course, that the guilty party was an unscrupulous individual with large wagers riding on the outcome of the race. He dismissed that possibility at once, however, reasoning that

187

had he or any of the horses been killed, the Steeplechase would almost certainly have been postponed or cancelled, which would not please a gambling enthusiast.

In the temporary stables, ostlers and grooms were busy; Roland Mathieson's splendid chestnut stallion was being fussed over by two grooms. A man cursed angrily and sprang from a stall, barely eluding the bared teeth of the tall bay gelding who lunged after him. Gresford Finchley's mount was showing its ferocity once again. "Like man, like beast," thought Cranford. A fine black was in the adjoining stall, its coat gleaming in the light of the lanterns as a groom combed the silken mane. The man nodded respectfully to Cranford, who said, "Mr. Valerian's mount, no? Why is he called Walker?"

"On account of the way he moves, sir. Picks up his hooves high, sorta like he goes on springs."

"I've seen him run. He's very fast."

The groom nodded and said with a grin that Flyer might have been a better name for the animal.

There was no sign of either Tio or his mare, but Cranford was pleasantly surprised to see a heavily veiled lady chatting with Sudbury while he brushed Tassels. Coming up beside her, he said, "You're early abroad, ma'am."

"Good morning, Lieutenant." Miss Mary Westerman turned to him and put out her hand and he held it briefly. "Yes. I knew His Grace meant to arrive early, so I dragged my poor aunt from her bed and bullied her into accompanying us. Sudbury has been telling me what transpired last night. Who would want to do so wicked a thing?"

The groom showed a very red face to his employer, then averted his eyes.

Cranford said, "I wish I knew, ma'am. Certainly, they didn't draw the line at murder. How do you go on today, Sudbury?"

The groom looked crestfallen and muttered sheepishly that he was willing to swear the ale was "right as rain" when he'd carried it to the barn. "Some artful cove must've slipped something into the tankard whilst I was busy with Tassels. Sorry I am, sir. I should'a been more careful."

The mare butted her head against Cranford affectionately, and he stroked her and assured her that she looked very well this morning. "You had no way of knowing there were murderers about," he told his groom. "Did you catch sight of anyone lurking near the barn? Or someone showing an unusual interest in Tassels?"

Sudbury said he'd noticed no suspicious characters.

Mary put in, "You would be hard put to it to find anyone who was not interested in Tassels, Mr. Cranford. She is so much admired. I came here to wish her well, and now can only be thankful you were unharmed."

Although her features were hidden, there was a warmth to her voice and he could picture her pretty smile. He said lightly, "We thank you. Though I fancy we're not the only recipients of your good wishes."

"True." Her tone was cooler now. "I had words with Roland Mathieson's Rumpelstiltskin, and I have to say I think him your most formidable competition."

She knew perfectly well that he'd not teased her about Mathieson's horse, but to persist would probably embarrass her, so he asked instead if she had already breakfasted.

Aware that she had been spared, and grateful for that courtesy, Mary answered, "No. And I am absolutely famished."

"I never allow my well-wishers to be famished," he declared, offering his arm.

Taking it, she murmured, "Are you not afraid of public opinion? Despite this stupid veil I may very well have been recognized. Even if I am still incognito, you will be criticized for accompanying a fast woman who dared attend such a male gathering as this."

He said with a chuckle, "Yes. Only think how my reputation will be enhanced. You ladies love a rake, do you not?"

She stiffened. "If you mean Valerian . . ."

189

"I hadn't, but it would certainly— Look out!"

They were strolling past a railed partition which now served as a stall for Major Finchley's tall bay. Mary's veil had fluttered over the side and the bad-tempered animal made a grab for it. Cranford jerked Mary away but the big horse had torn the veil from her hat.

A groom, leaning against a post and chewing on a straw, laughed.

Cranford said sharply, "Return the lady's veil, if you please."

"Beggin' yer pardin, sir," said the groom, his impertinent gaze fixed on Mary, "but it's more'n I dare do ter go in with that ugly brute. A man-killer he be!"

Stepping closer, Cranford snapped, "Remove your greasy stare from the lady, at once, or I'll throw you in there!"

The groom glanced at him, read the menace in the icy blue eyes and fled.

Cranford took up a rake that had been left propped against the wall and climbed over the stall's low gate.

Watching the restless stamping of the big animal, Mary cried anxiously, "No, no! Pray do not! The damage is done, and I don't need—"

Cranford thought, 'Oh, yes, you do!' and stepped inside.

The veil lay crumpled in the right front corner. The bay tossed his proud head about, pawed at the floor and snorted menacingly. "Easy, lad," said Cranford. Continuing to talk soothingly, he edged towards the veil, while keeping one eye on the horse and a firm grip on the rake.

The animal began to prance about and the ears were laid back.

Cranford reached for the veil, hearing Mary whisper, "Oh— my heavens!"

Teeth bared, the big bay plunged at him. He held the rake high and said sternly, "Down, you rogue!" The animal halted and edged back, as if confused, and Cranford added, "Yes, I know you're a fine fellow, and I mean you no harm, so be at ease and behave as you ought."

The great eyes watching him were fierce still, but the ears twitched erect again.

Still talking softly, Cranford took up the veil and backed towards the gate.

A harsh voice roared, "What the *devil* are you doing to my horse, damn you?"

It was all the high-strung animal needed. It gave a nervous jump and, squealing with rage, reared high. The ears lay flat against the head once more, the eyes glared hatred, and two lethal iron-shod hooves flailed at this puny man-creature who'd dared to challenge him.

Cranford ducked, then made a leap for the gate. He felt a rush of air beside his ear and a tug at the shoulder of his coat. Mary screamed, then he was over and Finchley and a scared-looking groom were attempting to control the animal's fury.

Mary sobbed, "Oh, Piers! Oh, Piers!" and threw herself into his arms.

The groom said in a very shaken voice, "Cor, sir! That were—it were close, that were!"

Finchley bellowed, "Curse you, Cranford! If you've interfered with my poor brute, I'll have you disqualified, be damned if I don't!" He went stamping off, passing Horatio Glendenning who ran up, saying wrathfully, "*Must* you persist in taking such confounded risks, Piers? Of all the reckless chawbacons I ever knew!"

Cranford scarcely heard any of them, most of his awareness centering on the surprisingly pleasurable sensation of holding Miss Mary Westerman close in his embrace.

Muffled against his cravat, she said, "Are you hurt? He tore your coat . . ."

"But not me, fortunately. Now I wish you will replace your veil, ma'am, else you'll not dare come back to the inn for breakfast."

Mary took the veil and rearranged it with hands that shook. "And his—his hooves nigh caught your head! If they had—"

"They didn't," he said firmly. "And you know the saying—" Smiling down at her, he offered his arm and patted the small hand that rested on it. " 'A miss is as good as a mile.' "

"Perhaps, but my heart missed several miles, I think! Pray do not take such risks. I am very frail, you know."

He chuckled. "I've noticed."

Glendenning complained, "Well, you don't notice me! Am I allowed to accompany you?"

His face suddenly very red, Cranford said, "But—of course, Tio. As if we'd exclude such a hungry fellow."

The viscount grunted, but brightened when Mary slipped her free hand through his arm and said cheerfully, "The more the merrier, eh, Mr. Piers?"

Cranford smiled but did not comment.

Breakfast was served in a parlour the duke had reserved, enabling both ladies to discard hats and veils. Glendenning joined them, his rich sense of humour endearing him to Mrs. Lucretia, who lost no time in advising him that he was "prodigious droll."

Cranford joined in the conversation cheerfully, but he was concerned for Tio's safety and determined to make a last effort to persuade him not to ride. He decided that the best time to make the attempt would be when the meal was over and they were returning to the stables. His plan was foiled, however, when Roland Mathieson took Glendenning aside as they left the inn and a moment later he himself was approached by Henry Shorewood, who warned that Gresford Finchley meant mischief. "Keep your wits about you, friend," the barrister cautioned. "The Major ain't the type to play fair if he fancies someone stands in his way."

"D'you mean he fears I'll win the race?"

Shorewood strolled off, tugging at his lop-sided wig and

thereby rendering it more lop-sided than ever. "That," he said over his shoulder. "Among other things."

⁓

That the dismal weather of this grey morning had not kept people away was very evident. The low hill which had been designated the starting point of the race was crowded with every conceivable type of vehicle, from luxurious coaches to farm waggons. Men of every style and condition mingled and jostled good-naturedly. Makeshift awnings had been erected to shelter the more elegant of the spectators, while the common folk contented themselves with hooded cloaks or broad-brimmed hats. Vendors moved through the throng loudly proclaiming the purity and deliciousness of their sweetmeats, cakes and biscuits; the damp air was enriched by the spicy smell of roasting chestnuts, and some enterprising gypsy youths were doing a brisk trade offering for a groat squares of sacking to "pertect yer noble nobs and dicers."

Making his way towards the roped-off enclosure at the crown of the hill where the judges and contestants would gather, Cranford remarked to Duncan Tiele that the crowd was twice the size he'd expected to turn out on this wintry morning.

"The size of the purse is what's lured 'em from their warm beds." Clad in a superbly cut mulberry-red habit and short cloak, his wide-brimmed hat graced by the down-curling plume of a golden feather, Gervaise Valerian, the epitome of The Sporting Gentleman, joined them. "I see some of our family have come to cheer us on, dear coz." He nodded to where General Lord Nugent was making his way towards them.

The General gestured and shouted something, and Herbert Turner hove into view from behind him, waving eagerly.

Valerian said, "Oh, deuce take it! The national bore is come amongst us! Fare-thee-well, cousin mine!"

Cranford grabbed his arm. "Wait up! It won't kill you to say hello to the poor lad!"

"You've my permission to say hello for me," said Valerian, wrenching free. "I haven't the time. Try if you can palm off that flea-bitten kitten you tried to foist onto me, he's just the type of gudgeon to take it!"

He melted into the crowd. Frowning, Cranford started to follow, but checked as his great-uncle and the young gardener came up with them. Turner looked wistfully after his fast-disappearing idol. The General slapped Cranford on the back and asked the reason for "that angry glare. If you was to ask me, I'd say your cousin had done you a favour. The Stansbury chit will make you a good wife, m'boy!"

Cranford murmured something appropriate, but the frown did not leave his eyes although his gaze had moved past Valerian. Farther down the hill, Henry Shorewood had been hailed by an individual he appeared wishful to avoid; a sturdy man clad in a long and voluminous cloak with the hood pulled close about his face. Even as Cranford watched, the barrister again attempted to walk on, only to be halted as the shorter man stepped directly and determinedly in front of him. Shorewood was obviously annoyed, but the cloaked individual refused to move aside. His face was lost in the shadow of his hood so that he was unrecognizable, but there was something about the tilt of his head and the way he moved that put Cranford in mind of someone: the alleged pedlar named Josuah. The sort of fellow whom so fiery and opinionated a man as Henry Shorewood should have been able to dismiss at once. But the lawyer was not dismissing him; in fact, he stood listening to the other man talk, and he looked increasingly troubled.

Cranford started down the hill, but his arm was seized and his great-uncle cried, "Are you gone deaf, boy? They've called your name twice—you're dashed well keeping everyone waiting!"

Herbert Turner said shyly, "The judges are getting cross, Mr. Piers."

Cranford glanced back. Sure enough, the other contestants

were already settling into their saddles, the horses sidling about restlessly. Glendenning, already mounted, waved, flourishing something, and two of the distinguished gentlemen who would judge the race were gesturing imperatively. Hesitating, Cranford again looked down the hill. Both Shorewood and his persistent companion were gone.

12

An excited shout went up as the riders began to fall into line. It was a crowded line and contained, besides many of Cranford's friends and acquaintances, some men he knew only slightly and a few he knew not at all. Glancing to either side, Cranford found Mathieson at his left, a smile on his dark face as he caught sight of his grandfather among the onlookers. Beyond Rumpelstiltskin, Glendenning's Flame stamped and cavorted. Duncan Tiele's white mare was a short distance to Cranford's right and behaving politely, with Finchley in the adjacent space keeping a hard grip on the reins of his mercurial big bay. Valerian swayed gracefully to the spirited antics of his black stallion, and on the far end Bertie Crisp held his chestnut mare nicely in check.

The horses, already restless, seemed to catch the excitement in the air. Even the gentle Tassels was quivering and dancing with eagerness, and the line was broken when Duncan Tiele's previously docile white mare suddenly bucked and spun, colliding with Finchley's bay. Finchley swore and roared at Tiele to control his "damned fat hammer-head who's as clumsy as she is ugly!" The white mare was not a hammer-head, but she was certainly on the plump side. Tiele looked affronted and manoeuvred her back into line, but Finchley's bay then plunged at Walker, Valerian's black stallion. Valerian promptly dealt the bay a hard rap on the nose. Finchley flailed his whip at Valerian, who deftly reined Walker aside, and the whip struck another contestant who at once howled *"Foul!"* The horses milled and plunged and snorted, the riders struggling to calm them. The judges were called upon, and in the ensuing uproar Cranford guided the buoyantly dancing Tassels closer to Glendenning.

"Great sport, eh?" said the viscount, laughing. "At least your pretty lady is behaving herself."

Cranford said urgently, "Never mind about that. I've been trying for a word with you. I've seen that pedlar fellow again, Tio. For heaven's sake slip away when you can and—"

"When?" interrupted Glendenning, the smile fading from his eyes. "Where?"

"Here! A few moments since. Talking with the barrister I told you of."

"Assuming it is he, why would our pseudo pedlar be talking with Shorewood?"

"Dashed if I know! Perchance because he saw *me* talking with the man and he knows you and I are friends. The thing is—"

"You saw his face? You're sure 'twas him?"

"He wore a hood and was turned away from me. But—"

"Then you're *not* sure, and I can't back out because of your 'perchances.' You know that. Furthermore, if you keep sending me dagger glances, I'll not give you this."

Cranford took the small, soft packet his friend thrust at him. "What is it?"

"I wasn't told. You'd best open it. I think we're forming up again."

Tearing open the paper wrapping, Cranford discovered a small square of cambric and lace with the initial *M* beautifully embroidered in one corner. His heart warmed and he suspected his face did also.

Glendenning chuckled. "Egad! So the lady has sent you a talisman. Shall you wear it as you ride into battle, Sir Knight?"

Cranford tucked the handkerchief into the curling brim of his hat and said with a defiant grin, "You may be sure I shall. Now tell me quickly, is Perry here? Have you seen him?"

The viscount shook his head. "No, but his future brother-in-law came and is in high gig wagering on you. I'd wish you luck, old fellow, except that the best I can offer you is to come in second to my—"

His words were lost in a new roar of excitement.

The rope barrier had been pulled aside; a large yellow flag was swung high, then swept down, and they were off.

Crouched low over the saddle-horn, Cranford scarcely touched his short-necked spurs to Tassels' sides. The mare was eager to run and sprang forward. They were down the hill in a flash, and he was exhilarated by the speed, the rush of cold air, the thunder of hooves, the drops of rain that struck his face like small hailstones. Tassels was moving very fast, her silken gait as smooth and unfaltering as ever. He held her to a steady pace. Mathieson and Finchley galloped past at great speed, neck and neck. Glancing back, he saw Tio and several others close behind, Valerian coming up fast and Bertie Crisp shortening the distance, while Duncan Tiele laboured along in the rear.

Across the meadow and over a low hedge. The first jump; not too difficult, but two horses balked and a rider was thrown. Now came a sharp swing to the right, across a rutted road with water gleaming ahead. Mathieson had the lead, with Finchley flailing his whip madly and his big bay charging along. Cranford stroked Tassels' neck and prepared her for the wide stream and she soared over it like a silver bird. "Well done," he exclaimed breathlessly, and felt the surge of her powerful muscles as if in response. Finchley was dropping back a little, and Tio's Flame moved up as they raced for the next hill. They were both ahead of Cranford and he saw Finchley's whip lash out at Flame's eyes. "Damned cheat!" he muttered furiously, and he let Tassels have her head, determined that even if he didn't win, that poor sportsman would not.

The contestants had thinned noticeably as they thundered through a hamlet, the occupants lined up at the sides of the lane, holding pieces of sacking over their heads, but waving and shouting encouragement. Finchley's bay took exception to the howls and the fluttering sacking and shied wildly, almost oversetting the viscount's Flame. Cranford had to swerve to avoid colliding with them, and inevitably, he lost ground.

The flag-marked route before them now was lightly wooded, the lane narrow and treacherous as it wound between trees, bounded on the right side by a steeply descending slope. One of the race stewards was mounted and watchful as the first seven riders raced up, vying for position. In the lead, the viscount and Mathieson shot past him neck and neck. Finchley came up in a burst of speed, and seconds later forced his way between them with ruthless determination and a complete lack of sportsmanship, so that Glendenning was crowded off the lane and down the slope. Fighting to stay upright and unable to avoid a tree, Flame slammed against it. Horse and rider went down, the chestnut rolling, pinning Glendenning beneath her.

Cranford knew that to stop would end his chance to win, but no race ever run was worth the life of a good man. Cursing savagely, his heart hammering with mingled rage and apprehension, he reined Tassels off the lane and down the slope. He dismounted while the mare yet ran, and rushed to kneel beside the fallen man and call his name. Flame was threshing about as though half stunned. Glendenning lay twisted under her, face down. For a terrifying instant Cranford thought his neck was broken, then he heard the faint gasped-out words, "Can't . . . breathe!" It would be futile, he realized, to try and pull his friend clear, and even as he reached out to calm her the chestnut rolled over, her shoulders falling heavily across Glendenning's head.

Springing up, Cranford talked to the mare as calmly as he could, praying that Tio wasn't suffocating. The frenzied threshing movements eased a little as he stroked her sweating neck, then tugged on the bit. "Up, Flame! Get up, girl!" The great eyes rolled at him in terror. He tugged again, saying firmly, "Don't dawdle about, pretty lady! Up! Now!"

Tassels wandered over and bent to snuffle at the fallen mare. As if embarrassed, Flame struggled to her knees, then with a lurch was standing, trembling violently.

Cranford bent to carefully straighten his friend's head and turn him. Glendenning's eyes were closed, his face covered with mud and blood from a cut on his brow. Reaching to feel for a heartbeat, Cranford saw the green eyes blink open. Intensely relieved, he whispered, "Thank God!"

"And . . . you," panted the viscount.

"Are you hurt? Anything broken?"

"Just my . . . pride. Flame . . . ?"

"She's up and looks to be all right."

"You saw?"

"I saw."

"Then—get after that—that bastard! Can—make up time if you take . . . left fork . . . through the woods. Looks impassable. Ain't. Mayn't be . . . purely legal, but—"

"Legal—hell! I'll come up with him, I promise. Will you be all right if—"

"I'll be mad as . . . fire if you let him win! Go!"

The steward was riding along the higher ground, peering down at them. 'Better late than never,' thought Cranford, and mounting up, he shouted, "Take care of him!"

The man looked shocked, nodded, and urged his horse down the slope.

Following Tio's directions, Cranford judged the left fork to be indeed impassable, but just as the viscount had said, a path opened unexpectedly. Risking everything on Tassels' unerring ability, Cranford urged her to a gallop. He held his breath as they shot through the trees, and emerging, discovered that the skies had darkened ominously, and that he was almost up with the other riders. Mathieson and Finchley now shared the lead. Valerian was close behind, surprisingly neck and neck with Duncan Tiele's white mare. They were close to the crossroads that marked the mid-point of the race. The lane was very muddy, but as he made the loop and started on the home stretch, Cranford spurred and Tassels streaked to catch up. Finchley yowled something profane, Mathieson looked surprised, Valerian, riding like a centaur and with not a hair out of place, was smiling his infuriatingly supercilious smile.

Cranford's one thought was that whoever should win, it must not be Gresford Finchley, who had almost brought about Tio's death. He passed Bertie Crisp and was gaining on Valerian and Tiele, whose white mare he guessed must be a mudder and had thus gained ground. Mathieson was alone in the lead now, with Finchley pressing hard, his whip flailing. A low stone wall loomed up, and beyond it a fast-flowing stream. Valerian and Tiele took the wall side by side. Walker almost cleared the stream but lost his stride at the bank and stumbled to regain his footing. Tiele's mare sailed high but short and came down in midstream. She was, as Cranford had noted, quite plump, and landing close beside Valerian, displaced a great sheet of muddy water, inundating the dandy. Flashing past as Tassels cleared the stream neatly, Cranford caught a glimpse of an unrecognizable man of mud and with a grin heard the dandy's spluttering howls of rage.

The rain began in earnest, but only two riders were ahead of him now and a quick backward glance showed very few others had survived thus far. Finchley turned a face contorted with fury to glare at him. Cranford shot past, avoiding the flail of the Major's whip to draw level with Mathieson's Rumpelstilt-skin. Mathieson glanced at him and, good sportsman that he was, his white teeth flashed in a grin.

Jubilant, Cranford gasped, "We can do it, Tassels! I knew you would win! Perry will have his home, after all, and we'll be able to—"

He reeled to a violent jolt and Tassels lost her stride. Even as he grabbed for her mane the saddle jerked sideways and he was hurled from the mare's back. The countryside became a spinning mix of green grasses, naked trees and blackening skies. He landed heavily, and sprawled, the breath knocked out of him. Dimly, he heard a triumphant shout as Finchley galloped past. Hard on his heels, the muddy Valerian yelled, "Sleeping, cousin?" Tiele rode up roaring, "All right, Cranford?" and he nodded, climbing giddily to his feet. Still persisting, Bertie Crisp called, "Are you done, Cranford?"

No, he wasn't done! By heaven, he wasn't done! He peered about and saw his saddle. Staggering to it, he saw also that it was useless; the girth strap had snapped. He whistled and Tassels trotted to him at once. Dizziness thwarted his first attempt to climb onto her back. The five-barred gate in a nearby fence offered a solution; leading the mare to it, he used one bar as a step and was able to hoist himself up.

A distant rumble of thunder set Tassels to dancing about uneasily. Patting her, he said, "Poor lass—you've had an unsettling day! But we must keep on!" A light touch with the spurs urged her forward at a canter coming quickly to the gallop, the pretty mare responding willingly as if she'd understood his words and his need. Cranford had ridden bareback as a boy and once or twice of necessity, during the retreat from Prestonpans and his desperate effort to bring his wounded brother through enemy lines. It seemed more of an effort now, perhaps because his battered head had not benefitted when he'd fallen from the saddle at speed. But the mare's gait was smooth, bless her, and the countryside blurred past until once again he could see the riders ahead. They were strung out now, Mathieson holding a good lead, then Finchley, and in third place Valerian, not riding as gracefully as usual. Tiele had fallen back, and three other surviving riders vied with Bertie Crisp to avoid the last place. Except, Cranford thought grimly, for himself. He recognized one of the landmarks, a big blue barn, which meant they were only a mile from the finish. He urged Tassels on, knowing he had no hope of winning, but determined to make sure that Finchley was held accountable for his shameful conduct.

His eyes were fixed on the cheating Major when Finchley appeared to overlook an opportunity to gain ground by keeping to the lane and instead swung his mount onto the turf at Mathieson's right. Momentarily puzzled, Cranford suddenly thought, 'It's Roly's blind side! That bastard means to cut Rump off at the turn before Roly sees him!' With an inarticulate shout of rage, he kicked home hard. Startled, Tassels all but flew, but it was too late. In flagrant violation of the rules, Finchley's big bay was cutting through the turn in the road directly in front of Mathieson, who failed to see him until the last instant. Rumpelstiltskin shied in alarm. A superb horseman, Mathieson was not thrown, but Finchley had raced into the lead. There remained only the last water jump and no hope that Mathieson could pass in time. Cranford swore, seething with frustration and fury.

The Major was braying his triumph and spurring hard.

A sudden brilliant lightning flash was followed by an ear-splitting clap of thunder. Perhaps Finchley's temperamental animal was afraid of thunderstorms, or perhaps he had suffered enough from those cruel rowelled spurs. Whatever the case, approaching the water jump at full gallop, he slowed suddenly, came to a dead stop and dug in his hooves.

The result was inevitable. Before Cranford's delighted eyes, Major Gresford Finchley soared without grace through the air, and splashed down in the muddy stream.

Not one of the contestants stopped to give him a helping hand.

~~~

The steady rain had failed to diminish the crowd and excitement knew no bounds when the riders came in sight. Mathieson was given a rousing cheer as Rumpelstiltskin flashed over the finish line. Valerian came in second and Tiele placed third. There was no sign of Major Finchley. Cranford was fourth and three others brought up the rear, among them Bertie Crisp.

Cranford congratulated Mathieson hurriedly, and was himself surrounded by a curious group demanding to know why he'd ridden in bareback. He said a terse "Girth snapped," and dispatched a stable-boy to ride back and discover if the steward needed help in caring for Lord Glendenning. His remarks were overheard and gave rise to a storm of anxious enquiries that turned to outrage when he described the behaviour of Gresford Finchley. Slipping away from the crowd then, he jerked his head at Sudbury, who was holding Tassels' bridle and watching him anxiously.

Cranford led the way to a less crowded area and interrupted the groom's questions about the broken strap. He said curtly, "It looked to me as if it had been cut near through. You noticed nothing amiss, I take it?"

Sudbury looked horrified and insisted he had given the master's saddle and bridle "extry special" attention before the race. "Nor the mare wasn't out o' my sight for a minute, sir. Save for when the gent fell down. A proper rasper he took, right outside that temp'ry stable what—"

Cranford interrupted tensely, "Which gent? And how were you involved?"

"Why—I dunno his name, Mr. Piers." Sudbury wrinkled his brows worriedly. "He seemed to have hit his head and for a minute or two I were thinking to call for a physician, but he wouldn't have none of it and said he'd just rest a minute and would do very nicely—as were the case, in fact. Wanted to see the horses, he said, but tripped on a rake what had fallen under the straw. A proper nice gent he were. Most respectable, and not the kind to—"

"What did this 'proper nice gent' look like?"

The groom sensed his employer's impatience and blinked unhappily. "Why—I—I didn't pay much heed, Mr. Piers, sir," he stammered. "Being as I were more anxious lest he'd hurt hisself."

"You must have *some* recollection. Think, man! Was he tall? Short? Fat? Thin? What was his voice like?"

"Well now, it were—just a voice, Mr. Piers. A nice soft-spoke gent, with a eddicated way of talk—like yourself. Nor he wasn't short, exact. Taller'n me, I think."

"Young? Old? Dark eyes? Light eyes?"

"Why, he weren't old, sir. Not what you'd call *old*. Though he weren't all that young, exack. He had eyes, a'course, but . . . Er—" Sudbury groaned. "Lor', sir. I'm that sorry. I just didn't pay no heed."

"Had you ever seen him before? In Muse Village, for instance?"

"Our *village? That* gent? Oh, no, sir! That I *is* sure of! If I ever see a swell like him in the village, I'd ha' noticed for sure!"

"Suppose he'd been dressed differently? Not a gentleman of fashion, for example?"

Sudbury scratched his head and, clearly bewildered, said, "I dunno about that, sir. But—what would a gent be doing dressing up in our village?"

Stifling a sigh, Cranford acknowledged to himself that it was hopeless. He sent the groom off to care for Tassels and find him another horse and saddle and to dispatch someone to retrieve his own saddle. "And my hat!" he added, anxious to rescue a certain small handkerchief. He snatched a quick wash and changed his linen and torn coat while he waited. A knock at his door announced the arrival of the steward who'd stayed with Glendenning. The man looked rather guilty, rightfully so, in Cranford's opinion, considering his tardiness in arriving at the scene of the accident. He reported that the viscount was not seriously injured, but had been carried to a nearby farm and an apothecary had been sent for. "I can direct you, Mr. Cranford, if you wish to see him." The directions were given, the steward, fully aware of the stern blue eyes that seemed to pierce him, took himself off, and Cranford hurried downstairs. Sudbury had a likely-looking bay gelding ready and he rode out anxious to assure himself that his friend was being properly cared for.

He found the farm easily enough. The viscount, his left arm splinted, had been settled into the feather bed in a small but immaculate bedchamber and was being fussed over by a buxom farm-wife. Her even more buxom daughter advised Cranford that "his lor'ship" had been treated by the local midwife. "He be in my bed, zur," she confided with a blush and a giggle.

Glendenning looked white and spent, but his ready smile dawned, and gripping Cranford's hand, he said rather wearily, "At it again, Piers! You'll do anything to place me in your debt, you rogue! And be damned if you don't look worse than I feel!"

"If that were truth they'd be burying me," argued Cranford lightly. "How badly is this pest damaged, ma'am?"

The farm-wife was round-eyed with shock that her highly born guest should be referred to as a pest, and preparing to carry out a tray of medical supplies said with faint reproof, "*His lor'ship* has suffered of a desecrated shoulder and his poor wrist do be broke, zur. Please to keep him quiet as may be is what Mrs. Blakeley said, zur. An' Matilda Blakeley, zur, be as good a midwife as you'll find even in Lunon Town. Quiet—as—may—be, she says. She do have just now left, more's the pity, else she could have told you herself."

"And that properly threw you 'gainst the ropes," murmured Glendenning, after Cranford had meekly ushered the kind-hearted woman into the passage and closed the door.

"You may believe it did," admitted Cranford. "Phew! The innate dignity of the British rustic never fails to put me in awe! And the lady was perfectly right, for I've always suspected you were 'desecrated.' "

The viscount's answering grin faded abruptly. "Sufficiently so to even the score with your damnable neighbour! He'll have my glove in his face as soon as I'm able, but if you mean to tell me he won that ridiculous race, I'm liable to have a spasm—at the very least!"

Cranford sat on the side of the bed and assured his friend that a spasm was not indicated. "Roly Mathieson won. My deplorable would-be cousin came in second." He grinned broadly. "And mud from head to toe!"

The viscount threw up a delaying hand. "*Valerian?* I thought he didn't believe in dirt and such. Elaborate, when you can stop gloating."

Cranford obliged with gusto and Glendenning gave a shout of mirth, then groaned that it was brutal to bring a man with numerous broken bones to laughter. "Go on, go on," he urged breathlessly, "but try to give me a more sober account."

"I'll try, noble martyr. Well, if you can believe it, Duncan Tiele's white and overweight lady mudded her way to third place. Finchley neither came up to the finish line, nor has he been seen since he—Oh, I forgot—but I suppose you couldn't endure it were I to describe his swan dive? . . ."

His eyes glinting with joyous anticipation, Glendenning commanded, "Tell me, you fiend!"

Cranford did so, once more reducing his friend to painful laughter and wails of regret that he'd not been present to see the Major meet his just desserts. Mopping a corner of the sheet at his brimming eyes, Glendenning sighed, "I'm sorry you didn't win, old fellow. My fault. If you hadn't stopped to help me—"

"Yes. Well, I'll hold it over you forever, you may be sure."

Horatio smiled and asked, "What shall you do now?"

Cranford shrugged. "Go home and see what else has fallen down or caught fire," he said with a rueful grin. "But I'll find a way to raise the funds, never fear."

Shifting painfully against his pillows, the viscount declared that he had no such fears. "Just don't take it upon yourself to call out the flying Major. That's my privilege. Dash it all, he could have put a period to me!"

"Which merely proves that you should have heeded my warning and not ridden in the race, you silly block. And how comes it about that you were treated by the Midwife Blakeley? We're not that far from Woking, and there's likely an accredited physician thereabouts."

"Yes, there is. But I chance to be acquainted with that particular gentleman. So does my sire."

"At your secrets again, are you, Tio?" Despite the stern words, Cranford had noted the strain in the green eyes and he added quietly, "Does this mean I am forbidden to notify your lady and your family of your latest little escapade?"

Glendenning hesitated, then asked, "Any more appearances by our infamous village pedlar?"

"Not to my knowledge, but I had little time to look about after the race. For some reason the fellows wanted to know about your mischance." He grinned in response to the viscount's indignation, and added, "So you want your people kept clear, do you? The Earl won't thank me, Tio."

"He will if you'll be good enough to send Florian up to Windsor. Amy will be glad to see him, and he can explain that I took a small spill."

The daughter of the house reappeared at this point with an urgent request from her mother that his lor'ship's friend be on his way. "We must not tire the poor genelman, zur," she said apologetically.

Glendenning advised her that she would be welcome to tire

him at any time, and having voiced a sinister threat to relay that provocative remark to his affianced bride, Cranford left him.

He delayed only long enough to seek out the mistress of the house and won her heart by insisting that she accept a generous sum for the extra work involved in caring for the injured man. "We will send word to his family and I doubt he'll be with you longer than a day or two, ma'am."

The lady was profuse in her gratitude and assured him that the poor gentleman would receive the best of care. "He might have to put up with my simple home cooking, zur," she said shyly. "I doesn't know how to cook Frenchy cargoes and such-like."

Knowing something of Horatio's perilous days as a fugitive from the King's justice and his diet of stolen carrots and berries, Cranford assured her that his lordship liked home cooking and would be very well pleased not to be offered such exotic dishes as "cargoes." He left the farm, sure that Tio was in good hands, and went out into the wet afternoon once more.

<hr>

At dusk the tap of the Golden Goose was crowded, and despite the storm that had returned to rage outside, was warm and cozy. Logs blazed and crackled on the wide hearth, pewter pots shone in the firelight, the air rang with talk and laughter, and the two comely serving maids were flushed and bright-eyed as they tripped nimbly among the company.

As winner of the steeplechase, Roland Mathieson ordered drinks all round, calling for another glass as Piers Cranford limped into the room.

"How does Glendenning go on?" he called.

Through the immediate well of silence, Cranford answered, "A dislocated shoulder, and one wrist is broken. But he's doing pretty well." His keen eyes raked the room, and he added a grim "No thanks to Gresford Finchley."

Mathieson said coolly, "You cannot slaughter the flying Major tonight, Cranford. For some odd reason he ain't among us."

"And if he had been," put in Valerian, de-mudded and immaculate as ever, "we'd have thrown him out, as he is doubtless aware."

There was a chorus of agreement. Gresford Finchley was denounced for a cheat and a poor sportsman; dishonourable conduct that would, as Valerian observed, almost certainly result in his being blackballed at every club in Town. "I hear that Glendenning claims you saved his life, coz," he drawled, sauntering to join Mathieson and Cranford.

Shocked, Mathieson exclaimed, "Jupiter! I'd not realized it was that chancy!"

Cranford, who had been staring at the dainty handkerchief now artistically pinned to the breast of Valerian's dark purple coat, said, "Sufficiently so that I've a bone to pick with the flying Major! That's a pretty thing you have on your coat, Valerian. Has it some special significance?"

"Oh, very special," said Valerian with his sly smile. "A lovely lady bestowed it upon me for luck in our ridiculous race. Is this not your faithful groom? . . ."

Sudbury hovered nearby.

Turning to him, Cranford asked if a fast messenger had been sent off with his note to Florian. Being reassured on this point he added, "Were you able to find my hat?"

"Sorry I am, but no, sir. But the lad which I sent to Sir Perry-Green's house this morning has come back, and he ain't there, Mr. Piers, sir. Gone to see relatives, they told the boy."

Peregrine had probably gone into the country to visit his fiancée's parent. Logical enough, with the wedding so close. But Cranford experienced an uneasy qualm. He'd accepted his twin's absence from the steeplechase as being due to his injury. On the other hand, if Perry was well enough to have gone all the way to Burford, one might think he could have detoured en route, at least to wish him luck in the race . . .

"... and said as I was to bring it to you, Lieutenant, sir."

Cranford started. Sudbury was offering a folded note. As he took it, Valerian drawled, "Ah, so you're invited as well, I see."

Murmuring an apology, Cranford read a brief and beautifully penned invitation to dine with the Duke of Marbury and his guests at nine o'clock.

Glancing up, he found Valerian watching with evident amusement.

" 'As well'?" he echoed, with little hope that his assumption would prove to be erroneous.

"Quite so," said the dandy, rearranging the snowy handkerchief over his heart so that the embroidered *M* was clearly visible. "I am so fortunate as to be one of the—ah, guests. That will cheer you, eh, coz?"

Scowling at that treacherous handkerchief, Cranford growled, "Not markedly, Valerian."

13

A liveried footman admitted Cranford to the suite the duke had reserved for his dinner party, thanks to the departure of several guests who had come just for the race. This was a surprisingly spacious area created by the removal of the door connecting two bedchambers. The beds had also been whisked away, replaced in one room by a good-sized dining-table tastefully adorned with snowy napery, and in the other by two sofas, small occasional tables, and three armchairs. Fires blazed on both hearths, and several candelabra sent their brightness to reflect on gleaming silverware and sparkling glasses. Small crystal vases held sprays of leaves and fern, with here and there the colourful splash of an early blossom or artificial flower. The rooms, which had previously been very clean but on the stark side, were now silent but eloquent testimonials to the artistry by which superior servants were able to transform the commonplace into the elegant for those who paid high wages for just such skills.

The instant the footman softly closed the door, Cranford realized that he was ill prepared for this gathering. The duke, known to dress in the height of fashion, was a vision of sartorial splendour in a magnificent French wig and a superbly tailored black velvet coat trimmed with gold lace. The heels of his shoes were very high and a great diamond-and-sapphire ring glowed on one thin hand. Scarcely less impressive, Valerian had chosen a coat of flame brocade threaded with silver; his thick hair was powdered and brushed into soft waves about his aquiline features, a silver patch accentuated the clear grey of his eyes and he wore a large ruby ring on one hand while the candle-light awoke glittering fires from the jewelled quizzing glass he swung idly by its silver chain. Cranford, who had not dreamt to find such a formal dinner party at a gathering of sportsmen, had bowed to fashion to the extent of requiring Sudbury to powder and tie back his hair, and had donned a simple dark blue habit. His only ornament consisted of the fine emerald ring his father had bequeathed him.

The duke welcomed him heartily, and apologized for the fact that his grandson had felt it necessary to return at once to his country home. "Just to be sure that his lovely bride and my great-grandson haven't run away during his absence," he said, a twinkle lighting his deep-set blue eyes.

Feeling like a country bumpkin, Cranford smiled responsively, but his smile faded as Valerian minced over to greet him with punctilious politeness—and with The Handkerchief pinned to the great cuff of his right sleeve. The quizzing glass was brought into play and Cranford was scanned from head to toe with studied insolence. "You military men," the dandy murmured, his eyes full of mocking laughter. "Austerity and no nonsense—whatever the occasion."

"Ah, here are our lovely ladies," said the duke.

Turning, Cranford was momentarily struck to silence. Both ladies carried masks, which they lowered as they entered. Mrs. Lucretia tripped in, giggling mischievously. Miss Mary looked more like Miss Cordelia tonight—elegant in a satin gown of a rich shade of deep pink not usually worn by unmarried girls, but surprisingly pretty for all that. Mrs. Lucretia wore gold silk that billowed out over large hoops while her bosom threatened to billow over the extremely *décolleté* bodice.

"Lovely, indeed," murmured Valerian, bowing over her plump little hand but with his eyes elsewhere.

"You are really thinking us very naughty to be here," she said archly.

"Yes, but then naughty ladies are so *fascinant*. Do you overnight here, ma'am?"

"We had not intended to do so, but Muffin thought 'twould be more convenient since we are to dine quite late this evening."

Touching his lips to Miss Cordelia's fingers, Cranford wondered for the hundredth time why Valerian was the duke's guest, and why Mary had given him a talisman after the way the clod had treated her. Not, he thought with a mental shrug, that it was any of his affair, of course.

They were ushered into what Marbury laughingly referred to as his "parlour pro tem," and the footman appeared with a tray of decanters, claret for the gentlemen and ratafia for the ladies.

Marbury proposed a toast to the absent winner of the race, and having sipped from her glass, Mrs. Lucretia observed that the barn fire was "just too, too shocking," and turning to Valerian, added, "I do not understand such horrid events, so you shall have to explain, dear boy, how that ghastly fire could have started."

Valerian said airily, "Ask my cousin, dear ma'am. He was there at the time."

"Whereby I was able to get my groom and my horse out," said Cranford, directing an irked glance at him. "Besides which, you made a remarkably prompt appearance."

"But of course." The picture of injured innocence, Valerian asked, "What did I say to provoke you, coz? Have I been so gauche as to already ruffle your military feathers?"

"Oh, but are they not *droll?*" trilled Mrs. Lucretia, waving her wineglass at the duke. "And so different. One would never take them for cousins, would one?"

"Distant—cousins," said Cranford with emphasis.

"Alas—he don't want us," sighed Valerian to no one in particular. "My withers are wrung."

His lips tight, Cranford indulged in a few scenarios on what he would like to do to the dandy's "withers."

"While you recover of your withering," said Mary, "perhaps Mr. Cranford will tell us of his friend's progress. My aunt and I were unable to see that area, but we heard about Lord Glendenning's accident. I trust he is not badly injured?"

"Fortunately no, and he is receiving excellent care." Cranford looked at her curiously. "Do you say you did see part of the race?"

"Pray do not shock the poor fellow by admitting such a breach of etiquette!" exclaimed Valerian, laughing. "My cousin—your pardon, Cranford—*distant* cousin places a high value on propriety."

"As do I, Gervaise," put in the duke. "And since I am responsible for the presence of these ladies, I hope you do not accuse me of a—how did you put it?—a breach of etiquette?" His tone was mild, but one eyebrow lifted and the glance slanted at Valerian caused that young man to become rather red in the face.

Mrs. Lucretia began to wield her large fan with nervous rapidity, and Mary said, "We were forbidden to attend the race, which I think very silly in this modern age. But His Grace was so kind as to loan us a glass and have us escorted to the top of Norman Hill."

"So that we were able to see *some* of it, at least," said Mrs. Lucretia. "How thrilling when your grandson came in first, Muffin!"

"But I suspect your wagers were not on Roland," the duke said with a smile. "Someone else flew your colours, eh, Mary?"

215

"And at least one of my champions still wears my talisman," she said pertly.

"You may believe that the other was most grateful for your good wishes," said Cranford.

"And although I treasure your talisman and shall keep it always, I have to own that I would treasure it more had I been the sole recipient of such a gift." Valerian sighed heavily. "Cruel, lovely one."

Clearly unrepentant, she said, "I have heard it said that there is safety in numbers. But much good it did me. Neither of you came near to winning. Indeed, one returned covered with mud, which is not at all romantical, and the other rode in muddy and bareback, which is even less romantical! So disappointing!"

Marbury laughed delightedly.

"Oh, I disagree, child, and think it indeed romantical." Curious, Mrs. Lucretia asked, "I cannot help but wonder why ever you did such a droll thing, Lieutenant Piers? I would have supposed it to be most difficult to ride without a saddle. Indeed, I am sure I never could do it! You must be a very skilled horseman."

"He probably learned it from his gypsy," murmured Valerian with a grin.

Cranford stiffened, then decided to ignore that barb. The dandy was evidently unaware of Mary's close friendship with Laura Finchley and her consequent sympathy for his young steward. Valerian, he thought, had made a mis-step.

He was right, for Mary's head had immediately tossed upward. Lowering the glass she had just lifted, she said, "If you refer to Mr. Florian Consett, sir, he was stolen by gypsies and not born into the tribe."

"Yes, I've heard that is his claim," drawled Valerian. "In truth, one could scarce blame him."

"For what?" demanded Mary, firing up. "For saying he was

216

kidnapped? Or for the possibility that he lies and is actually of gypsy blood?"

Valerian shrugged. "Either. Though I care not, whatever the case."

"Well, I do care," said Mary, her eyes sparkling. "I number Florian Consett among my friends and I believe what he says. Even if it were a fib, as you evidently conclude, he is an honourable and upright gentleman."

"Well said," exclaimed Cranford.

"Jolly well said," agreed Valerian, eyeing Mary admiringly. "I apologize, and beg your forgiveness, dear Miss Stansbury. Mr. Consett is pure as the driven snow!"

"Just because he has dark hair is not proof of gypsy blood," put in Mrs. Lucretia, who had been considering the case. "Only look at yourself, Gervaise. Your hair is dark. Oh, 'tis powdered now, of course, which is charming, I'll own, and quite in the mode, though you might do better to wear one of those high French wigs, like Muffin. Even so, you always look well, and are judged extreme handsome, as everyone knows, but your mama is very dark, being part French, or is it Italian? I forget, but Muffin will know, since his first wife was her cousin, as I recall. So only think how droll it would be if we fancied *you* to be a gypsy."

Cranford had listened in awe to this muddled monologue but Valerian said earnestly, "If 'twould commend me to you and your lovely niece, ma'am, I'd wear golden hoops in my ears and learn the Romany tongue!"

"Oh, very good," said Mary, laughing at him. "You may not wear golden earrings but you have a silver tongue, sir. At times."

Valerian looked at her mournfully and lifted one hand as a fencer might do in acknowledging a hit.

"I agree," said Mrs. Lucretia. "But Mr. Cranford is silent and has still failed to explain why he rode bareback in such an important race."

Risking another of the duke's warning glances, Valerian interpolated, "He claims the girth was cut. Which is—to say the least of it, most—um, odd."

Mrs. Lucretia's fan swung into action once more, creating quite a breeze.

Cranford, his eyes suddenly icy, drawled, "I feel sure you will explain what you mean by that, sir."

Frowning, the duke set down his wineglass and murmured, "Gervaise . . ."

"I certainly do not imply that I doubt your word, cousin," said Valerian hastily. "Acquit me of such a rude reaction. Everyone knows you are pure *et sans reproche.*" He smiled at Cranford, who met his angelic gaze with a steady stare. "The failure," Valerian went on, "seems rather to have been Miss Stansbury's."

"Mine!" exclaimed Mary indignantly. "How so?"

"Come now, dear lady. You must own that your talismen, both of the dainty things, rather—er, fell down on the job!"

The duke laughed, Mrs. Lucretia giggled, and the tense moment slid past, nor was there another until they had moved into the adjoining room and were all enjoying an excellent dinner.

Conversation went along smoothly. Perhaps because of a warning glance bestowed on him by the duke, Valerian restrained his caustic tongue. Seated next to Mrs. Lucretia, Cranford chatted easily with her and began to suspect that she was not nearly so foolish as she appeared. His breeding forbade any revelation of inner anxieties, and no one would have guessed that although he gave the impression of hanging on her every word, he was inwardly plagued by the awareness that the dandy seated across the table from him was flirting so outrageously with Miss Mary that any well-bred individual might have expected either Mrs. Lucretia or His Grace to put a stop to it.

The second course was carried in. The duke rose and began to carve the roast beef while asking that Cranford tell them more about the extraordinary race and how his saddle had been damaged.

The account was interrupted frequently, for Mary was full of questions, as was her aunt. Valerian looked thoughtful and commented that it certainly appeared as though some unknown person had not wanted his cousin to win the race. "Tassels was the runaway favourite," he acknowledged.

"As a result of which many people undoubtedly lost money," observed the duke.

Cranford flushed, and admitted, *"Mea culpa."*

Mary said defensively, "Not only because of Tassels, Your Grace. You had high hopes of coming in first, Mr. Valerian. I hope you did not suffer heavy losses?"

"Not at all, lovely one," he responded gaily. "In point of fact I came away with very plump pockets."

The duke handed a platter of sliced roast beef to the footman and sat down, saying in mild surprise, "You wagered that Roland would win?"

"My apologies, but I did not, sir," answered Valerian, chuckling. "I bet on my noble cousin—to lose."

The duke's right eyebrow shot up.

Mary exclaimed heatedly, "Well, I hold 'twas most unkind and shows a shocking lack of family loyalty!"

"But was so beautifully lucrative," said Valerian, unrepentant.

"For shame, sir!" Mary pushed the little vase at the centre of the table towards Cranford. "To you go the honours, Lieutenant."

Cranford said with a grin, "And are beyond price, ma'am. Flowers always brighten a table and these are arranged so charmingly."

"I might have guessed that you harbour a passion for weeds," mused Valerian.

"I grieve that my efforts do not please you," said Mary tartly.

219

"For my part, I find your efforts delightful," said Cranford. "You used fern here, I see, and admittedly the blue blossom is of silk, but the golden bloom is—"

"A dandelion," chortled Valerian.

Mary said, "Well, 'tis winter-time. One has to use what is available. Besides, I think dandelions are very pretty."

"And were created by the same Hand which gave us roses and lily of the valley," the duke pointed out. "I commend your taste, Miss Mary, and thank you for adding beauty to our table—in more ways than one."

"I couldn't have said it better," exclaimed Valerian, raising his glass to the duke.

"Very true," agreed Cranford.

Mrs. Lucretia remarked with an amused gesture that they all were very droll, and in so doing overset her wineglass. Claret splashed in all directions. Valerian leaped to his feet and jumped back, dabbing at his waistcoat; Marbury moved his chair aside and rang for the footman; Cranford used his napkin to divert the flow from Mary, and Mrs. Lucretia squealed with mirth and declared she was quite soaked and she dared not guess what her maid would say.

"She will likely say that you are—very droll, ma'am," said Valerian wickedly.

The lady was much too good-natured to take offence at this sarcasm, and laughed till she cried.

While the footman and a maid hurriedly replaced the covers, another maid led Mrs. Lucretia away to see what could be done to remove the claret from her gown. "Before it sets in proper-like, ma'am."

Marbury said smilingly, "Well, my little supper party has been more entertaining than I could have hoped. Now tell me, Cranford, what's all this about your trying to find a cat?"

"Would that be the mog you kicked in the stable, coz?" enquired the dandy.

Mary looked shocked, and Cranford said, "You really must

try to keep your facts straight, Valerian. Major Finchley was hastening to get his horse clear of the fire and the cat got in his way."

"So he kicked the poor little kitty, of course." Mary's lip curled. "Typical! Was it hurt, Lieutenant? Is that why you're trying to find it?"

"It was certainly very frightened. I've had my groom searching about, but I suppose, like all injured creatures, the kitten has found somewhere to hide itself."

He had not intended his remark to be double entendre, and was surprised to find Valerian watching him with a narrowed glare.

Mary said, "How very kind you are. Pray let me know if you arc able to find it."

He promised to do as she asked, and seeing the genuine anxiety in her really quite lovely eyes, was touched and promised himself to try for a private word with her after supper.

His hopes were soon dashed, however. Mrs. Lucretia returned as the third course was being set out and said with a meaningful nod that a gentleman waited to see him and had just been shown to his room.

Florian must have ridden like the wind, he thought, and murmuring an apology, left them.

He soon found that his optimistic interpretation of Mrs. Lucretia's nod was unfounded, for the gentleman who occupied the armchair in his bedchamber was several decades Florian's senior. Closing the door, Cranford noted that General Lord Nugent was flushed, and his face like a thunder-cloud. Hoping for the best, he said, "Good evening, sir. I'd thought perhaps you and Herbert had left. I didn't see you at the finish."

"Young Turner's gone off." With those barked-out words it became clear that brandy had played a large part in the General's evening. "Good thing. Though I didn't give him leave— to er, to l-leave. Prob'ly in a bottle somewhere if he was 's embarrassed as I was. That was a damned disgraceful exhibition you made of yourself, Left'nant, I don't scr-scruple t'tellya."

Cranford's heart sank. It had been a long day, and suddenly he ached with tiredness, but he said quietly, "Do you refer to the race, sir?"

"What the devil else would I refer to? It was—was dashed humiliating, I c'n tell you, to hear my friends laugh when you rid in bareback like some blasted performing cl-clown!"

Piers' jaw tightened. "The saddle girth broke, Uncle, and—"

"Then where in hell were your grooms? If you'd taught the lazy louts to take proper care of your equipment—"

"Your pardon, sir. Sudbury is a good man, but the girth was cut nigh through, probably at some time after he'd tightened the straps."

"Was the clod blind, then? If you'd used your wits you'd have had men watching the mare every m-minute. You certainly knew more than one rogue wished you ill."

"As you say, sir. I trust you did not lose a large sum."

The General grunted and shifted in his chair. "Did. But I didn't bet on you, at all events." Glowering, he added, "Nor did I expect to—to watch you make a curst cake of yourself!"

"My apologies." Piers clenched his hands and reminded himself of the times this man had helped his family, but his voice was clipped when he asked, "If that is all you came to say I should be going back to—"

"Do not *dare* use that tone to me!" The General stood, rocking slightly, but his eyes flashing wrath. "You came begging my aid once again, and tried to wriggle out of what I asked of you in return. Oh, I know that you counted on this stupid race to rescue you! Instead of which—"

Standing also, Piers said, "Instead of which I disgraced you—and the family, is that it, sir? Would you perhaps have preferred that I let Viscount Glendenning suffocate, as he surely would have done had I not stopped to—"

"In which case," roared the General, his flush deepening alarmingly, "Br-Britain would have rid herself of a rascally trai-

222

tor who fought under the banner of that Scottish upstart!"

Piers said sharply, "Not so loud, sir, I beg! Those charges have never been proven 'gainst Tio—"

"And if they were," said Lord Nugent, lowering his voice and glancing uneasily to the door. "If they were—'twould be another disgrace to our name, would it not? I know curst well that you all protected that fire-eater when he came within a whisker of being hauled off to the Tower. You'd be damned lucky not to lose your heads—the whole reckless lot of you! Much we owe to the Glendennings!"

Piers said doggedly, "The viscount has been our friend since we were in short coats. A sorry turn I'd have dealt him had I ridden past and left him to die."

"Well, a sorry turn he has dealt you, for you might very well have won the race in despite everything."

Meeting those accusing eyes, Piers said slowly, "Perhaps. But do you know, Uncle, I think your words are harsher than your heart. Had you been in my place you'd likely have done the same."

Mollified, the General sat down again and growled, "Do not think to turn me up sweet with your clever diplomacy. I'm alive on that suit! But—that's neither here nor there. Have you no brandy to offer me?"

Smothering a grin, Piers crossed to the sideboard and poured two glasses.

The General accepted the drink and stared down at it for a moment, saying nothing.

The old fellow was trying to compose himself. Something of import was coming. Piers waited.

"At all events, you are reprieved, m'boy." The tone now was benevolent and a faint smile was levelled at him. "It seems that Gervaise has—has seen the error of his ways and is willing to live up to his bargain and wed the Stansbury chit."

The glass sagged in Piers' hand. He gasped, "He told you as much?"

"Not personally. But his man chances to be related to my fellow and—"

"Servant-hall gossip . . ."

"Never look down your nose at it. 'Tis reliable as—er, as the Archbishop of Canterbury! Now why do you frown? Have you heard something unsavoury about the Archbishop?"

"I merely wonder what causes you to trust the likes of Gervaise Valerian."

"Trust that dandified rake-shame? Do you take me for a flat? 'Tis said nobody knows a man like his valet. That I do trust. Gad, but you're a hard man to fathom. I thought you'd be delighted." The reddened eyes scanned him suspiciously. "Ain't taken a fancy to the gel yourself, have you?"

It was a home question. Like a flash of light it dawned on Piers that he had indeed "taken a fancy" to Cordelia Mary Westerman Stansbury. All of 'em! He felt his face growing hot, and he said firmly, "Valerian doesn't deserve her."

"Not deserve a brazen hussy who cavorted about with cannibals for nigh to a year, and shows not a whit of shame for her wanton behaviour?"

"Mary is neither brazen nor a hussy, and has nothing to be ashamed of! If anyone should feel shame, it is Valerian!"

Staring at him, the General said, "Only listen to the heated defence! And in what cause? You may disabuse your mind of any hope if you've now changed your mind about offering for the gel. She won't have you."

"But you said only a few days ago that—"

"Perhaps I did. But that was before Valerian threw his hat in the ring, so to speak. Now hear me, young man. You are to back off at once! On *no* account think of courting the chit yourself. It will be much better for us if Valerian keeps his word and weds her. And of one thing you may be sure: That harpy mother of hers will stop at nothing to get her greedy claws on his fortune. On that count alone you'd be properly bowled out! You're a good-looking young fellow, I grant you, but he takes

224

the prize for looks, and fortune. And all London knows Miss Stansbury has adored the rascal since she was in the nursery. He has but to crook his little finger and she'll run to him. Never doubt it!"

Lying in bed that night, sleep eluding him, Cranford knew at last that he had more than "taken a fancy" to Miss Mary. 'Fool!' he thought, seething with frustration. 'I've loved her for weeks and never had the sense to know it!'

It was some time before he began to doze off, comforted by the determination that, fool or not, and whatever his great-uncle threatened, he would fight to win the girl he loved and do all he might to prevent her falling, dazzled, into the arms of . . . so worthless an individual as . . . Gervaise Valerian . . .

He slept the sleep of near exhaustion, and waking could not at first think what had disturbed him. He lay blinking into the darkness and decided drowsily that a rising wind was rattling the shutters.

The rattling persisted and grew louder. He tried to ignore it until it was augmented by a soft squealing sound that he at length realized was a voice; a woman's voice calling his name.

"Piers! . . . Lieutenant Cranford! Oh, *do* wake up! Please, *please* wake up!"

Mary! With a gasp he was fully awake, throwing back the blankets and snatching up his dressing-gown. It was pitch-dark, there was not so much as a glow from the fire on his hearth. It must be the middle of the night. She wouldn't come to his room at such an hour unless she was sleep-walking or there was some dire emergency. "Coming!" he called, and not stopping to put on his slippers, crossed swiftly to open the door, barely noticing the icy floor-boards under his bare feet.

Light flooded in from the candle Mary held high. She was clad in her night-rail, with a pretty beribboned cap tied under her chin, and a panicked look on her pale face. "Let me in!" she demanded, pushing past him.

"Whatever's wrong?" he asked anxiously. "It's not—"

"It's the shocking spinster," she said in a half-whisper. "And I know this is past forgiveness, so do pray close the door before the remnants of my reputation are in shreds."

"They will truly be in shreds if I do so," he said, hesitating. "You'd best tell me so I can—"

"It is—Florian!"

He closed the door.

"Something's happened to him?"

"Laura's abigail brought me a letter. Here." She thrust a rumpled paper at him. "Try if you can read it. She must have been in a dreadful state."

He lit his bedside candle from hers and unfolded the note. "She certainly must," he muttered, striving to decipher the blotched and ill-formed words. "Something about Helen and . . . her—*love*—is it? Who is Helen?"

"Not 'Helen'—*Heaven*! Standing beside him, Mary held her candle closer, and translated, " 'For the love of Heaven, find Lieutenant Piers Cranford and send him home! The most ghastly thing has chanced, Mary, and my father is raging and I dread lest he whips the people into—may God forbid!—into taking the law into their own hands. Our head groom, Sidney Grover—you know how he has always hated Florian—has been found beaten to death! Murdered! And my dearest love stands accused! He is innocent! I know it! But he was here and knocked Grover down this morning and Papa says he is a gypsy and has bad blood and—oh, Mary! Feeling is running very high. Please, *please* get word to Mr. Cranford before something dreadful happens! If I lose Florian I shall die of grief! The Lieutenant is our only hope! For pity's sake, help us. Your desolate friend, Laura."

Folding the letter mechanically, Cranford thought, 'Lord above! It would have be Grover!'

A small hand tugged at his arm; a sweet and anxious and beloved face peered up at him. "Will you go?"

"Of course. And you must go, Miss Mary. Quickly." Open-

226

ing the door, he looked up and down the passage. Aside from the bluster of the wind, all was quiet, and only one room showed a glow of light under the door. "Hurry," he whispered.

"Yes, but—you will let me know—"

Light flooded out as the other door swung open.

"Nobody will ask—" Stepping out, dressed for travel and pulling on his gauntlets, Gervaise Valerian's words were cut off abruptly. Halting as if briefly stunned, he then sauntered forward, his spurs jingling softly.

"Well, well, well," he sneered. "And what have I interrupted? A—um—tryst, perchance?"

Cranford said curtly, "Good night, ma'am," and hissed, "*Go*, dammit! Go!"

Mary hesitated. "Gervaise—'tis not what you think—"

He spread his hands, and purred, "But why should I think evil merely because I chance upon a chit leaving a fellow's bed-chamber—in the wee hours of the morning?"

Mary stared at him, then, with a helpless little shrug, hurried away.

Watching her, Valerian chuckled and murmured, "Truly, coz, you are a dark horse! I'd not have thought you had it in you to add the appellation 'strumpet' to the Stansbury's lurid repu——"

Cranford sprang forward and decked him.

14

Despite drifting clouds of fog, Cranford left word for Sudbury to return home as soon as the weather cleared, and rode out himself as the first hint of dawn glowed dimly in the veiled sky. The fog so altered the landscape that it was difficult to find his way. Twice, he took a wrong turn, and had all he could do to get back onto the Farnborough road. Fuming at these setbacks, he persisted stubbornly, but at length the vapours became so thick that he was forced to rein Tassels to a walk. Hours dragged past maddeningly before he came upon a small hedge tavern set back from the road and so wreathed in vapours as to be almost invisible. The air was penetratingly damp and chill, he was hungry and felt half frozen, and Tassels was shivering. He gave up and turned into the tavern yard. A solitary ostler ran out to him and as usual, Tassels was exclaimed over and made much of. Cranford left her in the hands of her admirer and went into the tavern.

It was a quaint little place, the beamed ceilings so low that they were but a few inches above his head. Copper bowls, kettles and plates set on shallow racks about the walls glowed in the light of the fire that crackled on the deep hearth. Several branches of candles sent out their soft radiance and the delectable aroma of freshly baked bread filled the air. There were only a few customers, most being obviously local people who were acquainted with one another. The host came forward to greet the new arrival. Shown to a settle in the ingle-nook, Cranford warmed his cold hands and ordered a tankard of home-brewed ale and the roast pork that was "almost ready."

The host, a round-faced, jolly little man, advised him to bespeak one of their two bedchambers. "This here fog has settled in, I can tell you, sir," he said cheerily. "Lived in this county man and boy for one and fifty year, I has, and I knows these here fogs, I do. Slide up the river from the sea, they does. Why, I've seen 'em set in so thick that folks has to wait days, sir, *days*, 'fore they can drive on." Cranford nodded but did not hire a room nor encourage more conversation, and after a shrewd glance at the stern young face, the host went off and advised his rosy-cheeked spouse that "the young gent in the ingle-nook has got Old Nick riding on his shoulders." He returned with the ale and set it before his troubled guest with a smile but without comment.

The ale was excellent and the fire warm. Cranford stretched out his legs gratefully and hoped that the host's meteorological predictions were not infallible. His heart sank when he drew out his timepiece and found that it was already past one o'clock. It was no use fretting against the fog, he had no choice but to wait, but the instant the beastly stuff thinned to the point that he could see his way, he would ride out and try to make up for lost time. He prayed that the fog was sufficiently widespread to keep his own people close to their hearths until he reached the village.

A plump serving maid came to announce with a shy and dimpling smile that dinner was ready and was set out on a table, "if y'worship would be so good as to come now, 'fore it gets cold."

Cranford followed her to a table set with a checkered cloth, a branch of candles, and a plate of fragrant roast pork with side dishes of roast potatoes, green beans, a loaf of still-warm bread, and a board of cheeses. He said it was a feast fit for a king, and found he had not exaggerated. While he ate, however, his thoughts inevitably turned to Florian. It was hard to believe that the gentle villagers would resort to violence, but he had witnessed the contagion of mass hysteria in the past, and knew the havoc a few cunning rabble-rousers could wreak. Constable Bragg would do his best to preserve law and order, he could count on that phlegmatic individual, and Bill Franck, also; the blacksmith liked Florian and would help. And if Oliver Dixon heard of the likelihood of mob violence, there was no doubt but that he'd leave the farm and go to the village, probably taking his sons and a couple of his men with him.

But it could not be denied that Gresford Finchley was a powerful landowner, accustomed to getting his own way, not above resorting to bullying or brutality if he deemed it necessary, and with only contempt for those he considered beneath his touch. Loathing the young steward, he would seize this opportunity to be rid of him forever, whether or not he was the murderer. And he was not! Of that Cranford was certain. There had been bad blood between the two men, admittedly, but at worst Florian would have acted only in self-defense. Grover had not been much liked and certainly not admired; even so, there had been a few rumblings of discontent when Florian had been appointed to the much-coveted position of Muse Manor steward. Those prejudices would be exacerbated by this unhappy development and played upon by the hostile Finchley.

He finished his dinner and was about to order coffee and a slice of sponge-cake when smoke billowed from the hearth. The wind must be getting up.

He strode quickly to the window, and his spirits lifted. The fog was indeed swirling about.

The host joined him. "Looks to be blowing clear, sir. But it might be local only, and thick again a few miles down the road. There's a cosy room with a nice soft bed above-stairs, and a warming pan 'twixt the sheets if you decide to stay."

"I wish I could," said Cranford briskly, "but I've urgent business. Be so good as to order up my mare at once, and my compliments to your cook for a most excellent meal. I've not enjoyed better in London."

Overcoming his disappointment, the host beamed with gratification and the serving maid beamed when she received a generous tip. Moments later, Cranford guided Tassels from the yard and they were off once more.

For some half-hour it was necessary to ride at a cautious speed, but gradually the fog dispersed, and at length he was able to give the mare her head. The miles slipped away and the fog was replaced by grey low-hanging clouds. The skies did not get much brighter; the air was cold, and occasional gusts of a bitter north-east wind deepened the chill.

More travellers were to be seen now, and soon a wooden belfry loomed against the sky. That would be the Parish Church of Farnborough, which meant he was nearly half-way home. If all went well, he would be in the village before dusk. But even as that optimistic thought crossed his mind, it was negated.

For years the authorities had ignored the advice of surveyors and had undertaken only token repairs on the rustic bridge that was a favourite route for local people. He himself had crossed it countless times rather than riding downstream to the new bridge; not to avoid the toll charge, but because the old structure was hump-backed and quaint, and situated where it offered sweeping views of the surrounding countryside. It had evidently succumbed at last to the ravages of wind and weather and fallen down, only some jagged planks remaining. It was a forlorn sight and a large sign warned redundantly that this bridge had collapsed and those wishing to cross the river should proceed to the new bridge some three miles to the west.

Cranford swore. The toll bridge was inexpertly run and he

had yet to cross it without encountering a long wait. The gate-keepers were notoriously slow in the best of weathers; on such an afternoon as this they were quite likely to have closed the gates when the fog was too thick for travel and might now be far behind in collecting the tolls. It could only mean another delay, delay neither he nor poor Florian could afford.

His apprehensions were confirmed when Tassels cantered to join the line of coaches, waggons, horsemen and pedestrians assembled with much grumbling before the still-closed gates. Even if the gatekeepers appeared now, reasoned Cranford ir-ritably, it would take an inordinate length of time for them to deal with all these people.

He reined Tassels aside and peered ahead.

"Be damned if I can see. They open up yet?" The deep growl emanated from a large coach and did not seem to match the skeletally thin gentleman who leaned from the window.

"No," answered Cranford. "What a stupid arrangement this is! If there were another way around—"

"Not lest you can fly, dear sir." The pretty but overdressed young woman seated next to the thin gentleman bent forward and eyed Cranford with pert and undisguised admiration, until she noticed the frown on the face of her companion. "Oh, what a lovely horsey!" she cooed then. "Do be a sweeting and buy me one like him, Pudding, dear."

"It ain't a him," growled the gentleman, with an embar-rassed glance at Cranford. "It's a her." And lowering his voice, he hissed, "And don't call me that in front of people!"

'Pudding?' thought Cranford, amused. The fellow looked more like a piece of string! But the words of the bold-eyed young woman whom one could only suppose to be his *chère amie,* echoed in his ears.

Someone at the head of the line was roaring a demand that the "curst stupid gates" be opened; a demand echoed at once by many irate voices.

Cranford scanned the gates thoughtfully. "... unless you can fly ..."

He reined around and cantered past the travellers who had already gathered behind him.

"Givin' it up, is yer, guv'nor?" enquired a wizened little man pushing a barrow laden with new brooms and brushes. "Can't say as I blames yer."

"Thank you, but I'm not." Cranford bent forward and stroked the mare's warm neck. "I must ask for your best effort again, lass," he murmured. "But you can do this, I know!"

Tassels whickered softly and tossed her head.

The man with the barrow, who had watched this exchange with interest, called, "Wotcher goin' ter do, milor'? You don't never mean ter try and—"

"Oh, yes, I do," said Cranford, and shouted, "Stand clear!"

Heads turned and people sprang back as Tassels thundered past the line, accompanied by whoops and shouts variously critical and encouraging.

Give 'em pitch, guv'nor!"

"No! It's too high!"

"Wake 'em up, sir!"

"... break your neck, you young fool!"

The gate was indeed high. Crouched in the saddle, leaning forward over Tassels' mane, Cranford talked to her, and with complete trust she obeyed the hands and heels that guided her so surely.

The cold air whipped at Cranford's hair.

They soared high into the air and cleared the gates with scant inches to spare under Tassels' tucked-up back hooves.

Cheers rent the air.

The mare stumbled, but with a heart-felt murmur of "Thank the Lord!" Cranford held her together and caressed her fondly. She was blowing but tossed her pretty head as if she understood and was proud of her achievement. He turned her and tapped her shoulder for her famous equine bow, and the cheers were louder.

Belatedly, a gatekeeper ran from the gatehouse, roaring, "Ey! You come back 'ere, me fine young nob!" which evoked jeers and laughter, whereupon he added something to the effect that "we don't allow none o' that 'ere!" and shouted demands for the fee or he would " 'ave the law on the owdacious criminal." Cranford threw him the fee, but responded that "the law" might be interested to hear of his laziness. He flourished his hat at the cheering onlookers, and told Tassels what a good girl she was as they resumed this desperate journey.

There were no more delays, and the mare did her gallant best, but he had to stop twice to rest her, knowing she would run until she dropped if he asked it. The roar and bustle of the city had long since been replaced by the gentle serenity of country woods and meadows. The chattering of birds, busied with their evening reunions, and the occasional voices of sheep or cattle were the only sounds to disturb the silence until they came upon a flock of geese waddling along, all talking at once. Cranford smiled and waved to the goose girl, who blushed and curtsied shyly.

The short winter afternoon had faded to dusk when they were at last turning onto the lane that led to the village. Above the trees Cranford could see smoke rising from cottage chimneys. He was still some distance away and he sighed with relief because thus far there was no sign of trouble.

Minutes later, the abbreviated church steeple loomed against the darkening sky, and with it a new and fearful sound. A distant muttering that grew to a confused uproar and became at last the voice he had dreaded to hear: the mindless howling of an infuriated mob.

As he came nearer, the darkness was lit by a flickering brightness. He could discern individual voices now, and as he rounded the last bend in the lane he beheld a sight he had never expected to see in this peaceful corner of England. A crowd of men was gathered in front of the tiny village gaol. The blazing torches they held aloft cast a lurid glow on faces so contorted with rage and hatred that he scarcely recognized them for his own people. Major Finchley was there, flanked by several of his men, all urging the crowd on, shouting epithets against "filthy thieving gypsies" and "foreign murderers." Cranford was astonished to see his twin, a cane in one hand and a riding crop in the other, standing resolutely with his back to the gaol. Peddars, their footman, was to his left side, and Oliver Dixon, appropriately wielding a long-tined hay-fork, stood at his right.

Peregrine was trying to talk some sense into the crowd, but Finchley's bull-like roars drowned his efforts.

"We all know the Cranfords welcome thieves and poachers," he bellowed. "Give 'em shelter even when we catch one of the worthless scum red-handed! Much they care if we're all robbed blind!"

"*They* ain't never bin robbed!" howled a man Cranford had never seen before. "What do they care if *we* is?"

Piers started Tassels forward.

Peregrine caught sight of him and gestured urgently for him to stay back.

Knowing his twin, Piers hesitated. Perry's message had been silent but clear, "Keep out of this, big brother! I can handle it!" Perhaps he could. Certainly, he wouldn't welcome interference. Piers reined Tassels to a halt. He would wait. For a minute or two. Unless this ugly mess became uglier.

A powerfully built stranger with a shock of curly hair shouted, "No, *they* ain't never robbed! And we knows why! 'Cause they offer the poaching swine pertection, *that's* why!"

"And now one of their gypsy friends has took the life of a good neighbour!"

"Aye! English-born and -bred!"

"So what we goin' ter do?" The tall ruffian who never seemed to talk below a howl stepped close to Peregrine, and

235

demanded, "What yer say, mates? Let 'em set him free? They will, mark me words! All in it together, they is and thinks 'emselves above the law what you and me has ter obey or be hung or transported!"

This brought shouts of approval and the crowd moved in, but paused as the gaol door opened.

Constable Bragg stepped outside, holding a musket. His pleasant face was stern and he said with the voice of authority, "Now, you men, get on home and don't do something as you'll be sorry for tomor——"

Someone threw a rock and the constable reeled back, his musket falling.

Peregrine snatched it up, but with a triumphant howl the crowd surged forward and the weapon was torn from his grasp. "Don't listen to these bullies!" he shouted, struggling desperately. "They've been brought in, don't you see? Major Finchley——"

But there was no stopping the crowd now; inflamed with blood-lust, they charged at Peregrine and his loyal supporters, shouting their intention to drag out "the dirty gypsy" and treat him to "some real justice!"

The deafening crack of a pistol shot stopped the charge, and the shouting ceased abruptly.

Major Gresford Finchley jerked around, his red face twisting with wrath as he saw Piers Cranford, mounted on Tassels, the pistol in his hand levelled and steady despite the mare's nervous sidling.

The attention of the crowd shifted as they all turned to face the new arrival. There were mutterings of "It do be the Squire! . . ." "Mr. Piers is come back! . . ."

Piers said sternly, "What are you fellows about? You don't behave like this! You're good, decent men. You know Constable Bragg will——"

From somewhere a man howled, "He'll do whatever you tell him! Aye, we knows that, Cranford! You rich folks is all alike! Come on, you chaps! Don't be cowed by that young nob! We're free men and we'll show his gypsy friends they can't get away with murder in our village!"

The Reverend Mr. Barrick tried to force his way through the crowd, his hands upraised and his falsetto voice warning of heavenly retribution if violence were committed, but he was surrounded, and, amid shouts that violence had already been committed, disappeared from view.

Major Finchley roared that Piers Cranford's pistol had been fired, "so you men have nothing to fear from him."

"But that was my other pistol," responded Piers, indicating the still-smoking weapon now in the saddle holster.

"Perhaps so," blustered Finchley. "But you're not the only man with a pistol! Have a look at this, friends!" He nodded to the tall curly-haired ruffian who had made his way ever closer and now sprang at Peregrine, levelling a long-barrelled weapon at his side.

Peddars and Dixon, who had started to his support, halted uncertainly.

"That good fellow don't mean to kill your brother," jeered Finchley. "But if you value his health, I advise you to put down your weapon."

Some of the local men drew back at this, markedly uneasy.

Piers sat motionless, knowing he had no choice. No matter what Finchley said, that curly-haired varmint looked savagely eager to fire, and another wound would very likely kill Perry. Helpless, he lowered the pistol, and it was torn from his hand by another of the imported bravos.

With a shout of triumph, Finchley urged the men to rush the gaol, braying that he would hold "the gypsy lovers" at bay while justice was done.

The curly-haired ruffian watched, grinning. Seizing his opportunity, Peregrine snatched for the pistol. The ruffian, stronger, tore it away, then flailed it at him in a vicious swipe that staggered him.

Enraged, Piers launched himself from the saddle and with a sizzling uppercut sent the ruffian sprawling. "You could hang for that, you cowardly varmint!" he cried furiously, then, seized by many hands, he was wrenched back.

Finchley sprang forward, levelling his pistol and bellowing, "My groom was brutally murdered! I'm within my rights to hang his killer!"

"Not on our property!" cried Piers. "You're trespassing, damn you! Consett is entitled to a fair trial!"

There were hoots of mocking laughter. Piers was immobilized by an arm twisted up behind him and a group of men overcame Dixon and Peddars and rushed into the gaol.

They emerged, dragging Florian. Battered and bruised, he met Piers' eyes in silent desperation, and whitened as a great shout of triumph greeted his appearance.

There was some discussion as to the method of his execution. A few put forward the suggestion to "drown the murderer in our pond!" Some yelled for a hanging. Little Ezra Sweet piped a ferocious demand that the gypsy warranted beheading and expressed the conviction that there were several fine axes in use in the neighbourhood.

Standing very straight, Florian listened in white-faced silence to all these proposals for his death.

It was clear that these men, most of whom were normally kind and law-abiding citizens had, at this moment, lost all semblance of rationality. Desperate, Piers stamped down on the toe of one of the bullies gripping his right arm, and as the man hopped and cursed luridly, swung his free fist at the burly stranger who had kept such a punishing grip on his left wrist.

He won clear, and fighting his way through the crowd, he shouted, "Don't bring this shame on our village! Don't let these hired bullies—"

A club struck at him, and the scene wavered and spun. Still striving, he was dully aware that there were too many. Finchley had won, and Florian would be murdered, in spite of—

A shrill scream.

Laughter.

Blinking dazedly, he saw Ezra Sweet's granddaughter, a militant expression on her comely face, dragging the wailing old man away by the ear.

A howl rent the air, and one of Finchley's bullies retreated before Mrs. Bragg, who swung a rolling-pin with verve while declaring fiercely, "I seed you throw that rock and knock my husband down, you great ugly villin! We don't want your kind in our village! Be off with ye!"

More shouts of alarm rang out as a small and familiar figure flailing a blazing torch to left and right, cried, "How *dare* you come here with your . . . wicked lies! Go back . . . where you belong, you nasty . . . creatures!"

His curls frizzing, the tall bully who had struck Peregrine let out a shriek and fled to stick his head in the pond.

"Don't be beaten by that shameless hussy," roared Finchley, in an effort to rally his troops. "She's the wench who lived with a lot of heathen cannibals on—"

Piers tore free of hands that seemed to have lost their strength and lunged for the Major. "*You* had that stable fire set and cut my saddle girth, you cowardly poltroon!" he roared, his fist whizzing for the Major's jaw.

Hurled backward, Finchley disappeared from view.

The village green was suddenly full of women carrying weapons that varied from a steaming kettle to a wet mop, and using them with enthusiastic vigour.

Finchley was no longer to be seen, and it was the beginning of the end. The ranks of vengeance-inspired would-be executioners split and, cowering, reverted to husbands and fathers caught making mischief.

The organizers of that mischief saw the writing on the wall, and following the example of the man who had hired them, drifted into the night.

Piers began an anxious search for Mary, but it appeared

239

that she also had left the scene. Oliver Dixon, a cut on his arm being attended to by his wife, imparted breathlessly that two coaches had pulled up soon after Cranford's arrival. He had seen a female leave one. He supposed it to have been Miss Westerman. "She's a rare plucked-un, that young lady," he said admiringly. "Blest if I know what the Major meant about . . . ow! Gently, woman! About her living with cannibals; d'you understand it, sir?"

"When Major Finchley is annoyed, there's no knowing what he'll say," Piers answered. "Pay it no heed, and— Did you say you saw *two* coaches? Who was in the second?"

Dixon said he didn't know, but his wife, who had been on the fringes of the crowd, said she'd seen a gentleman inside.

Piers asked sharply, "Did you know him?"

Mrs. Dixon shook her head. "He never got out of the coach, sir. And it were dark, y'know, so I couldn't see clear. Funny, though. I could swear as I'd seen him afore . . . though when or where, is what I can't put my finger on."

He thought grimly that it might well have been Joshua Pedlar sniffing about again, in which case the man was a safe distance from Tio.

Mary's lovely image commandeered his attention, as it so often did. Perhaps she had decided to overnight at the Westerman cottage. He would very much have liked to find her and thank her for her help in their battle, but it was late, and she must be tired. He decided to seek her out in the morning, and went instead to the gaol, where he found Florian occupying the solitary cell and talking with Peregrine and the constable. Mr. Bragg was pale and shaken, with a discoloured lump above his eye where the rock had hit home.

Piers said, "You'll have a fine bruise there, Bragg. You'd better get to your bed."

"I were just telling Sir Peregrine as I mean to lock up now, sir," said the constable. "Though I'll take my rest here tonight, just in case of more trouble. A fine state of affairs England's come to, when a gentleman hires Mohocks and the like to invade a peaceful village and get its honest citizens so drunk they forget who they are!"

"Drunk?" Piers turned to his brother. "What's all this?"

"It seems our generous neighbour hauled in three barrels of ale this afternoon," answered Peregrine grimly. "And set them up in the smithy, inviting everyone to celebrate."

"Celebrate what? The steeplechase? If he claimed to have won, he's a confounded liar. Roly Mathieson was the winner!"

"He was?" Peregrine looked disappointed and Florian said a dismayed "Jove, Mr. Piers! I was sure our Tassels would come in first."

Peregrine said, "So was I." Noting his brother's expression, he added, "There's a story to be told, I see. But to answer your question, Piers, Finchley claimed he was giving a party to honour Bragg."

"On account of I'd been so quick to get the murderer of his groom behind bars." The constable shook his head. "That ale were powerful strong and our folk hean't accustomed to making so free. In no time at all half the men was up in the world, which is why they got so ugly."

Piers muttered, "Why, that cunning rogue. So that's how he whipped up his hanging party! And damn near got his way!"

"I'm more grateful than I can say that you all helped me." Florian's voice was husky with emotion. "I didn't do it, Mr. Piers. I swear on my honour! Sid Grover was a mean-spirited bully with a vicious temper. I'll not pretend I didn't loathe him. But if I ever kill a man it won't be by bashing his head in from behind."

Peregrine asked, "Can you think of anyone with reason to murder him? And who would do the thing as you describe?"

Florian hesitated, and his dark eyes fell.

Bragg said, "I axed him the same, sir. He says he don't know of no one."

"Does he not, by Jove!" exclaimed Piers. "I could name you a dozen who thoroughly disliked the fellow, and there are very likely as many more! Where was it done?"

"I found him in the spinney just this side of the boundary line," said Florian.

"*You* found him? You silly clod! What the devil were you doing down there after I'd distinctly warned you— Oh, never mind, I know the answer to that. You went to see Laura Finchley again! Small wonder they charged you!"

Florian gripped the bars of his cell and said earnestly, "Yes, that's truth. I did hope to see her. I love her. If you had ever loved, sir, you'd know what it's like to be kept from the lady you care for. But on the way home I all but fell over the—the body." He shuddered and closed his eyes for an instant. "I hope I never see such a sight again. It was hideous!"

Piers stared at him blankly. "If you had ever loved . . ."

A male hand was tight on his shoulder. Peregrine said sternly, "Speaking of awful sights, you look burnt to the socket, and we have things to discuss, twin."

It was, thought Piers uneasily, the moment of truth.

Half an hour later, clad in his dressing-gown and seated before the fire in the Muse Manor drawing room, he accepted the glass of Madeira Peregrine handed him. It was as well that Aunt Jane had gone upstairs. She had been overjoyed to welcome her two "dear boys" home again, but she was greatly worried about Florian. They'd done what they might to allay her fears and she had kissed them good night and declared she would sleep easier knowing they were there. "You will want to talk," she'd said fondly, "so I'll leave you. I know you'll find a way to resolve this latest disaster." He had pretended not to see Perry's searching stare, and now, trying to sound indignant, he argued, "No such thing! In Town I told you about our leaky roof and the collapse of the steeple at St. Mark's."

"So you did. A bone for the poor dog, eh? What you did *not* see fit to impart was the flood that took our poor Gertrude, and the fire at old Ezra Sweet's cottage."

Piers shifted uneasily in his chair. He was ill prepared for this interrogation, for he ached with tiredness, his bruises throbbed unpleasantly, and he was beset by a nagging worry about Mary. Several people had told him they'd seen her coach drive away, but perhaps she had not gone to the cottage. Possibly, her Aunt Lucretia had accompanied her on the journey to the village and had insisted on an immediate return to London. His frown eased to a tender smile. He had no doubt but that it was Mary who'd inspired the Muse Village ladies to march to Florian's rescue. Bless her brave heart! But how she had managed to arrive so soon after him was a puzzle. Stifling a sigh, he realized that his brother was still speaking and that he sounded extremely vexed.

". . . may grin, but I am no longer a child, Piers! You saved my life after Prestonpans, for which I shall be eternally—"

"Oh, stubble it, for heaven's sake!"

"Very well. But I am sick to death of having you shoulder everything that goes awry and keeping me in the dark so as to protect me! I am eight and twenty—"

"Of which I'm very well aware, *twin!*"

"Then be aware that I do not need to be protected! I've the right to be told if problems arise concerning our estate. I'd hoped the part I played last year when Ross and Falcon and the rest of us were battling the Squire and his nest of traitors would have given you some respect for me!"

"Of course I respect you! I fancy all England respects you. You won yourself a knighthood, did you not? Don't be such a lunkhead!"

"There! You *do* choose to think of me as a lunkhead! And you continue to shut me out as if I were a frail child and you my steadfast guardian!"

"You're talking nonsense!" Irritated, Piers stood. "And I'm going to bed."

"Oh, no, you're not!" Peregrine stepped in front of him and said with rare harshness, "We'll have this out now, if you please. I want the whole, with no bark on it! I'll tell you that I already know more than you think."

"Tomorrow, Perry, I'm very tired and—"

"Yes, I can see that, and I know you've had a frightful day. But you deserve being called to account and the sooner we get this done, the better! Sit—down—big brother."

Looking into the angry glitter in the blue eyes that were, he knew, so much like his own, Piers heard again Mary's words when they'd been riding near the park that fateful morning. "I don't envy you when you must confess the whole."

With a rueful sigh he sat down.

Half an hour later, Peregrine looked aghast, and after a stunned silence exclaimed, "Why, you poor old birdwit! How in the name of Gabriel and all the angels did you carry on through such a tide of disasters? As God is my judge, Piers, I could deck you when I think— And speaking of decking someone— how did you leave Valerian?"

"Flat on his back."

"He'll challenge, you realize."

"Of course. I left him my card."

"Then I'll be your second."

"Thank you, kind sir. Am I permitted to seek out my bed at last?"

Peregrine pursed his lips, and as they both stood, he said thoughtfully, "I'm aware you don't like him, but you'll own he is no coward?"

"I'll own that, yes."

"Does it occur to you that he may really have come to care for Miss Stansbury and was dealt a leveller when he saw her leaving your bedchamber at that hour?"

"No. Gervaise Valerian has a love affair with only one person in this world. His dandified self."

Side by side, candlesticks in hand, they climbed the stairs.

"There's still much to be done," said Peregrine. "Finchley, for instance."

"Tio is claiming first right to call him out."

"From what you've told me, I fancy Tio may have to wait his turn. Our ignoble Major must have made a whole troop of enemies during that race!"

Piers smiled without mirth. "Assuredly. I must see how Tio goes on."

"I fancy his lady is with him. You *did* get word to his people?"

"He straitly forbade it. Don't look at me like that! He's a grown man and has a right to protect his family. I had asked Florian to tell Amy, but he never had the chance. Just as well."

"You're two of a kind," said Peregrine drily. "Very well, I'll seek out the chawbacon while you see what can be done for Florian and keep an eye on our sinister pedlar. Jupiter! What a bumble-broth we're in! But at least I have wrung the truth from you, twin."

Piers nodded. "We'll talk in the morning, when I can get my brain-box to work properly." He slapped his brother on the back. "Good night, Perry. It will be good to have your help in all this."

Turning into his bedchamber, he felt a twinge of guilt. Actually, he had not told his twin everything. He hadn't revealed his struggles to buy the river parcel and his reasons for wanting the property. He hadn't revealed his suspicions that both the flood and the attack on Perry and young Grainger had been contrived. Nor had he mentioned the shot that had so narrowly missed him when he'd been driving Florian home in the cart.

As the silent Blake pulled his boots off, Piers thought wearily that he had a right to keep his prospective wedding gift a secret. Also, he had no real proof about the flood, nor the rest of it. Only suspicion. And in the eyes of the law, suspicion paid no toll.

In bed at last, he stretched out gratefully. First thing tomorrow, he would discover if Mary had gone back to London. If she had instead decided to overnight at the cottage, he would have a chance to see her. Smiling at this thought, he fell asleep.

15

ranford awoke to pale winter sunshine and the awareness that he had added several more bruises to his colourful collection. He climbed stiffly out of bed, swore, and gripped his right arm, which the blow from a club had left lurid and painful. Taking up his timepiece, he groaned with vexation. It was nigh ten o'clock and he had intended to be at the village by eight.

Blake appeared in answer to his tug on the bell-pull. Suave and enigmatic as ever, the valet murmured his apologies for having failed to awaken his employer as instructed. "You looked so very worn, sir. When I was unable to wake you at six o'clock, I consulted Sir Peregrine and we thought it best to let you have your sleep out."

Cranford informed him in no uncertain terms that he expected his orders to be obeyed. Gathering the shaving impedimenta, Blake bowed and undertook to comply in future, and in response to Cranford's next enquiry divulged that Sir Peregrine had already left the Manor. "He apologized for his abrupt departure but said you would know where he is gone, and why."

Perry had said they would talk this morning. He had evidently changed his mind. Cranford tilted his head as soap was applied to his chin, and asked somewhat apprehensively, "Did my brother appear at all—out of sorts?"

"Not that I could tell, sir. A trifle preoccupied, perhaps, but he very kindly offered my nephew a seat in his coach for as far as Short Shrift, where Herbert can catch the stage-coach back to London."

"Your nephew was here? Did he bring a message from Lord Nugent?"

"No, sir. In fact, I fear he had—er, taken French leave, as they say. He is much attached to me and tends to bring me his troubles." The razor was swung aside. "If you will be so kind as to be still for a minute or two . . ."

In the interest of self-preservation Cranford complied with this request and tried to stifle his impatience. As Perry had said last night, there was much to be done, and time had a fiendish habit of slipping away.

The shave completed, Blake brushed and powdered Cranford's thick hair, and tied it back neatly. His later attempt to attach a snowy jabot to the stock was summarily rejected. Cranford said indignantly, "What are you about, you sly rascal? You know I do not care to have lace foaming out under my chin! Plain, if you please!"

The valet sighed. "If you would but wear a wig, sir. I fear you are sadly out of the fashion."

"Very likely," said Cranford shortly, and having shrugged into the riding coat Blake held for him, he hurried in search of his aunt.

Mrs. Burrows came into the breakfast parlour in answer to his ring. She explained that Peddars had sustained a black eye during the struggle at Muse Village and Miss Jane feared the footman may also have a broken nose, so had taken him to the apothecary. Setting a plate of eggs and sliced ham before him, she shook her head and said heavily, "By what I heard, that

248

was a shameful to-do last evening, Mr. Piers. Sir Peregrine looked quite pulled this morning, I thought."

"Did you!" In the act of removing a piece of toast from the rack, Cranford asked, "Was his limp worse?"

Devoted as ever, the housekeeper nodded. "Seemed to me as it was, sir. I know he was beaten in London, which surely did not help matters. He shouldn't be rushing about from pillar to post so soon afterwards. As I told him." She sniffed and filled his coffee cup. "Much good it did me. I can but be glad, sir, as you took no serious harm. The world's gone mad, so it has, when the Quality can be attacked on their own estate!"

He said gently, "And you're worried about Florian, are you not?"

"Fair worried sick, I am, Mr. Piers." Her voice trembled and she said shakily, "He's a fine young gentleman and wouldn't do such a heathen thing. Though—not wanting to speak ill of the dead, I'm bound to own that Sid Grover was not a good man and was bound to come to a bad end soon or late."

Cranford recalled her words as he rode Tassels into the village. He agreed with the housekeeper's sentiments but could wish that Grover had come to his "bad end" somewhere other than on Muse Manor land.

When he reached the village, his reception brought a furtive grin to his lips. Every female he encountered sent a smile his way, while the men avoided his eyes even as they touched their brows respectfully. Constable Bragg looked tired but was pleased to report that all was quiet today, and there had been no further trouble. "Keep alert," advised Cranford. "This being a case of murder, we'll have Runners down here today, I fancy. I may be out at the Westerman cottage for an hour or so this morning, but you can reach me there, or at the Manor, if you need me."

Bragg looked worried, but nodded and took Cranford back to the cell. Florian greeted him eagerly. There was a look of desperation in his dark eyes and when Cranford went inside and sat on the cot beside him he stammered that he could not endure to be locked up in such a confined space. "I suppose 'tis because I lived outdoors so much as a child," he muttered. "These walls suffocate me. If I am condemned to spend the rest of my life shut up . . . My God! I had sooner be dead!"

Cranford gripped his shoulder and shook it, saying sternly that he wanted to hear no more of such nonsense. "You've to deal with a nasty bump in life's road, Florian, but you have friends who will stand by you, and a sweet lady who cares for you. It was Miss Finchley sent me word of your trouble, you know."

Florian brightened and asked, "Is that why you came, Mr. Piers? I daren't hope you would get here in time." His eyes clouded again. "If you had not come . . ."

"Well, we did come. My brother and I, and Peddars and Oliver Dixon and others. Peddars is at the apothecary this very minute because he took a broken nose during the little—er, fracas."

"I shall have to thank him, poor fellow. And—the ladies! . . . Gad! Was that Miss Stansbury who swung the torch? What a swath she cut!"

Cranford chuckled. "She did, indeed. And trimmed the hair of one of the Major's hired bravos!" He paused, then asked quietly, "You have no notion of who really killed Grover?"

A brief pause, then, "None, sir."

Cranford looked at him steadily. "Why have I the feeling you protect someone?"

The dark eyes shifted. Gazing at the door, Florian answered, "I don't know, sir."

"I see." Standing, Cranford said, "If you should change your mind, lad, send for me at once."

In the small office he asked for the constable's view of the matter.

Bragg looked solemn. "If young Mr. Consett is shielding

someone, sir, he's a fool and will likely pay the full penalty under the law. The Bow Street men don't know him as we do, and since Grover was a commoner I fancy they'll not waste much time on looking for the guilty party. Consett will hang, sure as check. He hated the man and were found bending over the body with blood on his hands. 'Tis all the proof Bow Street will need."

"They won't hang my steward if I can help it," said Cranford grimly. He opened the door, then turned back. "By the bye, has that pedlar fellow come around lately?"

"Joshua, you mean?" Bragg took himself by the chin and considered. "Not for a week or thereabouts, I think. Likely on his rounds. Them as follows that trade don't stay in one place for long, y'know, sir. No telling where he might have gone."

'If I'm guessing rightly,' thought Cranford, 'Joshua has been in London Town these past two weeks. Hot on the trail of one foolhardy rebel!'

He retrieved Tassels and allowed several small hands to reach into his saddle-bag for the sweetmeats he carried there on such occasions. Their innocent squeaks of childish joy brought a grin to his face as he mounted up, returned their farewells, and then rode towards Quail Hill and the Westerman cottage. He had to rein in sharply, however, as a frail figure tottered out in front of him.

Ezra Sweet flourished his cane erratically, causing Tassels to shy in alarm. "What's to become of I, Squire?" he demanded in his shrill, querulous voice. "I axes ye! What's to become of a poor old chap like I be?"

"If you jump in front of a large horse in that foolish fashion you'll likely not be much older," snapped Cranford, stroking the mare's neck soothingly.

"Easy fer you to say," wailed the old man. "You got a fine roof over yer head, and yer own fire ter sit by of a evening. What has I got? Nought! Ye promised me a new cottage, Lieutenant Piers! Ye *promised!*" His voice quavered, and he went on

251

brokenly, "And I does not hesitate ter—ter say as—Squire or no, it bean't kindly fer a rich gent like you be . . . to go disappointing of a poor old chap as likely . . . won't live long enough to enjoy—" He broke off, dabbing a vivid purple kerchief at his eyes.

Touched, Cranford said in a kinder tone, "Never despair, Ezra. I keep my promises. You should know that."

"Aye, but—how? That's what I axes ye. How? And when? Now that yer gypsy steward's going to hang, as 'tis just and proper he should, though if I had my way—"

"Yes, well, we all know your way," interrupted Cranford. "But Mr. Consett is innocent, and will neither hang nor lose his head."

"So *ye* do say! There's them as says there'll be Runners from Bow Street come, roaring and stamping and clumping down here with pistols and handicuffs and chains ter drag him away and top him. What ye think 'bout that, Squire?"

"I think you would do well not to listen to such foolish gossip. I doubt very much if Bow Street will take Mr. Consett away. And if they do—"

"Or if they a'ready *has*," inserted Ezra, a sly grin creeping into his rheumy old eyes.

Cranford frowned at him. "Now what are you hinting?"

"Not *me,* Squire! Oh, never me! Minds his *p*'s and *q*'s, do Ezry Sweet. Allus has. 'Tis why he's lived to be such a very old man. But—" He stepped closer and, clinging to the stirrup, hissed, "There's them as holds Bow Street is here a'ready. And has been here many and many a day. Slithering about, axing questions, picking up a snip here and a snap there! And if 'tis truth, ye'd be wise, Squire, ter keep clear o' some of yer fine friends. 'Specially them as has unnatural strange green eyes and red hair under their fancy wigs!"

A chill shivered between Cranford's shoulder-blades. He said curtly, "You speak slander, and that can carry a gaol sentence, Sweet."

The old man quailed, and babbled nervously, "No, no, sir! Not me, Squire! And 'tis all woman talk and spoke in whispers, mind. Whispers as holds that Joshua pedlar bean't a pedlar 'tall, but a Army spy, hunting down Rebs." Recovering again, he said hoarsely, "And there be another whisper, jest a whisper, mind, as says that there lord friend o' yours—the one with them nasty green eyes—were out with Bonnie Charlie!"

"Nonsense! You shouldn't listen to such malicious gabble! And what is more, Ezra, you had best hope the gossips don't stir up trouble for his lordship. Viscount Glendenning is a splendid architect and has promised me that just in case Florian is delayed in building you a new cottage, he is willing to help. If he should hear how you speak against him, however—"

"Oh, don't ye go saying nothing, Squire! A poor feeble old man begs of ye!" The cane was thrown down. Raising gripped hands prayerfully, Sweet begged, "I do get took foolish-like at times, sir. My Bessie, she says I oughta be 'shamed. And I is, Squire. I won't say no more! I swear it! If ye'll just not tell his lor'ship—"

He looked really close to tears now, and Cranford said, "Very well. But think twice before you say such things, Ezra, or you may be living with Bessie longer than you plan!"

Ezra shuddered at this terrible prospect, and Cranford rode out followed by fervent vows never to lend his ears to gossip again.

The gates to the Westerman cottage were closed and there was no sign of life. Disappointed, he turned to leave, but decided to ride a short distance towards Quail Hill, just in case Mary was searching for her beads again. There was no feminine figure in sight today; no pretty pink gown rippling in the breeze. Dismounting, he began to walk, letting Tassels wander, while he sought about in the meadow grasses, hoping that he might please her by finding one of her precious beads. Luck was with him; he saw a small glint half-hidden under a weed and retrieved another bead, a blue one this time, larger than the others and smooth. He was cleaning it with his handkerchief when a shadow fell across the grass and he turned quickly.

Mary stood stroking Tassels and smiling at him. Today she wore a cloak of dark red velvet clasped high to the throat with large gold buttons; the hood, richly embroidered with gold thread, framed her face. There were roses in her cheeks and her bright eyes echoed her smile. Tongue-tied, he thought, "How lovely she is. And how could I have been such a fool as not to see it?"

"I am so glad you came, Lieutenant Piers," she said and reached out to him.

He thrust his handkerchief into his pocket hurriedly so as to take her hand. "And I am very . . ." His voice sounded strained and hoarse in his ears. He coughed and apologized, feeling clumsy and stupid, and stammered, "I am glad . . . also. Er—that *you* came, I mean. And—and—oh, Mary, you were splendid last evening! I tried to find you afterwards, but you'd gone. I wish you had not. I wanted to thank you."

"Thank *me?* You are the one stopped those dreadful men from murdering Florian! I think I have never been so angry as when that coward clubbed you down from behind."

"Even so, I was properly vanquished till you charged so bravely to the rescue."

She chuckled and they began to walk slowly up the hill together. "I had my little army, don't forget," she said.

"I am never like to forget such dauntless Amazons."

"From what I have read"—Mary glanced at him from under her lashes—"the Amazons were very warlike women, strong and aggressive and always fighting. Is that . . . how you think of me?"

" 'Tis a picture I shall carry to my grave! You swinging that blazing torch—cutting a swath through the crowd! I am all admiration!"

"Are you?" She stopped and looked up at him. "I would have

254

thought you the type of gentleman to admire a dainty and petite lady; the shy, gentle sort."

"Much good a dainty and petite lady would have done me last evening!"

"Oh." A small frown wrinkled her brow so briefly that he did not see it. Her lashes fell. Walking on again, she asked, "Do you think Florian has any chance of proving his innocence?"

"No. I think we must prove it for him. How is Miss Finchley taking all this?"

"She is shattered, poor dear. And what makes it worse is that her horrid papa is gloating and triumphant because he says the guilty party is in gaol and— Well, he delights to describe Florian's dreadful fate. If only we knew what really happened. Have you any suspicions at all?"

"Many. Grover was far from popular and several men had good reason to hold a grudge 'gainst him. But I had a strong impression last night that Florian knows more than he has said and is shielding someone."

"My goodness!" She touched his arm and asked urgently, "Did you tax him with it?"

"Yes." He put his hand over her fingers. "He denied it. I think the only person he might confide in would be his lady. Do you suppose Miss Finchley might be persuaded to visit him?"

"In *gaol?* Heavens—no! The Major would never permit it."

"If it were a matter of life and death . . ."

"And you think it might be?"

"If it were indeed—and if I were able to help her, would she dare to defy her father and slip away?"

Mary pondered worriedly, then shook her head. "I very much doubt it. She is a gentle creature." Another searching glance was slanted at him. "Not," she murmured, "an Amazon . . . like me."

"Very true." He drew her to a halt. She seemed a little flushed. He wondered if she guessed what he was going to say,

255

and taking a deep breath, nerved himself and began, "Miss Mary, it seems an age, but I know it is not long since I spoke, and I am probably rushing my fences. But—you know me a little better now, I think. Will you not consider my offer?"

Mary stood very still, gazing at a gorse bush, her face expressionless.

His heart pounding madly, Cranford waited through a pause that seemed endless.

Mary broke it at length, saying in a calm way, "The last time you offered, Mr. Cranford, you implied that you did so because your family felt responsible for my—disgrace. Is that why you have spoken again? Do you feel further obligated to rescue this . . . notorious Amazon?"

"Much I care about notoriety," he declared, staunchly if not wisely. "Besides, once you are a married lady, people will forgive your—er—"

"My torrid past? You fancy your name will offer me a shield 'gainst the condemnation of the *ton*? And what of yourself, sir? Would you not be criticized for wedding such a scarlet woman?"

He said with a shrug, "To say truth, we live rather 'out of the world' at Muse Manor. I seldom know what the rumour mills are brewing in London. Nor do I care. If you could be content with country life, we need seldom go into Town."

Her laugh sounded a trifle shrill. "La, sir! How uncomfortable for you to feel the need to keep your bride shut away from Society!"

Sensing belatedly that this was not going the way he had hoped, he said, "If I feel a need, it is to cherish and protect a very brave lady—"

"And to reward her bravery with a gold ring that will lift her from degradation to respectability!" She looked up at him, and he was dismayed to see that her hazel eyes were bright with wrath. "Thank you, kind sir," she said mockingly. "You are more than generous, but I am not so desperate as—"

"No!" Seizing both her arms he said, "Mary! I do not offer

for your hand as a 'reward'! Acquit me of such intolerable conceit!"

"Why, then?" she demanded fiercely. "Why would you wed me knowing I love another man?"

Cranford flinched. "Hoping that perhaps, in time, you might find you did not know your own heart."

"Stuff!" she said rudely, wrenching free. "Your pardon if I mistrust such unselfish generosity. I find it more likely that your great-uncle snapped his fingers under your nose again, so that once more you dance to his tune!"

"In point of fact, Lord Nugent forbade me to offer at all! He is convinced that Valerian has formed a *tendre* for you, which would—"

"Which would restore your family honour! Assuming, of course, that I accept such a belated offer, and, with floods of grateful tears, cast myself at his feet!"

Very pale now, Cranford said, "And you must pardon me if *I* find it questionable that you would reject such an offer!"

"I will not pardon you, sir! For you may believe I would reject *any* such offer from any so-called 'gentleman'!" Contemptuous, she added, "Whether he were the darling of Mayfair—or a nobody!"

"The latter being myself." He bowed stiffly. "Forgive me, Miss Stansbury, for wasting your time. I will relieve you of my unwanted presence."

He turned and strode down the hill, his hopes in fragments about him and his heart aching because she had dealt with him so unkindly.

"Wait!"

She had picked up her skirts and was running after him. Even as he looked back she tripped and fell headlong. He gave a horrified cry and ran to kneel and help her sit up. She clung to him. There were tears on her cheeks and he asked frantically, "My poor girl! Are you hurt?"

"No! Yes! Oh, Piers—I am so sorry! I was rude and vulgar

and horrid! It was just . . . I was so angry when you called me an Amazon and said I was not dainty or petite!"

"Did I say such stupid things?" He groaned and said remorsefully, "What a fool I am! Forgive!"

She put a finger across his lips. "You are not a fool. And I thank you for your very kind offer. But—"

"But you still want—him." He sighed, and sitting beside her said heavily, "I see."

"No. You do not see at all. I told you once that I had a Plan . . ."

"Yes. It worried me."

"My Plans always worry my friends. And you are my friend, Piers Cranford. I know that. The thing is well, if I go back to my mama, I am sure she will try to—to—"

"To arrange another—er, engagement for you?"

"To entrap some hapless male is what you really mean." She sighed and said ruefully, "And it is truth. My mother is not an evil lady, but—well, she is proud, and to hold her position as a Leader of Fashion, tends to outrun the constable. Papa tried to convince her to practice economies, but he gave up and went away to Egypt. Mama is very frightened now, I think. I spoilt her plan to marry me off to a rich man, but if I were under her roof she would try again, I am sure of it."

"You said you meant to reside with your aunts. Is that your Plan?"

"For a while. Six months . . . perhaps it will take a year."

"To do—what?"

"You say you do not follow the London gossip, so perhaps you've not heard. An East Indiaman went down a few years ago, and the survivors managed to reach an island somewhere. I forget the details, but not long ago another vessel found them and offered them rescue. One lady refused to come back to England. She said she knew she would be looked on with revulsion, and rather than endure such disgrace, she stayed with the savages."

He nodded. "Yes. I recollect. A very sad story."

"Perhaps. But"—her chin tossed upward—"I thought she must be very missish."

He touched one of the glossy curls that had come down when she fell, and said tenderly, "Is that why you resolved to come home and face whatever awaited you in Polite Society?"

"It is why I have resolved to"—she looked at him squarely, her eyes dancing with mischief—"to write a book, Piers! About my adventures."

He stared at her, speechless.

"I shall call it 'Spinster Amid the Savages,' she said musingly. "What do you think?"

He gasped, "You cannot mean it! You would really be ostracized! I doubt you could find a publisher! And your reputation would be in shreds!"

"Yes, but don't you see? That is the whole point. The more shocking I become, the more eager people will be to read my lurid tale! Oh, publicly they will shun me, I have no doubt, even as they devour the pages in private. Would it not be wonderful if it made lots of money? My future would be assured! I could set up a home of my own—with perhaps one of my aunts or cousins to play chaperone."

She clapped her hands triumphantly, and he was won to a smile. Taking her small hands within both of his, he said, "Do you know, Miss Mary, I think you are a little bit of a rascal! Oh, my dear—are you quite sure this is what you want? Would not your life be more peaceful if you were happily wed? Not to me—I know I am not your choice, though I had hoped—" He bit his lip. "But if Valerian does offer . . ."

"I will send him to the right-about," she said, with a defiant toss of her head. "And, yes, I know that is not a proper term for ladies. But I, you know, mean to be outrageous!"

Jane Guild heard Piers laughing while he was still above-stairs putting off his riding coat before coming down to a late luncheon. She had thought to see a wistfulness in his eyes when he'd arrived home, and she scanned him curiously as he came into the breakfast parlour.

He crossed to drop a kiss on her forehead, and she patted his arm fondly. "You must have had a good morning."

He paused for an instant, then said, "It could have been worse."

"You saw Florian? Poor lad, how does he go on?"

"Quietly. I told Bragg we must talk with Miss Finchley. If her sire objects, I shall sign a summons."

"Why, dear? Do you think Laura knows something of import?"

"I am convinced she knows *something*, and that Florian does, also. Since he won't confide in me, I hope to persuade her to tell me whom he is shielding."

Miss Guild was intrigued, and after Peddars had served them and left, she demanded to know what else Piers had done with his morning. His answers did not satisfy her and at length she said, "Yes, that is all well and good. I'm glad Constable Bragg was not badly hurt, and it is a pity Ezra Sweet has become so cantankerous in his old age. He was used to be a jolly fellow when he tended your dear mama's flowers. I cannot think, however, that his behaviour is what sent you into whoops just now."

Cranford said with a grin, "You are very right." He handed her a folded letter. "Here, my perceptive Aunt. You will see that I am properly driven to the ropes . . ."

Curious, she unfolded the letter, and read:

Mr. Cranford,

I have not been long in your service, and regret that I must now terminate my employment.

It is my hope, sir, that I have met your require-

260

ments. I have tried to please. However, I have my reputation to consider, and I feel it would be prejudicial to
my future were I to continue in the service of a gentleman who refuses to wear a wig, and objects to the refinement of lace on his jabots.

With the deepest appreciation of your many kindnesses,

I am

Yr. devoted ex-servant,
Rudolph M. Blake

~∞~

"Are ye quite sure as ye will not stay for supper, Mr. Cranford?"
Mrs. Dixon looked affectionately at her husband and added,
"We does not stand on ceremonials here, sir, nor ask that ye
change your garments 'afore sitting down at table."

"Not even these garments?" Cranford looked doubtfully at
his much-creased coat and muddy breeches.

"'Twould be hard to say which o' ye is dustier," acknowledged his would-be hostess. "Good clean dirt, sir, and ye've
worked so hard to help us these past five hours and more. You
deserve a good meal, so ye do."

Cranford had gone first to the church and assisted in clearing the rubble, and from there had proceeded to lend the
farmer a hand. He was tired and hungry, and the smells wafting
from Mrs. Dixon's kitchen were nigh irresistible. He said reluctantly, "Being acquainted with your cooking, ma'am, I am
more than tempted. But the light is almost gone and my brother
has likely returned to the Manor by this time. I am anxious to
learn of how he found Viscount Glendenning. His lordship was
badly injured during the steeplechase, you know."

Dixon and his wife did know and were quick to add their
good wishes for the viscount's speedy recovery. Walking with
Cranford to the barn, the farmer said, "I had thought, sir, as

that there Mr. Valerian, might win the race if Tassels didn't. A fine black he's got and goes like the wind."

"Yes. He rides well."

"That he do, sir. A bit too fast, though, or so I thought. Considering 'twas dark and only a half-moon for light when I see him. And the bridge repairs only just finished and not properly tested yet."

Adjusting Tassels' stirrups, Cranford checked and said sharply, "You saw Gervaise Valerian on the bridge at night? Are you sure?"

"Sure as may be. I were driving the cart home from Short Shrift. Mr. Valerian fairly shot past. I called to him, but I doubt he even saw me, he were thinking only on where he was bound." Dixon winked and said with a grin, "Knowing he has a eye for a pretty lass, I thought as he were likely going to visit a lady. Still, 'twas chancy to ride at that speed after dark."

Cranford mounted up and said lightly, "I've had the same thought, Oliver. Valerian takes too many chances."

The farmer chuckled. "Never think it, to look at him, would ye? He's not the man he pretends to be, not by a long way!"

It was dark when Cranford turned onto the lane leading to the Manor, his thoughts on Dixon's obvious admiration of the dandy. It was amazing what affectation and an expensive tailor could— He tensed suddenly. There were lights ahead. Many lights, and men's voices, shouting. God forbid this was another attack on the gaol and Florian! He saw Bobby Peale then, mounted on his old cob, and hailed the lad.

Riding to him at once, Bobby shouted excitedly, "We're all out looking, sir!"

"Looking for—what?" Cranford demanded, "Is there trouble at the house?"

Peddars ran up, holding a lantern high. "Father Barrick and half the village is searching for the lady, Mr. Piers, sir. Has ye come from the Home Farm?"

"Yes, I have."

"She's not there, is she?"

"Who is not there? Devil take it, will no one tell me? For whom do you all search? Is it my aunt?"

" 'Lor'—no, Lieutenant," exclaimed the boy. "She be safe in the Manor and were talking with the feathery lady."

"The feathery lady . . ." Suddenly cold as ice, Cranford gasped, "My dear God! Do you mean Miss Celeste Westerman?"

"Celeste?" echoed the footman, looking puzzled. "I thought as her name were Miss Mary."

Through his teeth Cranford snarled, "If someone does not tell me what this is all about—"

"But I did, Mr. Piers," answered Peddars hurriedly. " 'Tis Miss Mary Westerman. She did not go home for tea—nor for supper."

"They found her cloak on Quail Hill," supplied young Peale, his eyes round and solemn. "Her aunties come s'arternoon and is worried 'bout her."

"The feathery lady is fair aside of herself," confirmed the footman, as more men carrying torches or lanterns gathered about them. "It 'pears, sir, as the poor lady has been kidnapped!"

16

The gates stood wide, and despite the lateness of the hour, the Westerman cottage was a blaze of light when Cranford rode into the yard. He flung himself from the saddle and raced up the front steps. The door was opened before he knocked to reveal a liveried footman who scanned him anxiously, and beyond him Miss Celeste Westerman, who clutched her large fan as though it were an umbrella.

"Oh, 'tis you, dear sir," she said in obvious disappointment, and called, "It is only Lieutenant Cranford, sisters!"

"We can see who it is, Celeste," boomed Mrs. Caroline, appearing beside her, untidy as usual, and clearly distressed.

"So good of him to come," trilled Mrs. Lucretia, squeezing between them and shaking a teaspoon playfully in Cranford's face. "Come in, dear boy. Come along in. My, but how very worried you look, which is most appreciated! We are drinking tea in the large withdrawing-room. You must come and have a cup."

"Thank you, but—" said Cranford.

"No, 'buts.'" Miss Celeste took his arm as though they

were lifelong friends and led the way along the corridor.

"You are very kind," he said, containing his impatience with an effort. "But I only came to find out if you have heard anything of Miss Mary's whereabouts, or—"

"Nothing! We have heard nothing at all." Mrs. Lucretia wore a large dressing-gown of puce velvet trimmed with pink lace. With not a trace of embarrassment at entertaining a male caller *en déshabillé,* she sat down beside the low occasional table and took up a silver teapot. "Here you are," she said, handing Cranford a brimming cup. "If you will not sit down you shall have to drink it standing up. We expected, you know—"

"To receive a note," put in Miss Celeste, taking a chair and gazing soulfully at Cranford.

"Or a demand for ransom, or some such thing," said Mrs. Caroline, rearranging her perpetual shawl.

Gulping his tea before he realized it was scalding, Cranford gasped, "But you've had no word at all, which could indicate that your niece wandered away and became lost, perhaps?"

"None. And we doubt it," said Mrs. Caroline wearily. "We have thought and thought, and the curate came and Constable Bragg and our solicitor, and they all asked the same questions."

"And all we know—" said Miss Celeste.

"Is that our dear girl said she was going out for a minute to see the horses," Mrs. Lucretia imparted, "She is very fond of horses, you know."

"Which was at afternoon tea time," said Mrs. Caroline. "Soon after we arrived from Town."

"And they found her cloak in the meadow, and we've not laid eyes on her since!" Miss Celeste sniffed unaffectedly, and dabbed a handkerchief at her eyes.

"But—who would want to kidnap Mary?" wailed Mrs. Lucretia.

"She is not rich," Mrs. Caroline said heavily.

Miss Celeste waved her fan half-heartedly. "And her mama has not a penny to bless herself with."

"It is all so *very* droll," sighed Mrs. Lucretia.

Cranford stood. "I must go." He hesitated. "Would you wish that I ask Father Barrick to come back and stay with you?"

"It is nice to have a gentleman nearby at times of crisis," said Miss Celeste.

"And we are fortunate," observed Mrs. Caroline. "We have our solicitor."

"Shorewood?" Cranford asked, "He is still here?"

"In the kitchen," said Mrs. Lucretia. "He wanted to be sure that Cook served us a good meal, but he means to stay for dinner, you know, so he is probably looking to his own menu."

"And driving Cook demented," growled Mrs. Caroline.

Relieved that the barrister was present and would be able to guide them in the event of a new development, Cranford said his farewells.

Mrs. Lucretia accompanied him to the front door. In the entrance hall, as he took his hat and gauntlets from the table, she said, "You have lost your heart, I think, Lieutenant."

He drew a breath and said levelly, "I love your niece, ma'am."

"Poor boy." She shook her head. "You must find another lady. Mary is a dear child, but stubborn as was her grandmama. If she cannot have Gervaise, she will never marry. I am very sorry but—so it is."

Through the endless hours that followed, those words haunted Cranford. The moon had broken through the clouds, making it easier to find his way, but he was bedevilled by the knowledge that he knew not where to look. Constable Bragg had told him that many search parties were scouring the area searching for "the poor lost young lady"; thus far without result. The fact that Mary's cloak had been found caused the constable to shake his head bodingly and sigh that it was "a bad sign, Squire. A dreadful bad sign."

He returned home in the hope that Mary had gone there. His aunt informed him that Major Finchley had called to en-

266

quire if Miss Westerman-Stansbury had come to the Manor. "He actually looked concerned," she exclaimed, awed. "And said Miss Mary had long been a good friend to his daughter, who is greatly distressed by the news."

Having determined that every able-bodied man on his staff was assisting in the search, Cranford rode out again. Refusing to bow to weariness, he scoured the meadows, calling Mary's name. He stopped to investigate an abandoned cottage and several sheds where she might have taken shelter from the wintry night air, but at each location found only emptiness. He rode through the woods, calling her, straining his ears for the answer that never came, plagued by the awareness that it was cold and she was out somewhere without her cloak. He dismounted and climbed down into a small gorge, dreading what he might find, but succeeded only in disturbing a fox that scurried away, grumbling. Proceeding to the toll-road, he questioned the gate-keepers and met with irked responses that no such person had passed their way and that several other gents had already asked the same question. His offer of a generous reward for information leading to the lady's rescue evoked more cordial reactions, and he turned back towards his estate followed by promises to be on the alert for anyone answering Miss Stansbury's description.

". . . If she cannot have Gervaise, she will never marry . . ."

Almost, he could hear Mrs. Lucretia's mournful tones. She was wrong, he thought defiantly. Mary's nature was too affectionate to permit that she could choose to go through life alone, denied the blessing of children. If ever a lady was meant for motherhood . . . That picture brought an exquisite pang. He thought wretchedly, '*Why* did she have to give her heart to Gervaise Valerian?' If she had chosen a good man, a man like Tio, or Jamie Morris, or Roly Mathieson, he could have borne it—somehow. But—*Valerian?*

Perry's words echoed in his ears: "Does it occur to you that he may really have come to care for her?"

"No!" he told Tassels' left ear vehemently. "He is too much of a care-for-nobody!"

Tio had said, "I know you have never liked him . . ."

"They all think me prejudiced," he grumbled to Tassels' right ear.

Was it true? Why had he always so disliked the man? Because he was so dandified and affected? Because he cared not whom he offended, or how many feelings were hurt by his very lack of caring? Because Sir Simon still lived, and should be part of his life were he anything but a selfish ingrate? And now, having his choice of London's Toasts, Valerian had chosen the one lady to whom he himself had so completely given his heart!

Conscience argued, "Who set you up as judge and jury, Piers Cranford? Say truth! You envy him more than the fact that his father yet lives! You envy his carefree life and abundant fortune, his dashing manners and the way all the women adore him! Were you to be honest, you would admit that you are simply—"

"I am *not* jealous!" he declared to no one in particular.

Tassels tossed her head, and he sighed and said wearily, "You're in the right of it, lass. I'm talking nonsense which will—" He broke off as it dawned on him that they were on Hound's Tooth Hill. He had intended to seek high ground but had no recollection of guiding the mare up here.

"Good girl," he said, drawing her to a halt.

Bathed in the moon's soft glow, the countryside stretched out below him in a tidy patchwork; not clearly defined for more than a half-mile or so, but sufficiently to allow him to detect a coach or rider should anyone pass within that patchwork. All was still, all was quiet. Save for the hooting of an owl and the whisper of the night wind, it was so peaceful . . . His head bowed and his thoughts faded. Jerking his head up again, he acknowledged that he was very tired. Perhaps, if he were to close his eyes—just for a minute or two . . .

Tassels snorted, and moved restlessly. Cranford was at

once awake, and cursed himself for a fool. He had dropped off. And bless his silver lady for having woken him. Not that there was anyone in sight. But . . . there was a stirring on the air, more felt than heard. Muffled with distance at first, but drawing nearer until he could identify hoofbeats. Someone was travelling at the gallop—a chancy business at night, even with the moon. From the copse of trees where he had waited for fear of being silhouetted against the sky, he could see the horse now. A tall horse, and a rider who crouched low in the saddle and rode as if a troop of dragoons followed. Cranford's heart gave a spasmodic leap. He knew that fine black stallion. Beyond doubting, the horseman was his pseudo-kinsman—Gervaise Valerian! And what should bring the fellow here? At this hour? Unless . . .

It had surprised him to learn that Valerian was distantly related to Marbury and had thus been invited to accompany the duke and his party to the steeplechase. But had the dandy actually been courting Mary for some time? Both she and her aunt had seemed quite at ease in his company, rather than evincing the resentment they might logically have been expected to harbour against him. Had Valerian made a habit of crossing Muse Manor lands to visit the lady he was to have wed? Cranford scowled. He had been unable to summon much confidence in Mary's Plan to support herself by becoming a successful authoress. Had she in fact fobbed him off with that tale while keeping secret trysts with the man she loved? If that was the case, he had been a proper fool. Well, he would find out tonight. It would be better to know the truth, however bitter, than to keep on hoping.

His jaw tightening, he said, "Come on, girl," and guided Tassels down the hill.

It was a hare-and-hounds chase after that. Keeping to cover as far as possible, Cranford neither ventured too close nor ever lost sight of his quarry. It became clear that Valerian was doing all in his power to avoid any pursuit. He followed a wildly erratic route, often glancing behind him, abruptly turning about to re-trace his path until it was impossible to guess his ultimate des-tination. Twice, Cranford was almost caught, reining Tassels behind clumps of shrubs the first time, and next turning in amongst a copse of birch trees with scant seconds to spare. On the third near-miss, he hung back for longer than usual and it was thus he heard another rider approaching. At first he feared Valerian had seen his plunge into concealment and was return-ing to accuse him, but then he realized there was more than one horse and that they were not ahead, but behind him. He swung from the saddle and held Tassels' nostrils. A moment later, two horses came up at the gallop. They halted only a few feet from the copse. The first rider was leaning forward, scan-ning the meadow intently. Scarcely daring to breathe, Cranford heard an impassioned oath, followed by a frustrated "He's dished me again! Blast the fellow, he is slippery as any eel! A fine dance he's led us. D'you see him?"

A brief pause, then the second man said haltingly, "I see a rider, sir. About a mile straight ahead. There, by that small lake. But—I can't tell if it's our man!"

The first rider swore again. "Likely, he has an accomplice! Well, come on, Sergeant! Be damned if he'll give me the slip this time!"

Watching them ride on, Cranford knew that there was no longer room for doubt. The man giving the orders had been the elusive "pedlar," and Joshua was an officer of some sort: probably Military Intelligence. They had been following him in Town and again at the race. They must be hoping to catch Tio in a compromising situation—perhaps with a known fugitive. It was more than likely that the viscount had recovered suffi-ciently to leave the farmhouse and had either come here or they believed he would do so. They were persistent, confound the pair of 'em! Perhaps they had uncovered new evidence con-firming that Tio had fought for Prince Charlie. Or perhaps that wart Gresford Finchley had informed Military Intelligence of his suspicions.

Cranford sent Tassels out from the trees. Whatever their justification, they were dogging his steps, probably reasoning that eventually he would lead them to his friend. Staying well back, he followed the two hunters and smiled grimly when they came to the gallop once more. Clearly, they had caught sight of Valerian, who was riding like the wind. This development, Cranford told Tassels, might very well work to his own advantage. The two Intelligence agents, or whatever they were, would certainly help him to free Mary. He would give something, he thought, to see their faces when they came up with the far from amiable dandy!

Riding at the rear of the small procession, he was following the hunters now, rather than his cousin, but minutes later Valerian was briefly in sight as he rode headlong into a patch of woods. Recognizing his tactics, Cranford slowed and waited. The two hunters did not. In hot pursuit they tore in amongst the trees. Cranford grinned as, sure enough, after a very few minutes Valerian left the woods and rode northwards, almost immediately being lost to view. The hunters rushed from the trees, milled about for a minute, then galloped to the west. Cranford shook his head and, following Valerian, was able to catch a glimpse of him about a mile ahead. He observed his earlier precautions, this time also keeping a weather eye behind him in case Joshua "Pedlar" and his sergeant realized their mistake and changed course.

Clouds were drifting in, and the moonlight was often dimmed. Straining his eyes, Cranford was begining to wonder if the dandy's objective was the Scots border when, without warning, Valerian disappeared from sight.

"Where in Hades did the fellow go?" he muttered impotently.

Again, he waited, but this time it was as if the earth had

opened and swallowed up Walker and his devious rider, and the big black horse did not reappear.

Cranford rode forward cautiously. The ground was irregular now and he was obliged to slow. He came into an area of boulders and sudden deep hollows where grew holly and wild blackberry bushes and stunted trees. There were no woods to offer a place to hide. Valerian had probably skirted such a forbidding place . . . but if he had he would surely have reappeared from one direction or another. He had not reappeared; therefore . . . " 'Seek and ye shall find,' " Cranford muttered, and dismounted.

Leading Tassels, he wandered about. It was very dark and when the moon's light was extinguished he blundered into hidden obstacles. He trod carefully, which was fortunate, for without warning the rocky ground took a steep downward plunge, the slope becoming so precipitous that he had all he could do not to fall. He could hear Tassels struggling and sliding behind him; his legs were bombarded by the shower of rocks and shale she displaced, so that he was glad of the protection offered by his riding boots. He caught at a rocky outcropping to steady his balance, praying that this small but deep ravine did not end in a sheer drop, but within a few more steps he was relieved to find that he had reached more or less level ground.

The moon beamed forth once more, revealing stone cliff-like walls that rose, steep and forbidding, all around him. Tassels nuzzled him and whickered nervously. He told her how bravely she had made the difficult descent, but knew he had blundered into one of the deep hollows he had judged impenetrable. Valerian had come this way, certainly, but he was not in this particular hollow. Unless . . . He tethered the mare to a shrub and began to explore, pulling aside bushes and vines that grew at the foot of the cliffs but finding only solid rock behind them.

Determined to search elsewhere, he started back to Tassels, halting in astonishment because the mare appeared to have lost her head. He raced to her and discovered that she was still intact, having found such a delicious shrub that she had pushed her way into it. "You naughty glutton," he scolded, reaching for the reins. His arm progressed farther than the cliff face. With a jolt of the heart he pushed the branches away and discovered a deep fissure in the rock, sufficiently broad and high to admit a horse. "Clever girl," he murmured and, leaving her outside, crept forward.

Initially, the darkness was so intense that he could move only by feeling his way, but gradually the gloom eased to a sort of twilight and he was able to distinguish that he stood in a large natural cave. There must, he thought, have been water coursing through here in the distant past, for the rock had been moulded into strange shapes and forms. Once he encountered an arched doorway, standing unconnected and alone in the middle of the cave. A moment later he halted, his heart pounding as a tall man hove up before him, then drew a steadying breath when he saw that the "figure" did not move and was in fact a disconcertingly lifelike formation of twisted rock.

He saw then that at the far end of this cold but wondrous chamber there was a distinct glow on the wall. He took the pistol from his pocket and cocked it. Valerian must be the world's prize fool, he thought scornfully. Mary had loved the clod for years and when he'd had the chance to wed her he had drawn back. Now, having changed his mind and condescended to offer for her, she had rejected him. (Just as she should!) He must have realized too late what a gem he'd allowed to escape him. Mary, bless her independent spirit, had dared to humble him, and it was typical of his arrogance that he had determined to so compromise the lady that she would be forced to become his wife. Probably, it was the first time he had been handed such a set-down. One thing was certain: dandy or not, he would be unlikely to surrender her without a fight.

Following the light, Cranford trod with care over the uneven floor. Soon, he could hear talking; more than one male voice. So, as he'd suspected, Valerian did have an accomplice! The cave began to narrow, then turned sharply to become a passage from which shone the light. He heard Valerian say something about "leaving," and knowing he must not lose the element of surprise, he strode quickly around the corner and into a smaller and brightly lit inner cave.

Valerian was here, sure enough, bending over a rough bed. Enraged, Cranford forgot he had more than one man to deal with, and levelling the pistol shouted, "Take your hands from her, you miserable cur, or—"

With a snarl of rage, Valerian straightened. A sword seemed to leap into his hand. "Damn your eyes!" he cried furiously. "So it *was* you so hot on my trail! I might have guessed it!"

Cranford said nothing. His pistol sagged and he stared in stunned silence at the bed.

Cordelia Mary Westerman Stansbury was not the occupant. Instead, the last person he would have thought to see lay there. A man, emaciated, his drawn white face marked by suffering.

"Sir . . . Simon!" he gasped.

Sword levelled, Valerian sprang at him. "Do not count your blood money yet!"

Cranford leaped back, raising the pistol again.

"Gervaise! No!"

The dandy halted in reluctant obedience to that imperative command, then retreated to stand between his father and Cranford, crouching slightly, sword at the ready. "We've no choice, sir," he said in a gritty voice Cranford had never before heard. "Even were this pest not a reserve Army officer, he is greedy for gain and would hesitate not an instant to betray you for the bounty. He'll not send you to your death whilst I live to prevent him!"

"I very much doubt that Lieutenant Cranford intends to betray me," said Sir Simon feebly. "Do you, Piers?"

Staring at the small and sleek black kitten curled up in the

274

crook of the sick man's arm, Cranford said, mystified, "Betray you for—I mean—how? Why?"

"Oh, a fine performance," sneered Valerian. "If you do not mean to betray us, why did you follow me?"

"A home question," said Sir Simon. "Gervaise told me he changed direction frequently. You must have been quite determined to discover me."

"He is determined indeed, Father," agreed Valerian. "Determined to keep from losing his precious estate. He'd sell his own mother to prevent that!"

"The devil I would," said Cranford indignantly. "Much you know of it! And what is this talk of betrayal? You fought for the King in the Uprising. Glendenning saw you. And I know your father was not involved."

"I was not on any battlefield," Sir Simon declared wryly. "But then, neither was my friend, Geoff Boudreaux."

Cranford stared at him speechlessly. Lord Geoffrey Boudreaux had for long been suspected of aiding fugitive Jacobites to flee the retribution of an angry government. His grandnephew, Trevelyan de Villars, had been up to his aristocratic ears in such perilous activities and had escaped England badly wounded and barely one step ahead of a troop of dragoons.

"*You*—cry friends with—with *Treve de Villars*? . . ." said Cranford, incredulous.

The sick man stroked the kitten and glanced to his son. "I suppose you would prefer I not answer that, dear lad," he said apologetically.

"*Dear lad?*" Baffled, Cranford looked from one to the other, and reading the affection in each face, waited.

Valerian drawled, "Oh, by all means, sir. Tell him everything! He'll not leave here alive, at all events!"

"You must forgive my son," said Sir Simon. "He tends to become violent if I am threatened, you see."

"He . . . does? But—I thought— Everyone believes—"

"Yes, I am aware. Gervaise hatched that scheme early in

the game, but—pray be seated, Piers, and I'll let him tell you. I tire easily, I'm afraid."

Cranford uncocked the trigger carefully and returned the pistol to his pocket. His hands were muddied. Ignoring the sword that Valerian levelled at him, he sat on a makeshift chair that had been constructed of rocks and tree branches, drew out his handkerchief and began to wipe off his hands. Mary's lost bead had also come from his pocket, and he ran his thumb over it absently, intent on the drama unfolding before him.

The dandy scowled at him, but lowered his sword and growled, "Since you're said to have the brains in the family, Lieutenant, sir, I fancy you've already come at the root of it."

"Sir Simon is a Jacobite sympathizer and—"

"Not so! My father holds no brief for the Stuarts!"

"But I was horrified by Cumberland's tactics at, and after, Culloden," explained the invalid.

"That's when it started," resumed his son. "We were fairly sure that Lord Boudreaux was assisting fugitives, even then, and what must my reckless sire do but rush to join the effort. For some time I suspected where his sympathies lay. But when I realized how deeply he was involved, the chances he was taking—the very real possibility that he could be caught at any time! Well, in short, I manufactured our famous "quarrel" so that, if it became necessary, I—"

"Could come to my rescue," put in Sir Simon, with a fond smile at his heir. "And, alas, he has done so indeed—to his peril."

Vastly intrigued, Cranford asked, "You were caught, sir?"

"In the very act of driving a caravan full of refugees—yes. I was ambushed by dragoons, but fortunately being disguised, I was not identified. I took a pistol ball in my back, but managed to hide, and was for many months nursed and given shelter by my—friends. Gervaise searched for me, but . . ." He shrugged.

Gervaise said grimly, "The people who were shielding him

276

hid him too well. By the time I was able to find him, my father was a very sick man."

"And still being sought, no doubt." Cranford nodded. "The Army does not give up easily when traitors—" He bit his lip and broke off. "Your pardon, sir. But I am amazed that you have been able to survive for so long."

"Had it not been for Gervaise, I would have been dead long ago. But he bribed doctors, paid huge sums for medicines, places of refuge, and numerous conveyances, brought me down here by one desperate escape after another, and in so doing I fear has sadly depleted his inheritance."

"So there you have it," said Gervaise, watching Cranford narrowly. "And you will eagerly carry the word back to your noble great-uncle, no? Perchance it may restore the lustre to Lord Nugent's somewhat tarnished reputation. But you should not have put up your pistol, soldier. You cannot draw it now before I have you impaled on my sword!"

"Unless," said Sir Simon wearily, "Piers will give us his word not to betray us."

"For the love of God!" exclaimed Gervaise irritably. "How could we trust his word? Why do you think he followed me so persistently and even managed to negotiate the back entrance?"

Awed, Sir Simon exclaimed, "You never did! Not with your beautiful grey filly, I trust?"

"Yes. Though it was too dark when we started down for me to see how steep it would become. In fact, Tassels is still tied! I must go and—" He glanced down at the bead he held. "I must get on! I've already delayed too long! I came to rescue Miss Stansbury from your lecherous clutches, you great villain!"

"Rescue . . . Mary? What the deuce—" Gervaise sprang up, his sword glittering as he prepared to attack, and said thunderously, "I am neither lecherous, nor a—"

"Hush!" Sir Simon lifted his hand. "What is this you say, Piers? If the lady has been harmed, I promise you my son has no knowledge of it."

277

"I realize that now, sir. And I must admit I have sadly misjudged my—cousin, and owe him my apologies, but—"

"The devil with that!" said Gervaise, restoring his sword to the scabbard. "What of Miss Cordelia—or Mary, as you call her? Has she been harmed?"

"She went walking. When she failed to return at dusk, a search was launched. Her cloak was found on Quail Hill, where she often searches for the beads from a necklace that broke there."

"Has there been a ransom demanded? Any note or letter? Deuce take the filthy swine! If they dare harm her! . . . And why, devil take you, would you think I had stolen the lady?"

The kitten stretched and rolled over luxuriously.

Cranford pointed out with a slow smile, "You stole my cat."

"*Your* cat!" Gervaise, who had reached out to stroke the kitten, jerked his hand back and reddened. "I found Pixie and had a perfect right to adopt her!" He added with a trace of defiance, "I've no use for the foolish beasts, but my father chances to like cats."

"Which is neither here nor there," said Sir Simon. "Piers, do you really think someone has kidnapped the lady?"

"I fear it, sir. She has no fortune, nor, so far as I'm aware, any rich relatives. But she is a lovely young woman, and there are those today who can demand a high price for stolen English girls."

Sir Simon, who had been watching Cranford, said, "May I ask what you have there?"

" 'Tis one of the beads Miss Mary lost on Quail Hill." Cranford handed it to the invalid.

"So what has been done about the poor girl?" demanded Gervaise, snatching up a superbly tailored riding coat.

"Every able-bodied man for miles around is searching for her. I was seeking her myself until I saw you, and—Jupiter! Damned if I havent forgot! Two other men were hard after you, Gervaise!"

"That curst alleged 'pedlar,' I suppose! Did I give them the slip, or do they wait outside to take my father? I warn you—"

"Oh, have done! I'm not here to betray Sir Simon. Indeed, I will do all I may to help you both. But I must first go and see if Miss Mary has come home."

Sir Simon said, "I rather doubt that, I'm afraid. If the lady had a necklace of beads like this, she is a wealthy woman. This is an extremely old stone. I wonder you did not notice the strange forms and inscriptions engraved on the surface."

Piers said intently, "You think 'tis from ancient time, sir?"

"I would guess it is from a very ancient time, and more than likely came from a burial mound. A complete necklace like this would be worth a small fortune. And if there is a barrow, or mound—heaven only knows the riches it may contain!"

"Then may the Lord help her," groaned Cranford.

"Deuce take me for a gudgeon," said Gervaise. "I could have wed an heiress!"

17

Valerian said worriedly, "I don't like leaving him so often. Were it not for Mistress Hoylake, I would not dare take the risk."

The two young men were making their way along a dark tunnel-like passage so narrow that they had to walk single-file, Valerian in the lead, holding a lantern, Cranford following, and Tassels thudding along in the rear. Cranford had been considerably relieved when Sir Simon had told him there was a less perilous entrance to his sanctuary and a smaller cave which they had equipped as a makeshift stable for Walker. They had retrieved Cranford's beloved mare, leading her through the large caves and into this tunnel that sloped gradually upward.

"Am I permitted to know who is Mistress Hoylake?" he asked. "She seemed a very kind lady, but has she to stay hid in the caves all the time?"

"Fancying me to be a merciless tyrant, are you?" snapped Valerian. "Well, I ain't! And you may believe the lady is perfectly content to be there. And to be safe."

"Ah. She is a Jacobite?"

"Her son is. She sheltered him, for which she could lose her head. My father was able to whisk her son to safety with the aid of a very gallant gentleman who called himself Lingun Doone—which is not his real name, so do not be thinking to sell it to—"

"His real name being Geoff Delavale."

"*Sapristi!*" Valerian turned an astonished face. "You know?"

"I know. He chances to be a very good friend of my brother-in-law, and since I have as yet not sold his head to the Army—"

"You are not likely to do so now—which places your own head at risk, you realize? But, of course, you are already at risk, crying friends with that hot-headed rebel Glendenning."

"You were saying your father rescued Mrs. Hoylake's son. Were there others?"

"Many others. I'll have you know my sire is a prodigious gallant gentleman."

"I have always thought that. I'm very glad to find that you appreciate him. No, don't fly into the boughs. 'Tis a tribute to your acting skill that you have convinced all London you despise the gentleman."

Valerian was silent a moment, then said with quiet dignity, "He is the most courageous and selfless man I shall ever know."

"I envy you. We scarcely had time to know our father. But you surely don't plan that he stay forever in the cave. What do you mean to do?"

"Get him over to France—or Italy—as soon as may be. The lady also. Careful here, there are fallen rocks . . . Mistress Hoylake has her own skill; she is a splendid nurse. But our desperate flights and often miserable hiding-places have brought about relapses. We came nigh to losing him again last autumn."

Cranford said thoughtfully, "Last autumn. That would be when rumor had it you were sharing an Italian villa with your latest bird of paradise."

"The gossip-mongers have their uses. In point of fact, I was finding this place, smuggling my father here, and bringing

Mistress Hoylake to him, whereby he goes along better. But he is still very weak." A pause, then he said rather too heartily, "I dare to believe he will improve when he can get out in the fresh air and sunshine."

"I have no doubt he will. Perry did, you know. It was touch-and-go with him several times, but he's quite recovered now and is soon to be wed in fact."

"So our great-uncle told me. Speaking of which, Cranford, the fact that you now so graciously admit our kinship changes nothing. I trust you understand that."

"In what way? You still mean to challenge me to a duel?"

"Blast your eyes! You know very well what I mean! Your supercilious attitude towards me—"

"Supercilious! Contemptuous, rather. Which you earned with your clever masquerade!"

"Even so, in public you shall have to continue to regard me as though I were something less than a slug. And another thing—when Cordelia Stansbury is wed, it will be to *me*, so do not cherish empty hopes."

Cranford said grimly, "We'll see about that. But we have to find her first!"

"It is my opinion your wits are to let," grumbled Valerian, standing with the horses and watching Cranford scramble down from the top of the rise. "Look at you! You cannot even command your feet! When did you eat or sleep last?"

"Your father's cognac has stood me in good stead."

"Or made you so lushy you don't know what you're about! Why are we on Finchley's estate? You told me the Hall had already been searched. If Mary were there she would have been rescued long since."

"*If* she had been there. 'Tis my belief the Major would not want his daughter to know of his infamous behaviour and has Mary hid somewhere close by."

282

"Now what are you about? Do you mean to leave the horses here? Why?"

"So that we can keep watch from the top of the rise." Following his example, Valerian secured Walker to a nearby shrub, and said, "Why would the old duffer take such a risk as to kidnap a lady of Quality? He don't know about the precious necklace, so what would he stand to gain?"

"He very probably does know about the necklace. His daughter Laura and Mary are bosom bows, don't forget. If Mary told Laura about the beads and Laura chanced to mention it to her father, he may very well have put two and two together."

Valerian gave a disparaging snort as they walked up the rise side by side. "You give the malevolent Major higher marks for intelligence than do I. Nor did his daughter impress me as being needle-witted. Laura . . . Hi! Ain't she the lady your gypsy steward fancies?"

"Yes. And she may not be clever, but Laura Finchley has a kind heart and is a charming young woman."

"Not charming enough to risk hanging for, in my humble opinion."

"Florian did not kill Grover, though he had plenty of provocation. And nor is he the only man to admire Miss Finchley's charms."

"So I've heard. Among them, another of your odd retainers, if somewhat indirectly."

Cranford turned and looked at him. "Now what do you imply? Young Peale perhaps, or Sudbury?"

"I don't imply. I state. And I refer to our great-uncle's bastard."

"What the devil—"

"Did you not know?" Valerian laughed softly. "Why do you suppose a proud man like General Lord Nugent Cranford would keep a gardener who is short of a sheet?"

"If you mean Herbert Turner, he is an excellent gardener

and the son of my great-uncle's housekeeper—"

"And our great-uncle! Oh, never look so taken aback. These things happen. If you paid heed to *ton* gossip you would have learned one or two of our family's more lurid secrets. If you don't believe me, ask your valet. Blake knows. Young Turner was crying on his shoulder Monday. I chanced to see them when I was cutting across your pristine acres to visit my father, after the race."

"And—Turner was really distraught?"

"Nigh hysterical, I thought. Almost, I felt sorry for the poor clod."

Cranford said nothing, but his tired mind was slowly fitting the pieces together. Grover had tormented Herbert Turner for years . . . poor Herbert had always worshipped Laura Finchley and knew of her unhappy home life . . . and Blake, the boy's uncle, had left his service very abruptly shortly after Grover's murder . . .

"What are you staring at down there?" demanded Valerian. "Whose hovel is that?"

"The late Sidney Grover lived there."

"Finchley gave his groom a cottage of his own? That's odd."

"Especially odd for a clutchfist like the charming Major. It might serve him to keep Mary there. The local people are superstitious and would very likely have drawn back from searching the home of a murdered man."

"But if he does have her, why has there been no ransom demand?"

"I doubt he would risk such a move. He may believe she knows the location of the barrow."

"*If* there is such an article. My father is brilliant, never doubt it, but he could be mistaken."

"Or he could be right, which would explain everything. There are rumours that Finchley is deep under the hatches. He has a surfeit of pride and loves his estate, and if he is really rolled up, I think he'd stop at nothing to lay his hands on a possible fortune in ancient jewels and artifacts."

"I thought all buried treasure belonged to the crown—but if, as you say, he is really desperate, he'd find a way to conceal . . . My God! He may be trying to force Mary to tell him where to find it! Come on!"

Whirling about, he ran down the slope, tore Walker's reins free and sprang into the saddle.

Coming up with him, Cranford caught at the stallion's bridle. "Wait! We don't know how many may be down there! We'll do Mary no favour if we are outnumbered. Better to take them by surpri——"

"Surprise—hell!" snarled Valerian, and was off, up the rise and down the far side, riding towards the cottage at the gallop.

Groaning anathemas on his reckless cousin, Cranford followed.

"I do not understand why you keep me waiting for so long." Sitting on the shabby sofa before the hearth in this cheerless parlour, Mary complained, " 'Tis freezing in this dirty cottage. What is behind that half-wall? The scullery?"

Gresford Finchley nodded. "And wash-house. Though I doubt Grover ever washed anything."

"I believe you." She shivered. "Can you not light a fire at least?"

Finchley spread his large hands and said with an ingratiating grin that he had sent his men out to find firewood. "Poor Sid Grover was an indifferent housekeeper, I own."

"Yes, but you have only just arrived. And if, as you claim, your daughter is so desperate to see me, why has she not come? The groom who brought me her message said 'twas a matter of life and death, so I came at once. But 'tis past dinnertime. I am hungry and my aunts will be worried." Standing, she said firmly, "I must get home, Major Finchley. When Laura comes—"

"No, but you must not go." He walked over to a rickety table set by the half-wall to the scullery and took up a covered basket. "I have fetched you some bread and ham, and a jug of milk. But I cannot light the fire; Laura insisted we must not, lest the smoke be seen."

"Oh, my!" Mary moved to occupy the chair he pulled out for her, and asked breathlessly, "Is this to do with Florian, then? Does she hope to free him? How?"

Finchley took off his riding coat and wrapped it solicitously about her shoulders. "There, my dear. Now you may be warm and comfortable while you eat the poor supper I've brought. There's a little pot of mustard if you want it, and a spoon."

Mary did want it, and added mustard to her ham with a lavish hand.

Watching her, the major shook his head and said enviously, "You young people have cast-iron insides. I wish I could eat such highly spiced food."

'If you drank less, you might be able to do so, and would likely not have such a red nose,' thought Mary, but she smiled and made no comment.

"I've no least notion why Laura is taking such a time," he muttered. "I only hope she has not made a mull of things. 'Twould have been better to let me handle the business, and so I told her, but she would have it that old Bragg would treat her more kindly, especially if she has to resort to bribery."

"Dear heavens!" Looking up from retrieving a plate with some thickly buttered slices of bread, Mary said, "The constable is an honest man—he would never agree to break the law! Is Laura all about in her head?"

"An apt term, Miss Stansbury, if rather naughty. I forbid Laura to use cant expressions. But I have to admit I fear that very thing. She is so devoted to this young fellow, you know, and held that if she offered a large enough sum . . ." He sighed. "Alas, 'twould likely require more than I was able to give her. My finances are not . . ." He shrugged.

Incredulous, Mary bit hungrily into her bread, and taking up a forkful of the ham, said rather indistinctly, "You gave Laura funds to—to bribe Constable Bragg?"

Finchley nodded sadly.

The bread was newly baked and delicious, and the ham tender. Much as Mary disliked and mistrusted this man she enjoyed her impromptu supper, and said at length, "But—you have always objected, most violently, to Florian Consett's courtship and Laura's affection for him."

He sighed again. "As any well-meaning parent would do, you must admit. Especially in view of these dreadful charges 'gainst him. But it has been borne in upon me that their attachment will prove lasting. I love my daughter too dearly to break her gentle heart. So—I gave her all I had."

His eyes were downcast; he looked despairing. Watching him narrowly, Mary continued to do justice to the food, then asked, "If Laura succeeds in freeing him, where will they go? Do you dare to hide them here?"

"No, no! I am assured this would be the first place the law would seek them. There are Runners coming from London, as I fancy you know. And those hounds will never rest until they are taken. I have arranged for passage to France. How they will go on after they reach land, I dare not contemplate. I can give them no more and there is no one I can ask for a loan without betraying them, alas."

The Major, thought Mary, was just trying to prevent the young couple from escaping. She said, "But they must have funds! Perhaps I can help."

Finchley's eyes shot to her face. "You are kind. But—your mama will surely not allow it."

"No, nor would I approach her. But I have a little money of my own, and—some pieces of jewellery they might be able to sell in France."

He clasped his hands and exclaimed, "How good a friend! And such generosity! Now that I recall, Laura did mention

287

something about a—what was it, a necklace? But if your mama gave it to you? . . ."

In the act of pouring some milk into her mug, Mary's hand paused for an instant and from under her lashes she slanted an oblique glance at the Major's face. "My mother did not give me the necklace. In point of fact, I chanced to find it—that is to say, I found some beads. I supposed they were just glass, and indeed they may be. But they are quite old, I believe, and may have some value. My papa will know, for he studies antiquities."

"But—so do I, my dear child! If you would allow me to see the beads, we could know their value at once! And we could then go to where you—you did say you—found them? . . ."

Mary lifted her head and looked at him levelly. His heavy features were flushed, the small eyes glittering with avarice and—triumph. She said softly, "Why, you deceitful creature! Laura never sent for me! It is all a hum!"

Finchley started and his sugary smile became fixed but, striving still, he purred, "Now that is not a proper term for a young lady to use, my dear."

"Nor was it proper for you to lure me here with your wicked lies—only so as to find out where I found my beads!"

The smile lost its sugar and became a snarl. Leaning to grasp her wrist he shouted, "Insolent chit! With your be-smirched reputation you dare to censure me? You'll tell me where you found that necklace—if you don't want to wind up in the river!"

"Oh!" she gasped, paling. "You are just trying to frighten me! You never would do such an evil thing! You would surely be hanged!" But despite the brave words, she sank down into the chair again, her eyes closing.

"Do not tempt me," he said, throwing down her wrist con-temptuously. "When you were found everyone would believe you had decided to end your shamed life. No one would suspect me of—"

Springing to her feet, Mary declared unequivocally, "You

are a bad man!" and seizing the heavy glass milk jug, dashed the contents into his face.

Reeling back a pace, spluttering with astonishment and disgust, he gulped, "Wretched . . . doxy! What lady would—would do such a thing!"

"My sort of lady! And here is something for you to cleanse your dirty self," cried Mary, and slapped several slices of ham and the second piece of bread at his variously milky and purpling face.

Roaring profanities, the Major grabbed for her with one hand, while pawing frantically at his buttery eyes with the other. He failed to recall that the ham had been liberally spread with mustard. His furious attempts ceased abruptly and he let out an anguished howl. "Morgan! Brackett! To me! Quickly. You—you stupid fools! This unnatural witch has—has blinded me!"

Mary heard the front door open and ran quickly around the half-wall to the scullery and the back door. Reaching for the latch, she gave a gasp of dismay and jumped back as the door burst open.

Flourishing his sword, Gervaise Valerian plunged into the dark scullery and rushed past her, roaring, "Where is she, you unconscionable villain? What have you done with her?"

"I'm here, Gervaise," called Mary, but her words were drowned as four men ran in from the front. They were a rough-looking crew, all armed with knives or clubs, and she recognized one, who carried both weapons, as having been with the supposed Mohocks who had attacked her and Piers Cranford during their ride in the park.

Undaunted by the formidable odds against him, Valerian positioned himself in the corner of the wall and cried, "Come on, you ill-dressed bravos! Have at me, and die young!"

They whooped and shouted as they rushed him. Breathless with anxiety, Mary knew he was hopelessly outnumbered and must fall, but his sword flashed and darted and their clubs failed to beat that deadly blade from his hand. In a lightning attack, he sprang forward, sword thrusting, and an unshaven rogue screamed and went down.

Mary gave a small cry of shock as a strong hand gripped her arm.

Piers Cranford said, "Come," and led her to the door.

"No!" she exclaimed, pulling away. "Help him!"

"I shall. When you are safe."

Finchley dodged his way to the fireplace and tugged on a rope, and somewhere outside a bell clanged stridently.

Dismayed, Mary cried, "He has called in his men! Make Gervaise come—now!"

"I mean to. Do you take Tassels and bring my people!"

She hesitated, but even with Cranford to aid him they would be sadly outnumbered. She nodded and ran through the scullery.

Cranford swung around, and drawing his sword sprang to his cousin's side.

Glancing at him from the corner of his eye, Valerian shouted, "Hey! This is my battle!"

Deflecting the club that would have brained him, Piers answered, "Aye, and if you don't pay heed and abandon it, 'twill be your last!"

Major Finchley mopped at his streaming eyes, and howled, "Use your knives, you thrice-damned blockheads!"

Two heavy daggers were hurled almost simultaneously. Valerian staggered slightly. At once Cranford closed the gap between them but they were losing the protection of the corner and with shouts of triumph Finchley's bullies moved to each side of them.

Cranford shouted, "Blooded?"

"Naught to matter. Guard your side!"

The rogue who badly needed a shave was on his feet again. Beside him, a squat, powerfully built man snatched up a chair and flung it, and again the cousins were separated.

Valerian reeled, and another ruffian with long greasy hair

ran in from the front door and sprang for him, dagger upraised.

Cranford leaped, and with a crouch and a stamp forward drove his blade under the descending dagger and struck home. There was a gurgling cry and they faced one less bravo.

Valerian cried breathlessly, "Jolly good!" and the battle raged on, the cousins now fighting back to back.

Finchley retreated to the battered sideboard and wrenched open a drawer.

Mary had gone no farther than the scullery. She whispered, "Oh, my Lord! He has a pistol hid!"

She looked about in desperation, and her eyes lit on the milk jug. After she'd hurled the contents at Finchley, the jug had fallen to the table. She darted into that violent room, only to dance back again as a heavy club, aimed at Cranford's head, barely missed her.

Howling threats and obscenities, the tall man from the park jumped clear of Valerian's next lunge and hurled his dagger.

Valerian sprang aside.

Finchley drew his pistol and aimed it at Cranford's back.

"Oh, no, you don't!" Mary ran forward, snatched up the milk jug and brought it crashing down on the Major's head.

With an odd little grunt, Finchley half turned, folded up, and sprawled across the table, his pistol falling from his lax hand.

Mary picked it up and levelled it at the tall man from the park. He was facing Valerian, a confident leer on his coarse features, but his expression changed as he saw the girl aiming that very large pistol with two small and inexperienced hands. Backing away, he whined, "Now, ma'am . . . now, missy. Put it down, do, 'fore ye hurts yer pretty young self."

Risking a swift glance behind him, Cranford groaned, "I told you—"

Mary cried shrilly, "Surrender, you wicked creatures, else I'll shoot your friend!"

"Shoot away, mistress," howled a youthful rogue with a

loose mouth and an evil grin. "You only got one shot and I'll wager you don't rightly know how to use that there wepping!"

"You are very likely right," said a deep and familiar voice from behind Mary. "But I do. Allow me to relieve you of that nasty thing, Miss Stansbury."

She relinquished the pistol gladly into Henry Shorewood's hand and the ruffians drew back, watching murderously as the barrister aimed the weapon with steady assurance.

"Are you much hurt, Valerian?" he enquired.

"No," panted Gervaise.

"And you, my inept Major?"

Clutching his head, Finchley dragged himself up. "Much . . . you care," he moaned.

"True. I've no patience with stupidity. You might have known Cranford would suspect you. Ah, but here come the rest of your rogues, so we are not quite undone."

Cranford's eyes narrowed and he swore under his breath.

From the open front door came the sound of running feet and men shouting.

Staring in bewilderment from the barrister to Finchley, Mary stammered, "What—what do you mean? Can it be that—"

Cranford knew just what he meant. Whirling on Shorewood, he flailed his sword at the pistol and as the weapon fell from the barrister's grasp he snatched it up. "I always thought Finchley had someone with brains backing him," he cried, ducking a flying meat cleaver. "Get her out of this, Gervaise! Hurry!"

"I think you won't get very far," said Shorewood gratingly, clutching his wrist, but very aware of the steady hand that aimed the pistol at his heart.

Valerian gasped, "What—about you, Piers?"

"I'll hold them as long as I can—then follow. *Go!* If they take her we're done!"

Valerian jumped out of range, seized Mary's hand, and ran through the open rear door.

Finchley's bravos howled their rage and plunged forward, and more men raced in from the front.

Shorewood's great voice boomed, "Hold up, lads. Our former Lieutenant is a crack shot and I've no wish to die today."

They halted at once, glaring ragefully at Cranford, but not daring to disobey their employer.

Cranford knew that sooner or later Finchley or one of these ruffians would challenge him and that once he fired the pistol he would be speedily overwhelmed. He could only hope to delay them for as long as possible. He said, "So 'tis you I have to thank for all my disasters, eh, *gentleman* of the law?"

Shorewood gave a careless shrug. "Not all. And you are ungrateful, Cranford. Do but consider the lengths to which we went so that you would be encouraged to sell without the need to do you an injury."

"You were the rogue bidding on my estate," accused Cranford. "*You* caused the floods!"

"I mean to have your lands," admitted the barrister. "To which end I did arrange for the landslide, but I promise you my own hand was nowhere near the scene."

"You confounded villain! You murdered Gertrude!"

"The devil," exclaimed Shorewood indignantly. "I never harmed a lady in my life!"

"Gertrude is—was—a cow, you fool," snarled Finchley.

"To judge me a fool, my dear Major, is a risky error," said the barrister silkily. "I warned you our Lieutenant was a fighter and that we'd have done well to move faster. You enjoyed your little ploys to whittle him down gradually, but it took too long, and that business with his brother was quite ineffectual."

"You curst lawyers all talk too much," growled Finchley, staring balefully at Cranford. "And don't put it all off on my head. You were the one set the stable fire and had that yokel's cottage burnt down."

"*Mea culpa,*" acknowledged the barrister with an unrepentant grin. "A neat step, though later events proved it unnecessary. I will admit that your poor sportsmanship at the steeplechase took Cranford out of the race very tidily."

"Damn your eyes, do not dare name me a poor sportsman!"

"Can I perhaps assume you have at least succeeded in learning the whereabouts of the burial mound? Or did you botch that simple task also?"

"I'll tell you what I have *not* botched," snarled Finchley, his hatred for the barrister very apparent. "All these months you've talked to me as if I were dirt beneath your feet. And all these months you've thought to cheat me at the end, and get your greedy paws on Muse Manor and the hidden fortune! Did you fancy me too stupid to see it?"

"I knew exactly how stupid you are, dear partner," purred the barrister, "and planned accordingly."

With a lightning move he reached to an inner pocket.

Finchley grabbed a fallen dagger and hurled it at his partner's heart.

The barrister's face turned an ashen hue. He clutched at the handle of the dagger protruding from his chest, choked something incomprehensible, and collapsed.

Seizing his chance, Cranford leaped for the opening to the scullery, only to find it barred by a brute of a man flourishing a scythe. He sprang aside but the scythe whistled for his throat, and behind him Finchley shouted, "Finish the swine!" Another sweep of the deadly scythe. Cranford had no choice; he fired point-blank. The big man was hurled back and fell heavily.

Finchley roared, "Three of you new fellows go out to the backyard and surround him!"

The youth with the lecherous grin complained, "There's a curst tall fence back there, guv'nor!"

"Then run around it, you lazy clod! You four, get after Valerian and the girl. They can hang the lot of us!"

The new arrivals obeyed at once. The remainder, numbering about six now, closed on Cranford. Fighting them off desperately, his sword whirling, but retreating step by step, he knew there were too many. His only chance was to escape before he was completely surrounded.

The big ruffian from the park attack yelled exultantly, "We got him, mates!"

They plunged eagerly at their solitary opponent.

Cranford leaped onto the table and the lamp on it flickered. The lamp! Snatching it up, he shouted, "You like to play with fire! Here!" and hurled it at that lusting charge. It shattered and exploded into flame.

The joy had gone out of the attackers; howling with fear, they drew back. The big man's breeches were ablaze and his shrieks added to the uproar.

Not waiting to see the result, praying he had bought Mary and his cousin sufficient time, Cranford sprinted out of the back door, across a weedy and overgrown garden and through an open gate. He could discern men jumping down from the side fence and running at him. There was no sign of Walker or Tassels, but, confident that Valerian would not have left him without a mount, he ran swiftly from the cottage and, gathering his breath, whistled.

The shouts behind him were closer and louder. He recognized Finchley's howl and guessed the Major would have appropriated Shorewood's pistol.

A silver horse cantered to him.

"Bless you, my beauty!" he panted and vaulted to her back.

An enraged roar went up from the cottage.

There came the ear-splitting crack of a shot and a mighty unseen hand almost knocked him from the saddle.

He gasped, "Come on, lass! Faster!"

And, as always, Tassels obeyed.

Finchley and his ruffians would lose no time in following, and the villainous Major had already sent some of his men in pursuit of Mary and Valerian. The dandy would head for the nearest source of help, which would be the Manor. Cranford turned Tassels in that direction. The moon was brighter now.

Leaning forward, he scanned the meadows for other riders. Valerian had been hit, he was sure; God send he would have sufficient strength to protect Mary!

Racing at breakneck speed, he saw four horsemen ahead, apparently making for the village. He swung Tassels to the east and Muse Manor. It was taking the deuce of a time to get there. Tassels was doing her best, that was certain, but she had developed an odd gait and at times seemed almost to float through the air. He could hear hoofbeats behind him again, and tried to look back, but abandoned the attempt when pain, sudden and sharp, reminded him that Finchley had shot straight. Wearily, he urged the mare to greater speed. There were lights everywhere, waving about, and voices shouting. He wondered in a detached fashion if the Major's bullet had actually killed him and he was riding Tassels to the next plane of existence. For some reason that amused him, and he chuckled to himself.

"Piers! Thank goodness!"

Mary's voice, sounding very relieved.

Mary's face, glowing in the light of all the lanterns.

He blinked, and saw that Valerian stood beside Walker, talking to Tio Glendenning. There were others there now. Familiar faces drifted at him: Perry, dismounting; Constable Bragg in his cart; Bobby Peale, riding his old hack; all peering at him anxiously.

Mary looked frightened, but thank the Lord, she was safe now. Eager to tell her this, he swung down from the saddle, then caught at the stirrup, irritated because his right side hurt so fiercely.

Perry came up and threw an arm about him. "You clunch! Why did you not send for—"

Piers said in a faraway voice, "Mary . . . you're quite . . ."

Valerian swayed and sank down like a puppet whose string had snapped.

With a shrill cry of terror, Mary ran to kneel beside him. Looking up, her eyes frantic and full of tears, she stretched out a blood-stained hand and sobbed, "He is hurt! Please help! Oh—please!"

The viscount slanted a quick glance at Piers' white and enigmatic face. Catching his eye, Peregrine tightened his arm about his brother. "Look after her, please, Tio. Bobby, perhaps you and Mr. Bragg can carry Mr. Valerian into the house. Can you manage, if you lean on me, twin?"

With a great effort, Piers said wearily, "I can manage."

18

❧

"My dear boy!" Alarmed, General Lord Nugent Cranford rose rapidly from behind the desk in his study and hurried to pat his grandnephew gently on the shoulder and pull up a chair for him. "Whatever can you be thinking of? Only a week since you were shot and you've essayed a tiring journey into Town? I wonder Peregrine didn't put a stop to it! Be dashed if I can see what could be so curst urgent!"

Piers drew a slow breath and sat down cautiously. His side was stiff and painful and the journey to town in the rocking coach had been a good deal less than pleasant. He'd felt it both an obligation and a vital necessity, however, and not to be delegated to his twin, who was for the third and hopefully final time planning for his wedding. He said, "Perry doesn't know I'm here, sir."

"Nor should you be! Look at you! A regular death's head, and weak as a cat! You and your cousin are two of a kind, I declare! Here you've journeyed to Town for no *sensible* reason, and he's gone frippering off to Italy for no *possible* reason! Italy! When he should be recruiting his strength here in Town, and tending to nuptial arrangements. You'll know he has offered for Cordelia Stansbury?"

Piers tried not to flinch, but he was weaker than he knew and his eyes betrayed him. "I supposed he would, sir. You must be pleased."

The General had seen that briefly desolate look and to conceal his own sense of guilt said with forced heartiness, "And there's a massive understatement! I'm delighted! Purely delighted that the young rascal came up to scratch and honoured his obligation at last! But—there, I know you've never liked him and I think you cherished a *tendre* for the girl, so I'll say no more on that head. Though why he must dash off to *Italy* . . . of all places, baffles me!"

Piers could have enlightened him but he said, "Have you seen Miss Stansbury, sir?"

"Oh, yes. Delightful girl. A bit on the—er, harum-scarum side. But—these modern women, y'know. Like to take the bit 'twixt their teeth. Not demure and gentle like your grandmama, eh?"

Startled, Piers thought, '*Demure and gentle? Grandmama?*' and tried to equate that description with a large lady with a large voice and a domineering personality, who had ruled her husband and the family with a rod of iron. He smiled and kept his reservations to himself, which was as well because the General had not waited for comments.

"Even so, Miss Stansbury is charming. And much prettier than I had remembered. Good God! Do you say she ain't been to see you? After you and Gervaise risked your lives to wrench her from the hands of that dastardly Gresford Finchley?"

Actually, Mary had come to see him. It had been a difficult visit, for although, at his insistence, he had been allowed to get out of bed and sit in an armchair to receive her, and had made light of his wound, she had wept. Had she not allowed herself to be hornswoggled by the horrid Major, she'd said, scattering tears, neither Gervaise nor Piers would have been hurt. He had assured her she was talking nonsense, and had then been really hurt when she had blown her little nose and said earnestly that he was the *best friend* a lady could ever wish for. He pushed that bitter recollection from his mind and tried to concentrate on what his great-uncle was saying.

"... fine example of an Army officer, he showed himself to be! Small wonder he made a run for it. He'll be clapped into prison if he ever dares set foot on British soil again! As will that murderous solicitor should he recover of his wound. He is opinionated as ever, I'm told. Shows no whit of shame for his crimes, and means to conduct his own defence in Court. Much good will it do him! You might know that Nathan Stansbury would make such a mull of choosing his man of the law. A proper rogue he picked, eh? Though that don't surprise me. Lawyers ain't to be trusted. Too clever for their own good, most of 'em. Bear that in mind, my boy."

"Yes, I will, but—"

"Well, speak up, speak up! Why are you here? And don't say 'tis out of filial affection, for I shall not believe you!" He laughed heartily at this good joke, then asked, "Do you expect someone? You keep watching the door."

"I had sent for young Turner, sir."

"Herbert? Why? You'll not get a sensible conversation out of that poor fellow. He's likely talking to his cabbages. He does, y'know."

"Then perhaps we could send for him again. I've some questions he may be able to—"

"Pish! Nonsense! As well ask a snail. What the deuce are you about? Sit down, lad! Oh, very well. I'll send for him." The General reached behind him and tugged on the bell-pull, and when the butler appeared, sent him off to find his gardener. "Meanwhile," he said, apparently in an expansive mood, "you shall have a glass of cognac, Piers. Put some colour in your cheeks!"

He poured the brandy, handed Piers a glass, and was grumbling at the tardiness of his servants when the housekeeper came in.

She shot a quick glance at Piers and said in a nervous flurry of words, "Did you wish to see me, sir?"

"No, Eliza," said the General. "Lieutenant Piers wants a word with Herbert. Be so good as to desire him to—"

"He's—he's not here, sir. He has—er, gone out. In fact, I doubt he will return to—er, today, so you had best not wait for him, Mr. Piers."

"Not—return?" echoed the General, mystified. "What gobbledegook are you mouthing, woman? Send the boy here at once. I know he's about—I saw him just minutes ago in the back garden!"

"No, no, you must be mistaken, sir. Herbert's away. If there's something the Lieutenant wants to ask him, why, I can relay a message when—er, when he comes home."

"Which will be—tomorrow?" asked Piers gently. "Or never, perhaps? And why do you not look at me, Eliza?"

"Look at you?" said the General. "Why should Mrs. Turner look at you? Seen you before. Lots of times. In fact, I—"

"Your pardon, sir," interrupted Piers. "It's of no use for him to run, Eliza. Better for him to talk to me than to Bow Street."

Lord Nugent's jaw dropped and he half-whispered, *"Bow Street?"*

The housekeeper quailed, and wringing her apron said fiercely, "Oh, but you're a wicked young man, Piers Cranford! All these years being so friendly and kind, and now you try to get my boy into trouble only to help your worthless gypsy friend! Nugent! You must not let him make up his lies and deceits and false accusations!"

"What in the name of all that's wonderful are you blathering at?" demanded the General, having reached the end of his patience. "And what the deuce has Bow Street to do with my gardener, Piers?"

"I had hoped Herbert would tell you that himself, sir. It would be better were he to do so, Eliza."

"It's all lies, Nugent," cried the housekeeper shrilly. "Don't believe a word he says! He'll do anything to—"

"Hold your tongue, woman! And whether for better or worse, Piers, the boy's not here, so let's come at the root of all this backing and filling."

A timid voice interjected, "I—I'm here, Lieutenant Piers."

"No!" The housekeeper's scream was piercing, and she flew to throw her arms around her tall son and demand in near hysteria that he say nothing, that he had done nothing, and that Piers Cranford was cruelly trying to make him the scapegoat to protect his murdering steward.

The General, at his sternest, said, "That . . . will . . . do, Eliza! Herbert, have the goodness to explain all this rigmarole."

Herbert said, " 'Tis of no use, Mother. They'll find out anyhow." He put her from him firmly, and said, "I'm the guilty one, my lord. I killed Sidney Grover!"

Mrs. Turner burst into a flood of weeping.

The General said softly, "Now did you, by God! I wouldn't have thought you had it in you . . ."

"Because he so mercilessly tormented you?" asked Piers.

"No, sir! He was a bully and a beast, but I could have stood that. It was when he kept bragging and saying such evil things about Miss—Miss Laura. She is so beautiful and—and so pure. And the things he said . . . Vile, loathsome things about what he would do when she was his wife."

"Sidney Grover?" exploded the General incredulously. "Finchley's groom fancied he would wed a lady of Quality? Fella must have been demented."

"He claimed he knew things Major Finchley had done, sir. Bad things that could have ruined the Major, and very likely got him hung. He said the Major wouldn't dare deny him. Miss Laura was as good as—as in his bed!"

"Pretty talk, and so much hot air, likely," said the General with a snort of disgust. Scowling, he added sombrely, "Black-mail must be the most vicious crime under the sun . . . Still, you'd have done well to laugh at him rather than ruin your life by beating him to death."

"He didn't, my lord," declared the housekeeper between sobs. "My poor son knows not what he says. Don't pay heed to—"

"Mother—stop," said Herbert with surprising resolution. "I did indeed put an end to the filthy beast. I have no regrets. He wanted killing."

Over the housekeeper's distraught wails, Piers observed, "He was a strong and powerful man. What did you hit him with, Herbert?"

Turner held up a fist. It was large and muscular, and he said, "I can kill a bull with this, sir. I did once, when Farmer Milling's bull tried to gore me in the meadow. I knew when Grover went down, I'd hit hard."

"Straight to the jaw, eh?"

"That's right, sir."

"No," said Piers intently. "That's wrong, Bert. Sidney Grover was beaten to death from behind. His skull was crushed not by a fist but by some heavy object."

Through a hushed moment they all stared at him.

Herbert said haltingly, "Then . . . is it possible I . . ."

"You *didn't* murder that evil man," cried the housekeeper, smiling through her tears as she hugged him. "You would never attack a man from behind!"

"No. Never. But—I did knock him down."

"And someone else came along," said Piers thoughtfully. "Someone wanting to be rid of him, who saw him, perhaps try-ing to get up, and finished the business."

"Finchley!" The General drove a fist so hard at the desktop that his quill-pen leaped from the standish. "Grover was a threat and very likely blackmailing him, so as you said, Piers, the man saw a chance to end his persecution. And persecution it is!

Almost I can sanction his action. If ever I lay my hands on who is—" He broke off hurriedly, turned very red, and said, "Well, you may be at ease, Eliza. Your son has not a man's blood on his hands. I'd thought we might have to smuggle him out of the country, but by what my clever grandnephew has found, we've but to take our case to Bow Street, and—"

"You'll not have far to go, my lord."

The new voice came from the doorway. Turning, Piers was touched by a chill apprehension.

Joshua "Pedlar," clad in a dark brown coat and red waistcoat and distinguished by a neat powdered wig, advanced to show the General a small staff surmounted by a crown.

"Bow Street?" The General scowled. "How dare you march into my study unannounced, sir?"

The Runner handed him a card. "You may be glad I did come unannounced, Lord Cranford. I heard enough to convince me of young Turner's innocence."

Reading the card, the General muttered, "Joshua Swift. Hmm . . . I've heard that name, I think."

Joshua Swift, who had other names and identities, smiled a tight smile. " 'Not always swift, but sure,' perhaps, sir? I've been so called."

"And with reason, by what I hear," said Piers. "Does this solve your case, Swift? Or are we still to see you—er, peddling around my village?"

"Time alone will tell, Mr. Cranford. Although, actually, this was not the case I have been following. As I think you are aware."

The General said sharply, "What's this? More trouble?"

"Mr. Swift appears to believe that is the case," said Piers with a bored smile. "What will be your next move, Swift?"

"In this particular case, Mr. Cranford?"

"Unless you are able to prove another," said Piers, his gaze challenging. For just an instant, frustration banished the Runner's bland and enigmatic smile. Recovering, he said that Herbert must accompany him to Bow Street, though he doubted the youth would be detained.

Piers said, "I'll go with you, Bert."

"You will do no such thing," said the General vehemently. "You run along, Mr. Swift. I shall escort Turner to the Court."

Piers put up his hand to hide a grin and the Runner looked considerably taken aback at having been told to "run along," but after a momentary hesitation he bowed and followed Mrs. Turner to the door.

When they were gone Herbert moved very fast to take up Piers hand and before he could be prevented had pressed a kiss on it.

"Come now," said Piers, red-faced with embarrassment. "There's no call for that, lad."

"For that and more, sir," said Turner, his fine eyes shining with unshed tears. "Always, you have been so kind and—and stood between me and those who despised me. Now—you have saved my life! I really thought I had killed Sidney Grover and I was resigned to pay the penalty! If you *knew* what it meant to find I had not . . . ! I shall never be able to thank you enough!"

Piers directed a steady look at his great uncle. "Why, that's what families are all about, eh, sir? We stand by our own."

The General's jaw sagged once again.

Turner said uncertainly, "Do you—do you really think of me as—as part of your family, Mr. Cranford?"

"I do, and so do we all. Now you had best go and comfort your poor mama; she has had a wrenching time of it, I make no doubt."

Herbert nodded and walked quickly from the room, head up and step sprightly.

Lord Nugent, still staring glassy-eyed at Piers, mumbled, "You . . . know!"

"Gervaise told me."

"My dear God! Then the whole *ton* will know!"

"Not so. He is an honourable man. He'll keep a still tongue— if that's what you wish."

"Do you say Gervaise is . . . honourable?" Even more glassy-eyed, the General stammered, "But—I thought—you— and—he— Now, by Zeus and all his confounded thunders and lightnings! I demand to be told— Oh, Gad! I apologize, Eliza, but you should not come creeping in if you don't want to hear me swear at my infuriatingly sly grandnephew. What do you have in that great box? Some of Herbert's clothes, just in case?"

"No, sir. Something of your own, which I now return and can only pray you will forgive me."

"Well, I won't," roared the General, waving the box away. "I'll endure no more soul-bearings, and so I tell you! I am a poor gentle old soul, and—" His impassioned and questionable declaration was cut short as his housekeeper allowed Piers to take the box from her. It was heavier than he'd guessed and momentarily he had forgotten his wound. With a gasp he dropped the box and, falling, it burst open.

"Great . . . saints!" gasped Lord Nugent, his eyes goggling.

Scarcely less astonished, Piers stared down at the small fortune in golden guineas and hand-written bank notes that had tumbled from the box. "Why, Eliza," he exclaimed, "you are a wealthy woman! But Herbert won't need a tenth of this to his defence, even if he is bound over for trial, which I—"

His great-uncle, who had been gazing down at the pile, interrupted frowningly. "This is *my* signature! See here! My note for five hundred guineas . . . And this one for two hundred . . . These were amounts I paid to—"

"To your blackmailing housekeeper!" Sinking to her knees before him, Mrs. Turner said brokenly, "Yes, unlike my son, I am guilty, Nugent. But 'tis all here. I touched not a penny."

Piers said quietly, "I'll leave you alone, sir," and started to the door.

"Oh, no, you don't," growled the General, throwing out an

arresting hand. "I want a witness to this chicanery!"

"I rather doubt Eliza intended the money for herself, Uncle."

The General scowled from his grandnephew to his house-keeper. "What then? This woman has been blackmailing me for years!"

Mrs. Turner raised a woeful, tear-streaked face. "For our—son, Nugent." She glanced at Piers. "There—now you know."

"He already knew! Our guilty secret is doubtless being bruited about from Land's End to John o'Groat's by now! What has it to say to anything? You didn't rob me on the grounds of our natural son—poor fellow."

"No, sir. But—because of, and for—him. Yes, I know how you must despise me. It was only—only that . . . Well, I knew of your unhappy involvement with that treasonable League of Jewelled Men— No! Do not turn from me, I beg! I know you were unaware of their real purpose and had managed to conceal your connection with them. Only—you did so much for the Cranfords when their parents died. You sent the boys to University. You gave Dimity a generous dowry when she wed Sir Anthony Farrar. But—year after year, not a penny for poor Herbert. Oh, I know he was an embarrassment to you because of his accident—"

"No, no," mumbled the General, avoiding his nephew's eyes. "He is a good lad. I—I kept him here, did I not?"

"Yes. And out of sight as much as was possible. And would acknowledge to none that he is your own flesh and blood." She held up her hands prayerfully and begged, "You are a proud man. I understood how you have felt. But—oh, Nugent, do pray forgive me! I never meant you harm. I was just so afraid that if—if anything should happen to me there would be no one to—to provide for my dearest boy."

"Well, and there you misjudge me," said the General, bending to take her hands and adding gruffly, "Come now, m'dear, get up, do. And there is no call for such censorious looks from you, nephew! I had every intention to provide for Herbert. He's a fine-looking lad—do you deny that, sir?"

"No, indeed," said Piers meekly.

"And but for the accident with that stupid nag would have turned into a son I'd be proud to acknowledge. What d'ye say to that, sir?"

"I say there is plenty to be proud of now, Uncle."

"Then you may keep a civil tongue in your head if you expect me to use this great windfall to fund your purchase of the Quail Hill property—*and* to tow you comfortably out of the River Tick! Your church steeple and the flood and the cow and the whole blasted rest of it. And there I go—looking after you again! D'ye object, m'dear? 'Twould be curst lonely in this house if you were to go off and leave me! We shall see Herbert well secure for all his days. I swear it!"

Mrs. Turner buried her face in her hands, and he threw an affectionate arm about her even as he scowled defiantly at his grandnephew.

Piers said, "Sir—how can I thank you?"

"By relieving me of my Trusteeship and taking on all the burdens of your damned nuisance of an estate! I'm done with it as of this minute. Oh, curse and confound it, she's at it again! *Why* must females always become watering-pots when they're happy, I wonder . . ."

Cranford left them and walked slowly along the flagway. There was no sign of his coach and he deduced that Bobby must be walking the pair. Was little Mary weeping because she was happy? He thought wistfully that hers was a more sunny nature; she would most likely be smiling. Such a delightful smile with those pretty lips that curved so adorably . . . He shook himself mentally. It was stupid to scourge himself so. The die was cast. He must be happy—for her dear sake. At least, he had the satisfaction of knowing he had been of some small service to her. And she was fond of him. At least, she had seemed genuinely affected when she'd come to visit him. He would have that memory, and eventually this crushing sense of loss and a grey lonely existence must fade and—

"Good day to you, Lieutenant Piers Cranford!"

The harsh accents told him who had spoken, and his heavy heart grew heavier. "Good day, Mrs. Stansbury," he said, removing his tricorne and essaying a bow.

Mary's mother was, as usual, clad in the height of fashion and had to bend her head to avoid displacing her high French wig as the footman handed her from the luxurious coach. They were some distance from the General's house and she said with marked condescension, "You may escort me to Lord Nugent's door. Oh dear. You carry your arm in a sling, I see. If you are not able . . ."

He assured her he was able, and was inwardly glad she did not lean on him as he offered his good arm and retraced his steps. "You are looking very well, ma'am," he said.

"Oh, yes. It is expected of me, and so I contrive. I wish I could return the compliment, but you do not look well at all. Perhaps you will regain your looks in time. Some people do, you know, so do not be in despair. I am here to see your great-uncle so as to set his mind at rest. You will know that my daughter, bless her gentle heart, has received a most flattering offer?"

He acknowledged that he was aware.

"But you do not say you wish them happy," she scolded, slapping his wrist with her gloved hand. "Very mean-spirited in you, sir!"

"I apologize, ma'am. Pray believe I wish them every happiness. Shall Mr. Stansbury return to England for the—the wedding?"

"But of course," she said, halting her graceful progress along the flagway and opening her eyes at him. "What a foolish question. He will have to give the bride away. If he does not, I suppose . . . Hmm. Perchance Lord Nugent would accept that honour. Now *that* would serve very well . . . I must ask him."

"Is Miss Stansbury in town, ma'am?"

The wig shivered to the suggestion of a nod. "She has to choose her bridals. Lucky girl. I vow all London's ladies will envy her such a fine match. Well, I cannot stand here keeping you company. I wish you good day, Lieutenant. You might have done well to emulate dear Gervaise and spend a little time in sunny Italy. He did not look near as poorly as you, but—you *might* perhaps benefit from a rest."

Her tone said clearly that he had one foot in the grave. She was in *alt*, of course, but he could not refrain from thinking she could at least have said something kind about his efforts to rescue her daughter. 'Mean-spirited, Cranford,' he thought. He bowed awkwardly over the hand that was thrust at him imperiously. It was a thin hand and it turned suddenly to grip his own in a claw-like clutch even as the lady uttered a faint squawk.

Fearing she had suffered some kind of seizure, he looked up.

Mrs. Stansbury was holding her large fur muff to her cheek. Shielded by it, she exclaimed, "*Disgusting!* It offends *every* sense of propriety!"

Bewildered, he stammered, "It—does? I mean—what does, ma'am?"

She glared at him. "Are you blind? Do you not see that I am hiding?"

The only person he could see nearby was an elderly lady. Wrapped in a voluminous cloak and followed by a servant, she led a small dog by means of a long scarlet riband.

"I see Lady Bottesdale and her footman," he said softly. "Has she offended you, ma'am?"

She hissed, "Of course she offends me, as she offends every person with a modicum of refinement! Oh, how *can* you look so *stupid?* Do you not *see* it?"

Striving, he said, "It . . . Er, do you mean her little pug-dog, ma'am? It does stop frequently, but I promise you it has not behaved—er, improperly."

310

Her muff flailed agitatedly and he had to jerk back to avoid being struck. "It *walks about!*" she declared with a fierce gesture of emphasis. "It offends by *being!* I might know that a man—a soldier, especially—would be blind to such vulgar conduct, but Elmira Bottesdale knows I am repulsed by the creature and I vow it delights her to distress a person of sensitivity and discrimination. Here we are, thank heaven! You may escort me up these steps. Hurry, before she comes up with us! You can walk quicker than that, surely?"

Lengthening his stride, he asked, "Do you disapprove of people walking their dogs in Town, Mrs. Stansbury?"

"I refuse to acknowledge that it is a dog!" she declared. "How *any* person of sensitivity could choose a pet that holds its tail curled up over its back so that all its—its *nether regions* are clear to see—Ugh! 'Tis beyond my comprehension! One wonders how Elmira was bred up. As a lady of culture and refinement, I cannot forgive such a deliberate offence to the eye! Ring the bell if you please, and so farewell, Lieutenant!"

Biting his lip hard and somehow suppressing the laughter that fought to escape him, Cranford bowed and made his way back down the steps.

The dowager Lady Bottesdale was level now, and as he drew aside and said a polite "Good day, my lady," she looked up into his face. She replied as politely, but a pair of dark roguish eyes met his own; one of them winked.

It was all Cranford could do to control himself.

Bobby Peale tooled the coach around the corner and Peddars sprang down to assist his employer to climb inside. As the door closed, Cranford delighted his retainers by breaking into whoops of laughter. His mood was lightened and the day seemed less dark. Thank the good Lord for elderly ladies with a sense of humour! He could scarce wait to tell Aunt Jane of the shocking behaviour of the Dowager Lady Bottesdale.

As he had expected, when they reached Muse Manor he was in deep disgrace. His aunt was angry and really upset because he had disobeyed all the doctor's orders and gone racketing off to London.

"But I left you a note, dear," he protested feebly.

"A note! Which I found after you had gone, having deceived me into believing you had just stepped out for a breath of air!"

His efforts to explain were ignored. The good lady had been terribly distressed and worried. Piers' declarations of love were not to be heeded. He had demonstrated that he gave not a button for the feelings of those who *really* loved him, and he had to endure a royal raking down before he was able to tell her of Florian's innocence. Her mood at once changed from martyrdom to joy, and when he described his encounter with Mrs. Regina Stansbury and the abandoned behaviour of Lady Elmira Bottesdale, Jane Guild laughed till she cried.

Her relief, however, was soon tempered by concern. She knew her nephew too well to be unaware that his brisk energy had faded. In the days that followed, he was almost unnaturally bright and cheerful but several times when he was unaware that she watched him, she thought to detect a deep sadness in his eyes. Convinced that he was grieving, she called in the local apothecary and an indignant Piers was advised he had over-taxed his strength and was ordered to rest for at least a week. He did not protest this edict too forcefully, but developed the habit of sitting on a chaise longue by the window in his room, reading. Peeping in on him from time to time, his aunt noted that his gaze was seldom on the printed page, but that he looked instead towards the north-east and Quail Hill.

Troubled, she decided to send off a note to Peregrine, wedding or not, but on that very afternoon Florian drove up in a fine coach, accompanied by a radiantly happy Laura Finchley and a hawk-faced older gentleman. It seemed to Miss Guild that from the moment the coach door swung open, the house came to life again. Piers came downstairs and was embraced by his young friend and by Miss Finchley. The older gentleman was introduced as Signor Gabriele San Sebastiano. He offered a magnificent bow and smiled constantly, seeming a very cheerful individual although he spoke little English.

They all adjourned to the withdrawing-room and Miss Guild rang for tea, whereupon Miss Finchley suddenly burst into tears and threw herself into Piers arms, declaring her undying gratitude for all he had done in their behalf.

"And Valerian also," put in Florian, seating himself on the sofa beside his love and dabbing tenderly at her tearful eyes.

"Gervaise?" said Piers, obeying his aunt's militant gesture and occupying his favourite wing chair. "Is he back in England already?"

"Not so far as I'm aware," replied Florian. "But he sent a servant to escort this gentleman, and—oh, how can I tell you? It is so wonderful!"

They waited eagerly and although rather incoherent at times, the handsome young man so many had taken for a foundling or a gypsy was able at last to control his emotion and tell his story. While in Italy, Valerian had chanced to meet a youth who so resembled Florian that the likeness astounded him. His new acquaintance was a member of a family of wealthy vintners and was only too pleased to invite his English friend to their large and charming villa. It had taken Valerian very little time to discover that while a small boy, the eldest son, who also was named Florian, had been taken to England on holiday and a summer boat ride had turned to disaster. They knew the child had been rescued, but despite all their efforts to trace the men who had snatched him from the river, they were never found. The little boy had been the pride of his house and the family had never given up hope that their prayers would be answered and the beloved lost one would be restored to them. Valerian, who knew some Italian, had told them as much as he knew of Florian's history, and imbued with new hope, the patriarch had at once travelled to England accompanied by his priest and servants who were fluent in the language. No sooner had the old gentleman set eyes on Florian than he'd been sure of his identity, and the youth's faint recollections of a big bed and a dog and a white pony had confirmed that he was indeed the missing heir and that his true name was Florian Gabriele San Sebastiano.

Thus, the fortunes of Miss Laura Finchley and Florian Consett had been reversed; Miss Finchley was the daughter of an accused murderer who had fled the country leaving only debts and disgrace behind him, and the penniless gypsy lad was now the heir to a fortune and member of a large and loving family who were waiting eagerly to welcome him home.

The occupants of Muse Manor were overjoyed. The entire staff was assembled, Piers called for champagne and refreshments, toasts were drunk, and the rest of the day passed in celebration and congratulations. Unable to sue for the hand of his beloved in the usual way, Florian intended to approach Laura's maternal grandmother. Once her permission was obtained, they would return to Italy in the company of his newfound grandfather where, in due course, Miss Laura Finchley would become Signora Florian San Sebastiano.

Dinner that night was a merry occasion; Mrs. Burrows summoned helpers from the village and outdid herself in providing a splendid five-course meal. The elderly Italian demanded Mrs. Burrows' presence, kissed the blushing cook's hand, and embarked on what was obviously a heartfelt appreciation of her skills at having created fare un banchetto-superbo!

It was an evening to be long remembered, and the participants went happily to their beds. The following morning farewells were said, promises of visits exchanged, and the guests drove off to share their glad tidings with Peregrine and the many friends of whom Florian was deeply fond, some of whom had constituted the only family he had known.

Standing with Piers' arm about her as they watched the coach rumble down the drivepath, Miss Guild said sighfully, "What a blessing that they have found their happiness at last.

'Twill be a whole new life for Laura. She will lose many friends, but I suppose she will find new ones to replace them."

"She did not lose the one she loves," he said. "That is a loss that can never be replaced."

19

I t was a dull, grey afternoon, windy and chill, but Cranford paused to rest at the top of the bridge, gazing at the cottage, now deserted, where his beloved had dwelt with her eccentric but warm-hearted aunts.

His cloak billowed and he drew it closer with a guilty awareness that if Aunt Jane had already missed him she would be worrying again. He'd not intended to walk so far, but the house had become unendurable after Florian and his party had left. He flattered himself that he'd carried it off well enough, and heaven knows he was glad for their happiness. But he knew himself for an envious man, because that very happiness had brought a keener awareness of his own empty future. All this past week he had tried to tell himself that someday he would find another lady—and known it for a lie. Mary was in truth a *rara avis*. How could he hope ever to find someone with so bright and resolute a spirit? Who else would possess the same lilting little laugh? What other lips would curve so prettily into that mischievous but so sweet smile? He had found his true love at last and given her his heart, and although he had known little of women, he knew he would never—could never—love again. And he had so hoped for children of his own . . . Still, not to despair! He had a brother he loved and who was soon to be wed. Hopefully he would at least be an uncle, and Perry would, he knew, allow him to have a part in the lives of his nieces and nephews.

The cottage had a desolate and abandoned air. Soon after his return home he had sent Sudbury down there to learn if any of the aunts were in residence and the groom had returned saying the cottage was empty. He had therefore sent off a letter to Mrs. Caroline Westerman at the London house, stating his desire to purchase the river parcel. The lady had responded with a prompt and cordial offer to negotiate with his solicitor, since she and her sisters were now in agreement to sell. He had instructed his own man of the law, Barnabas Evans, to represent him in the matter, and being acquainted with legal processes had been mildly surprised by the speed of the various transactions. It now appeared that with luck the sale would be finalized in time for his twin's wedding. Peregrine and Zoe could live in the cottage while their new home was being built—just where Perry had so longed to see it, atop Quail Hill.

Mary was doubtless still in Town. He had learned that the choosing of bride clothes was a lengthy business. He had no least desire to visit the cottage and reawaken all the memories it held for him, and so turned his steps instead up the hill. This was where he first had met the lady he had not wanted, and had come to want with every fibre of his being. He wandered about, determined not to be tormented by memory, but surrendering at last when her lovely image persistently invaded his mind; feeling very close to her in these familiar surroundings; loving her; searching, out of habit, for one of her beads . . .

⁓

The sound of galloping hooves brought Jane Guild running to the door Peddars was already swinging open.

317

"Perry!" she gasped. "Oh, thank heaven!"

Sir Peregrine dismounted, thrust the reins at Sudbury, who came hurrying to take them, and limped rapidly up the steps and through the front door. His face was grim as he demanded, "Where is he? Is it very bad? What happened? A relapse?"

"No, no." Miss Guild caught his arm as he started to make his awkward way up the stairs. "He is not here, Perry!"

"Not here? But I thought—I was *sure* he is in much pain! Do you say he is no worse?"

"He is not . . . better. Exactly. But—oh, never look so afraid. Come into the morning room."

He followed her and took the armchair beside her, saying impatiently, "For heaven's sake, Aunt Jane. Tell me! Something is very wrong with my twin. I have felt it more keenly every day and should have come sooner, I know. Have I failed him utterly?"

"No, my very dear. There is nothing you, or anyone, can do to help him, though I believe you are right. The poor boy is suffering cruelly, but—it is worse than a physical pain. He loved her, you see. And—and she had given her heart to Gervaise Valerian."

Sir Peregrine stared at her in bewilderment. "Cordelia Stansbury? But—Piers knew she loved Gervaise. Everyone knows. Why on earth—"

She shook her head helplessly. "Who can say why a man loves one particular lady? Or why he goes on hoping she will return his affection even when 'tis perfectly clear she is deep in love with another man?"

Baffled, he muttered, "He thought her plain . . ."

"He sees her now with the eyes of love. In truth she is no beauty, but she has—I suppose one could describe it as a—a sort of glow."

"He offered for her, and she laughed at him. Heavens above, how could he love her after that?" Springing up, he began to limp about distractedly. "I might have known! Always he has been the quiet one, comforting and caring for us all, shouldering our burdens, and never a word of his own hopes. I know—I *knew* that if he once threw his heart over the hedge it would be a forever thing with him. That notorious jade has broken his generous heart. And he let her, the idiot!" Pausing to look down at her, he said miserably, "My poor idealistic twin! Aunt Jane, whatever are we to do? How can we help him?"

She said sadly, "I think we cannot. We can only wait and pray he finds his own happiness someday."

<hr />

"Well, and did you find it, sir?"

The clear voice caused Piers' heart to give a spasmodic leap. His head jerked up. He half-whispered, "Mary . . . !"

For an instant she was dismayed by the change in him, then she said cheerily, "Yes. I'm glad you recognize me."

She wore blue today; a soft blue gown under a thick cloak of darker blue. Her curls blew softly under her hood, her cheeks were rosy, and her eyes held a warm smile. He forced himself to look away, and said lightly, "Of course I recognize you. If I appeared surprised, 'twas because I had understood you were in London, choos——Oh, Jupiter! You will have missed your friend! Florian and Laura came to—"

"To tell you their news. I know. They came here first." She stepped closer and took his arm, then, noticing how he shrank from her touch, drew back and said in alarm, "Oh, how stupid of me. Have I hurt you?"

"Only by removing your hand. My arm is not damaged. Our apothecary is something of a tyrant and demands that I not use the arm for a short while."

Smiling, she took his arm again, but very gently. "Is it not wonderful, Piers? I was quite worried for Laura. She is too softhearted and—"

"Not an Amazon like someone I could name," he said, struggling to appear at ease and yearning to pull her close and kiss those rosy lips.

"As I was saying," she said, giving him a stern glance, "Laura is easily crushed, and her father's disgrace could well have sent her into a decline. Now—it has all worked out beautifully, do you not agree?"

"I do. She is—is very fortunate."

"As is he! Your friend has won himself a gentle and kind lady who will make him a wonderful wife."

"Oh, I agree. I did not mean—I only mean that—"

"That marriage will solve all her problems? One can but hope."

"It certainly will bring her happiness—and Florian also. When two people really love one another, as they do, I would think they've the chance for a joyous sharing through the years. Surely—you entertain such—hopes for your own future?"

She was silent, her lips pursed thoughtfully as they made their way higher up the softly undulating hillside. Then she said, "There is the barrow! Over there."

He turned at once to look at the green mound she indicated. "Oh, Gad! Then there really is one! And it *is* on the river parcel! Small wonder old Finchley was so desperate to buy it!"

They approached the mound together and Cranford gazed down at the line that was visible in the turf. "To think people—centuries ago—buried their treasures here . . ."

"And their bones," she said, twinkling at him. "I did not disturb those, but you may be sure Major Finchley would have felt no such qualms."

"True. Did you really—dig here, Mary? It seems almost sacrilegious."

"I suppose," she said, firing up, "had you been a pirate and found bones and treasure hid on a desert island, you'd have been too noble to dig them up! However badly scorched you were!"

He could not restrain a grin. "Such terms you use, Miss Stansbury!"

"I am not Miss Stansbury at this moment, sir. I am the outrageous Miss Westerman, who dwelt with savages and flouted all the conventions with not a *soupçon* of shame!"

"There is no need for that Plan now, surely?" But reminded of Valerian's now straitened circumstances, he asked, "And if you should stand in need of funds, will you be allowed to benefit from your treasure?"

She turned and they began to walk slowly down the hill. Joying in her nearness, and with a not very sincere mental apology to his absent cousin, he reached out and took up her hand, managing to restore it to his arm.

Mary watched this procedure with interest and replied, "Buried treasure belongs to the Crown, as you know. But our solicitor—we've a new one, by the bye—is disputing that ruling because he says it applies only to gold coins and golden objects—not to gems."

"Does he entertain hopes of the outcome?"

"Yes. But I think 'tis rather in the way of splitting hairs, don't you agree?"

"I'm afraid I do. But there is a reward—no?"

"Quite a large one. And if you do not betray me, I shall keep the ill-gotten gains I have accumulated thus far."

"Rascal!" He patted her hand, his mind hoarding that pert little smile. "What does my cousin have to say to this?"

"Oh, you know Gervaise." She glanced up at him from under her lashes. "He has not the least respect for the laws of the land. If he had his way we would dig up the entire mound at dead of night and have a boat waiting to carry us over to France!"

"Likely you're in the right of it. But he has many—good qualities, and—and—you will be able to reform him, I've no doubt."

"Good gracious me! Why ever should I wish to do such a

321

thing? The female who weds a man with the intent to change his ways is a widgeon! On the other hand, I have to admit that the lady who weds Lieutenant Piers Cranford will *have* to change him to save her own sanity."

Taken aback by this unkind remark, he said, "You must judge me a very vexing fellow, ma'am. What have I done to give you so poor an opinion of me?"

"You have a truly dreadful habit of flinging yourself into danger! Constantly! With no thought of how that trait distresses others!"

"No! You are unreasonable! Because I chanced to—"

"No one takes such chances! When you are not fighting Mohocks or charging into burning barns—"

He said hurriedly, "You know very well I had no choice in either instance! Truly, I am not such a fool as to court danger, Mary."

"Perhaps not, but nor do you run from it. I vow your poor wife will live in terror that you are risking your life to save someone or something, without a thought for—"

"Yet knowing Valerian's volatile nature, it does not concern you that he is—er, not exactly law-abiding?"

"Do not change the subject! However, I own that I wish he showed more sense, for I am very fond of him. But I have to tend to my own affairs, and cannot—"

"Mary!" Halting, he faced her and, heart racing, said, "I had understood you were in Town, choosing your bride clothes."

She said mischieviously, "You have met my mama."

"Yes. Is she—I mean, is there any hope she is—is mistaken?"

Resuming their much interrupted stroll, she said judicially, "Mama, you know, tends to live as though events that suited her were happening—regardless of whether they actually are."

"Then—" He drew her to a halt again. "You were not in Town buying clothes?"

"Oh, yes. I have quite a sum, for I was able to sell one of my beads. Never say you are going to object?"

He put his available hand on her shoulder, and looking deep into her lovely eyes said firmly, "For mercy's sake, stop teasing me and tell me the truth. Are you or are you not betrothed to Gervaise?"

Her brows arching, she said, "Oh, no."

He gave a gasp and his own eyes closed for an instant, so that he missed the tender smile that was bestowed on him.

"I had thought you understood," she said, all innocence, "that I have a Plan. I have already looked at two small houses. In Kensington Village. And—"

"Kensington Village? You little scamp! Do you say you intend to move there and write your shipwreck book?"

"But of course. Aunt Celeste means to be my chaperone."

"My dear God! If ever there was a lady unsuited to—"

"Be so kind as to not speak unkindly of my aunt, sir!"

"No—I should not, I don't mean—Mary, Mary! Have you even *started* this famous book of yours?"

She walked on, taking his arm uninvited. "Well . . . not exactly. But I have written to my papa asking him to advise me about life on a desert island. When I receive his reply I shall be able to begin."

"But—surely you know more of the subject than does he?"

"How should I? I have never so much as set eyes on one!"

"But—you said—I understood—"

Mary smiled, and lifting one hand, touched his cheek gently. "Poor boy who looks so haggard and ill."

It was very hard, and he could not resist kissing those caressing fingers, but he said sternly, "Never mind about that. Cordelia Mary, I want the truth. Were you ever shipwrecked?"

She folded her hands demurely before her and shook her bowed head, looking, he thought achingly, like a little girl knowing she is about to be spanked.

"Then—good heavens! Where were you during the year you were believed to be on your desert island?"

"In the New World." She looked up, her eyes dancing. "And do you know, Piers, it is the nicest place, full of the most friendly and kind people! You would—"

"Never mind what I 'would' or 'would not,' Miss Sauce! What were you doing in the New World?"

"Well, I had decided to run away, you see, so Mama put it about that I had gone to Egypt to find my papa. But actually, I chanced to meet a very pretty lady from a place called Boston, and she had two darling children but no governess, so I—"

"Lord above! You became a *governess?*"

"Yes, sir," she said, dimples peeping.

"In Boston."

"Yes. And it is a most interesting—"

"If it is so nice and interesting, why did you come home?"

She opened her eyes very wide and said an astonished, "I am an English lady! Where else should I go? Oh, I see what you mean. Well, Piers dear—"

He started. "What?"

"No, pray do not interrupt. The thing was—the children were very pretty but—so indulged and *naughty!* And their silly mama would not permit— What are you doing?"

"I am about to kiss you. If you are quite sure you do not still love Gervaise."

"But I do. I always will."

He drew back and the arm that had slipped around her waist was withdrawn.

"That," she said, "is why I could not come to see you again while you were ill."

He said dully, "I think you are playing a very unkind game with me, Mary. You said you rejected his offer."

"Well, of course. How could I marry him unless I loved him in that—very special way?" Peeping at his white and drawn face, she went on, "But I had been so silly, do you see? As a

324

young girl I fell in love—not with Gervaise, but with his beauty and charm and debonair ways. I lacked the sense to know I had fallen in love with a handsome face and a gentleman I did not begin to know. And by the time I found a gentleman who was—everything Gervaise was not . . . I had made such a cake of myself . . ."

He looked up at her, scarcely daring to hope.

Sudden tears sprang into her eyes. She said huskily, "Oh, my dear. I am so conceited as to be sure you love me and— No, wait! You must allow me to finish while I still have the courage. I began to love you, I think, when I saw you jousting that ugly warning sign. Through Laura I learned much more about you. I found out how you had struggled with your problems. I saw how bravely you fought those horrid ruffians in the park. If you knew how my heart was wrung when, needing desperately to win the steeplechase, you ruined your chances so as to help your friend. No! Do not tell me any man would have done the same. They did not, did they? *You* were the one to aid him."

Feeling decidedly light-headed, he mumbled, "I think the other riders did not see or they would've stopped. I'm sure Bertie Crisp, for instance—"

"Bertie Crisp! What chance had he of winning, I should like to know! You were the favourite—you could have come in first! You rushed home to help poor Florian, and fought off that howling mob! You were the one to rescue me from that horrid Major. And do not, sir, claim that Gervaise would have done so, for he came charging in so recklessly that he almost ruined—"

Piers could restrain himself no longer. Mary was seized in a grip of iron and crushed against him despite her smothered pleas that he not hurt his poor side. She was then kissed so long and hard that she would have protested had she not been so enjoying it. When at last she was released she was as dazed as he, and sinking down beside him on a convenient mound, she gasped, "Are you quite sure, my dearest love? I really am a shamed woman and held in contempt by the *ton,* and you are so very honourable a man."

"I am more sure than I have been sure of anything in my life. Oh, Mary—Miss Cordelia Mary Westerman Stansbury—I do so adore you. I would go down on my knees save that I am not sure I have the strength to get up! Will you, my love, do me the great honour of becoming just plain Mrs. Piers Cranford?"

Her lips gave him his answer though they did not utter a word.

Some indeterminate time later, safely locked in his good arm, Mary said dreamily, "Will you still love me if I am sent to prison for keeping some of the jewels I found?"

He had long since removed her bonnet and now kissed the top of her ear. "I shall visit you every day," he promised fondly.

"Hmmm . . ."

"I think I must be alarmed by that particular 'hmmm.' What is your inventive mind scheming now?"

"Well, do you know, Piers, even if my mama sanctions our match—"

"Oh, egad! I'd forgot your mama! And much as I love you, my dearest one, I will not allow the lady to bully either of us! If she senses that resolve, we may have to wait for your father's permission."

"Not so. I am an elderly spinster of one and twenty, my darling, so I am free to wed whomever I choose. The problem is that I know how badly you are in need of funds and I shall probably not bring a great dowry to—"

"Be still! I care not for great dowries, and besides—"

"As I was about to say, it occurs to me that were I to write a book about my experiences in some ghastly prison cell, it might provide an even better income than the one about the desert— Oh . . . *Piers!*"

Rattling along in Constable Bragg's cart, Ezra Sweet grumbled, "It be comin' on to rain. That won't help matters."

The constable said patiently, "There was no need for ye to come, Ezra. I can give Lieutenant Cranford the note."

"I s'pose ye begrudge me comin', Jeremiah Bragg. A proper Jeremiah ye be. Spoilin' everyone's hopes and plans! Me poor old bones bean't hurtin' this here cart, nor my weight taxin' yer nag undue."

"No. But if you mean to pinch at the Squire when he already promised you—"

"That were weeks ago, Jeremiah! Months, I dessay! I got a right to *ax* him, don't I? Careful-like, for Squire have growed hisself into a hasty-tempered young sprig!"

"He was shot, Ezra, and he's been very ill. Mrs. Franck said Mrs. Burrows was weeping over it and says he looks so thin and tries so hard to be cheerful that she's afraid they may lose him."

"Well, that won't do, that won't! Who's goin' to look after me if he goes away, I should like to know! Where's he goin' to go? We need him here! But if he's pulled you've likely chose a bad time to come, Jeremiah!"

"Well, p'raps this here note will cheer him up. Though what it may mean is more than I can come at."

Sweet peered at the paper in the constable's large hand. "What's it say, then? I got a good head fer puzzles. I'll help ye, Jeremiah."

Bragg took up the letter and unfolded it. "Seal must've falled off," he said rather sheepishly. "But it don't make much sense anyhow. It says—" He read laboriously, " 'Father and Pixie soon moving to Milan. If you expect me to wish you well, do not refine on it!' "

"Lor'," exclaimed Ezra. "That bean't a nice thing to say! Who writ it?"

"It's signed—'De-plor-able D.' "

"I dunno what that jaw-breaker means, but whoever it is

bean't no friend to Squire, that's for certain! I knew it, Jeremiah! You've chose a bad time to take me to Muse Manor. It be a shocking bad time! Squire will be in one of his ugly tempers, surely!"

In this instance, however, Ezra could not have been more mistaken.

"Halfling!"

Sir Peregrine sprang up from the morning-room sofa as that glad cry rang out. Beside him, Jane Guild gripped her hands and looked with dawning hope from the radiant young lady to the nephew whose blue eyes fairly hurled a joy she had despaired of ever again seeing there.

Peregrine limped forward and seized the hand that Piers held out to him. Scanning that haggard but beaming face, he said wonderingly, "Cawker! I've been worried to death! Now what are you about?"

"About to make you known to my future wife, twin!"

"Praise the good Lord!" whispered Miss Guild, joining them and lifting her cheek for Piers' kiss.

"We met once before, Miss Stansbury," said Peregrine, enormously relieved. "How very glad I am to welcome you to our family, dear ma'am."

"You must call me Mary," she said, adding, "I am a scarlet woman, you must know."

"I'll explain about that directly." Piers turned to his aunt. "And do you wish me happy, my dear?"

"With all my heart," she answered, shedding tears as she embraced him and then Mary.

Somebody coughed politely.

Glancing up, Piers saw his erstwhile valet, neat as ever, but with a pleased gleam in his dark eyes as he proffered a letter upon a silver salver. "Your pardon if I intrude, sir," he murmured. "But I am advised this is most urgent."

"Are you, indeed?" said Piers, taking up the letter. "Am I to assume you have returned to work out the notice you never gave me?"

"I thought I might reapply for the position, Mr. Cranford, if you would not object."

"What? Despite my wigless head and lace-less jabots?"

Blake said with faint scolding, "You will appreciate that, under the—er, circumstances, sir, at that juncture I dare not detail my true reasons for leaving your service. I was obliged to go at once to support my poor sister."

"So you deceived me," said Piers, but he was so engulfed in joy that he added, "You are come in time to be presented to my future wife. Mary, this is Rudolph Blake—my here-and-thereian of a valet."

Mary, who was now sitting on the sofa holding a soft-voiced conversation with Jane Guild, smiled and acknowledged Blake's bow, and he murmured his compliments and took himself off.

Peregrine said sternly, "I'll have some explanations, twin. I left my marriage preparations to—"

"Yes, well, I'm sorry to say that you are going to have to postpone them yet again," said Piers, failing to look in the least sorry.

"*What?*" demanded his twin, who had better success in looking enraged, although he was inwardly delighted.

"I had thought, you know, Perry," said Piers shyly, "that—well, that we might have a double wedding."

"Jove! That would be splendid, but—" Peregrine hesitated. "When? In August? I don't know—"

"Not in August, I hope. Either Marbury or our great-uncle will be willing, I feel sure, to help me procure a special licence. It may take a week or two, however." Piers turned anxiously to his love. "Shall you object, dearest?"

"Good gracious," exclaimed Mary. "You are very sudden, sir. What a good thing I have spent the past week and more in London, buying my bride clothes."

He stared at her mischievous smile and so ached with love for her that he had to tear his eyes away. "I know that will discommode you and your Zoe," he said to his brother. "So I have arranged a bribe for you . . ."

He handed over the letter Blake had brought.

Reading it, Peregrine became very pale, then flushed, and uttered a cheer of delight. "Quail Hill! You old rascal! You have bought it back!"

"Yes, though you will note, if you read on . . ."

Peregrine read on, then looked up, awed. "In—*my* name? Do you mean it, twin? The property is mine?"

"And the funds to build your house, Perry. Your wedding gift from the family, including, I am glad to say, a generous contribution from our great-uncle! What do you say to that, halfling?"

Mary stood and crossed to slip her hand in his. "Do you not see, my dear one?" she said lovingly. "He cannot say anything at all."

Gazing at that adored face now entrusted forever to his care, Piers put his usable arm about her and the depth of his happiness overwhelmed him.

Jane Guild watched "her" boys, and said a silent but heartfelt prayer of gratitude.

Over the top of Mary's curly head, Piers met the blaze of joy in the eyes of his twin; a joy that was, he knew, reflected in his own eyes.

The brothers grinned at each other, but said nothing. There was, indeed, no need for words.